THE
MISTAKE

About the Author

Katie McMahon wrote *The Mistake* while attending a masterclass run by the internationally bestselling author Fiona McIntosh. Previous writers discovered at the masterclasses include Tania Blanchard, author of the runaway bestseller *The Girl from Munich*. Katie lives with her family in Hobart, Tasmania, where she works as a GP and teaches communication skills to medical students. She is a lapsed Masters of Creative Writing student, and her hobbies include reading and drinking tea. Katie has previously published articles in *The Age* and *The Quarry*. *The Mistake* is her first novel.

THE
MISTAKE

KATIE McMAHON

ZAFFRE

First published in the UK in 2021 by
ZAFFRE
An imprint of Bonnier Books UK
80–81 Wimpole St, London W1G 9RE
Owned by Bonnier Books
Sveavägen 56, Stockholm, Sweden

A CIP catalogue record for this book is
available from the British Library.

ISBN: 978–1–83877–378–6

Also available as an ebook and an audiobook

1 3 5 7 9 10 8 6 4 2

Typeset by IDSUK (Data Connection) Ltd
Printed and bound in Great Britain by Clays Ltd, Elcograf S.p.A.

Zaffre is an imprint of Bonnier Books UK
www.bonnierbooks.co.uk

For Phill

Bec

I never thought of myself as smug. That's the really humiliating bit.

I didn't plaster a BRIARWOOD: INDEPENDENT AND OUTSTANDING sticker on our car's back window. ('Not everyone needs to know where you go to school, darlings.')

I wore my engagement ring – of course I was going to wear it – but my wedding band was as discreet and unassuming as a light switch.

I was careful never to mention how easily I fell pregnant (yes, all three times) or that, after twelve years of marriage, Stuart and I still had sex at least once a week. I didn't say things like, 'The kids are doing long-haul so much better these days' or, 'My dermatologist is excellent, but I'm too much of a scaredy-cat for filler before forty'. (Those are actual quotes from the school gate, by the way. You can see where my baseline was.)

I thought I was way too humble and sensitive and *grounded* for any of that sort of talk. And anyway, I felt the opposite of smug. I felt like someone who had to try really hard just to manage the minimum.

But I was smug. Insufferably.

Lots of people probably think I got exactly what was coming to me.

And I agree with them.

Kate

Mum once said Bec was the easy one. Even when we were little, she was one of those people who never put a foot out of line. At least not deliberately.

But when she makes a mistake, it's a really, really big one.

Chapter One

Kate

Eventually, I decided to try online dating.

'So,' I said, casual as anything, 'I'm going on Tinder.'

It goes to show how strong the urge to procreate is, because just about everything I'd heard about internet hook-ups was bad. Stories about ghosting and photos and genuinely frightening weirdos. It was almost enough to make you look back with fondness on the days of smoke-filled nightclubs where your bottom was pinched by simple, honest menfolk with beery breath and heads like red capsicums.

'Oh right,' Bec said. 'Aren't you on it already?'

We were talking on the phone, and I could tell she was cooking dinner. She sounded a bit distracted: probably worried she'd accidentally put non-organic kale in the kids' frittata.

'Well, if you meet someone nice, you can bring him to Stu's fortieth. As your plus-one.'

Hearing Bec use the term 'plus-one' without irony was almost enough to make me cry. I loved my sister, but honestly, there were moments when I felt I didn't know her anymore.

In any case, I didn't want a 'plus-one' for social events. I also didn't want: walks along the beach, red wine in front of fires, or even sperm for my (no doubt rapidly dwindling) 39-year-old supply of eggs. I was just yearning, absolutely yearning, to have sex. (Intercourse, to be more specific.)

3

Of course I know – believe me, I know – that intercourse is Just One Of The Many Ways Human Beings Can Enjoy Their Sexuality. But I felt I'd fully explored my personal sexual identity – if you catch my drift – and it was well past time to involve someone else. A man, in my case.

Anyway, the yearning. For skin and touch and eye contact and that quiet, concentrated breathing. For the way some men know how to look at you and say – all level and effective – 'God, I want you' or 'Been dying to get you alone' or something like that. It hardly matters what they say. It's all in the tone. And I wanted to wake up with urgent hands on me. I wanted to be undressed. I wanted to be dragged across a bed. But you just can't say stuff like that to someone who uses the term 'plus-one' in general conversation.

'Ha! Maybe,' I said instead. 'Listen, I'd better go.'

I hung up, feeling a bit sad, as if I'd given someone a really thoughtful present that they hadn't bothered to open. But it was hardly Bec's fault she didn't know what was going on with me.

Far below my apartment windows, Melbourne gleamed. Lights were starting to come on: they snaked along the coast, all the way around Port Phillip Bay. So many headlights. So many houses and banks and football grounds and beaches and delis and trams and apartments and offices and building sites.

I will go on as many dates as it takes, I thought, until I find one man to have sex with. The only criteria are that I must want to have sex with him, and he must want to have sex with me.

I would give it three months, then reassess.

I wasn't optimistic.

'Kate!' said Juliet. 'There will be right-swiping a go-go! You'll have so much fun!'

Juliet – my main Melbourne confidante, given Bec lives in Hobart – is enthusiastic about most things, especially if they have to do with me. She is extremely kind.

'I'm putting just my face in my photo,' I said, looking at my cauliflower salad.

Juliet chewed a cherry tomato. (We were having lunch at a café with second-hand chairs, butterscotch walls and a we'll-accept-you-even-if-you-eat-gluten vibe.)

'Whatever you're comfortable with.' She used a strident tone, as if someone had suggested I should do something I was *un*comfortable with, and pushed her hair out of her face. She has curly red hair, like Nicole Kidman's was before Hollywood.

Just then her phone rang. Juliet is a travel agent. You would think that travel agents would have all perished of the internet, but a few of them hang on, battered and defiant. They are like survivors in a ye olde English village after the Black Death has galloped through. (The reason Juliet survived is the high-end retiree market. Her clients are elderly, but not sweet, easily-fobbed-off, grateful-for-any-old-rubbish-because-at-least-it's-not-The-War elderly. More like: 'I'm paying top dollar for this Northern Lights helicopter jaunt, so why is the Moët non-vintage?' elderly.)

'So when's your first date?' said Juliet, when she'd finished explaining to the man on the phone why he didn't want a balcony the size of a postage stamp.

'You sure? About just my face in the photo?'

'You don't owe anyone anything.' She gave me a sweet smile, then started eating fast. She would have an appointment to talk about Copenhagen, Iceland or Budapest at two.

'All right,' I said.

'Just don't show your bazookas,' she added, with her mouth full. 'Tinder would actually burst into flames.'

That's Juliet. Exceptionally kind.

Two weeks later, both Bec and Juliet had texted to ask me if I had met any 'cuties' (Bec) or 'contenders' (Juliet).

No luck yet, I texted back, to both of them. I sent the emoji with the crossed eyes, as if the whole thing was a hilarious adventure.

I didn't know how to tell them there's a certain look men get. It's the look that probably crosses your face when you think you've spotted an amazingly good deal and then realise you missed a zero on the price tag, or when you grasp that the $14 is per oyster, not per six oysters. And that's the look from the *polite* men – the ones with nice mums and dads, the ones who weren't the coolest boys in school.

The others – the ones used to getting their own way – look annoyed, as if they've been duped by a shoddy naturopath into buying herbs that do nothing. Date Number Seven fake-yawned as I said, 'Hello.' So I'd know it was a fake yawn, he raised four straight fingers to his wide-open mouth and gave his lips several slow taps. Date Twelve – cuffs flipped back revealing tanned wrists – looked at his watch as I sat down and said, 'I need to be elsewhere.' He gave his head a little shake, the way you might when your team loses because the referee made a stupid decision.

On the way home that night I remembered the time David Hillman – the film producer – invited me out for Italian and I said no. I told him it was because I was off to New York in the morning, but really it was because he pulls his shirt collars out over the necklines of his jumpers. (That's a really bad look; I stand by my judgement there. Even he couldn't pull it off. And he still wears them like that, too; I saw him interviewed recently. Handsome as ever. He's aging well.)

I listened to a podcast the other day, about aging. Some women thought it was easier to age if you hadn't been good-looking to start with. You would have based your self-esteem and your sense of identity on your intelligence or your sense of humour or your kind heart or whatever. But other women thought that it was easier to age if you'd been hot in your youth. They said that hotties, having been hot for their allotted two decades (late-teens to late-thirties, or thereabouts) inevitably realised the limitations of hotness. They saw through it. Understood hotness never buys happiness.

I wondered if I would, eventually, have come to believe that.

Adam Cincotta was the seventeenth date. No one can say I don't persevere.

We met at a newish restaurant with good black-and-white drawings on the walls and sensible – by which I mean dim – lighting. It was crowded, but not too noisy. Well-designed acoustics. I was wearing a pale-green mohair sweater, black skinny jeans and my favourite black ankle boots. Also the earrings Bec and Stuart gave me for Christmas. They were dangly and sparkly and, having been chosen by Bec, much more tasteful than they sound.

I was first to arrive, partly because I wanted to get it over with. I waited, facing the door, watching plates of gnocchi go past and thinking I'd definitely stay and have dinner even if he left straight away. When he arrived I was reading the menu.

'Kate?' he said.

He was standing behind the chair opposite me, one capable-looking hand resting across each of its polished wooden knobs. His black polar fleece was the sort of thing I'd wear for a bushwalk, if I were to suddenly become the bushwalking type. He was skinny, but not in a bad way, and at least as tall as me.

'Adam?' I said.

He sat down and asked me what looked good. I immediately noticed he hadn't done The Look and that he had very definitely grey eyes. He had a sort of alert, quick-reflex way about him that could have made him look like a meerkat but didn't, because his gaze was grave and his shoulders were relaxed. Meerkats are cute, with their babysitting among the tribe and their big roundy eyes, but you just wouldn't want that frantic, bouncy sort of vibe when it comes to sex.

We talked about my family (a mere seventy-minute flight away in Hobart) and budget airlines (generally not too shabby) and Melbourne's inner-city traffic (we both tried to walk everywhere). Then we somehow got onto his hobby: rock-climbing. He had done something called free-climb Arapiles, and seemed to think I would know what that meant.

'I have no idea what you're talking about,' I said. 'Scrambling illegally up an ancient ruin?'

'No, Arapiles the mountain,' he said. 'In the Grampians?'

He didn't immediately reach for his phone to show me a photo, which was nice. Instead, he tilted one of his forearms to indicate a steep cliff-face.

'You climbed it without a rope?'

'No. With a rope.'

'But you said, "free climb".'

'Yeah. You have ropes. Gear. It means you don't—'

'Not that impressive, really, then,' I said. I was smiling though.

'Bugger.' He had a smile that came and went fast. 'That's all I've got.'

There was a little silence until I started talking about a holiday I'd been on near the Grampians. I made it sound as if I'd been camping with friends, although it had actually been a health retreat where I'd eaten a great deal of chef-prepared fermented stuff and resisted pressure to discuss my 'bowel actions' with the On-site

Qualified Ayurvedic Therapist. Since she was about twenty, I did not believe she could be that well-qualified.

When the waiter told us there was only one panna cotta left, Adam asked me if I wanted it. I said, God no, I was having the chocolate thing, and he said, well, thank Christ, and did you notice how chivalrous that was? I laughed and so did the waiter.

While I was eating my chocolate tortino, I found myself thinking about my underwear. I was wearing a matching maroon ensemble from Victoria's Secret. The bra only partially concealed my nipples; the knickers were called the Very Sexy Strappy Cheeky Panty, which made me think of *The Very Hungry Caterpillar*. Curled up in my drawer, the entire Very Sexy Strappy set had looked like a top-quality version of the shoebox of hair ribbons that Bec and I shared during primary school. On me, it looked pretty much the way it does on the VS models.

Pretty much.

Adam said he could walk me back to my apartment. I said that would be beyond chivalrous, we were now heading into gallant territory. He smiled his quick smile again. We ambled along a wide, busy-ish street. Necklaces of headlights shimmered past, and a tram with an ad featuring a beautiful, curvy twenty-something whose hips presumably represented the brand's Very Genuine Commitment to diversity. It was raining, but we were on a wide footpath, under the awnings of lovely old shops. They mostly sold expensive kitchenware, expensive shoes or expensive haircuts. I was thinking, if he turns out to be a nutter, at least we will have been captured on CCTV and in tasteful environs.

As we waited to cross a road, a shiny black four-wheel drive with a numberplate saying GELUZ? went past.

'Do you have a personalised number plate?' I asked. He looked at me and shook his head. 'Would you ever get one?' I went on.

'Maybe. If I first had a lobotomy.' Then he squinted his eyes and said, 'You?'

'Mine says "For Kate Not You", with K 8 for Kate,' I said. I drew a squiggle in the air to show the '8'. 'And the number four, and the letter U,' I clarified. He looked at me for a moment.

'Kay Eight, I know U R joking,' he replied, and did his quick smile again.

The lights changed. He put his hand on my back, just for a second, as I stepped off the kerb. It felt nice. After a minute I stopped to look in a window (boring knitted things, but I needed to collect myself for a bit) and when we started walking again, he took my hand. His hand felt Very Subtly Lively. I felt very something. Not nervous. Not excited. A bit scared. A bit hopeful. Turned on. I felt very turned on.

It was that delicious time when you sort of want to talk but there's nothing to say, when it feels as if your bodies are swooshing your minds along. A familiar feeling, lovely and painful at the same time, an echo of a long time ago. From early on at dinner I'd been able to tell the sort of lover he'd be. Agile and strong; quiet, purposeful, competent.

'Here we are,' I said. I dropped his hand to fiddle with the coded gate into my apartment complex.

It was when we turned down the path that I saw us in the double glass doors that lead to the lobby. My hair, which as usual was down, had got a bit wet and gone very frizzy. It felt suddenly, unbearably itchy against my face, and I became aware that a few strands were stuck to my lip. The doors glinted at us with malevolent accuracy.

We didn't hold hands again. As soon as we reached the bright fluorescent glow of the vestibule, I turned to him.

'Thanks for a fun evening,' I said. I was aiming for dignified.

'Thank *you*, Kate.' He put one of his hands on my waist. 'Shall we go in?'

He obviously hadn't noticed that my forehead was all tight, the way it goes when I need to cry. I felt the pressure he was putting through the base of his palm, onto my jeans, through to the upper-most strap of my ludicrous knickers.

I shook my head. Not flirtily. Not maybe-next-time promisingly. Just the way Mum used to when I asked her for a treat before dinner. Firm, routine, with the chance of some mild irritation just around the corner.

'Possibly an unchivalrous suggestion,' he said, not letting go of my waist.

'No problem at all. Thank you for walking me home.' He let go. 'In such a gentlemanly manner,' I managed to add.

Then, as I turned away, I somehow pulled out my best smile. The dazzling one. The iconic, stunning, light-up-the-room, insert-any-other-superlative-here one, just as if I were still a true professional. And I did it over my shoulder, in a manoeuvre that was a perfect imitation of a normal – of a *sexy* – woman flirting. As if there was nothing marring my anticipation of all the fun we were planning to have When We Were Both Ready.

When I got into the lift, I pressed the button and leaned back against the wall and closed my eyes. But I'd missed the moment and now the tears wouldn't come.

In the morning I made myself do all the usual things. No phone in the bedroom. Yoga in the yoga room. Ancient-grain porridge with stewed apricots for breakfast in the sun. The whole time bracing for disappointment. Telling myself he probably wouldn't have texted, and if he hadn't it could just be because I'd acted weird, and in any case that it didn't really matter either way, and also that, if he hadn't, it was his loss.

Finally, I checked my messages. Bec had sent a photo of Essie wearing the bright-green wig I'd given her for her birthday, one of Lachlan with his bike and one of Mathilda dressed up as Harry Potter. There was a reminder about a hair appointment.

And him.

Well. Seeing his name on my screen unleashed a lot of happy feelings. It was like opening the door on an overstuffed cupboard and standing there while the huge stack of towels – the ones you shoved in and hoped for the best about – falls out all over you.

I took a deep breath and replied 'Y' to the hair. Then I sent a lot of my specially downloaded unicorn emojis for Essie. (Mathilda, being eight, is too grown-up for unicorns, so I sent her some blue and green hearts, and a double thumbs up to Lachy.)

Then I read it. He had sent it at 11.37 p.m. the night before.

Thanks for dinner. Sorry for any lack of gallantry. I got carried away.

I picked my phone up off its special mat. I put it to my chest and squeezed it hard.

My pleasure, I typed back. My finger hovered over the Send button for three minutes. I said, 'For God's sake, Kate,' out loud. I deleted the words, stood up and made tea and when I sat back down I texted, *Come over?* as fast as I could and sent it. I was telling myself it was just a game, just a bit of fun, even though I could still feel the exact spot where he'd touched my back.

He replied straight away: *Can't. At work. Tonight?*

Of course he would be working; it was 10.14 a.m. on a Wednesday.

Yes, I texted back. I hesitated. *CU at 7? K8 x*

OK K8. GR8. x

Don't B L8 x, I wrote, and then I stepped away from the phone before I could do anything to spoil it all.

*

'Your front door's the same as mine,' he said.

He arrived at ten past seven, carrying a bottle of Spanish red wine.

'But your apartment's a lot nicer,' he added, as I led him into the living area.

He sounded a bit impressed. Thank God. The only thing more annoying than people asking, 'So, where are you based?' is when you tell them and then they try to hide the fact that they're impressed.

'Thanks. I love it here.'

My apartment is nicer than most people's, I forbore to say. My apartment is worth several million dollars, and I have spent a lot of time decorating it. (I've tried to go for New-York-loft style: lots of light and white and space, and then beautiful bits of furniture, the sorts of things that an interiors magazine would describe as eclectic, quirky or bohemian.)

We were in the living room by this time. I had planned that the icebreaker would be pointing out interesting bits of the view, because everyone gravitates to the windows. But he didn't come over to the windows; he went towards the kitchen.

'I'll open the wine,' he offered. I decided not to make a big deal of that in my head. Men like doing things for women, apparently, and anyway I really wanted a drink. So I just told him where the glasses were and sat down on the couch.

'So you were a model back in the day?'

He set down the wine glasses on the kitchen counter. He was wearing a dark-green shirt that fit him properly and was not (praise the Lord) tucked into his jeans. Call me a traditionalist, but if the occasion requires that your shirt be tucked in, then you should not be wearing jeans. A little triangle of grey T-shirt peeked out from near his collar.

13

'Yeah.' I guess he'd googled me. I felt flattered – and also glad, because the pictures that still come up on Google are far from unbecoming. 'Didn't you know that last night?'

He shook his head and I believed him.

'What did you get up to today?' I said. For some reason I had decided it'd be good to change the subject. Modest. Also, I didn't have a clear idea exactly what work he did. He'd talked about a science degree.

He shrugged. 'Just work. Taking photos, actually. Not fashion though. Lots of boring waiting around stuff today.'

I liked that he didn't say, Of-course-I'm-not-in-Demarchelier's-league or any of that crap. He left the wine bottle open on the counter. You could tell by the way he handed over my glass that my Persian rug and taupe leather couch inspired no apprehension in him. Some people just don't spill drinks.

As he sat down, he put his hand on my thigh. Knew he'd be competent, I thought, as triumphant as if I'd guessed his star sign. It was just as well, because I really needed to get the sex done and I'd accidentally sat down on the left side of the couch, and anyway, I was holding my wine. I took a big gulp. I had not eaten since the ancient grains.

'Was that when you looked at my pictures?' I said. When I try to act modest, I can never keep it up for long. 'In the waiting-around bit?'

'Yep.'

I couldn't tell if he was embarrassed or what. His hand on my leg was like an entire planet. I wished – yearned, craved, ached – to slide my own hand along it, slip a delicate, teasing, pseudo-casual finger along the margin of his heavy silver watch. Instead I turned a bit so I was sort of facing him.

'They're pretty amazing, Kate,' he said. I wondered if he'd seen the undone silk shirt ones. Prada let me keep that shirt, but I don't have it anymore.

'I know.' I sounded so wistful that I quickly added, 'Good old airbrushing.'

He made a little face that could have meant either *airbrushing alone can't make people look like that* or, alternatively, *no amount of airbrushing will ever make you look like that again*. Both those sentiments are true, of course. I slurped my drink.

He was still holding his glass in one hand, and he lifted his other one off my leg and used it to brush my hair behind my ear. He stroked my cheekbone with three attentive fingers, then ran his thumb over my lip. I opened my mouth and he turned his wrist. He moved his thumb a little way into my mouth, deliberately, gradually. He was watching my face. I skimmed my tongue along his thumb.

I felt as if I was impersonating a woman who knew what to do, but I must have been getting something right, because after a moment he made a tiny little sighing sound. He took my wine glass out of my hand, and put both our drinks on the coffee table, in the middle, where we wouldn't knock them.

He put his hands on the back of my neck. I could feel his palms on my skin. Then he slid them down to my shoulders. Our faces were close together. Even with the wine on board, I remembered to raise only my left arm to go around his neck. When I saw that his eyes were closed, I closed mine, and we started kissing.

'So, what do you do with yourself now you've stopped bringing playful Aussie naturalness to the catwalks of Paris?' said Adam.

It was later that night, and we were in my bed.

I laughed. My most famous campaign showed me with slightly unkempt-looking hair and minimal make-up. At least it had looked minimal in the pictures. Around that time everyone else was doing glossy crimson lips and glossy enormous hair, so just about all the stories written about me used the words 'playful', 'natural', or (in the more high-end publications) 'insouciant'. 'Sultry' got a red hot go as well. He must have read quite a lot about me on Google.

'I study medieval history,' I said. My Masters degree is about the types of textiles ordinary women wore – and made – in the 1500s, and how that influenced the economy. Even I knew that was not great post-sex conversation, so I said, 'King Henry VIII sort of era?' Then I added something about treason and Anne Boleyn. (I've noticed that Anne is the one most people remember, perhaps because she was the first of Henry's wives to be executed. Catherine Howard – fifth wife; probably still a teenager when Henry had her head lopped off for extra-marital shagging – seems to have been largely forgotten.)

'Brutal times,' said Adam. Then he looked around my room and said, 'Student flats have certainly moved on.'

I shrugged. I didn't want to tell him that I hadn't made all the money through modelling. I made lots, obviously, and because I had my dad advising-slash-nagging me, I managed to keep most of it. The pound was very strong then. I had income protection insurance and excellent, excellent lawyers. I made sensible investments. All adds up.

'Yep. But you better get dressed, my flatmates'll be back around now.'

It took him much less than half a second to realise I was teasing. He laughed, probably more than he would have if we hadn't just had really very good sex. At least, it had seemed good to me. But maybe community standards had changed, the way they have regarding home cooking and smacking children.

'Want some tea or something?' I said, sitting up and shaking out my hair.

He looked a bit surprised, but said, yeah thanks, that tea would be nice. I could see him making an effort to keep his eyes on my face as he spoke. I smiled and looped my knickers around my foot and then pulled them up my legs and on. Retrieved from under my pillow the T-shirt that I'd placed there earlier – in anticipation of exactly this moment – and found my way into that. Awkward but whatever.

Before, I had never minded being undressed in front of lovers. It just seemed to me to be part of the intimacy, part of the whole thing. For years I couldn't understand what all the fuss was about. Now, of course, I understand. But my bottom in a G-string is still more an asset than a liability, in my honest opinion, so once my T-shirt was on I stood up and walked into the kitchen. He whistled, in a parody of a bogan guy driving past in a car. It was nice. A couple of times when people – men – have whistled, they've stopped halfway through, as if they've made a mistake. It's sort of heart-breaking and funny at the same time.

When I came back with his tea, he had his grey T-shirt back on and was sitting up, leaning back against the pillows. He has the kind of very short hair that is impossible to mess up, so he looked pretty much the way he had when he arrived. I handed him his drink and went back to the kitchen for mine.

He was staring so much that when I got back into bed, I leaned against the bed-head, sipped my Milo and said, 'What?'

'Sorry,' he said. He gave his head a quick shake. 'I was thinking about work stuff.'

'Oh right!'

'Kay Eight? That was a joke. I was thinking how nice you look.'

'Thank you.' He'd made *nice* sound the opposite of boring. I let the silence stretch out.

'What's that you're drinking?' he said, comfortably.

'Milo. Want to taste?' I held out my cup. He used one of his hands to steady it as he had a sip.

'Yum. I'm having Milo next time.'

'Well, that's rather presumptuous,' I said. I would have thought it was obvious that he was on safe ground, but he looked a bit embarrassed.

'Sorry.' He smiled a quick smile. 'You – want to catch up again later in the week?'

'OK,' I said, and sipped my drink. 'That might be nice.'

I was as cool and sexy as anything, like Anne Boleyn was, at the beginning.

Chapter Two

Bec

'It's so hard not to!' Bec heard herself say.

She was talking about towels, and had just implied to Allie Vincent, her best friend out of the school mums, that it was practically a super-human act to *not* spend the afternoon buying bags full of top-quality manchester. As if Allie deserved some sort of Everyday Hero community award because she'd spent only $220 at Bed Bath N' Table.

The two women were sitting on a low sandstone wall that bordered some flowerbeds, waiting to collect their daughters from school. The afternoon air was perfumed with heirloom roses, and voices of what sounded like the senior choir floated through unseen windows. It might have done some of the girls good, Bec thought, to see a bit of graffiti or a dented old station wagon, but they certainly wouldn't be exposed to such atrocities within the grounds of Briarwood Independent Girls' Grammar.

'They sound pretty good actually, don't they?' said Allie.

Allie was wearing black exercise leggings with muscle-supporting panels in the sides; her sunglasses flashed, but in a discreet sort of way. It was almost impossible to tell whether she was naturally pretty or just so well-pampered she had achieved the appearance of being so. Some days, the way Allie seemed so happy about herself and her life was almost inspiring. Other times, Bec felt she'd rather stab out her own eyes than spend another second hearing about how much genuine personal fulfilment Allie got out of her new 'job' as a Thermomix consultant. ('It's just so *me*. So who I *am*. Totally re*ward*ing!' she'd said, the day after she'd hosted her first party.)

'So how are the plans coming on?' Allie asked. There was a conspiratorial edge to her voice, as if they were discussing a mission to liberate political prisoners instead of Stuart's fortieth birthday party.

That was the nice thing about Allie: you could chat to her about slightly trivial stuff and she would take it seriously. Stuart, on the other hand, would say things like, 'Just tell Essie she's younger, so she doesn't get to go,' or 'No one's going to care if the pass-the-parcel's not perfectly fair.'

Kate was good to talk to, but she knew straight away if you were hiding something. 'Why are you doing your Kylie-Minogue-after-the-cancer voice?' she'd ask. (Kate thought Kylie's bubbliness masked a whole lot of tension.) And Bec's best friend from medical school, Laura, had become so direct and so serious and so lacking in *humour* that you simply couldn't hold a normal conversation with her.

Anyway, it wasn't that Bec didn't like Allie. When Stuart once joked that her initials stood for Absolutely Vacuous, Bec had defended her, even though she sort of knew what he meant. Allie tended to take personal grooming and the need to eat superfoods just that bit too seriously. Still. She was a really sweet friend, so Bec looked down at her new ballet flats and allowed the trace of a wince to cross her face.

'What?' Allie looked suddenly, genuinely horrified. She turned to Bec and gripped her arm. 'Not the caterers?'

'The catering's great.' Bec watched one of the teachers carry a cardboard box along a camellia-lined path. The junior school girls – blazer-ed and boater-ed and carrying enormous navy-blue backpacks – would be arriving any minute. She turned to Allie.

'A couple of weeks ago, Stuart announced he wanted to have a fire-eater.' She kept her tone very light and very girly. She met Allie's gaze and shrugged in a husbands-what-can-you-do-with-them? way.

'No!' said Allie. 'I love how Stuart is so *ran*dom!'

'I *know*,' Bec said, and paused.

She thought back to last year's Easter Lantern Parade. Lily Pianno's dad and his New Young Girlfriend had unexpectedly turned up, and Allie had been almost manic with industrious delight. Within thirty seconds, she had dragooned Bec into keeping Lily's mother engaged in conversation and hissed at one of the grade fours to go and offer the girlfriend a mini pizza from the oval plastic platter. Later, while they were helping wipe crumbs off the kindergarten tables, the two of them discussed it. 'Major crisis avoided.' 'Well done us!' 'Can I just say, what is he even thinking, though?' The whole thing was so exciting that it had been a struggle to keep their voices sufficiently low. But the next morning, recalling it all, Bec had felt sick. What a pair of petty bitches we are, she'd thought.

She suddenly decided not to say anything.

Texts were so hard to interpret anyway, and she'd probably got the wrong idea. After all, she was hardly in the business of deciphering the sexual intentions of gorgeous young fire-eaters. She and Stuart had been together forever. Fourteen years, in fact. God. She was thirty-*eight*.

'So,' she back-pedalled, making a flicking gesture with her hand, 'I've had to track a suitable person down.'

Allie's face implied Bec was an admirably stoic survivor of a violent crime.

'It's been so hard.' Sometimes she really hated herself. 'And apparently, I need to meet him at some point, which of course is yet to be made clear, and I've just got so much else to do this week.' Her angst sounded entirely authentic, which was sort of a worry.

'Hair. Waxing. The dry cleaning. God, the coffee van. And, of course, Stuart never notices things like the spare room and the deck and what have you, so that'll all fall to me. I'm going to look like a wreck by the time Saturday night rolls around.' She threw that in for good measure, and realised too late it probably sounded as if she was fishing for a compliment.

'Oh, you'll look fabulous.' There was the thinnest possible strand of envy in Allie's voice, more heart-warming than any flattery. 'But can I just say again, you really do need to engage with laser hair-removal once all this is over, Bec.'

'Mmm. I really must.' Bec waved a hand to indicate she'd hogged the conversation long enough, and was about to make time for Allie's issues. 'Now. Have you decided yet about the holidays?'

Allie started to say something about Vanuatu, but just then a smiling Mrs Wilkinson opened the child-proof gate, and three dozen back-pack-laden girls from the junior school came lumpily along the concrete path towards them for the sweet, never-to-be-taken-for-granted flurry of hellos and chat-laters and hurry-because-we've-got-to-go-and-get-your-brother-straight-aways.

She hustled Essie (exhausted and grumpy about everything, mainly because she was five, but also because of the thick cheese Bec'd accidentally put in her sandwich) and Mathilda (uncharacteristically excited for reasons that remained elusive) all the way across to the car and into the back seat. On the road to Lachlan's school, she gave up trying to get the girls to tell her anything significant about their days. They were looking out of the windows.

Diving back into her own thoughts was a vast relief, like snuggling into bed.

That you on facebook? Cos nice bikini
Oh god years ago now

She'd omitted the punctuation on purpose, obviously.

There was only one bikini photo of her on Facebook – Stuart's sister had posted it after their family holiday in the Cook Islands, and Bec hadn't worked out how to get it off her public profile. Actually, she hadn't tried all that hard. She was still breast-feeding Essie a bit when it had been taken – Essie had gone on and on forever – and the light was good. It was really a very flattering photo.

Sorry boundaries. Normal bloke, have had a beer and from WA, let's blame that, sure you want a lad like me entertaining at your fancy party? There was a winking emoji.

All good.

That felt like a youthfully casual thing to say, but the full stop definitely conveyed something. Polite, mature, unimpressed.

He didn't reply for ages, and then wrote:

We should meet before the party. Make sure we on same page about fire stuff

Certainly. Let me know when suits!

She just couldn't bring herself to send it without the exclamation mark. Too unfriendly.

Mmmm. Will do.

Well.

It wasn't just the stuff about the photo. It was that you could interpret the *mmmm* in so many different ways.

'Essie. Get in the car,' Stuart said, the next morning.

'I *AM*!' Essie yelled.

Bec sighed. Her car was at the mechanic's, so, unusually, the family were all leaving together that day.

Essie stayed where she was and poked the garage wall with her ladybird umbrella. Stuart looked at Bec. Bec undid her seatbelt and got out.

'Essie.' Bec squatted in front of her little girl, and managed to keep the rising agitation out of her voice. 'It is time to go right now. Daddy

23

has to be at work. You're the only one keeping us waiting. Now,' she took a deep breath, 'you can get yourself in, or I will carry you.'

'I'm COMING I SAID!' Essie boomed.

'You have until ten.' Her voice was admirably level. In fact, she sounded like someone who had made a very sincere effort to learn about effective parenting strategies. Which, she supposed, she had.

'One. Two . . .'

Essie put the umbrella down ever so carefully.

'Three. Four . . .'

Essie started moving faster. Bec counted a bit more slowly.

'Five . . . Six . . .'

Essie's navy-blue school dress hit her seat.

'Well done, kiddo!'

Essie beamed, and Bec was smiling too. She felt quite ridiculously proud, to be honest. 'You made it.'

Bec hurried back to her seat and smiled over at Stuart, but he was apparently too busy to notice her exemplary five-year-old management skills, or to smile back. No doubt he was thinking about his terribly crucial operating list or someone's splenectomy or something.

Not that his job wasn't important. Being a surgeon was very demanding. Obviously.

'Remind me, Bec,' he said, as he dropped them all off at the girls' school. 'Next time your car's in for service? I'll just book you guys an Uber.'

She knew it was ridiculous, because he was just being practical, but she felt so hurt that she got tears in her eyes. She had to pretend to Mathilda that she was allergic to her new eyeliner.

The next day, she collected Stuart's favourite suit, bought milk and bananas – which she did so frequently it was practically a hobby – picked up Lachlan's eczema cream and was almost back to her car when her phone vibrated. When she saw who it was, she got in very quickly, and for some reason, locked the doors.

'Hi. Ryan, is it?' Outside, the street was going on as usual. Traffic passed the neat lawn of the old army barracks, and a pub with brightly painted signs offered Free Kids Meals on Mondays.

'Hey, Bec,' he said, not even checking he had the right person. 'How you going today?'

It had been a long time since anyone except Kate or her mum had asked her that on the phone. Usually it was all, 'So, how may I help you this morning?' or 'I guess you're calling about so-and-so's play-date/sprained ankle/swimming lesson.' In fact, she hardly ever *talked* on the phone anymore. Everyone texted.

'Oh. Fine. Just bought some bananas.' Good grief. 'I'm sitting in my car now, though. Too much detail!' She dug her fingernails into her hand to prevent herself from thanking him, from apologising for nothing, from speaking at all.

'No worries. I've just waxed my board.' He paused, and she considered saying something about how she mustn't take up his time if he was busy, but then he spoke again. 'Glad I caught you. I'm heading out of phone range in a bit.'

She imagined him at a beach car park somewhere remote, leaning back against a sexily dented ute.

'Great waves out at Lion Rock today. Going to walk there. Really long way.' His voice was without any sort of irony, and she thought of the rocky path down to the wild, remote beach. She hadn't visited there since the kids.

'Well, anyway, Ryan. How can I help you?' Being nice to clients was his *job*, she reminded herself, and he was ringing about his official fire-eating duties.

25

'Yeahhh,' he said. 'I was just calling to say, how about we meet Friday morning? If I cruise by your place about ten, we can have a cuppa or whatever, and I can get a sense of what you're after.'

'Oh. OK. Maybe.' She practically yelped the words, then tried to pull herself together by sitting up straight and frowning analytically at her steering wheel. Because the simple fact was that he was a *service provider*, and now he needed to come to his fire-eating venue and be briefed by her, his *employer*. It was exactly the same as when Greg the plumber came to look at the downstairs bathroom tap. She always made Greg tea – often more than one cup, and he took four sugars, which possibly accounted for him being fairly porky even though he was a manual labourer – and then, when he brought his cup back, she asked him down-to-earth questions about his boat, which was called *Reel Livin'*.

And what about the volunteering she'd done in Nepal? Once upon a time, she'd shared meals and walks and even youth-hostel rooms with various beautiful medical-student boys without there ever being any question of anything sexual happening. Well. Maybe there had sometimes been a *question*. But still. The point about Nepal was that even if there was a slightly flirty undercurrent, you simply put that to one side and got on with the practicalities.

'Sure,' she said, more levelly. 'We could just have some tea while I show you the deck and the running sheet and things.'

You were single in Nepal, a stern voice reminded her. *And twenty-something. And definitely not a mother. And by the way, Rebecca Henderson –* Stern Voice really knew how to go for the jugular – *I hope you're aware that your pubic hair had no greys in it back then!*

'Nice,' he said.

And that's when she realised she could justify it however she wanted, but Stern Voice was entirely correct. She should have said she was busy on Friday – which, by the way, was true – and that it'd be better if he came over and talked to both her and Stuart on the Saturday morning. 'My husband would love to meet you, too,' she could have said. 'We're both so delighted you'll be performing at our gathering.' No. Even she didn't sound quite that middle-aged. But 'Come Saturday morning and meet the fam' would have worked just fine.

Anyway, it was too late.

'See you Friday then,' he said. He checked the address. 'Be good to meet you, Bec.'

Stern Voice made a tutting sound.

Three hours later, Kate rang. Bec was in her kitchen, doing the online grocery shopping.

'How did Essie's assembly go?' Kate asked, after they had discussed their mother's recent tendency to suggest Lebanese food for every family get-together. 'Did you get a picture?'

Bec's free hand flew to the phone, so that she was clutching it to her ear with both hands.

'Oh my God!' There was no need for her to say the actual words.

'Tell her the car broke down,' said Kate. 'Tell her ... tell her the neighbours' cat went missing and you had to help look for it.'

'I can't believe I forgot! I've never missed a Wednesday assembly. Never!'

'It's all right,' Kate soothed. 'Essie was probably too busy remembering the words to even notice.'

Neither of them believed that.

'Maybe I can tell her I was there in the crowd.'

Kate made an uncertain sort of *eaaa* noise. Tears filled Bec's eyes.

'How could I have done this?' she said.

'It's not *that* bad,' said Kate. 'Lots of mums don't go every week. Stuart hardly ever goes.'

Stuart had possibly been literally saving a life while the five-year-olds were singing 'The Grand Old Duke of York'.

'Stuart would have been busy doing something worthwhile. I was just ...' she paused. What had she actually been doing at four minutes to midday, when she was supposed to be taking her seat for the Prep Assembly?

She'd been in the laundry. She'd been bleaching Mathilda's socks. She'd been scraping dirt off Lachlan's runners.

She'd been thinking about the fire-eater.

Of course, Essie noticed, and of course, Essie cried. And of course, Bec felt so guilty that she almost texted Ryan and cancelled. But she did actually need a fire-eater, and they did, after all, need to meet. In the end she decided to compromise by wearing a very unflattering purple jumper. ('You painting the cubby or something today?' Allie asked, at drop-off.)

At just after nine-thirty, she paused in front of the lounge-room mirror. At ten o'clock on the dot the doorbell rang. She was now dressed in a clingy white knit she loved but hadn't worn for a while. She really had far too many clothes.

When she opened the front door, the fire-eater was bending down to examine the pot of rhododendrons on the porch.

'Hey,' he said, looking up. In fact, he seemed to uncoil himself from the plant, and give all his attention to her.

'Come in!' Too chirpy. 'Come in, Ryan.'

He followed her along the corridor to her kitchen. At the bench, he leaned forward on the heels of his hands.

'Can I offer you a tea?' she asked.

'Any chance of a coffee?' Mischievous grin.

'Of course! Sit down.'

'I can spot a good machine.' He tucked one of his ankles around the leg of the nearest stool, dragged it a bit closer, and sat. She was about to start up her usual speech, about how much coffee they drank and how it had seemed sensible to invest – as if the actual point of a coffee machine like that was to economise on household expenditure – but he said, 'Your kids do those?'

He was looking up at the wall, where she Blu Tack'd the kids' work. There were drawings and paintings and feathers-stuck-to-paper. There were bits of embroidered hessian and pipe-cleaner butterflies and misspelt notes about love and mummy and fambly. Everything was higgledy-piggledy and overlapping. She loved that wall.

'Yeah.' She looked up at it with him. 'Bit chaotic. The kids are craft-crazy.'

Ryan met her eyes. He smiled in an approving way.

'Lot of happiness in this house,' he said.

'Oh yes.' She turned to the coffee.

'Just a shame about the visual clutter.' He was joking.

'I really must pare back the pipe cleaners,' she replied, and they smiled at each other again.

He was so good-looking, in his shabby black jeans and his faded down-jacket, with his shoulders and that jaw and those *lips*, that it felt like an achievement to participate in any sort of banter. She was fairly proud of herself, in fact. She passed him his coffee.

'Looks great,' he said, and gave her a little nod. Of course, she couldn't think how to respond, so there was quiet for a few terrifying seconds. Kate would have known what to say. The fact fell into her head like a thud. She got on with making her tea.

He sipped his coffee, then said, 'So, what did you have in mind?'

She dinged the teaspoon on the side of her cup a couple of times, and then used her most matter-of-fact voice to say perhaps he could start his 'act' at ten, just before the speeches. 'I was thinking the deck?' she suggested.

He turned his head, looked through the sliding glass door, and said he thought the deck'd be a bit small. 'But stunning garden. We'll find a good place,' he added, as he turned back to her.

So Bec talked about maybe the lawn or perhaps the terrace or possibly even the tennis court, and the whole time she was thinking: does he think I grew *up* in a house like this? Is his life full of rich ladies like me? Does he joke about visual clutter with all of them? Am I different from the others? Can he tell?

'Let's go check it out,' he said. He finished his coffee in a long swallow, and flipped himself off the stool. She left her half-drunk tea on the counter. Near the sliding door, he made a tiny after-you gesture, and stood well aside for her. He even turned his eyes down as she passed him. Maybe he'd forgotten all about the bikini comment.

Outside, the air was damp and the sun seemed precious and thin. They walked side by side across the deck, and down the steps. At the rose garden, he said, 'This place must smell amazing in summer,' and, when they crossed the main lawn, 'Do you ever just lie on the grass and watch the water?' ('Once I did,' she said, trying not to sound apologetic. He would think she was a poor little rich girl. Or, more accurately, and more pathetically, a poor older rich lady.)

In the end, they decided his act would be best on the terrace.

'And anything in particular you want me to do?' he said. He was lounging against an old sandstone wall.

'Oh, you know. Just whatever's most spectacular without actually setting anyone alight.'

He laughed. He had a very tiny chip out of one of his front teeth. It was tempting to think she'd always found those attractive.

They went back inside, talked about payment, and then she saw him to the front door.

'Thanks for coming round,' she said.

'My pleasure.' And then he gave her a not-particularly-subtle up-and-down look. If he'd been fat and fortyish, it might even have seemed sleazy. But coming from Ryan, it was just a look full of . . . not quite lust, but *appreciation*.

His eyes were back on her face. But he was quirking his mouth, as if they'd just shared a private joke. *And* they both had their hands in the back pockets of their jeans.

'I'll look forward to Saturday, then,' he said, very innocently. 'Bec.'

Chapter Three

Kate

'Well, let's get started.'

It was about thirty-six hours after Adam and I had slept together, and I was about to give a tutorial to the first years. Thank God: it gave me something to focus on. I generally over-prepare, even though the first-year co-ordinator – Professor Penelope Purcell – once said I could do it blindfolded.

I hadn't told Adam this, but I only got into Tudor history to try to make myself feel better. I knew, straight after the operation, that I didn't want therapy. Not saying therapy's bad, as, for one thing, that would be just about illegal. But I always felt it would not have helped me. Apart from Bec's husband Stuart, practically everyone I know has at some stage suggested I 'might want to talk to someone'. It's a bit of a sore point. Also one reason I like Stuart so very, very much.

(When I first met him, I assumed Stuart would be horrible, because he's handsome, wears ironed Ralph Lauren polo shirts on weekends, went to Glenferrie College and is a surgeon, but I was being too judgemental. He is actually properly smart and thoughtful, not just privately educated and venal. He really loves Bec, is the other thing. Sometimes I wonder if it's because she's the only woman who ever turned him down. When they first met – she was an intern at the hospital where they both worked – she was very feisty and earnest, always dashing off to Nepal in her holidays and then coming home and fund-raising for tube wells and giving presentations with graphs about horrifying tuberculosis rates and lots of photos of rashes. At first, she thought Stuart was an entitled tosser, then a bit too charming to be true, and then she started saying things like, 'It's not his fault he was born into privilege,' and 'His mum *is* a judge. I think she shaped his values.')

Since I didn't want counselling, quite a few years ago I decided to have a crack at 'putting things into perspective' by thinking of people worse off than myself. It took a while to find the right worse-off people. (War crimes: too terrible, literally made me vomit halfway through the first chapter of the book I'd bought. Witches burned at stakes: too infuriating; women still aren't supposed to be opinionated, middle-aged and ordinary-looking, in case anyone hasn't noticed. Starving/homeless/no-money-for-school-uniforms women and children: I just kept donating money and crying. The donating thing continues, I might add.)

Tudor England was far enough away to bear, and quite interesting, but bad enough to make me feel a bit better about my own situation. Being chopped up while you're still awake and in public would have to be marginally worse than months of occupational therapy. Marginally. So, once I'd read a few novels and watched a couple of films, I enrolled in a part-time Arts degree where I could pretty much just do the History subjects, and now I was doing my Masters. Last year I started tutoring the first years in research methods, and once, I contributed to an article that got published in a historical journal where it was no doubt read by anywhere up to twelve people. But Mum pinned that article to the kitchen noticeboard, something she never did with any of my magazine covers.

A good tutor has to know the material, and a bit more to cover unexpected questions. She should also find a way to inspire the students with a love of the subject, even though most of them mainly care about whether the person they like has texted them, finishing up in time to grab their car before their parking meter expires or, at best, how to pass the next exam.

Exams these days are called Competencies, and anyone who fails is deemed 'Not Yet Competent'. (The 'Yet' is optimistic in some cases, believe me. I think there should be a category called 'You Clearly Don't Want To Be Here You Are Wasting Everyone's Time Leave Now' or else just 'Terrible. You're Expelled.')

It was odd, the first time I had to stand up in front of ten 18-year-olds and act knowledgeable and grown up, and it's not as if I could have a wine beforehand. I wore seamless white underwear, black Capri trousers, black brogues and a brand-new ice-blue knit. It was what *Vogue* might have called pragmatic chic: everything was Chanel, to intimidate any empowered millennials who – I feared – might otherwise ask me stern, pernickety questions about the importance of peer review versus the validity of lived experience. (I was inexperienced and very nervous. Obviously none of them asked any such thing.)

Today I was wearing the same black pants, olive suede flats and a soft dark-brown sweater that I bought second-hand at a market in Hobart. Also really beautiful olive-green lace-edged underwear. I always choose underwear to reflect what I'm doing and my mood. I realise that makes me sound both annoying and tragic, and also indicates that I have way too much time on my hands. In my defence, it sort of started as a way to survive. Anyway, today's green silk was all about exquisitely worked detail and being gentle with myself. Adam had Not Yet Called.

The students dribbed and drabbed in. I was definitely old enough to realise that I was pretty much invisible to them, so I didn't feel self-conscious just sitting silent at the big square table until the clock clicked over to eleven. Then we started. It was a blessed relief to have to give all my attention to something other than Adam Xavier Cincotta.

I enquired what they had made of the week's readings and asked if anyone had any thoughts to share. Of course none of them did, so I had to ask some of them directly.

'So, Amy,' I said, 'would you call that a primary or a secondary text?' and, later, 'Kyra, how else could someone go about finding that information?' (Some of them had very weird names. Kyra Kiernan, I ask you. There was a Delphine-April too, and yes, she preferred to be called by her full name.)

'You're on the right track,' I replied, to all but the most ridiculous answers. Even then I tried to twist their words to make it sound as if they'd said something sensible. It's hard to talk in front of people when you're eighteen. I don't know why everyone makes such a big deal about extreme youth; in real life, most people are far more attractive at thirty.

'Thank you ... Kate,' some of the students said, as they left. Mostly they are polite but shy; they're still learning how to use teachers' first names.

'Nice earrings, Kate!' said one of the more confident girls.

'Bye. Thank you. My pleasure. Bye. Yes, no problem. Bye, now,' I said.

As the last student left – 'Thank you very much!' – I realised how very, very intensely I wanted to hear from Adam. The worst of it was the *shame*: I was bordering on forty and still waiting breathlessly for a text from a guy I'd pretty much had a one-night stand with. The kids I tutored probably imagined I was respectably shacked-up with a sustainable-design architect. They surely believed I had a more prestigious place in the world than spinster aunt, casual tutor, Masters candidate. I looked down at my posh suede shoes in an effort to steady myself, but everyone knows that only the most horrible sort of people rely on expensive possessions to feel good about themselves, so that was no help. I reminded myself about not being defined by a man and blah-blah-liberated-effing-blah, but by the time I was outside, the mild euphoria of the 'Thank you very much!' had worn off. I was fighting a grey, dragging sense of being pathetic.

My favourite route home is also the longest, past nice cafés and through a park that, for some reason, always makes me think of an American ivy league college. I wouldn't be all that surprised if a couple of twenty-something girls with big white teeth and that straight, bouncy American hair appeared out of the undergrowth, flicking their bangs and chatting about sororities.

I was walking past the fountain at the same time as I was remembering the moment Adam undid my bra (one-handed) at the same time as I was battling the all-consuming-ness of the hope that he'd text me at the same time as I was thinking I really should try to eat at least one piece of sushi for lunch. My phone rang. I managed to grab it and swipe to answer before it stopped.

'Hi, Kate,' said Adam. 'It's Adam Cincotta.'

'Yes,' I said. I peered quickly at my phone screen. NO CALLER ID, it said. I sat down at a handy park bench. He said something about eating lunch at his computer, and I said something about just being on my way home from work myself. 'I'm in that park with the fountain and the elm trees.'

'Pretty.' Did I imagine a compliment?

'Yes,' I managed.

'You want to have dinner tonight?'

'Yes.'

'With me, I mean,' he said. I couldn't quite tell if he was joking.

'Yes.'

'Seven? At that Japanese place near yours?'

36

My mind scrambled around. He must mean the one we'd walked past the other night.

'Yes.'

'OK. I'll book. Bye, Kate.'

'Yes. Bye.' I hung up.

No wonder everyone texts. At least you have time to think about what you're going to say.

'The problem,' Adam was saying, 'is that she point-blank refuses to ask for help.' He was acting all droll, but there was real concern on his face.

'Bugger,' I said. We were at the Japanese place, and he was telling me a story about his grandmother in a nursing home and her tendency to fall over a lot. We'd been talking about our families.

'Indeed. The nurse told me she's supposed to press a buzzer when she wants to go for a walk, but Nonna just hops up and gets going. I said, she's ninety-one, I don't think there's any chance of turning things around at this point.' He half laughed, half grimaced. 'She had to have an X-ray of her wrist today.'

'Your poor nonna,' I said. It can be hard to ask for help, I almost added.

'Yeah. Anyway, that's her. My papa died seven years ago; Mum and Dad and my sister are in Ballarat; my brother's in Adelaide. They can all walk very competently.'

I nodded.

We were leaning towards each other. The table was small and the restaurant, even though it was almost full, felt subdued and tranquil.

Adam was wearing a different fleecy top, one of those expensive quick-drying things that you buy from outdoorsy shops. It had a short zip at the top, with a bit of navy T-shirt visible underneath.

Jeans and work boots. It would not have worked on everyone, but he managed to look attractive in a non-fashionable way. In my view – which I know is sexist and old-fashioned, but I can't seem to change it – there's nothing that says unmanly like a guy who follows trends.

I thought: it would be way too soon to invite him to Stuart's fortieth.

I re-crossed my legs and accidentally brushed his shin with mine. He looked up from his teriyaki at me and smiled his quick and really rather lovely smile.

I moved my leg a tiny bit, and let it relax against his. We were still looking at each other. He took quite a big swallow of his beer. His throat, when he tilted his chin up, was all of a sudden mesmerising. I found myself still staring at it when he placed his glass back on the table.

He put his hands on his cutlery. We had both stopped eating.

'I had a really nice time the other night,' he said.

'Me too.' A pause.

'*Really* nice, Kate.'

Oh God, the look he gave me.

In my mind, I was the kind of woman who could say things like, 'Adam, why don't we go home right now?' or 'I think we probably need to find a bed sooner rather than later.' But in real life it seemed I couldn't say any of that stuff, not even just, 'How about we skip dessert?' I've also lost the ability to do my trademark 'sultry' pout. The best I could manage was to flip my hair back and smile in a way I hoped was inviting, warm and confident, as if I was doing a turn-of-millennium-era ad for organic skin care. (Never did those. My look was considered too sexy. Ha.)

'We should go,' he said, very quietly. The organic skin care look has its niche, clearly.

'Yes.' I turned to find my coat, saw it wasn't on the back of my chair, and then remembered that the waitress had whisked it away. It seemed to take ages for her to bring it back and it was a bit of a fluster to put it on with her trying to help and Adam sort of watching. He said he'd pay and I had to fumble around to find cash for my half, which he said he wouldn't take, but in the end did.

He held my hand as soon as we stepped out into the very-much-colder-than-earlier night. We started walking pretty quickly towards my house. To my un-surprise and pleasure, he did not make any ridiculous exclamations about how on earth did I manage to walk in those shoes. (Subtext: you are vain and frivolous and/or I'm threatened by your height and/or you're obviously not a proper feminist.) Of course, before sleeping with him I had formed the view that he was not the sort of person to make high-heel-judgement remarks, but it was good to be reassured. Also: he was taller than me, even in my heels.

This time, when we got to my apartment building, I made the effort not to look at my reflection in the glass doors. Instead, I looked at the path that leads to them. Box hedges grow on either side, so tidy and perfect that they don't even look alive.

Quick mental appraisal of my underwear. I had gone the whole hog: black floral lace bustier with attached suspenders, black V-string, black stockings. I was wearing a really quite short stretch-knit black skirt. Bec has a sweet-slash-annoying friend called Allie who talks frequently about how you have to make the most of your assets. Well, Allie would approve.

I beeped open the door; we got into the lift; I beeped the lift security thing. He took my hand again and pressed the button to my floor. I assumed we would start kissing as soon as the lift doors slid closed. Instead, he looked at me and said, 'Seventeen floors.'

Wry. Complicit. Wanting me. God.

I couldn't look at him, but I could feel that, like me, he was watching the numbers above the doors. They illuminated, one by one, as we ascended. I read the various round buttons. STOP said a red one. ALARM said another. I had often wondered what would make anyone press STOP. Surely few emergency situations could be improved by the elevator grinding to a halt.

The doors opened.

'After you, Kate,' he said. I have a special identification code thingy for my front door. As I was zapping it unlocked, he stood very close behind me and laid one of his hands on my hip bone. He smelt nice. Something herbal and ethical.

My apartment was dimly lit – after all, his being there was not unforeseen – and nice and warm. He closed the door behind us with one hand and held my hip with the other. Then he leaned back against the door and pulled me in. I turned to face him and he pressed me up against him.

'Kate,' he said, still very quietly.

His face was near to mine. I felt desperate to kiss him. I brushed my lips on his, and he said, 'Mmmm,' and started kissing me. He does the ravenous-yet-controlled, communicative sort of vibe that is, in my opinion, the essence of excellent kissing.

His hands slid down to the hem of my skirt, slipped up under it, and skimmed along my legs. He broke off the kiss for long enough to murmur, 'I've been thinking about this all day.' Right tone, too. When he got to the top of my stockings, he made a small sound of pleasure in his throat.

'Shall we go to bed?' I mustered.

'Mmmm,' he said again, this time in a way that meant, yes, definitely, that sounds like a truly excellent idea. Still kissing, still with his hands on me, we sort of veered through the lounge room, past my beautiful umbrella plant – I talk to that plant sometimes;

in fact, I call her Philomena, and I had a ridiculous spasm of embarrassment that Philomena was seeing us like this – and into my room. Somehow we both ended up lying on the bed facing each other. He slid down my skirt and I kicked it off.

'Come here.' He took hold of one of my thighs and pulled it between his legs. Still in his jeans. The whole me-more-naked-than-him thing was proving to be quite arousing. Surprising.

'Out of this,' he said. His hands moved to the buttons of my shirt (caramel-coloured, silky, Zara) and he undid them one at a time, starting from the top. Pretty slowly. Whenever he undid a button, he'd look down my shirt, then up at my face. When my shirt was completely open, he swished it back over my shoulders and off. I made a definite effort not to think about how my stump must have felt under his hand. It wasn't that difficult, because I was pretty much swept up in the way his fingertips had begun skimming along the top of my bustier.

'Goodness me,' he said, as he pulled the lace down. How he managed to make that sound sexy, I will never know, but he did. He flicked a glance into my eyes, kissed my lips once – no tongue, teasing – then brought his mouth down onto my breasts. It felt so delicious I said, 'Ohhh.'

After that, we both started saying 'goodness me' a lot, and it meant things like *what you're doing feels quite glorious* and *please do keep going* and *that feels so nice you'd better stop pretty soon*. Eventually I said, 'Take off my...' Then I paused. Undies was what kids call them, knickers sounded a bit old-fashioned-governess, panties would scream escort-service advertisement, he wouldn't know what a V-string even was – '... Undress me.' I settled on. I wriggled up against him so he'd know which bit I meant.

'Yep,' he said. Not casually.

I thought he might get all tangled up with the suspenders but he snapped them open as easily as Bec flicks up lids on the kids' drink bottles, grabbed my knickers by the front bit and slipped them down. I could feel the aching loveliness of his warmth all along my side. My stump was in close to him, where it wouldn't be all that visible. He was looking – with yearning, it has to be said – along my body.

'Goodness me,' he said again, as he stroked me. (*You look beautiful. You feel wonderful. I'm glad you're enjoying that. I am going to have to have sex with you almost immediately but I am making a reference to our earlier teasing, which I know you will like.*)

He stood up and finished taking off his clothes. Looking down at me all the time. I rolled a bit further onto my side, so my stump was pressed down invisibly into the mattress. I kept forgetting about it then remembering.

I hadn't properly looked last time but he had really quite a nice body. Wiry and long-limbed. Good amount of dark hair. He had a condom in one of his many pockets and he rolled it on, lay on top of me, took hold of my wrist, held it against the pillow, took hold of himself with his other hand and eased into me.

'Oh,' he said. His voice was all thick and crackly. 'Oh. Kate. Jesus.' It was very obvious that the time for goodness-me banter had passed.

He started moving, and I moved too, and it felt so, *so* lovely, and I was so very, very into it. He was kissing me; he had one hand on my face, it was all unbearably gorgeous, but I just couldn't seem to get the right bit on the right bit. I wriggled around more and felt a bit nearer to coming but I could feel that it wasn't going to work because I needed to be rubbed somewhere altogether else.

'Kate,' he said, after a bit. Then, 'I'm going to . . .' and then, 'Oh, oh, ohhhh.'

He flopped on top of me for a moment, then propped himself up and dropped two gentle kisses onto my lips.

'You all right?' he said. Very tender. Hand still on my face. Quick smile. Then, 'Did you . . . ?'

I was nowhere near ready to tell him the whole truth. I hesitated for a split second, which of course is all it takes. He grimaced.

'Unchivalrous,' he said. 'Sorry.'

'It's totally fine,' I said.

Obviously (or perhaps not) it had occurred to me, at some point, that I could re-arrange us so that I was on top, in what had always been my most orgasm-friendly position. But I don't think I can be up there, anymore. Face intent, hair swishing, breasts bouncing. I would look ridiculous, like a lovely old house with a tasteless extension or a sweet young man with terrible acne. I'd be that thing that makes people look away to either wince or smirk. Embarrassing. *Pitiable.* The essence of un-sexy.

'Well,' he said, in a what-on-earth-shall-we-do-now? sort of a voice. He started nuzzling me, and in the end I came very quickly.

'Thank you,' I said, after a little while, my hand still in his hair. I wondered vaguely whether 'thank you' was too effusive. Probably oral sex is standard Aussie bedroom fare nowadays. No doubt it's one of those things – like lattes and men wearing scarves – that used to be slightly European and edgy but has been commonplace for years.

I gripped Adam's hair a bit tighter.

'Thank you,' I said again. Too bad if I was being too effusive. I'd just had my first orgasm with another person since before the amputation. Adam was my first lover since then.

Fourteen years.

Chapter Four

Bec

'What's more annoying?' Kate said.

It was the night of Stuart's fortieth, and they were in Bec's en suite doing their make-up. Kate was applying bronzer along one of her formerly famous cheekbones.

'Women who talk about how they never bother wearing make-up or blow-drying their hair,' Kate went on, 'or men who say they think women having Botox is terrible?'

'I thought we weren't doing tearing-down-of-other-women?' Bec loved their 'What's More Annoying?' game, but Kate always encouraged her to listen to podcasts about being a good feminist, so surely the least Kate could do was follow their advice.

Kate put down her make-up brush and turned to Bec. 'Or women who insist on living their bloody values every single second of every single day for ever and ever? That's not tearing down, anyway.' She picked up her brush again and pouted at her reflection. 'Is this too much?'

'No,' Bec said, aware she was already blending a bit more highlighter onto her own cheekbone.

'You look nice,' Kate said. 'Wearing a dress like that when you've had three kids is just showing off.' She always said things like that, presumably so Bec would know she wasn't *at all* jealous of the children. Bec would've understood if Kate had been jealous. It wouldn't have been a crime.

'Thank you,' Bec said.

To be honest, standing next to Kate in front of a mirror was not all that easy. It wasn't that she begrudged Kate her looks. Not exactly. And Bec knew she looked pretty enough, in her beautiful bronze silk dress. In fact, she looked a bit like Kate's first draft, which was still quite nice. They both had blondy-browny hair and undemanding, tanned skin. Bec's legs were normal (Stuart said they were gorgeous); Kate's very long (Stuart made a closed, I-hadn't-noticed-them face). Bec's boobs were small and perky; Kate's were big and perky. Bec's eyes were averagely blue; Kate's were enormous and aqua. Bec's features were 'regular'; Kate's were ludicrously enjoyable to look at. Occasionally, Bec lost track of what Kate was saying because she was too busy marvelling at Kate's cheekbones – not envying them, but actually *marvelling* at them. And Kate was her *sister*.

'But what about the Botox thing?' Kate said, now. '"I just think it's a shame she's not aging gracefully", and crap like that.' She finished with her cheeks. 'And can I just say, I'm definitely getting to the age where I'm going to have to fall back on my bone structure.'

She wasn't looking for reassurance. That was the thing. Kate knew how beautiful she was.

Just then, Stuart came in and said that the kids had been disposed of – they were having a sleepover with Allie's kids; Allie's mum was in charge – and that they both looked gorgeous and to bugger off so he could have a shower. He gave Bec a little kiss on the lips as she left. It might have been nice to return it more enthusiastically, but she was too busy crossing her fingers about Mathilda's bed-wetting and wondering whether she'd imagined things with the fire-eater.

Kate and Bec repaired to another – equally 'statement' – bathroom. After she won her scholarship – *ambitious, optimistic, idealistic, fifteen* was how she'd described herself in her application – Bec used to ride her bike to school past the house that was now her home. The properties along the winding, beach-front avenue always held a vague sort of fascination for her. She used to wonder what sort of homes lay behind the tasteful, electrically operated gates, and what sort of lives were lived in them.

Now she knew. Their gate opened onto an asphalt driveway that wound through very soft, very green lawns. It passed under old European trees and around terraced flower beds to arrive at their extensively (expensively) renovated 1931 house. From the driveway, you couldn't quite see the lap pool, the raised vegetable beds, the new trampoline, the old rose garden or the gate that opened onto a private sandy path to the beach.

It was all very lovely, and it made her feel scared and sick.

Her ambitious, optimistic, idealistic, 15-year-old self hadn't known anything about enormous mortgages.

It was 9.42 p.m. Bec was feeling a bit weary.

'Everything going all right?' she asked a black-aproned waitress, who was dispensing chorizo-and-prawn skewers off a slate tray.

'Yes,' said the waitress, blandly. Clearly, she was wondering who Bec was and why Bec was talking to her. 'Would you care for a savoury prawn skewer?' Bec shook her head and moved through the kitchen.

Among the round plastic tubs of ice that stood on the floor of the butler's pantry was a rather gormless-looking girl scraping plates into a bin, and a young man called Brody, who had multiple uncom-fortable-looking piercings in his face but was the *owner* of the catering operation. Bec asked him if he had everything he needed, even though it was clear she was in his way.

'Yes thanks, Rebecca.' Presumably he had just finished a self-help book – or a YouTube tutorial, more likely – about getting ahead by remembering names. 'And the entertainer was just in here,' he added. The gormless girl jerked her head up. She had her tongue out; it was curled up, touching her top lip. 'He was looking for you, Rebecca.'

Bec was suddenly very much more awake. She still wasn't sure whether Ryan had been flirting with her. It *was* sort of impossible to believe. Or did that just indicate she was ageist and had unfashionably low self-esteem?

The gormless girl turned back to the bin. Bec checked her reflection in the mirror inside the spare mugs cupboard and then walked out into the kitchen, stepping aside for a waitress who was carrying a tray of delicious-smelling little patties made out of something unrecognisable. The waitress looked so *unconsciously* young and beautiful that Bec had to admit to feeling a bit hopeless for a second. Then she saw that Ryan was standing on the other side of the bench, staring not at the waitress, but at her.

He was at least three inches taller than the man nearest to him, and was wearing a pair of low-slung, caramel-coloured cords which had been cut and left unhemmed just above his ankles. His feet were bare. His sleeves were short. Bracelets with tiny shells and turquoise beads circled his wrists. On the floor next to him was a large black box with a faded rainforest sticker on it. He was so self-contained and so handsome and so out of place and so very *young* that she felt an immediate stab of foolishness that she had even considered that he might want to sleep with her. Not that she'd *seriously* considered it. But her fantasies crashed up against reality in a way that made her extremely glad that fantasies were private. She very much hoped Kate wasn't watching as she said, 'Hello, Ryan.'

'Hey there, Bec,' he said. He smiled slowly, for all the world as if they'd just woken up together. She put a hand to her throat, removed it instantly, and managed to ask him if he needed anything and whether he knew where he was supposed to be.

'All good,' he said. 'I'll go set up.' He raised a casual hand, and his T-shirt lifted enough for her to see his flat, tanned abdomen. 'I'll see you after, though, Bec.'

'Sure thing,' she said. There was a definite moment. He broke the eye contact first, but reluctantly, it seemed.

She swallowed.

Rebecca? said Stern Voice. *May I remind you that when you sneeze, sometimes several drops of urine leak out?*

That made her pull herself together quick smart.

Still. *See you after.* And he'd sounded as if he was looking forward to it.

In the living area, she was relieved to see that the party was precisely as dim and exactly as noisy as fortieths should be. Snippets of conversation reached her ears: 'apparently talks way too much about his own bowel flora and' . . . 'knows her digital footprint just terrifies me, but she' . . . 'No! He didn't! She'd never even told him!' Bec couldn't help but notice that some of the guests were laughing as if they'd been under a lot of pressure at work lately.

Near the door to the deck, the pretty waitress was offering prawn skewers to a handful of men that Stuart called the Old Guard. Bec could tell from everyone's posture that they were asking her what she did when she wasn't waitressing, or some nonsense like that. Bec sniffed tartly, even though, all things considered, she was perhaps not in a position to take the high moral ground. She went over.

'Thanks so much for your help,' she said to the young woman. Then she turned to the assembled men and said, 'Now, Ted, what's this I've been hearing about a new barbecue?'

48

The waitress made brief eye contact with Bec. A man in a pair of navy-blue suspenders that cut into his chest fat took a skewer – 'Thank *you*!' – from the waitress's tray, slid a plump prawn between his lips and contemplated her departing bottom. Then Ted talked about his new barbecue until Stuart – mercifully – arrived. He slipped his arm around Bec's waist; his fingers rested on her tummy in an intimate, firm way that made her realise he'd had more to drink than usual.

'Your lovely wife's looking after us so well!' said Blue Suspenders, interrupting Ted's musings on the benefits of the six-burner system. 'And when are you going to dance with her? It's not everyone whose wife still has the body of an 18-year-old.'

'Car park redevelopment's as chaotic as expected, isn't it?' replied Stuart, in a tone that Bec recognised as being Middle Class for *Shut up, cockhead, or I will deck you.*

'I think Miranda's had a bit too much, just quietly.' Blue Suspenders seemed in a poor position to criticise, but there was no doubt that Miranda – who Bec had known vaguely since university and who had once been fragile and elfin with fairy-floss hair – was very drunk. She was sitting on the edge of a potted lemon tree with her head bowed, her upper arms blotchy and her large white thighs well apart. 'Always had a liking for the bubbly, Miranda did, just quietly,' Blue Suspenders added.

'I might pop over and see how she's getting on.' Bec used an amused voice, as if they were all in on a joke. She really behaved despicably sometimes. 'Have a good night, gentlemen.' Horrible men.

As Bec moved away, Blue Suspenders said something else – something too quiet for her to catch – and the men (possibly even Stuart, it was hard to be sure) all laughed loud and unapologetic laughs. What were they all even doing in her house?

Ryan was suddenly visible over the edge of the balcony. He was standing by the terrace in the half-dark, doing something purposeful and fluid with long sticks and pieces of cloth. *See you after*. That had sounded very definite. Much more so than *See you later*.

Once Bec had deposited Miranda safely in the front sitting room – she took the precaution of placing both a vomit bowl and a glass of water at Miranda's elbow – she made her way back towards the noise of the party. Halfway along the corridor, Kate came fizzling out of a bathroom.

'How's it going?' Kate said. The corridor was an oasis of quiet. They leaned against the wall, standing so close that their hips were touching.

'Fine.' Bec shrugged. 'Just the usual. Don't know how Stuart puts up with them.' She adjusted her sleeve. 'The fire-eater's arrived.'

'I *saw* him,' said Kate, in that tone she could do.

'He—'

'Why did Stuart want a fire-eater?'

'You know what Stuart's like about parties. So—'

Kate snorted. 'Remember when he organised that whole Peter Rabbit thing?'

About a year earlier, at Essie's fourth birthday party, Stuart had organised a troupe of actors – dressed up as Mr Todd and so on – to chase the children around the garden. Essie's little friends had been terrified; only Essie had shown any spirit. ('Back to the burrow! Back to the burrow!' she'd shouted, shepherding her screaming peers towards the hidey old mulberry tree.) Stuart had been infuriatingly preoccupied with something work-related that day; it was Kate, Bec and their mum who'd had to bring out the fairy bread prematurely to calm everyone down. To top it off, the actors needed to be paid cash, which Stuart of course hadn't thought through, and while Bec was sorting that out, the radish-shaped profiterole cake collapsed. ('Croquembouche down,' her dad had muttered, like a fighter-pilot, which had made her mother start laughing. Bec had been far too frazzled to join in.) Still. Essie said it was her best party ever, which was great, even though all the kids said that every year, like the officials after the Olympics.

'Can I just say one thing?' said Kate. They turned to look at each other. 'I have never slept with a fire-eater.' She smiled her languid smile and tossed her hair.

'I need to check on the deck.' She really had no desire for yet another I'm-so-much-sexier-than-you-Bec conversation.

See you after, she was thinking, as she walked away.

Out on the deck, she stopped to talk to one of the school dads about the grade-six trip to Canberra, and gave a hectic chat-later-love-you smile to her parents. She was discussing how challenging it was going to be to keep internet porn away from their children with one of the book club mums, when she chanced a glance over the balustrade to the lawn.

Ryan was standing in front of one of the terrace's sandstone walls. The wall was lit from below with small brass lights; it loomed out of the dark lawn; his lean body was silhouetted against it. She heard herself breathe in. She felt free and reckless, like a river going over a waterfall. She was the cloud of droplets dispersed by its onward rush, the water and the spray and the plunge and the deep, dark pool at the bottom. She looked away.

'And meanwhile, you're praying they never get on a motorbike, aren't you?' she chirped, merrily. 'Now, goodness. It's ten already. And believe it or not, that means it's time for a spot of fire-eating!'

After that, it would be time to see him.

'And she's up!' Kate said.

It was the next morning, and Bec had finally shuffled into the kitchen, pulling her dressing gown around her. Kate was drinking coffee at the dining table. Stuart was standing at the stove frying eggs.

'Coffee?' he said. 'And of course you'll have eggs.' He was always way too chipper in the mornings. He cracked a couple more eggs into the frying pan.

'Oh God, have you been for a run already?' Bec asked him. She stood behind him and put her arms around his waist. His stomach was flat under his T-shirt, and she tried to feel appreciative: Stuart was not one of those gone-to-seed middle-aged men. 'And yes, please.' She kissed the back of his neck and sat next to Kate. At least the kitchen wasn't too messy. The caterers had done a reasonably good job cleaning up.

'How'd you sleep?' Bec asked Kate. Kate had slept pretty well. They talked in a desultory, Sunday-morning way about the dancing and the left-overs and Kate's flight back to Melbourne that afternoon and when the kids would be home.

'Oh my GOD!' said Kate, suddenly. 'How sexy was that fire-eater?'

'Not really my type,' Bec said. She had actually practised that phrase in the mirror before coming into the kitchen. It came out pretty well. Stuart put a cup of coffee down in front of her and went back to the stove. Kate rolled her eyes.

'She was always so conservative,' she told Stuart. 'Which is just as well for you, I s'pose.'

Bec sipped her coffee. Demure as a doctor's wife. Ha.

'Not that you're not attractive, Stuart,' Kate went on, to his back. 'You're more the hardware-store-Father's-Day-catalogue type, though. He's more the Gucci.'

Stuart laughed easily. He turned, leaned against the counter so he was facing the two women.

'How's your love life?' he asked Kate.

'Fine.'

Bec would have sworn she felt Kate start, but her voice held the trace of a shrug.

'*Is* there someone?' Bec said. Someone particular, she meant. 'What's he like?'

'Sort of,' said Kate. 'But early days.'

No doubt about it. Kate was definitely being cagey. Not like her at all.

'He should come and visit,' said Stuart. He threw a tea towel over his shoulder and gave the pan a brisk shake. He believed fried eggs shouldn't get too crispy on the bottom. 'Why didn't you bring him last night?'

'Yeah,' said Bec. 'You never bring your hotties home to meet the family.'

'Are you still not into the . . . hashtag relationship goals?' Stuart raised his eyebrows at Bec and took a mischievous slurp of his coffee. 'Madam Kate, will you ever stop torturing poor Melbourne men?'

'Or is he just not into the social chit-chat?' said Bec, getting the giggles. 'Better things to do with your time together? Is it more just Netflix and Chill?'

'You two do realise that you talk like repressed teenagers when your kids aren't around?' said Kate, and Stuart and Bec had a microsecond of shit-do-we-really? eye contact.

'Sorry,' said Bec. How very mortifying. She put on her most progressive, respectful-of-all-choices face. 'But just to say, you know, if you wanted to invite him down, we'd love to meet him. Or anyone you like.'

''Course we would,' said Stuart. He'd always had such a lot of time for Kate. 'Bring him down soon. What's his name? I'll vet him for you.'

'Adam,' said Kate. 'All right. Maybe. I'll ask him.' She tilted her head, one way, then the other, as if she had a crick in her perfect neck. 'Thanks, that might be nice.'

The only sound was the eggs frying and the fan above the stove. Bec sipped her coffee and looked out over the Derwent.

It had been a great party. People had wondered aloud why on earth they'd never thought of having a fire-eater; she was pretty sure that Ryan was about to be besieged by Sandy Bay residents booking him for their next 'event'. There were rhapsodies about the espresso van that arrived at eleven. At least two dozen people were dancing on the deck at 1 a.m. and several couples who'd been planning to drive home took Ubers. Even Kate – on her way to bed at almost three – commented that it was one of the best parties she could remember. 'Which is a miracle, really,' she'd added, with a yawn. 'Considering who you had to work with.'

Stuart had almost had tears in his eyes when he made his speech. He'd thanked Bec for 'making his world'. Allie had listened with her hand flat against her chest and her head tilted a little bit to one side. He was *such* a lovely husband, but listening to him, Bec had felt a wave of something else, too: something unfamiliar and unexpected. Something that was close to pity.

Because. Even though the whole party thing was moderately satisfying, and even though people were looking at her as if she was the luckiest – and even, inexplicably, the most *admirable* – woman in the universe, she was really just waiting for the formalities to wind up so she could see Ryan.

He had finished his 'bit' as he called it. He packed up while the speeches were going on, and then stayed to sing 'Happy Birthday' – it was that kind of night; even the catering staff were singing – and finally he was following her along the corridor to the front door. Even once the party noise lessened, their footsteps were inaudible on the clean beige carpet. They stood together just inside the doorway. He looked so comfortable, and somehow *real* against the spotless walls.

'Won't your feet be cold?' she asked him as she was about to undo the deadlock. He just shook his head. She couldn't help but be aware that he was standing quite close to her. Was that just what twenty-something people did?

'Well, thank you again,' she said. As brightly interested as a business-class flight attendant. And so cringingly polished, with her clever, grown-up social skills.

'All good.' He kept his eyes on her face, and exhaled, loud enough so that she could hear.

'I've paid you, right?' She was flustered. He nodded. They were still facing each other in front of the door; his chest was centimetres away from hers. She glanced down the corridor: it was empty. Surfie types like him often seemed to be comfortable with silence.

'What?' she said. Was there cake around her mouth? Chorizo in her teeth? She put a hand up to her face. Really, she was not at all suited to being a sexy older woman.

'When did you meet your husband?' he asked.

'Sorry?'

'When did you two meet?'

'Oh. Stuart. I was twenty-four.'

He nodded. It felt as if he wanted to chat, chat to *her*, and she got a surge of courage.

'What about you? Are you . . . attached?'

She'd already imagined his type. She – certainly a she – would have artless hair and wide green eyes. She'd have one of those long, taut abdomens and small, perfect breasts and manage to look gorgeous in an Indian cotton slip dress thrown over bathers. She'd go surfing in a serious, meaningful sort of a way, be vegan and take occasional party drugs. She and Ryan would have pledged their love at sunrise on a cliff top, with rings Ryan had whittled out of a whale bone that they'd found washed up on a remote beach.

'I'm single. Never married. No children.' She hadn't even considered that he might have children; he didn't look old enough somehow. Which was silly. He had to be at least twenty-five.

'And you came to Tassie for the surf?' He'd told her that the other day. She really was an excellent active listener – *which of course*, said Stern Voice, *is exactly what young men look for in sexual partners.*

'Yeah,' he said. He kept staring at her, and she accidentally twirled her hair around her forefinger. His chest was just muscly enough.

She let go of her hair and wondered about something else to say. Or maybe it was fine to stay silent. Weren't older women supposed to exude a sort of enigmatic knowingness? Wasn't that supposed to make up for the fact that they were no longer as nubile as the too-insecure-to-be-truly-sexy 19-to-25-year-old sector?

'Been good to meet you,' he said, at last, and there was a moment of meaningful eye contact that she definitely did not imagine. 'Really. Very good.'

'Yes. It has. And now' – on purpose she sounded extremely reluctant, which was unforgivable – 'you'd better go.'

She opened the front door and stayed standing where she was, all the while thinking: I am wearing a dress Stuart earned the money to pay for! All $590 of it! While Stuart is thirty metres away! At his own fortieth! Possibly chatting to my dad about compost, even though he finds compost tedious but has somehow fallen into the trap of letting my parents believe he finds it fascinating!

Ryan was still standing there. He made an eloquent gesture. Like a shrug. An obviously-we-want-to-kiss-but-oh-well-we're-too-honourable sort of a gesture.

And she knew she should have opened the door briskly and nodded curtly and walked back down the corridor purposefully to her lovely husband. But she didn't do any of those things.

Instead, she stood still and watched as Ryan shifted the large black box to his other hand. He had to pass really close to get through the front door. As he passed, he looked into her eyes. With his free hand, he *grazed the side of her waist*. It was the sort of gesture Kate or Allie might have made – intimate, affectionate – but was it also underscored with something else? That something else being – since she was allowed to *think* it, whatever Stern Voice may say – the desire to peel her beautiful dress right off.

'See you around,' he said.

'See you around.' She'd made it sound like an agreement to meet again, and she hadn't sounded like a flight attendant.

'Your eggs are done,' said Stuart.

'Are you all right?' Kate asked.

'I'm fine!' Now her voice was like a cheerleader's. 'Just a teensy bit hung-over.'

She drank her coffee, and when Stuart brought the eggs she thanked him, and when it got a bit later she had a shower, and the whole despicable fizzy time she was wondering where, and when, and how, she might manage to see him around again.

Chapter Five

Kate

'Penny?' I said, putting my head around her door. I had to force myself to use her first name. I'm as timid as the students when it comes to PPP, and we usually communicated by email.

Professor Penelope Purcell had summoned me to a meeting in her office. It was very tidy, as always. There were archived academic journals in colourful cardboard magazine holders, and folders with handwritten labels – very attractive writing, all done in the same black felt-tip pen – arranged on shelves. She had one of those noticeboards that is half cork, half whiteboard. The cork half displayed tasteful postcards – line drawings and such, not aerial photographs of hotels and sea – and photos. There was one of her in a big group with Julia Gillard. The white board said things like: *ASHM Hong Kong presentation – make a start* and *Delegate lit review for SV*. Today, sixth item from the top, it said: *KL re future plans*. Items one to five had been crossed off and it was only 11.45 a.m.

'Hello, Kate,' she said. As she spoke, she took her fingertips off her keyboard, swivelled in her chair and gestured for me to sit on a tiny, hard-looking couch. She has an excellent haircut (short) and a very slight English accent, as if her parents grew up around the corner from the Beatles.

'Thanks for coming in. I thought it was time we touched base about next semester.' It was March. 'Would you be available to give a course of lectures to the second years? Some stuff about data extraction methods, qualitative versus quantitative research, what constitutes valid references . . .' She waved a hand to indicate we both knew what she was talking about. 'The kids are very black-and-white still at that stage; you'll do them good.'

She spoke as if she knew my situation exactly. That I didn't need the money. That I had enough time. That I'd be reticent. As if she knew all that, but it was still a forgone conclusion that I'd say yes.

'Sure, Penny,' I heard myself say. 'Certainly, I can.' Mum, and a million podcasts, always talk about how women tend to doubt their own capacity.

'Good. Prudence-Rose will be on maternity leave again, and this is a good opportunity for PhD candidates. I'm assuming you'll be continuing with a doctorate next year?'

'Um. Well. To be honest, I—' I paused. I thought PPP would jump in the way people usually do, and say something like, 'Well, no pressure obviously, but you might like to consider it when you're ready,' or, 'Of course, there's no need to tell *me* your career plans.' But she stayed perfectly still and silent. Looking at me.

'Maybe,' I said, even though I'd always believed PhDs were not for people like me. 'I'll need to think that over.' It was pretty exciting.

'Good.' She sounded satisfied. She gave me some concise instructions about what to do next, should I decide to go ahead. 'Of course,' she finished, sounding a bit weary, 'everyone in the department will have an agenda.'

I looked at her. I had no idea what she meant. 'Thank you,' I said. I stood up to go.

'One more thing,' she said. I sat back down. 'I understand you spoke to Claire Simpson last Wednesday?'

'Yes.' Claire was one of my first years. The poor girl had nearly been in tears during the presentation she was doing. 'How is she?'

'She's fine. Just be mindful. If a student has mental health issues, you need to give them the helpline number rather than get involved yourself.'

Unexpected steel clenched inside me, even though she was Professor Penelope Purcell.

'I beg your pardon?' I said. Once I read that that is a good reply when someone says something outrageous. It's to buy you time to come up with a good 'riposte'.

'None of us are trained in crisis management. Anxiety. Suicidality.'

'She's not suicidal,' I riposted. (Go, me.) 'She hasn't got "mental health issues". She was upset because she broke up with her boyfriend and her family is in Shepparton or somewhere, and now she's sharing a house with a lunatic girl who wakes her up at 3 a.m. with terrible music and she's worried her ex won't be feeding their dog.'

'Well, it may not be appropriate for us to involve ourselves in pastoral care. It's really for the helpline to sort out those sorts of issues.'

'No it is *not*.' My words surprised me, and I think PPP was surprised too, even though she didn't move. 'Not everyone needs counselling,' I went on, as if I knew what I was talking about. 'Sometimes people just need a friendly chat with a . . . a grown-up.'

'I can see you feel very strongly about this, Kate,' she said. She was obviously buying *her*self time by reverting to some sort of gold-standard conflict-management evidence-based reflective-listening technique. I hate that. In fact, *I* can see that *I* feel hugely bloody irritated when people pull out that sort of tiresome crap. Rage rose in me. Familiar, even though it had been a while. I took a deep breath.

'Listen. Penny. Claire was fine. Really. I asked her if she was thinking of topping herself and she said she wasn't. She apologised for crying and I gave her some tissues and we had a cup of tea. I told her about my horrible ex-boyfriend' – still known to Bec and me as Horrible

Hayden – 'from when I was at uni. We had a laugh. She said she knew she was better off single.' (I'd made the tea at the staff tea station; it was the first time I'd ever drunk it; it was execrable, as bad as hospital stuff.) 'It's not abnormal to cry when you're sad and exhausted. You don't need a helpline for that. You need a cup of tea with sugar and a hug.' I'd given her that too.

PPP kept sitting still and looking at her interlocked hands.

'Please remember we've had this conversation.' Then she smiled and sat back in her chair. 'Claire told me you'd been very helpful. And they're all adults after all,' she added, half to herself. 'Look, Kate. Just – be careful.'

'I will,' I said. Then I added – maybe rather dramatically; I was wearing magenta silk high-waisted knickers and no bra, plus the whole new-lover-sex-orgasm thing was still wrapped around me like an invisible cloak – 'But I also am going to be *human.*' Perhaps I am becoming a sort of oddball academic. This is a worry: my hair is too naturally messy for any personal eccentricity to creep in. I would appear unhinged.

PPP gave a single nod. We said goodbye. I stood up to go as she turned back to her computer.

'Oh, thank God! I've finally placed you,' she said, as I reached the door. She whirled around on her chair to face me, her hands in fists with the forefingers pointing up. 'It's been bugging me for *months.* You were in *Sports Illustrated!*'

'Oh,' I said. 'Yes.' It was one of my last shoots. I'd been disappointed not to make the cover.

'My little brother had your picture on his wall. He was in love with you in high school.'

It is very odd to pretty much be told that your boss's brother spent a goodly portion of the early noughties masturbating while looking at a picture of you in bathers.

'Another life,' I said. My standard response. It's the best I've been able to come up with. This sort of thing had happened a few times. (The being-recognised thing; the boss-brother-masturbation angle was a first.)

'So that's how you manage shoes like that on a tutor's wage. Good for you.' It's possible she'd taken my rant about being human too far, but I found I liked it. Is there anything more annoying than people whose main life goal is to be *appropriate*?

'My dad was in ethical investment, before it was a thing,' I found myself saying. 'He kept me on the straight and narrow.'

'And what does your mother do?' she asked, as interested as if she were doing field work.

'She's a social worker. Migrants and refugees.'

'Ah. I bet they were mortified about the modelling,' said Penny.

'Yes!' I said. 'They were!' (They were. No one else had ever acknowledged that.)

'Well,' said PPP. 'That's a relief.' She meant that she'd finally placed me. Then she waved a hand. 'I'll let you get on.'

I walked down the corridor, aware that I'd just fallen into deep and platonic love with Professor Penelope Purcell.

It was the following week, and I was lying on my favourite rug, talking on the phone to Bec.

When I'd finished telling her about the PhD (she thought I should definitely go for it, which was nice), I said, 'So, about bringing Adam down to meet you?'

'Oh!' said Bec. 'How *are* things with Adam?'

She didn't wait for an answer, but launched into her standard spiel, which is along the lines of: my life here in suburban Hobart is so boring and married and middle-class that the only way for me to have any excitement at all is by hearing about your crazy single-girl Melbourne hijinks, kiddo!

It's all the more annoying because I am the older sister.

'So, we're coming to Tassie?' I said. 'We're thinking the sixteenth?' *We're,* I thought. Listen to me.

'That soon?' said Bec.

Adam had seemed pretty keen, actually. I'd given him a warehouse-sized amount of room to say no – regrettably, I used the phrase 'no pressure' at least twice – but he'd cut me off and said, 'I love Hobart. Let's do it.'

'Yes,' I told Bec, now. 'But before you offer, we won't stay at your place this time. Thanks and all, but we're very much in the wanting-privacy phase.'

'Of course!' Then Bec launched into her routine about soccer, crazy, swimming lessons, busy, Stuart on call, nits, joint calendar, parent-teacher interviews, how can it be March already!, orthodontics, expensive, busy. Finally she said, 'Maybe afternoon tea at our house on the Saturday afternoon? And then lunch at Mum and Dad's on the Sunday? So you'd have the mornings to yourselves? And the evenings? Or would two events be too much for him? Too boring? Because we cou—'

'Who cares if he's bored?' I said. Nonchalance about men is *my* standard schtick, obviously. 'That all sounds lovely.'

We couldn't leave Melbourne until Adam finished work, which wasn't until after seven, so we didn't arrive until late at our hotel in Hobart. It was all recycled wood and tastefully dull brass and organic moisturiser in bigger-than-usual matte plastic bottles.

On Saturday, at just after three, we knocked on the door of Bec's house. Mathilda answered. There were hugs, Lego, hair-clips, slime kits – I am a present-giving aunty; I'll do whatever it takes to main-tain their adoration of me – and exclamations over the length of Essie's legs and Lachlan's new braces and my braid. (I'd had it done the day before in Melbourne.)

Then the children dispersed to do the healthful, wholesome sorts of things they tend to do on Saturday afternoons. (Lachlan: practise handball in the garage or ride his bike in the driveway. Mathilda: engineer slime in the laundry. Essie: help Mathilda with slime.)

I had assumed Bec would be so happy that I was introducing *anyone* to her that she'd serve some sort of gin with the word 'artisan' on the label and six different cheeses (also 'artisan'). I'd presumed she'd say over-intimate things like, 'Has Kate told you about Horrible Hayden yet?' or 'When is Kate going to drag you to London and make you look at the torture instruments?' I'd thought we'd end up staying for dinner.

'Tea?' she said. 'And want to put those out, Kate?' She indicated a brown paper bag of vanilla slices (Mathilda's favourite). 'Sorry Stuart – my husband – couldn't be here. He's at work,' she told Adam. When she said 'at work' she made it sound as if the words had Capital Letters. Or maybe – I concede it's possible – it only sounded like that to me.

Adam said something about Stuart's job being very demanding and Bec laughed her best Sandy Bay tinkly laugh and said, 'Well, he loves it. Surgeons all seem to be like that. And you're a photographer, I understand?'

She was pouring boiling water into the teapot that used to be our grandmother's, otherwise it's possible I would have smacked her in the head – maybe with one of the vanilla slices – while saying, 'Shut up, Bec, because you sound exactly like the person you never wanted to be.'

I didn't. I transferred the six luscious-looking custard-y treats onto one of Bec's big white platters and enjoyed the silence while Adam considered his response. He seemed more like a relaxed tiger than a meerkat right then, I was delighted to note.

'Three kids, eh?' he said, in the end. 'Kate tells me you're very busy.'

It was just the right thing to say. Bec managed to start acting normal and told a funny story about Mathilda's school's Flourish Program – that's what sex education is called now, apparently – while she put the teapot and milk and sugar and cups onto the bench.

'I'm exhausted,' she said, at one point. 'Bloody Mathilda wet the bloody bed last night – bloody 3 a.m. – and bloody Stuart's been on bloody call all week.' That probably explained the vanilla slices. She was wearing more make-up than usual and I felt a stab of love for her.

Forty minutes passed. We discussed Adam's nephew who is Mathilda's age and still wets the bed, the extreme sexism yet entertaining-ness of the Enid Blyton book that Mathilda had somehow got her hands on (Bec hadn't given it to her; she hates Enid Blyton), rock-climbing, my current essay, and Bec's cleaning lady who Bec thinks might be in a domestic violence relationship and Bec is wondering if she should talk to her about it (which I told her I can't believe she even has to think about). Adam said domestic violence was a huge problem and I chimed in with something about mental-health funding and Adam said his parents lived in the country and things about farmers and firearms. Bec said a patient of Stuart's had killed herself the year before. 'I mean,' she added, looking horrified, 'the suicide was made public. We're not breaching confidentiality or anything.'

I was just about to tell them about a podcast I'd listened to on men's sheds, but then Bec said, 'People say surgeons don't care. But Stuart certainly takes things to heart. Such a perfectionist.'

'I guess even doctors are only human,' I said.

Bec looked like I'd smacked her, so I put my hand on her arm and added, 'I know Stuart cares, Bec. Sorry. Of course, he does.' He really does.

Around then, Stuart himself arrived back from the hospital.

'Madam Kate!'

He was all bonhomie and, I could tell, genuinely happy to see me. He looked at Adam as if he was trying to decide what football code Adam followed. Bec flicked the kettle back on.

The two men then got into an oddly lengthy discussion about sourdough bread. Bec and I had a good but similarly too-long chat about Essie's lovely teacher who is letting her hair go grey as a statement. Then Bec and Stuart started talking about the Melbourne photography scene. They said names, all knowledge-able and show-offy. They talked about exhibitions and galleries and artists-in-residence.

'And what sort of stuff do you do, Adam?' Stuart said.

'I tend to do urban streetscapes. A few people. Nothing too arty.' Adam reached across me – leaning in so close I could smell him – and took a vanilla slice. 'So, on the way here, we—'

'Would we know your work?' Stuart asked. 'Sounds as if it might be that gritty Chris McLaren aesthetic?'

Adam looked blank. 'That's not really what I do,' he said.

'You involved in that *Laneways* book? The Fred Delia anthology?'

'That's not really what I do,' said Adam, again.

'Weddings and stuff like that, is it, then, mate?' said Stuart. He tilted his chin back a tiny bit, and his tone made me understand why some people hate private-school parents.

'Well.' Adam swallowed. He sipped his tea.

'You must have some interesting wedding stories,' Bec said, as if it was a cross examination. 'Do tell us more, Adam.'

66

'Ah,' said Adam. 'Nothing much comes to mind. How was—?'

'So, how long have you *been* a photographer?' she said.

There was a silence.

'I did a science degree first. And then sort of segued into it after that.' For the first time since I met Adam – admittedly not that long ago – he looked less than completely self-assured.

Stuart nodded. 'I see,' he said.

'That so?' said Bec, also nodding.

I looked at Bec in this certain way I do (furious), and she immediately said, 'Anyway, speaking of weddings! We've been invited to one in Brisbane.'

'How nice,' I said, very sweetly. But something in Adam's posture had changed. Enough to make me feel a little bit sick about him.

I said we'd better go, and that I'd just have a quick chat to the children. Bec decided to come with me.

'So, um, how serious are you guys?' she asked, as we walked down the corridor.

Her face was so smooth and *compassionate* that I shrugged my most nonchalant shrug and said, 'You know what I'm like.'

Later, as she hugged me goodbye, she said, 'Thanks for fitting us into your dirty weekend.' She was trying for light and girly but didn't quite manage it. With her forearm still on mine, she looked into my eyes – all serious and meaningful – and said, 'As long as you're happy. That's all we care about.'

I moved my arm away.

'I didn't mean—' she said, innocently. Pretending she *adored* Adam. Pretending we'd all just had a perfectly *marvellous* chat.

'Don't worry about it. We'll see you tomorrow at Mum and Dad's.' I sounded like Jane Seymour. (King Henry VIII's third wife. Haughty and poised, yet forgiving of others' foibles.)

What is more annoying? I asked myself, as Adam reversed our hire car out of their twisty-turny driveway like he'd been doing it all his life. People who say 'we' when 'I' would suffice, people who talk about your 'dirty' weekend away, or people who say they 'just want you to be happy' when they're not even your parents?

But I didn't laugh with Adam about any of that, the way I might have done only a few hours before.

The next day, Sunday, I felt a bit better about things. Perhaps I had strategically re-aligned my goals with the current environment, or nimbly adjusted my priorities in the face of changing conditions, or resiliently accepted the world's harsh realities, or whatever.

'Ready for the parents?' I said, from around my toothbrush.

'I'm really crap with parents,' he said. He was in the bedroom, buttoning up his shirt. 'But I'll give it a crack. Your mum's Marion, right?'

'Correct. And Dad is Rob, but we all call him BFG. He's really tall.'

'Got names wrong once before.'

'You dill. Don't today.'

'Won't.'

'Because *my* parents notice everything.'

'No resemblance, then.' Affectionately.

We weren't looking at each other, but we were having a really nice time.

It turned out Mum had made lamb shoulder (Lebanese flavours, as predicted) and her Earl Grey tea cake. The cake was a nice surprise, as it's my favourite dessert and I'd been anticipating cardamom rice pudding or some such.

She was friendly – 'How do you go with pine nuts, Adam?' and then, 'Be a love and pop the couscous on the table' – but she didn't ask him for his views on Extinction Rebellion, food additives or Scrabble. I could, therefore, tell that Bec had phoned a report in, and that it hadn't been positive. Bec smiled at me and helped Mum with the pilaki and the water jugs. Innocent as a strawberry. Whatever, I thought.

During lunch, Adam pointed out BFG's recently completed chook enclosure, which admittedly is very well-engineered. 'That pre-fab?' Adam said. BFG was delighted, because he never uses pre-fab, and he therefore gave a very lengthy answer – at least ten seconds – involving the terms load-bearing and Z-something. Adam tilted his jaw in an attentive, man-to-man way and then said something about tensile strength. Stuart made a well-informed remark about the begonias.

After lunch, while the kids were up various trees – Bec and Stuart embrace a limited-screen, free-play parenting style – Adam went outside with Mum and BFG to be shown the coriander patch and the tomato vines (as featured in the lamb) and to have a closer look at the chook enclosure.

The rest of us cleaned up. Mum and BFG don't own a dishwasher: their kitchen is little, with old cupboards – freshly painted blue – and an excellent gas cooker. I was happily putting Mum's cups away, when Stuart said, 'So, have you met *his* family?' I was pretty sure Bec would already have told him I hadn't. Of course, she'd wheedled that out of me days ago.

'They're out past Ballarat,' I replied. Ballarat is an unpleasant three-hour drive from where we live.

'So, what's his place like?'

'Pardon?' I said. Imperiously.

'Stu.' Bec sounded like a warning beacon. She's unbelievably two-faced sometimes.

'All part of my standard vetting procedure.' He was aiming to sound light.

'No idea,' I said. I put Mum's favourite green teacup back on its hook. 'Haven't seen it.'

Bec froze. '*Really?*'

'Really?' echoed Stuart. He stopped trying to be light, which was a vast relief as he's not that good at it. He frowned, as if he was my father (the sort of vigilant-about-marriage-prospects father who would fight a duel over his daughter's virtue) and I could practically hear him reminding himself of my ample net worth.

Just then his phone rang, and he said a few brisk, surgeon-y things about normal saline and keep them fasted, and then told us he had to go off to work. (Pretty much all he ever says on the phone is normal saline and fasted. I could do it.)

'Give my apologies to your mum and dad,' he said to Bec. 'Give the kids a kiss.' He didn't mention Adam. He didn't go outside to shake his hand goodbye. At the kitchen door, he gave me a hug, which included a bear-up-old-girl pat on the back.

'Hope work goes well,' I said, wishing it would involve pus in someone's bottom or something like that.

Bec and I went back to the sink in silence. She dried items very thoroughly, and I put them away very neatly. Through the window, we heard Essie yelling, 'Is Ms Tillack meaner than Mrs Syme?' and Mathilda bawling back, 'WHAT?' several times. (Eventually they came up onto Mum's tiny deck and it was established that no, Ms Tillack was kind yet firm, while Mrs Syme was the meanest teacher in the whole junior school, and had once been known to insist on a grade-six girl retrieving her untouched ham sandwich from a *bin* and taking it home to show her mother.)

'"Kind yet firm",' Bec said. She hates confrontation. 'Bloody Enid Blyton. The other day I heard them call someone thin-lipped and cruel. And Mathilda keeps asking for ginger bloody beer.'

I laughed, but tightly.

By the time we'd finished the cutlery, the others were all on the deck, looking down towards the river and up towards the mountain. BFG appeared to be pointing out the road up to the summit. Just about every house in Hobart has a really good view and a biggish garden, but Adam of course wasn't used to that and was staring around in an impressed, only-ten-minutes-from-the-CBD! way.

Bec folded up the tea towel and hung it neatly over the middle of the oven rail, the way she and Mum and I always do with tea towels. Then we stood together, looking out of the kitchen window at the little group on the balcony. Adam was now squatting on his haunches to talk to Essie.

'He's really cute, though, isn't he?' she said, eventually.

'Yep.' I said it icily, with a very pronounced 'p' sound.

She looked down at her fingers, which were twisted together the way they always are when she's under pressure. 'Kate, Stuart just wants to make sure you—'

'Not everyone even wants a cookie-cutter perfect relationship, Bec, you know.' The sentence started off sounding cosmopolitan and scornful but finished up a bit broken. It's a stupid saying anyway, because everyone likes cookies, and how else would you even make them?

'Of course!' she said. 'Well, like I said, he's really cute, and as long as you're happy.'

'I am.' Then I gathered my now unbraided hair so it fell over my shoulder and gave her a modest-yet-suggestive little smile. I nudged her with my hip and lowered my voice in an experienced-urban-older-sister way. 'It is just *ridiculous*, the chemistry.'

Which had the dual advantage of being true and of wiping the appraising, superior shrewdness right off her face.

'Babe, I can't make it to dinner tonight,' Adam said, the very next Tuesday. 'Sorry.'

It was almost five. I told myself that he wasn't to know there was beef stew simmering on my little-used stove, or how hard I'd worked to finely chop two large onions, or that, while I'd been re-drafting my essay on late-sixteenth-century concepts of household roles, a whole separate part of my mind had been polishing up my delight in the idea that, like a genuine bachelor girl, I'd be finishing up at my desk by around five and having a quick shower before sitting down to a casual dinner with the guy I was seeing.

'No worries,' I said. Against all the boring advice about men that has ever been given, I added, 'How come?'

'Work stuff,' he said.

'What work stuff?' Lightly.

'Should I come by later? Say eleven?'

There was a silence. I considered my options.

'All right,' I said. My tone was as breezy as a small-car commercial. 'I'll save you some stew.'

I planned to leave the stew on the counter and be smooth and scented and asleep (or at least fake-asleep) when he buzzed. Unfortunately, he appeared an hour early, at just after ten, and I was sitting on the couch, un-showered and crying. My eyes always go red when I cry.

'Hey. Kate. Babe. What's wrong?' He put down his backpack and gave me a hug.

'Where've you been?' I said, into his shoulder. When I could smell that he'd just had a shower, I totally dropped my bundle. My snot went all over his black thermal.

'I told you.' His voice was tender. 'Work stuff.' I stood back and looked at him the way Bec looks at the kids when there are Tim Tams missing from the treats shelf.

'How dumb do you think I am?' I said. In my head I was Catherine of Aragon (first wife): intelligent, dignified, moral-high-ground occupier extraordinaire. But out loud my voice was the unhinged shriek of the vacuous and contemptible (in my humble opinion) Catherine Howard (fifth wife) on her way to the Tower. I saw my stump waggling in my peripheral vision. It's very difficult not to talk with your hands when you're upset, even if you don't still have a hand. My jigging stump made me cry more.

'Kate. I promise. I was working.' He gave me a gentle kiss on the forehead, and put his arms around me again. After a bit he kissed the top of my head. 'Now. Go and blow your nose,' he said. I didn't feel like moving, but I turned around and went towards the bathroom.

I had a shower, and thought about how, that evening, I'd discovered that even if you went through every single entry on the first six pages, Google had nary a mention of a Melbourne photographer called Adam Cincotta.

I stood under the hot water and tried to decide what to do. What sort of urban wilderness artiste doesn't have a bafflingly solemn website that takes minutes to load? I could ask him, in a teasing voice, as if I was joking. And – I could say, a bit more seriously, as if I was concerned about industrial exploitation in the creative sector – what sort of photographer has to be at work at nine o'clock on a Tuesday evening without warning?

When I got back to the lounge room, he was just finishing his stew. I hovered for a moment. He turned around and smiled at me, and I decided not to ask any of my questions.

You see, I had been lonely for such a very, very long time.

Chapter Six

Bec

It was after ten by the time Bec arrived home from dropping off the kids. She was vacuuming the lounge room when her phone rang.

'Mrs Henderson.' His voice sounded intimate and jokey, as if they'd agreed on that as a private nickname. The vacuum cleaner finished its brief decrescendo; there was silence.

'Hi, Ryan,' she said. She stayed standing up, even though she was right next to her own couch.

'Thanks again for the other night,' he said. It was more than three weeks since Stuart's party. 'How'd you all go the next morning?'

'Yeah. Bit dusty.' What was she saying? Why was she using that knowing, sardonic tone? She used to talk like that when she was at university. 'I think Stuart had a very sore head.' That was the right response. And it would remind them both who the party had been for.

'Fun night,' he said. She was still trying to work out exactly how he meant that, and also, how to agree in a not-overly-eager way, when he said, 'Life settled down now, then?'

'Oh well, you know, there's always something, isn't there?' she said. 'Things are as cray-cray as usual.' Dear God, she was sounding more like Allie every day.

'Ah yeah. My mum always reckons it's women who carry the burden of the universe.'

'Sounds like the sort of thing my mum'd say.' Her mum would have put it more like, Women perform the majority of domestic labour and have hardly any superannuation. But really, similar sentiment.

'Would she?' He sounded intrigued, almost as if he thought that implied some sort of connection between them.

'I can just imagine your mum,' Bec said, on an impulse. She actually could, too. 'I bet she knits beanies – in a cool way – and makes those beeswax sandwich wraps. I bet she used to let you climb really high on play equipment but hardly watch any TV and I bet . . . I bet she doesn't believe in vaccination.' She used a shock-horror voice when she said the vaccination line, so he'd know that she was not judging his mum's choices on that issue. Even though she was judging her head off, and obviously *her* children had had every vaccine going.

'Pretty right,' he said. 'She weaves. And does cool pottery.' He laughed. 'Just don't tell your husband about the vaccination thing.'

'Hate to break it to you, but I'm a doctor too, Ryan. So you're in big trouble now.' She didn't know what was worse: that she sounded as jolly as all-get-out, or that she sounded so pathetically show-offy.

(Once, when she was in year ten, Bec had been on the kitchen phone to the boy she had a crush on. When she hung up, Kate – then in year twelve – said, 'Were you *trying* to be un-sexy, Bec?')

'Are you? Really?' said Ryan. He sounded intrigued again, and as if he didn't think she was being too jolly or too show-offy at all.

'No. Not really. I mean, I was. But I don't – I'm not even registered anymore.'

'Because of the kids?'

'Partly, I suppose. I don't quite carry the burden of the entire universe, but definitely the burden of an average-sized household.'

Less jolly now, thank goodness. 'And the kids are young still, and I sort of believe they need me. Not that it's not great. I mean, I know I'm very fortunate. To have that choice.'

Even as she was saying all that, she knew that later she would regret being so forthcoming and unguarded and sincere. All the stuff about their mums, too. But it somehow felt as if she *had* to be – had to be light and open and confiding – to make the conversation take the right shape, so he wouldn't feel disappointed in her. So he wouldn't think, Why did I bother ringing that uptight Sandy Bay lady? and instead would think, That woman is down to earth and *enchanting*. And then he might ring her again, or at least keep using that impressed, intrigued tone.

'Sounds to me like your family are really fortunate too,' he said.

'Oh well. Surgeons have to work very hard.' She kept saying that lately, as if a surgeon was all Stuart was. 'How long have you been in Hobart?'

'Two or three months. WA originally. Then I was up northern New South Wales. Just time for a change.'

'So, do you support yourself with fire-eating work?'

'Nah. I own a property near Byron Bay.' Perhaps he'd inherited it. 'Airbnb. That keeps me going. I do a bit of circus-skills stuff and labouring. A couple of gardens.'

'I sound like the mother in *Titanic*,' she said, remembering when poor-but-charming Leonardo DiCaprio went to dinner in first class. 'Checking your credentials.' Good grief, she was probably nearly the mother's age by now too. 'Have you even seen *Titanic*?'

''Course I have,' he said. 'That scene in the car.' He gave a tiny groan. 'Sexy, sexy Kate Winslet. Beautiful woman.'

Bec went very still inside. His appreciative, knowing tone. The way he hadn't said *still* beautiful. The way he hadn't said *was* sexy. There was a pause.

'To be honest,' she said, 'I wasn't at all dusty after the other night. I barely drank.'

He was quiet for a second too. Then he said, "Course. Loads of work for you. Man. Putting everyone at ease, making sure things flowed right, directing the troops.' There was a smile in his voice. 'Me included. What else? Oh yeah, wrapping all the grumpy old men round your little finger. Helping that poor drunk lady.'

'You saw that?' Miranda had re-surfaced during the fire-eating.

'Yeah. Nights like that don't just happen, right? It was a slick operation. And it actually had heart. Beautiful outside and in, I thought.'

'Wow. Thanks.'

'It's true.' A little beat. 'Yeah, so I was just calling. To thank you, really. I've had lots of calls, new business. Been good for me.' Bec was aware of an indefensible stab of disappointment. 'And also to say, maybe you and I could catch up one time?'

She swallowed.

'I know, like, six people in Hobart,' he added.

(Bec couldn't imagine he wouldn't be able to find dozens of people to be friends with – men like him were always part of a tribe of young people, all practising acrobatics in a way that barely concealed the sexual tension everyone was feeling. There was also usually a posse of their children, who all had mohawks and grown-up nicknames, and who were preternaturally good at either surfing or guitar.)

'Um,' she said.

Don't you dare! cried Stern Voice.

'Probably not this week,' Bec said.

It was like being in a car accident. The type in which you were all right, but you couldn't believe it had happened. You just sort of sat there, in your car, feeling shocked and brave and waiting for someone to help you.

'It's tricky, isn't it?' he said, eventually. 'This thing. You and me.'

She didn't know how to respond. It took a lot of effort not to default to, 'I know!' or 'Sorry!'

'I'll let you go then, Bec. Take care, won't you, hey?'

'I will. You too, Ryan.'

They said goodbye. More fondly than was standard, but still. Very decorously. And as if they both thought it was for the last time.

'Oh my word, you have got to be joking!' It was later that afternoon. Bec turned in her seat to meet Essie's eyes. 'Two certificates in one day!'

'Mum! Watch the road!' screeched Mathilda. Bec had just collected the girls from school. Essie was telling a long, excited story about the Premier's Choir Challenge and her Star of the Week award, punctuating her sentences with kicks to the back of Bec's seat. Bec inched the car forward towards the roundabout, and twiddled her fingers at Rachel (Amelia's Mum) Linton who was stowing a backpack into the boot of her enormous four-wheel drive. Rachel gave Bec a sort of half-smile, half-grimace, as if they were Anzacs about to go over the top.

'Well, that's just wonderful,' Bec said. 'Darling, have you got magical shoes on? Is it them that I can feel tap dancing on my back?'

Mathilda giggled. Essie giggled.

In that moment, she knew she was crazy to have taken that call from Ryan. Stuart was really a wonderful husband, and they had a wonderful family. She had to put the fire-eater out of her mind, the way you sacked a piano teacher or a cleaner who wasn't working out. Because she had never been of the view that fantasies were all right and crushes were to be expected and innocent flirting was simply a normal part of being married. Just her opinion, but surely you were better off putting your heart and mind into whatever you were actually doing.

She looked again at Essie and Mathilda (Lachlan was at soccer training). The two of them were talking about someone called Zora whose little sister had broken her arm. Essie was gazing at Mathilda as if she was trying to remember everything Mathilda did so she could tell someone all about it later. It was so very cute, and Bec made a mental note to mention it to Stuart. ('They're gorgeous at the moment, aren't they?' he'd say, his eyes crinkling up as he imagined them. Stuart'd been saying 'gorgeous at the moment' since the kids were born. With any luck, he'd still be saying it at their fiftieths. 'Hey, Bec, just look at the way Lachy's hairline's receding. Gorgeous at the moment, isn't he?')

She'd delete Ryan from her contacts. She'd block his number.

But when they pulled into the garage, Essie was busting for the toilet and Bec had to rush to unlock the front door, and then there was the milk to bring inside and yet another lot of books had arrived from Amazon and Mathilda was suddenly starving to actual death and Nicole (Oscar's mum) Zhao texted to say she wouldn't be allowed to collect Lachlan from training unless Bec messaged Paul-the-Coach straight away.

By the time she was making dinner (pouring an entire pan of cheese sauce over a small dish of broccoli; it was the only way she ever got anyone to eat green vegetables) she couldn't believe she'd planned to block Ryan's number. For one thing, he might need to talk to her about a fire-eating reference or something. And for another, she was allowed to make a *friend*. Heaven's sake. She spent the vast majority of her life looking after her family; making cheese sauce on a Wednesday night was honestly the tip of the iceberg.

She scorched her hand on the side of the saucepan and the pain barely even registered.

'Dinner's ready!' she called. Being a weeknight, it was just the kids and her for dinner.

'There's no need to squawk, Mummy,' said Mathilda, severely. She'd been sitting silently on the daybed near the kitchen. Bec hadn't realised.

By the time the children were asleep, her burnt hand had started to throb. She took two paracetamol and decided to pour herself a white wine. (She preferred red, but around the time she turned thirty-five it started giving her migraines, just in case the post-baby pelvic-floor situation wasn't enough to be going on with.)

With the sort of clarity that comes when you're just a little bit drunk, she realised she'd better get rid of Ryan's number. And that she should talk to Kate. Or to her mum. Or – why hadn't she thought of it earlier? – to Stuart. They'd always promised to *communicate*. They'd always thought that most problems could be solved if couples only *talked*. Sitting in the quiet, darkened house, drinking her wine and folding the washing, the idea of opening up to her husband – 'Something sort of silly's happening, and I think I'd probably better just tell you' – seemed completely feasible.

'That cheeky little prick!' Stuart would say, as if Ryan was a high school student who'd written lewd graffiti about a teacher. 'In his dreams.' There'd be a contemptuous sort of snort, as if Ryan was from a different species. Then Stuart would dismiss the subject completely and ask, 'How'd Lachy go at training?' or 'Has Essie been back to the dentist yet?' or, to be fair, 'When's your next walk with Allie?' Stuart would be *amused*, she realised, more than threatened. He'd be totally secure in her love for him, and take it for granted he'd be informed immediately in the very unlikely event of anything remotely salacious happening in her life.

Unexpectedly, that really wasn't a very good feeling.

'Mummy! I think Goldy is dead!' Mathilda's voice from the kitchen was a wail.

It was Thursday afternoon. Bec staggered through the front door, put down two school bags, one soccer bag and her handbag, and joined Mathilda by the fish tank. Goldy the goldfish was floating on top of the water.

'Is she, Mummy? Is she?' Essie had appeared. Her eyes were full of tears: she looked imploringly up at Bec. Lachlan came trooping in.

'What can have happened?' Mathilda was as dramatic as it's possible to be when you're eight.

'I'm afraid Goldy's died, darlings,' Bec said, solemnly.

All three children – even Lachlan, who was ten and hardly ever wanted to hold her hand anymore, and certainly never in public – started crying real, copious tears. She squatted down, balancing awkwardly on her ridiculous wedge heels – what sort of person got dressed in shoes like that just to buy a new hose and then pick kids up from school? – while all three children collapsed onto her lap.

She felt a horrible urge to laugh. Then she remembered how they'd given Essie the goldfish tank – with the yet-to-be-named Goldy in it – for her fourth birthday and felt the urge to cry herself.

'But she had a good, long life. Sixteen months is a very old age for a goldfish.' Bec had no idea whether that was true. 'We'll bury Goldy in the garden,' she told them. 'You can pick some flowers to go on her grave.' She was also not entirely sure of Goldy's gender, and hearing her own solemn use of the word 'grave' almost made her want to laugh again.

Just then, her phone rang in her handbag. Of course, she carefully ignored it in her best not-letting-technology-take-over-life way. She patted Essie's back and Lachlan's arm and shifted her weight slightly so that all four of them didn't fall on top of the tank, in which Goldy's surviving relatives (Daisy and Patchy) were still swimming. She waited for the sobbing to subside. She really must give the fish tank a clean. It was very hard to not ask Mathilda what on earth the bright red mark on her school dress was.

That was when the landline rang. Three rings, then stopped, then rang again. It was their signal. Stuart thought Bec was a bit hopeless at answering his calls and replying to his texts, which was true, because she sometimes had her phone on silent. (She rarely bothered texting him. He couldn't get at his phone when he was operating, and there was no point asking a theatre nurse to read, 'Essie's banged her head, and Lachlan needs new school bathers by tomorrow, and Mathilda's on her bed crying about something someone said to her at lunchtime, and I'm exhausted, so can you please call me?' to the operating theatre at large. Obviously. She tended to just get on with things.)

'I'll have to get this, darlings,' she said. She disentangled herself. 'Daddy must be needing to talk to me.'

'Bec?' Stuart's voice was only a tiny bit different from normal.

'No, it's your mistress. You've called me by mistake.' This was one of her standard wifely jokes. It was the harsh reality that Stuart was far more eligible than she was.

Stuart didn't laugh. There was a silence.

'What?' She lowered her voice and turned so that her back was to the children.

'Something weird's happened,' he said. 'There's been a complaint.'

'What?' Her stomach twisted.

'Not about work,' he said, quickly. 'Well, sort of not about work.'

'Stuart. What?' There was a breaking, flaking feeling in her chest, like honeycomb coming apart in her mouth.

'Some girl. A girl from my party? One of the waitresses, I think. She reckons that I—' He made a sound like a laugh. 'She reckons I told her I'd do a lap band in exchange for a blow job.'

'Oh no.' Bec paused. 'You didn't, did you?'

'Of course I didn't.' He sounded affronted. 'But it's a really bad look. She's seventeen, apparently. She's complained to the hospital, it looks like she's going to go to MPRA, she's posted on *Facebook* about it.'

'*What?*' Bec felt sweat come onto the hand that was gripping the telephone. 'She can't do that! It's ... surely it's defamation or something?' And even she knew that being reported to the Medical Practitioner Regulation Authority was pretty much every doctor's worst nightmare.

'What's *wrong*, Mum?' screeched Mathilda.

Bec turned around to find all three children were staring at her. She was so upset that she made an impatient 'run along' gesture at them.

'Maybe,' Stuart said. 'I'm seeing Rodney in the morning.'

Rodney was their lawyer. He mainly advised them about insurance and tax and their wills. (She'd never really got used to the idea of having a family lawyer, but as far as Stuart was concerned, that was just what you did.)

Stuart said a few more things that she couldn't quite hold on to: it was as if his words were falling through her head like water through a colander. 'I'll be home about six.'

'All right.' She didn't even register that that was very early for a weekday.

She said her goodbyes and hung up, making an effort to compose her face before she turned and faced the children. They were standing

84

in front of her, like skittles about to be toppled. Goldy floated on top of the water behind them.

Essie's warm little hands were around Bec's thighs within seconds.

'Don't cry, Mummy,' she said, earnestly. 'Goldy will be happy in the sky now, and we can put her near the mulberry tree.'

'OK. Sure,' Bec said. 'How about you guys go and dig a little hole? I'll bring Goldy out in just a second.'

Of course they wouldn't go without her. Of course she had to hold it together long enough to go with the three of them to make a hollow under the canopy of the mulberry tree and preside over the funeral.

When they got back inside, she said, 'How about, for a treat, you go and watch a movie?'

'But it's a school night,' said Mathilda. 'What's for dinner? Mummy! We haven't even had afternoon tea!'

'For a *treat*.' Dear God, she just had to get away from her poor, lovely children for five single minutes. 'To celebrate Goldy's life.' She was improvising. 'And let's have take-away chicken for dinner: I'll nip down and get it now. Lachlan can be in charge.'

Only when she was back from the corner deli and had checked they were all safe in front of *Harry Potter* (the third one, not too scary) did she pick up her phone to see what Facebook said. She had a lot more messages and notifications than usual. Her whole body seemed to squeeze in on itself.

Bec have you seen this? Very concerning, one of the school mums had messaged. She'd shared a post with Bec. It had a photo of Stuart, the one that was on his website, where he was wearing a College of Surgeons tie and looking professional and serious and just the tiniest bit self-satisfied. ('Only a third-generation surgeon could pull off that expression,' she'd told him, more than a year ago, when she first saw the picture. 'I don't look like too much of a tosser, do I?' he'd replied, a bit sheepishly.)

The post seemed to be from one of the party's waitresses. Bec couldn't tell which one: her profile photo was of someone in a platinum wig and big sunglasses. Her name was given as Stef Hanni. The post said:

I did a waitressing job approximately three weeks ago at the house of this surgeon. DO NOT go to this man. He said he would do a FREE lap band on me WHICH I DON'T EVEN WANT if I performed ORAL SEX on him.

There were 246 reactions. There were seventy-seven shares. There were 154 comments.

Just not acceptable in this day and age!!!

Typical culture of entitlement in that profession i'm sorry to say.

There was no sound in the room now; it was as if Bec was alone on the planet. She scrolled.

Appalling behaviour. Thanks for posting, will change my appointment.

Known him since he did my husband's bowel operation, cannot believe it, I am so sorry this happened to you.

She scrolled on. Surely there'd be at least some posts in Stuart's defence. His practice manager and the receptionists (none of whom, she now recalled, had been invited to the party) would stick up for him. Or at least his nurses. Someone would say, 'This is ridiculous. Stuart respects women. Stuart would never have said that.' One of his patients might put in a good word. Just last week he had brought home a jar of home-made jam, with a gift-tag attached that said, 'Words can never express my gratitude. You are a truly wonderful doctor. Tasmania is so lucky to have you!' And in his study, on the mantelpiece, was a heavy, expensive card with a Tasmanian water-colour on the front, and inside, a message that said, 'I know you couldn't save our beautiful Jessica, but thank you, Mr Henderson, for explaining everything about her condition so clearly. It was a source of considerable comfort to me and my wife on that most dreadful of days.'

But that night, only merciless black-and-grey type stared out at her.

You poor girl, no one deserves to be treated like that. Good on you for speaking out, it takes guts.

Will ask my GP to refer me to someone who RESPECTS women.

Hashtag sexualharassment. Hashtag baddoctors. Hashtag collegeofsurgeons. Hashtag MeToo.

Believe the woman, her mum had always said. You have to listen, and you have to believe.

Yes, Bec had always thought. Yes. Of course you do.

One comment said, *I found him fine, certainly no complaints about my scar or experience.* Another said, *He removed half of my colon for bowel cancer, very traumatic, but no problems with him myself, but I am older.* Another said, *I think these complaints / allegations should go through the proper channels.*

That was as much support as he was going to get, it seemed.

Does not deserve the title of doctor. How is this not illegal?

Makes me feel sick to think this predator operated on my teenage daughter.

Bec went into the toilet and vomited. It was the second time in her life bad news had made her do that.

Before Stuart got home, she realised that she'd better pull herself together, brush her teeth and at the very least make a salad. She was standing at the bench, cutting cherry tomatoes into leaky halves, when he came into the kitchen.

'I got a roast chicken,' she said, as if that was the most important thing in their world. 'We can get the kids to bed earlier, that way.' When he didn't reply, she glanced up at him. Bless his heart, he looked like a 12-year-old at his first disco.

'Where are they?' His voice sounded so hearty that it made her want to start crying again.

'Upstairs.' To give him a bit of privacy, she turned back to the tomatoes. 'They're watching a movie.' He probably wouldn't realise that that was a special treat.

'Bec? Bec, you believe me, don't you?'

She put down the knife and met his eyes.

'I believe you think you're telling the truth,' she replied. 'But you were pretty drunk, Stuart.' He had been. Not falling-down drunk but a fair bit drunker than her. 'And I do know you wouldn't ever have gone through with ... with it. But the way you were all carrying on, the way those horrible men were talking ... well, I mean, things like that do get said, Stuart, and not everyone who says them has "rapist" tattooed on his forehead.' She sounded angry by the end. She picked up the knife and went back to her tomatoes.

'Right.' He used the same tone as when interns were incompetent. Hard. Exasperated. Polite. As if *she* was the one who'd done something wrong.

'I'm just getting dinner ready.' She snapped the knife back down onto the chopping board. He had absolutely no idea what her evenings were like. 'Then I'll put the kids to bed. *Then* we can talk. All right?'

'OK.' His voice had softened. 'Whatever you want, Bec.'

'What I want is for this to have not happened.' She picked up the knife again. 'And I don't know if you're planning on saying anything to the children. I can't do it.' She knew she was being horribly unsupportive. But her kids. Her kids her kids her kids.

He didn't say anything. She chopped tomatoes (so snippily, so tensely, as if she was in a neat-salad-ingredients competition) for a while. When she looked up again, he'd tilted his head back so that his face was towards the ceiling. His eyes were closed.

Much later, she would remember him like that. Still beautifully dressed, handsome, still such a believer in his own ability to solve problems. She always remembered that night as a sort of turning point, where her life contained both the normal – the unplanned free-range chicken, the self-satisfied ache that came after the gym, the beautiful kitchen with its view over the Derwent – and the beginning of all the things that came after.

In a way, it was the worst of all the nights.

Chapter Seven

Kate

'Here we are then,' Adam said.

It was a few days after our weekend in Hobart, and I was at Adam's place for the first time. Bec and Stuart would be practically apoplectic; I was tempted to text them a selfie of me giving a thumbs-up next to his fridge.

Seeing where Adam lived was honestly not that big a deal as far as I was concerned. I mean, I was a bit curious, but I already knew what made him laugh (toilet humour; certain political cartoons) and what made him cross (dangerous driving; poor journalism) and that he liked manual cars and disliked board games. I knew what sort of sex he liked, for heaven's sake (will spare details. Nothing outlandish though. But: not boring). So it wasn't as if seeing what he had in his fridge was going to give me any huge insights into his personality, and it certainly wouldn't allay the concerns I had about him shagging multiple other women, trying to steal my millions and generally being an entirely different man to the one I thought he was.

Juliet – who'd fielded a large number of my Adam-related questions over coffee that morning – reckoned that unless two people confirmed they were 'exclusive' then you had to assume sex with other people was going on. Meeting families made no difference at all, she said, shaking her head like a New York doorman. 'It's not the olden days, Kate, unfortunately,' she informed me. I didn't bother telling her that everyone slept around in the olden days too, and without any protection, which is probably why lots of them got syphilis and, in the absence of modern medicine, then went mad.

Instead, I just said it was no wonder there's no prospect of peace in the Middle East, when even sorting out something as simple as 'dating' is so difficult. Also, with today's ready availability of dating apps, all the UN people probably bonk their heads off while at Middle East summits and are therefore too knackered to even do proper diplomacy. (Juliet said she was sure they were all very responsible and capable people who were far too dedicated to important social justice issues to stay up late having sex, but I got the impression she was being sarcastic. She once dated a logistician who worked for the UN, and that was apparently the best thing about him.)

'The trouble is,' I told her, 'you can use the word "dating" for just about anything. No one actually knows what it means.'

'That's the whole point of it, Kate,' she said, as if I was a loveable kid who was a little bit slow. Juliet has done a lot of 'dating'. She says she would like to be in a proper relationship, but she somehow isn't. (The men lose interest, she says.)

I didn't bring up gold-digger issue with Juliet. It was too unbearable.

Anyway. We went through his boring front door (yes, exactly the same as mine) into what seemed like a perfectly fine sort of apartment. The kitchen had an almost-bare Formica breakfast bench and a white plastic bin with a swing-top lid and two rather crappy metal swivelling stools. Everything was clean, down to the clear plastic salt-and-pepper grinders and an almost-full bottle of olive oil next to the cooker. There was nothing else on the counter except a white toaster, a white kettle and a pristine green cylinder of Milo. I wondered if it was possible that the Milo had been bought for me.

'Let's sit down,' he said. He indicated a grey, fabric-covered couch.

'OK.' I kept the surprise out of my voice.

He looked very serious, even though over dinner, when we'd been laughing about the waiter's overuse of the term ASAP, he'd muttered something about being keen to take me home as soon as possible. His implication had not been that he was feeling an urgent desire to converse with me. (It had been really quite sexy, and I'd started to think: maybe tonight I could even go up on top of him. I really wanted to have an orgasm with him – well, I was having orgasms with him right, left and centre; my nervous system was probably in a state of near-exhaustion – but I wanted one during actual intercourse. And I could tell he wanted that, too. He'd put a little bit of pressure on my hip and turn over onto his back and say, 'Come up here,' or 'Want to watch you' or some such. But I hadn't quite managed it yet. It is less easy than I once assumed, to get that carried away.)

So I sat down on his couch. That was when I properly noticed that there were no pictures on the walls. No cushions or rugs or plants. Stacked on the edge of the television cabinet, in a neat way that suggested that it was their allocated spot, were a book about London bars, a book about road trips in Europe, and a book by Barack Obama.

'I need to tell you something,' he said.

Of course, it occurred to me that perhaps he was married. Could this be his double-life flat? Maybe somewhere in the suburbs he had a proper family home, with bookshelves and lampshades and a kitchen bench cluttered with school readers and bills and batteries and, obviously, somewhere in that house – possibly running a vacuum cleaner or wrestling a fitted sheet – a harried-but-loving wife whose boobies were not as perky as mine but only because she had borne two or three of Adam's adorable primary-school-aged children. Was I about to become someone who appeared in podcasts about serial liars?

'I'm not a photographer,' he said.

I reflex-nodded because although I had obviously suspected as much, I still had absolutely no idea how to respond. I wasn't, for some reason, at all concerned for my safety. I didn't stand up or even think about where the nearest exit was or if his bare walls would be soundproof. I believed he wouldn't hurt me, is all I can say. There was no logic about that. Probably just a lucky guess.

'OK,' I said, for the second time.

'I'm a data analyst,' he said. 'I work for the public service. I tend to avoid talking about it, because it's kind of boring, to some people.' He was looking at me with his eyes moving rapidly back and forth, as if he was alive with strategies to cope with my fury. 'The time I said about photography, I'd been taking photos that day. For a project we were working on. I didn't exactly lie. I just—'

'Wow,' I said. 'Oh right. Wow.' I stood up.

Nothing like this had ever happened to me before. I looked down at him, and I suppose I probably looked appalled, because he said, 'I am so, so sorry.' I just stood there in front of him, very possibly with my mouth unappealingly open. 'Kate. Look. As I said. I didn't mean to lie.'

I snapped my face into shape (wrathful, feisty, empowered) and stood up straight.

'We've known each other more than a month, Adam.' If I'd had both my arms they would definitely have been crossed. 'And I *knew* you were lying, by the way. You're really bad at it. Have you not heard of the internet?'

'I know.' He looked utterly miserable. 'It was just – it's not as if we even talk about work much. And things rolled on and it was hard to find a moment. A couple of times I was just, look, I'd see you and it'd be nice, and I didn't want to start up the whole conversation.'

'And yet, somehow, you managed to find plenty of *moments* to fuck me.' That time I really did sound like Catherine of Aragon.

Regal and righteous as all hell, although I'm pretty sure she wouldn't have used the eff word.

'Yeah.' He nodded at the floor. Very chastened.

Then he looked up, raised his eyebrows and shrugged in a way that meant, *Well, I'm only human after all.* Very, very annoyingly – where the eff were my effing principles? – a glimmer of a smile forced its way onto my face. I met his eyes for a second and we grinned.

'Whatever,' I said, coming to my senses. 'Don't try your charming . . . smirk stuff on me. I am not . . . nineteen.' Now I sounded like Anne of Cleves (fourth wife). Sturdy defender of the truth but not particularly good at English.

His smile vanished. He turned his head to the side, and I could see from the way he raised his hand halfway to his face and then lowered it back into his lap that he was actually very, very upset.

'Were you worried about seeming boring or, or geeky, or something? Were you trying to, I don't know, impress me?'

'Nah. Honestly. It wasn't premeditated. I blurted that out, and then – as I said – I didn't find a moment to correct myself.'

'Why would you say it then? The photography thing?'

'I was maybe a bit overwhelmed. You're a gorgeous woman, Kate.' He swallowed. 'And you asked what I'd been doing that day, and, I swear, that's what I'd been doing. Traffic movements in various parts of Melbourne. Very boring.'

'Whatever,' I said, again. 'You made me look stupid in front of my sister. You lied to my family.'

'I know I did, Kate. I'm sorry.' We were both quiet for a moment. 'But I hadn't told you, and I couldn't tell you in front of them. I thought that'd make it worse.'

'And are you "seeing" other women?' The air-quotes were very, very nasty ones.

'No. Not since we met.'

'Really?' I was so surprised I didn't even sound angry anymore.

He nodded once, in a take-it-or-leave-it-I'm-not-going-to-reassure-you-further sort of way. Interesting.

'What about your grandma in the nursing home. Is that true?'

'God, yeah.' He rubbed his forehead. 'You couldn't make that stuff up.'

'Your family, all the stuff about your parents and nephews and everyone?'

'Absolutely. Yes. They want to meet you, in fact.'

'Where do you even work?'

'Office block off St Kilda Road.'

'Which one?'

'On the South Melbourne side.'

'You did the science degree before, like you said?'

'Yes.'

I nodded, but I must have looked sceptical, because he stood up, opened a smoothly moving, almost-empty drawer in the TV cabinet and extracted a photo album, the sort that comes bound and printed from an online service. FORTY WHOLE YEARS OF MEMORIES!!! was written in bright green on the cover.

'My sister just made me that,' Adam said. He didn't show me the photos, but extracted, from inside the back cover of the album, one of those cardboard slip-covers with a university crest on the front. I sat back down, and he sat next to me and opened it. Inside, was a single picture: a younger looking Adam – toothier, somehow, and if anything, less attractive – wearing a black cap and gown, and holding a rolled degree.

'They your parents?'

He nodded. A man with Adam's grey eyes, who was valiantly restraining a small paunch, and a woman with bright lipstick, stood behind Adam. The two of them were beaming in a brimming, unpractised way; each had a hand on Adam's shoulder. You could tell that his mum had been to the hairdresser's especially. I leaned closer. She was resting her hand lightly, obediently, just the way the photographer would have asked her to. But his dad had his hand clenched, hard, around his son.

Their baby. The words came into my head all by themselves, and I suddenly had tears in my eyes. It was just that they looked so proud.

'Parents in graduation photos,' I sat up straighter, 'look very much more youthful than they once did.'

'Yeah.' His tone was so tender I knew he'd noticed the tears. 'They certainly do.' We exchanged a very quick we're-not-all-that-young-anymore-are-we? glance.

'So, is that all?' I said. I looked at him, right into his eyes. It was as if I was Thomas Cromwell, or at the very least an extremely canny high school teacher.

'That's all.' We kept looking at each other. 'It's usually just a busy eight-to-whenever sort of job. Longer hours sometimes. Irregular. When it gets busy.' He smiled his quick smile. 'When your sister and her husband were asking me ...' He made a face like a scrunched-up ball of paper. 'Very uncomfortable. I'm very, very sorry.'

''S OK,' I said. 'They were being a bit ...'

At exactly the same moment I said, 'Dickhead-ish' and he said, 'Supercilious.'

'Yes, that.' I shrugged. He has an excellent vocabulary, actually.

He kept his hands in his lap, and, once more, I considered my options.

I was smart enough that he wouldn't get my money. I could just wait, and see, and enjoy the nice bits. Because maybe, *maybe* he was telling me the truth. It can be hard to undo lies we tell about ourselves, God knows, and was it really so very impossible to believe that a man could like me, and be nervous around me, and tangle himself up like that?

'Well,' I said. 'No harm done. So can we please go to bed?' I was already touching his shirt.

'Sure you don't want to hear some statistics or see a pie-chart or something first?'

'I'm pretty right for data analysis, just this minute, thanks, Adam.'

He looked so relieved, and so *loving*, and his hands on me already felt so familiar and so knowing, that I found it impossible to believe that he could be deceiving me.

Except. He hadn't told me his department or his title or even his field. He'd been evasive about his office address. And the beautiful photo told me pretty much nothing about his life as it was now.

I wanted to believe him. I very much did.

But people do bad things. And I am very wealthy. And I am also not an idiot.

It was a Monday evening, and we'd just finished watching a movie about a twenty-something woman who falls for a forty-something man. Of course, the age difference was not part of the plot, which was to do with espionage, corrupt politicians and Eastern European nightclubs. Is there anything more annoying than the way movie producers seem to think that beautiful young women find ordinary-looking middle-aged men irresistible? There are very few things more annoying, but of course it is purely coincidental that most movie producers are middle-aged men.

'Just so you know, Adam,' I said, 'in real life, women who go out with forty-ish men usually don't look like *that*. They usually look like me.' I raised my forefinger and drew a circle in the air around my face.

'No, they don't,' said Adam, lazily, flicking off the TV with my remote control. He looked at me. 'Because you are exceptionally beautiful.'

'Yeah, but you know what I mean,' I said, a bit impatiently. 'Age-wise.'

He smiled. He says he likes how I'm not fake-modest about how I look. (I've never said things like, 'Oh, we all want what we can't have. Look at your beautiful teeth,' or 'I believe every woman is beautiful,' or 'God, you should see me without my make-up on!' Any of that just would've made me sound either dumb or really, really fake. And now I know what it's like to actually, desperately want what you can't have, I'm extra glad I never said any of that stuff.) (Also, I am proud to say that I never once complained about my beauty 'defining me'. I mean, for God's sake. How could that sound anything other than enraging to someone who has to work all day as a cleaner or a hotel receptionist?)

'Hey,' Adam said. He wasn't quite looking at me. 'Want to come and meet my nonna some time?'

'All right.'

'Great.' He sounded completely natural.

Then I said, 'And want to go to Hobart again? One day?'

I needed to see Bec, who was having a totally crap time, or, to put it in the most annoying way possible, facing some very significant challenges on her journey. We'd been speaking every day. And I thought it might be reasonable to give Adam another try with the family.

'OK,' Adam said. He sat up and cracked his knuckles. 'Yeah. I could do that.'

But he made a little face. A sort of I've-been-worried-you-were-going-to-suggest-that face.

'What?' I felt a bit scared, actually. Every time I started to feel comfortable ('exceptionally beautiful', 'meet my nonna'), something – his phone beeping with a late-night text, another last-minute dinner cancellation – would remind me that I couldn't afford to take him for granted. I was see-sawing between letting myself go and firm self-talk about being self-reliant and self-fulfilled and this is all just about the sex.

I'd been springing questions on him, including when he was nearly asleep. Questions like, 'So how was your meeting?' and 'What did Scottie say about your proposal?' So far he had always answered to my satisfaction. And when he'd met me for lunch a couple of times, he'd had a very convincing miasma of office about him: an almost-smooth shirt, air-conditioner-y facial skin. He never let me treat him to anything, either, to the point where it was almost becoming annoying. But his place was so spartan – there was a whole empty cupboard in his bathroom – and whenever I suggested meeting him at his office, he'd say something like, 'I've been wanting to try Such and Such. How about I see you there?'

'What?' I said, again. He adjusted his posture, the way you do when you want your body to catch a cool breeze, and sat with his hands on his thighs. I was next to him on the couch.

'There's some good rock-climbing in Hobart,' he said.

'Really?'

'Yep. We haven't talked about it much, but I love climbing. I need it.' He did ironic air quotes around 'need'. 'I used to go all the time. Like, every weekend. It's kind of a different state of mind.' No air quotes this time. In fact, the way he spoke – sheepish, sincere – reminded me of Stuart when he got chatting about something sweet the kids had done. 'So in Hobart, you've got the Organ

Pipes. You've got dolerite bouldering on the mountain. You've got the Lost World.'

'Right.' I would have looked as blank as I felt. Apart from anything else, I was hoping that starting multiple sentences with 'you've got' was not going to become standard.

'I try to get down there for climbing at least once a year. And I've been thinking, if we go to Hobart again, the two of us, maybe I could go climbing for a day. Or part of a day, anyway.'

'OK.' I nodded rather vigorously. I was waiting for him to say something about personal space, or that he felt it was unwise for him to spend more time with my family this early, or that his ex-girlfriends (he'd alluded to an Annabelle and a Carla) had never understood his love of mountaineering and had therefore driven him away.

'And the thing is, Kate, babe, it's not that I don't want you to come with me. But . . . I don't think you'd probably be able to manage it. I had a look, a think. Even the easier climbs – you really need . . .'

The penny dropped but I decided, for some reason, that I'd stay quiet. I kept looking at him, expectantly.

'You really need two hands.'

I wished I hadn't made him speak, because it felt as if he'd hit me. Honestly. I can't put it any better than that.

'I understand,' I said. I jumped up and started clearing the coffee table, self-conscious about looping my fingers through both our empty tea cups, stacking the wine glasses on the plates, managing the whole pile, in the end, with my left (non-effing-dominant, wouldn't you know it?) hand. Left-over, I call it, when I'm feeling sad.

'Of course!' – with my back to him – 'Sure. I don't need to come. Climbing's your thing. That's totally fine!'

I clattered the stuff into the sink and swallowed and then turned around. He was sitting in the same position, looking up at me. I could tell he was deciding what to say. Quick to think and slow to speak was his way, I'd noticed. Which was just as well, because I have been accused of being on the hot-tempered side.

'Good,' he settled on. Level, casual. No histrionics to see here. 'OK. I could go climbing on the Saturday morning, first thing, then we'd hang out the rest of the time. Something like that.'

'OK,' I said, more steadily. 'Sounds good.' I opened the dishwasher and started positioning things inside.

By the time I'd done the cutlery, I found myself thinking that there were bound to be inspiring people with missing limbs who scaled mountains, but that I really had no desire to be one of them. Even if I had a right arm, I would be much happier at home with my Tudors than out testing the limits of human endurance or appreciating my place in the vast mystery that is nature or whatever.

After a while, Adam walked over and gave me a big hug. His jumper was soft, and he put his forearms firmly on my back, behind my heart. He kept them there until I moved away. Quite a long time.

That was the first night he stayed over and we didn't have sex. We did in the morning though, and I thought we were reasonably quick – in a good way – about it. But apparently not quite quick enough, because he texted me later, and his text said: *Late to morning meeting. First time in at least a decade. It was so worth it, lovely Kate.* x

I caught myself wishing very much – more than anything, just about – that I could be sure that it all was real.

And then I thought: Kate Leicester! Stop it. This is just a physical thing.

I was always pretty amazing at denial.

Chapter Eight

Bec

Bec was doing tacos for dinner, and the onions were making her cry. Since it was a screen day, she could hear, from the lounge room, the theme music from *Mr Maker*. She was just reflecting that Essie would very soon burst into the kitchen and ask for an old shoebox and/ or different coloured tubes of glitter and/or corrugated cardboard, when her phone rang. It was Kate.

'Are you chopping onions?' she said, as soon as Bec answered.

'What's more annoying?' Bec replied. 'The fact that I'm chopping onions, or that next I have to shred practically a whole lettuce into Mathilda-friendly pieces?' Or, she could have added, that then I'll grate a vast amount of cheese, and after dinner, load the dishwasher, wipe down the table, sweep the inevitable taco splinters up off the floor, hear Essie's reader, watch all three of them brush their teeth, use a detangling brush on Mathilda's hair, listen to Lachlan's piano practice, kiss them all goodnight and then make another dinner. Stuart did not like what he called Mock-Mex, and even though he had never actually asked Bec to make a second meal – in fact, she didn't think he quite realised that she did that sometimes – she wanted him to come home to something he'd enjoy.

'How're things?' said Kate. 'Tell me everything right now, before the kids come in.'

'Oh, you know. Not too bad.'

There was a short, irritated pause. Kate had always had a colossal ability to affect silence, but how she did it was a mystery to Bec, frankly. Also hard to understand was the way Kate didn't seem to care about making conversations go smoothly.

'What do you even mean? What. Is. Happening. Today?'

'I don't—' Bec said. She walked around the bench and shut the lounge-room door. 'I've just . . . look, I've been thinking, today, and I just don't know what to think.'

'What are you talking about?'

'I s'pose, just. I always thought I'd be the one to take the woman's side in a thing like this.'

'Really?' Kate said.

'Um. Yes. Of course.'

'Because I always thought you'd be the one to take the side of the person telling the *truth*,' Kate said, as if Bec was a total idiot.

'It's not that simple though, is it?'

'Of course it is!' Kate said. 'And don't start on about how 96 per cent of women are telling the truth, because I know all that already, probably better than you do, and it's not 100 per cent.'

'Mmm.' Bec knew she sounded non-committal. It was a deliberate choice. Kate was a self-proclaimed authority on all matters to do with feminism and minority-group welfare, and at the best of times she was very hard to argue with.

'Bec. Are you seriously telling me that you don't *believe* him?'

Sometimes Kate and Stuart sort of ganged up on her. They did it in a we-both-love-you-so-much-Bec-this-is-for-your-own-good way, as if they were the grown-ups.

Bec shrugged dramatically, like a surly teenager. Then, very calmly, she said, 'I'm just not sure what to think. As I said.'

'Oh. I see. As you *said*.' Kate imitated her voice.

103

'Look, Kate. Did you ever stop to think that I might know Stuart just a little bit better than you do?'

Kate stayed silent, but Bec could tell she was cross.

'He's not perfect,' Bec went on. 'Nobody's perf—'

'He would not have said it.'

'Nobody's perfect, Kate, and you know, in a marriage, you get to see that and realise that. And *I* can tell you that it's not absolutely out of the question that even the wonderful Stuart might have slipped up.'

'He wouldn't have said it.'

'Fine. Whatever you think. How's Adam? How long you been seeing him now? Must be at least six weeks.'

'I might not know anything about Sandy Bay marriages, Bec,' Kate said, 'but I can—'

'No. You don't. And maybe they're nothing like they seem to – to outsiders.'

'But I *can* tell you that if poor old Stuart wanted a half-decent blow job – and I concede *that's* certainly not impossible – he'd be smart enough not to get caught organising it.'

'Well,' Bec said, aware that her lips were actually trembling, 'one thing I can tell *you* is that Stuart and I think that Adam is not a smart choice. We call him Adamdick. Did you know *that*?'

There was a longer pause, difficult to interpret. For once.

Then, 'Perhaps if we'd both been just a little bit smarter, Bec, we wouldn't be having this conversation.' Kate's voice had gone stringy.

There was nothing Bec could say to that. In fact, it was a struggle to get enough air down her throat.

'I'm pretty sure we both regret certain choices, Kate,' she eventually managed.

'Some of us more than others, presumably,' Kate replied, and hung up.

Both of them were crying, at the end.

'What are you doing here?' Bec said.

She was still in the middle of making the kids' afternoon tea when Stuart arrived home. It had been three weeks since the complaint.

'Bit quiet today. Left early.'

Before she could react, he reached into the internal pocket of his jacket, and then held out an envelope, already slit along its top. It was an easy gesture, so competent and assured and *manly*. Which was somehow heartbreaking.

'My . . . letter came today.'

It wasn't as if they hadn't been expecting it, but still.

'What's it say?' But she was already unfolding it from its official-looking thirds. 'Actually, could you possibly finish that?' She indicated the chopping board and a few kiwi fruit. It really wouldn't kill him, she told herself, and if the kids didn't eat soon then both Essie and Lachlan would get tearful and grumpy, and no one would benefit from that.

She needed to hold the letter in both her hands, but to her surprise, the sentences did not swim before her eyes. Even though her breath was coming a bit fast, her brain felt as clear and receptive as a glass of water. She read silently with, she knew, her lips moving – they'd always done that when she was concentrating – and let the facts arrange themselves in her mind. Stuart, meanwhile, was chopping up kiwi fruit and sitting the kids down at the table on the deck, and then opening the fridge. When she next looked over at him, he was standing at the bench, with a beer in his hand.

'Like a drink?' he asked, through a mouthful. It was possibly the first time in their lives that Stuart had failed to offer her a drink before getting his own.

She shook her head, and turned her eyes back to the letter.

A notification had been made. It was pursuant to Section 144 of the National Law. The notification related to an incident that had occurred at a private residence. There was their address. There was the date of the party – the successful, confusing, frivolous, *fabulous* birthday party – she had organised. The notification related to Stuart's professional conduct. The notifier alleged that Stuart had offered his professional services in exchange for a sexual favour, namely oral sex. The notifier had not consented for his/her identity to be disclosed to Stuart. The notification was being assessed by the Board. When the assessment phase was complete, there may be either no further action, immediate action or an investigation.

Of course, Bec had already phoned the caterer. Brody had said, embarrassed, that he wasn't able to give her any contact details of individual staff.

'But we all thank you for your custom, Rebecca,' he'd said.

'I quite understand,' she'd replied, sympathetically. 'Thank you anyway.'

'The whole thing could take months,' Stuart said. 'I looked it up. Only half of even the initial assessments are done in under ninety days. Sounds like a total shit-show. If they decide to investigate further then . . .'

He was toying with the dirty fruit knife, and he suddenly smacked its tip down hard into the marble bench. His fist slid down the handle and onto the blade.

'Your hand!' she said, reflexively. 'Sweetheart. Your hand.'

The knife clattered onto the floor, and she checked the deck. The children hadn't noticed. (Miraculously, all three of them were eating their fruit as if they thought it was delicious and had forgotten biscuits even existed. No doubt Stuart would assume things were always this easy.)

'Sorry, Bec,' he said. He sounded mystified, as if he couldn't believe what had happened. 'I'm really sorry about that.' He looked down at his upturned hands. There was a thin arc of bright blood seeping from his right palm. 'If it's all right with you,' he said, 'I might go for a walk on the beach.'

'OK.' She swallowed her shock. A *walk* on the *beach*? And his hand. His precious surgeon's hand. His hands were the reason they had a stack of surgical gloves in the shed, because even top-quality gardening gloves let dirt in under your nails. The reason she always bought expensive, allergen-free soap. The reason he'd given up cycling; the reason he'd jog up flights of stairs without thinking twice, but would never, ever put his hand in an elevator to keep the doors open.

'But is your hand OK?' she said. 'Don't you want at least . . . a Band-Aid or something?'

'It's just superficial.' He was still looking down at his palms. He walked towards the front door – apparently avoiding the deck and the kids – as if he wasn't going to say anything else. But as he left the kitchen, he turned and looked at her.

'I am an *excellent* surgeon, Bec,' he said. He shook his head. 'I'll be back in a bit.'

'Of course.' She picked the knife up off the floor. She rinsed it and popped it in the dishwasher. Then she started on dinner. At that point, it seemed that getting the kids to bed early was the most helpful thing she could do.

'Time for dinner soon!' she was calling, when Stuart appeared in the kitchen a few days later.

It wasn't just that he was home early, this time. She could tell by the way he was walking that something was wrong.

'You OK?' She washed raw chicken off her hands and flicked on the kettle.

'Can we please have a quick talk?' He glanced in the direction of the playroom and the children.

She sat, facing him across the kitchen bench. He stayed standing up.

'*What?*' she said. She took a breath. 'Sorry, darling. What?'

'At the clinic? My waiting list is down to a week.' He scrunched his eyebrows and looked out of the window, over her shoulder. Then back to her. 'Sorry. I should have told you earlier that things have been slow.'

'Seriously?' she said, as shocked as if he'd told her his parents were divorcing. 'Really?'

'I guess it's the referrers,' he said. He looked like a hurt little boy who was trying to be brave and grown up. 'The GPs. They don't . . . no one probably . . .' He could see she wasn't understanding what he meant, and he said, like a confession, 'They'd be concerned about being tarred with the sexual-harasser-supporter brush.' He shrugged. 'So. They're not referring patients to me anymore.'

'Oh, Stuart.'

And the worst part about it was that all this time, when Stuart must have known how bad things were, *her* life had been going on almost as normal. Allie was being a bit weird, hurrying back to her car at drop-off with a curt raise of the hand, hurting Bec very much more than Bec would have thought. But otherwise, people were still polite to her. Stuart still went off to work in the mornings. And hadn't she always told the kids to ignore it when people said mean things about you? She'd thought she should just keep on smiling and making nutritious meals and doing the school run and that eventually it would all die down. That bureaucratic wheels would turn, Stuart would be vindicated and the gossip would go away. But now she saw she'd been an idiot, a stupid, pampered woman who tutted and turned up her air-conditioner while a bushfire raged outside.

'What does this mean, exactly?'

Never in her life, had she had even the flickeriest flicker of a worry about Stuart being out of a job. The difficulty, always, was him having too *much* work. It was almost impossible to imagine a world in which Mr (surgeons were never mere 'Drs') Stuart Henderson FRACS wasn't striding from one demand to the next, incising and deciding and ligating and advising, dealing with a ceaseless flow of elective cholecystectomies and key-note presentations and acute bowel obstructions. In fact, the two of them had had endless conversations about what they called 'the quest for work-life balance', but what she privately thought of as Stuart's unwillingness to prioritise their family. He loved his job; that was the real issue.

'It costs thousands of dollars a week to keep that clinic open. If I'm not generating enough income . . .' His voice trailed off. She waited for him to say, 'So what I'm going to do is . . .' or 'The way round it will be . . .' but he didn't. He closed his eyes and rubbed both his palms over his face. Then he sat down at a stool by the recently wiped bench. It was empty apart from the chopping board where she was working.

'Right. You're having a wine,' she said, cheerfully. She would be stoic and practical. And also calm, unfazed and reassuring.

Stuart smiled, his face like a stretched plastic bag.

'Yep,' he said. 'It's time for a wine.' When they clinked glasses, it felt like a parody of times gone by.

'Have you told your dad about all this?' she asked, after a few moments. Stuart's dad thought social media was a waste of valuable time. He was seventy-four and lived with Stuart's mum in Sydney, where he played golf and bridge, ran popular hypotheticals for medical students about the ethics of health-care – purely to keep his mind active, he said, because he was just a retired neurosurgeon and not one of your clever ethicists. He also wrote charming, perfectly pitched letters and sent charming, perfectly pitched books to all five of his grandchildren.

'No.' Stuart didn't look at her.

'Do you think . . . ? Are you going to tell them?' Her tone was soft.

'God, Bec. I don't know.' He slugged his wine. 'They'll find out eventually. Have we got any, like, cheese?'

''Course.' She brought out some crackers and a slab of smoked cheddar. He never ate cheese during the week. Watching him cut, too quick and too jagged, into the yellow cube made her feel so panicked that she had to look away.

'The kids had a pretty good time at school today, I think.' Surprisingly, that seemed the logical thing to say. Keep calm and carry on. All that. She launched into a story about Essie's excursion to the Shot Tower. He nodded along.

When she got to the bit about the bus ride back, she saw he had a flake of cracker on his cheek. Usually she would have said, 'Look at you, you hopeless grub!' or 'You do realise that is not an attractive look, don't you?' but that evening she just finished her story and then walked around to his side of the bench. She gave him a little kiss on the lips and brushed the flake away. He'd never know it had been there.

Her face was still close to his when he spoke.

'Jane says . . .' He paused.

Jane Payne was his practice manager. Bec had never particularly liked her, to be honest, because she was always complaining about

110

the receptionists needing time off when their kids got sick. 'All these children!' she'd say, like a noblewoman complaining about overly fertile peasants. Jane Payne seemed to expect the receptionists to stay childless so they could dedicate themselves unreservedly to her roster for their twelve-to-fifteen hours a week.

'Jane says that the clinic needs to take on a locum who can generate more work. The wages for the receptionists, the nurses – they have to be paid.'

'OK then.'

'So, I've written to the referrers, saying I'm taking a short sabbatical.'

Bec looked over at the half-chopped chicken, just to keep the shock off her face. 'Well, that sounds like a – a reasonable idea.'

'With paying the locum, there won't be much income left over for me, that's all.'

'I'm sure we can—'

'And Bec. There's something else. I – look, as a sort of arse-covering exercise – I've been suspended from the Royal. Without pay.'

The Royal Tasmania Hospital was where he did his public work, the essential operations on people who didn't have private health insurance. In contrast with his lucrative private clinic, it had always seemed poorly paid, but that, of course, was only relative.

'Income protection doesn't cover you against this type of stuff,' he added, as if he was answering a question. But she hadn't even thought that far.

To her extreme annoyance, Bec found herself trying to call to mind all the sorts of things Kate would have said. Things about injustice and innocent-until-proven-guilty and risk-averse bureaucracy. But Bec never felt as if she *knew* enough to say things like that. The thing is, pretty much everyone had always stopped talking and looked at Kate whenever Kate opened her mouth. Even growing up, it had been obvious that Kate was mildly surprised when people spoke over her, or when anyone failed to snap to attention whenever she said, 'What I think is . . .' Maybe that was why Kate always sounded so definite. It wasn't her fault: it was simply what she was used to. If Kate grew up believing that her opinions counted for just a little bit more than most people's, then that was probably because most people she met seemed to believe that too.

'We can manage,' Bec said. She was his wife, anyway, not his lawyer. 'We can drink rubbish wine and go without new clothes for six months.'

He nodded, glumly. She couldn't blame him. She sounded fatuous, not cheerful.

'I'm used to being poor, don't forget,' she babbled on. 'I can show you how it's done.' (Her childhood had been the sort where there was enough money for both the girls to have piano lessons, but only just. Stuart's was the sort where his parents didn't know exactly how much music tuition cost, only that they really must discuss how much to anonymously donate to the Sydney Symphony Orchestra that year, and who the very best cello teachers were.)

'Yeah.' He was trying – for her sake, she knew – to appear optimistic. It was heartbreaking, actually, much worse than the glum look.

'We can maybe re-mortgage,' she said. 'A little bit, we probably could. And I can, you know, cook economical recipes and learn to darn. The kids can have a break from piano and ballet and things, if we need to do that. It'll be *good* for them.' But she wondered if he was thinking of the two investment properties that they'd sold to buy – and to excitedly and oh-*so*-expensively renovate – their beautiful house. They now had marble splashbacks and bespoke couches and absolutely no source of income except him.

That was when he smiled in a terrible sort of way and said, 'And where are we at with the school fees?'

And her mind suddenly felt blank and stuck, like the roundy-roundy symbol that appears when the internet goes down.

It was the next afternoon, and she was waiting for the girls to come trooping out of their classrooms. She'd left her phone in the car on purpose, so she wouldn't be tempted to look at it. So she might catch someone's eye. So she would seem approachable.

Allie was nowhere to be seen – she was always collecting Olivia from the side-gate now – but the other mums' conversation drifted over. Tomorrow, Claire Davis would find it too easy to pick up Anna McIntyre's children, since Anna's husband would be in Sydney *again* all week. Lydia Campbell clucked supportively. (If Bec had Anna's husband, she would vastly prefer him to be in Sydney on a permanent basis. He was a gymnasium-chain owner who used his Range Rover's horn in the school car park. Often.) Another mum, who Bec didn't know but who had expensive jeans and sleek blonde hair, was also standing alone. She gave Bec a tentative smile, and Bec felt profoundly grateful.

'Mummy!' yelled Essie. Lately, it was always a bit of a relief when the kids came out.

Mathilda said a more dignified hello, then launched into a story about a missing Freddo frog, and Bec nodded and smiled and said, 'Bye, ladies,' to the general direction of the chatting mums.

'Bye, Bec,' they all said, with antiseptic smiles. Politeness. Sometimes it wasn't all that great.

On the way home, they stopped at the corner deli. Today – in addition to the usual bananas and milk – she needed to buy more spanakopita for Mathilda, whose vegetarian phase was lasting longer than expected. Fortunately, all three children were inclined to wait in the car.

While she was standing in the fruit section, trying to decide about blueberries, a voice said, 'Bec?'

'Hi.' She was turning around and smiling before she even realised who it was. 'Ryan!'

'Hey there.' He did his slow, sexy grin and she realised that it didn't matter at all that Claire and Lydia and Anna had been so mean. 'How's it going with you guys?' His voice was very quiet, and he didn't move his lips much.

'It's going well,' she said. She gave him a slightly awkward punch on the arm. 'I always quite like getting to Friday.' She wondered if he'd tell her not to wish her life away. He seemed like the live-in-the-moment type.

'Yeah. Fridays. Always good.' He was holding two avocados in one hand, and had a box of organic-y looking pasta under his arm. 'Whatcha up to this weekend?'

'Oh, you know. Soccer with the kids. I'll probably watch a movie or something with Stuart.' She met his eyes very steadily as she said Stuart's name. 'I think the weather's going to turn on Sunday. Maybe even a storm.' Well, what did he expect? She was a married, middle-class mother. It was pretty much mandatory for her to talk about soccer and her husband and the weather. And what did he imagine she'd be doing with her weekend, anyway? Going to a beach party and drinking tequila? Receiving texts containing eggplant emojis?

(She had only recently found out – from Kate, of course – that eggplant emojis had something to do with penises. What, she'd wondered, was she supposed to do if she genuinely needed to ask a shop assistant whether he had any eggplants out the back? Also, were there any other vegetables she needed to know about? Zucchini, for instance? Carrots? In fact, why had eggplant even been selected in the first place? It seemed rather a *bulky* choice.)

Ryan nodded. She got the feeling he was letting the silence run its course. A man in a high-vis vest reached between them for a bag of lettuce. She wondered whether Ryan actually was attracted to her. She knew he could tell what she was thinking, and she didn't care. In fact, she met his eyes and thought, deliberately, *God I'd love to sleep with you.* Because she actually would. Kate wasn't the only one who could think things like that, it turned out. She tried it again. The eff word came into her head. In its non-child-friendly format.

'Come visit me Monday morning,' he said, as if it was a perfectly respectable suggestion. 'I'll brew us up some chai.'

Kate's voice sounded. *Is there anywhere on the planet a less manly drink than chai?* Also, *Chai and sex, he means.*

'All right,' she said. Kate could just shut up and keep having her ridiculous-chemistry Melbourne sex. 'I'll bring us some biscuits or something.'

She half-hoped he'd say something pathetic about dairy intolerance or trying to eat clean, but he didn't.

'Nice. Get chocolate ones.' He smiled a much too intimate smile and then stepped past her, towards the cheese fridge.

On Monday, she put on her favourite jumper (very dark red, roll-neck, fitted but not tight) and skinny jeans. Hair in a high ponytail, gloss on her lips. When Stuart told her she looked nice, she smiled a genuine smile.

'Thanks, sweetheart,' she said, and gave him a pleasant, lingering kiss. She could tell by the way he didn't put his hands on her straight away that she'd caught him by surprise. Or maybe it was just that he was distracted. He was going into work to 'finish a few things off' but there was no doubt that he had a bewildered, pale air about him, and they both knew that soon he'd be home all day. It was a bit like watching a tidal wave coming in.

She dropped off the kids. She bought a packet of chocolate biscuits – deliberately not thinking about whether he'd prefer caramel or dark or milk. She parked her car brazenly, right on his street, and walked down a concrete pathway alongside a renovated Federation house. It was one of those houses that looked like a cute old-fashioned worker's cottage from the street, but inside would be all modernity and space and thousands upon thousands of dollars' worth of sweeping, architectural lines. Rhododendron leaves brushed her face. She threw a glance at the sliding glass doors of the house. Nobody seemed to be home.

Ryan's bungalow stood in one corner of the long, narrow back-yard. A shallow concrete ramp with a metal rail along one side led to a front door that had been painted a flawless, high-gloss green. Several well-kept pots of herbs were grouped by the door. Two types of parsley. Mint. Rosemary.

It wasn't as if she didn't know this was wrong. Of course she knew. She felt – not twinges of shame or stabs of remorse – but a feeble sort of anguish that she supposed must be guilt. It was like a shadow. But the thing was, the shadow didn't seem to matter very much. She could easily live under a shadow. The main thing was that she wanted to see him. Nothing else mattered, there, in that garden, on that morning.

She swallowed and knocked on the door.

Oh goodness, he was young. Even with the morning sun slanting onto his face there were no lines. Even when he smiled there was nothing in the way of crows' feet. She fought the desire to shade her own face with her hand and straightened her back in an unapologetic way.

'Good to see you,' he said. His limbs were loose, his voice pitched low and slow. He stood aside for her to enter. The green door shut behind her with a well-oiled click. The room – a sort of kitchen-dining-living area – smelt of cloves, cardamom and laundry detergent. Sunlight came in. By the window was a wooden clothes horse that held a sandy wetsuit and a clean – at least, she hoped they were clean – pair of brown woollen socks. A door to the left led to a bedroom: she glimpsed the foot of a blue-and-white covered bed.

She perched on a stool at a breakfast bar while he poured soy milk and loose tea into a pan and stood it on an old-fashioned electric cooker. It would take forever to boil.

'I really like this street,' she said. 'Lovely old houses.'

'Yeah, me too.' He came and leaned against the other side of the bench, and they talked about the weekend (he'd been surfing; she'd watched *Mulan*, which had proved every bit as bad as she'd expected) and yesterday's frost and the South Coast. He passed her a shell he'd found. It was broken along one edge, and in a way unremarkable, but when she looked at it for a while she saw that its underside was a very shiny grey, and the ridges along its surface faded magically from dusky pink to cream.

'Beautiful, eh?' he said.

She nodded, and noticed that she wasn't rushing to fill the silence. She'd sort of forgotten how to have a conversation, or something, but that didn't seem to matter. It felt nice.

'You look pretty in that red,' he said.

'Thanks.' She blushed. She knew it would be very noticeable; she'd always been a blusher. 'I blush a lot, Ryan.'

'Sure.' He was unapologetic and calm. 'Very, very pretty, though.'

Bec remembered a time, just after she'd left her job at the hospital, back when she'd been working at the shoe shop. She'd been on the way to pick Kate up from physio and her terrible old car had broken down. An Englishman had helped her push it to the side of the road and then invited her to dinner ('Fancy having something to eat with me?'). His accent. Those forearms. That unflustered drift of his eyes. But she'd said no, because Kate was expecting her. She hadn't even mentioned the man to Kate. Ben, his name had been. An electrician.

Ryan poured chai from a saucepan into two heavy ceramic cups, the vase-shaped sort that had been popular in the eighties and that had probably been bought from an op-shop.

'Let's sit,' he said, indicating the one small couch. Oh goodness.

Ben-the-Electrician had leaned back against his ute with his arms folded. The thing was, she hadn't realised, at the time, that it *mattered*. How could she have known, then, that she would remember him all these years later? That she'd *regret* not saying yes?

In the end, they ignored the furniture and arranged themselves on the floor. Bec leaned back against the couch. He lay on his side, propped up on one elbow with his drink in front of him. Biscuits – still in the packet – in between them. It reminded Bec of her parents, who, when she'd been a child, always seemed to end up sitting on the floor when their friends came over. She bit her lips, hard, so they'd be swollen and pinker.

After two biscuits each he came and sat next to her. Now they both had their knees drawn up in front of them, both leaning back against the couch, their four feet in a line.

While he was telling her more about his mum – a potter, she hadn't made the cups, though – he slid a hand around her ankle. She had a leather boot on, but still. She went right on telling him about her own mum – who would be protesting about climate change the next day – without pausing, without even losing her train of thought. It was as if she was an audacious teenager, the sort who accepts dares to do really scary things on a skateboard and then does them with a shrug.

They talked a bit about bushwalks in Tasmania, and Ryan's sore shoulder from labouring until he said, 'Want more chai?'

'OK,' she said. What else could she say, really? She didn't want chai. She wanted him to stay there, with his hand around her ankle. She wanted him to slide his palm up her leg.

'Take your shoes off if you want,' he added. 'Be comfy.'

And then, just before he stood up, he leaned in and gave her a tiny, casual kiss on the lips. Dear God, it was honestly just such a *relief*, in the end. Out of my system! she thought, hopefully.

'Glad we finally got around to that, Bec,' he said, as if he'd read her mind. Then he slouched off towards the stove. She took off her boots – and, after a very short hesitation, her socks – and put them off to the side of the couch.

When he came back with the chai, he sat down next to her again and slid his arm around her shoulders. He was closer this time, so close to her that their hips were touching.

'So what do you think'll happen about the cable car?' he asked. (Some developer wanted to build a cable car up the mountain; most people in Hobart had an opinion about it.) He put his hand onto the back of her neck, where her skin was bare, right near her hairline, and moved his fingertips very softly, just behind her ear. Bec thought about how that sort of touching could be extremely irritating, but in this case, very much wasn't. He took another sip of chai. 'I don't think I'd want to go on a cable car.'

'Not your thing?' she said. She laid her hand on his thigh. Really quite far up. He leaned forward, so his chest nearly brushed the back of her hand, and took another biscuit.

'Want one?' he said, still leaning forward. She shook her head.

He sat back again, put his arm back around her – although not, unfortunately, on the back of her neck this time – finished his biscuit, drank more chai. The whole time, they were talking about things: her vivacious neighbour who was all for the cable car, a pub he knew that Bec said used to be very seedy, how nice the man who ran the local café was, Netflix, *The Avengers*. At some point in the Netflix bit she finished her chai and put down her cup. She was letting her body soften against his. She'd obviously been very tense when they'd first sat down.

'I think I ate too much,' he said, after they'd talked about *Thor* and Byron Bay.

'Me too,' she said.

'Yep. Good though.' He dropped his shoulder and tilted his chin down – only a tiny bit – so he could kiss her lips. Brief, firm, gentle. 'You taste like chocolate,' he said. 'Nice.'

Then he unfolded himself and went and washed up the cups.

She stayed where she was for a few minutes. He said he should go and check out someone's garden while the weather stayed dry. So she put on her boots and said goodbye.

'Good to see you,' he said, at the door. He kissed her again – only a short kiss. His hands stayed on the back of her neck the whole time, even though she let her chest compress against his.

'Come back soon,' he said, lightly.

She'd thought she'd be the one who would have to put a stop to things, that morning. But, as she walked back up the concrete path, she realised she would have been very happy to stay.

There were roadworks, so it took ages to get out of his street. She inched her car forward towards the roundabout. There was always going to be chemistry at the beginning, she reminded herself. That sort of chemistry didn't mean anything. It didn't mean there was a real heart-to-heart connection. It certainly wasn't worth risking a solid marriage for.

Beginnings weren't what mattered. And anyway, it was pointless to compare meeting Stuart with meeting Ryan, because she'd been an entirely different person back then.

And not only because she'd been young.

She'd been an intern. Dr Rebecca Leicester, with a pager clipped to her belt, and a stethoscope around her neck and a white ID card she could use to zap herself through the automatic double doors that led to the intensive care unit, to the operating theatres, to the residents' quarters of the Royal Tasmania Hospital.

From the time her alarm clock went off, she was running. She used to leave her hair to dry itself on the bike ride to the hospital. She used to twist it into a ponytail in the residents' bathroom before morning hand-over. She used to say, 'I'll check her creatinine,' and 'So has he had the frusemide yet?' and 'Better grab an ECG.'

'Exhausting!' she'd say. 'Ridiculous! Why can't I start at nine like a normal person?' But even she could hear that she sounded the way Kate did when she complained about the early starts and the boring make-up sessions and how modelling wasn't really as glamorous as everyone thought. Like a mum whose kid had just made the Olympic squad, complaining about having to wash all the uniforms.

Bec met Stuart on a Friday. She was wearing this nice blue sweater that Kate had sent her from London, in the days when it was a novelty to receive packages in the mail. It was after five o'clock, and she was doing what all the efficient interns did: checking a pile of drug charts before she went home for the weekend. You had to do that, because it caused headaches for the nurses and the weekend doctors, if a patient ran out of an order when you weren't there.

She was sitting on ward 5D, in a tiny alcove that was known as a work station. It had apparently been designed by someone who had no idea what it was actually used for. The white Formica ledge that was supposed to be the desk was criss-crossed with telephone cords and precarious piles of patient files, and an enormous computer monitor took up the rest of the space. In fact, it hung over the edge of the 'desk' by several inches.

She'd just taken a half-finished Cherry Ripe – the healthiest chocolate bar, also the flattest – from inside the slip-cover of her *Oxford Handbook of Clinical Medicine* and had a bite. She'd missed lunch, which happened pretty often.

'Hi,' Stuart said. 'I don't think we've met.'

Stuart was from Sydney. She found out much later that, on that Friday, he was two weeks into a three-month 'regional area' stint in Hobart. At the time, all she knew was that he was a tall surgical registrar with curly dark hair and shoulders that went right out to the edge of his scrubs, and she surmised he was not exactly having trouble attracting women. He was sitting on a wheelie chair at the other end of the work station, and had just finished making a phone call. He'd been using phrases like 'stat dose' and 'absolutely out of the question' in a way that was as impressive and authoritative as possible, although – tragically – she'd been able to tell that the conversation was about a patient with an infected ingrown toenail.

'I'm Stuart,' he said. He used a fake-humble voice, as if he thought she already knew his name. She was very glad that she didn't.

'Born to rule,' her mum would have said. 'Sexy wanker,' Kate would have said. 'Can't hurt to go on a date, though, darling,' Marion would have added, with an encouraging look. Marion had always been a firm believer in embracing new experiences, within reason, and at that point in history she thought it was high time Bec got over James Le Dieu, the beautiful Canadian backpacker she'd met in Nepal. (Something sexual *had* actually happened, in James's case.

Very much so. Not in a youth hostel, though. In a yellow-painted hotel in Kathmandu, among other places.)

Bec smiled at Stuart, swallowed her Cherry Ripe, and introduced herself as Rebecca Leicester, the orthopaedic intern.

'D'you want to grab a drink after work?' He wasn't actually leaning back with his hands behind his head and his knees apart, but he might as well have been.

'No, thanks.' She smiled at him as warmly as she could (not very; it'd been a long day and he clearly didn't *need* a smile) and went on with her drug chart rewrite.

'Oh. OK.' Stuart stood up. He told her later that no one had ever turned him down for a date before. 'Have a good weekend,' he said. And he walked off.

'Bye.' She turned back to her drug charts, and then something made her glance up again. As he made his way along the hospital corridor, he looked back at her over his shoulder. He gave her a quick, awkward smile and kept going. It was, she told Kate when she phoned from London a few days later, just the tiniest bit endearing.

But after that, she didn't meet Stuart again until much later, when Kate wasn't calling from London anymore. When Kate was back in Hobart. When everything had changed.

The evening after visiting Ryan's house, it felt as if her whole life was flying out into space, almost as if the planet itself had exploded. Bits of everything disappearing. No centre. All the certainties gone.

She decided to ring Kate. They hadn't spoken since their fight – nearly a fortnight ago – and Bec missed her, very much. It was only a matter of time anyway. One of them always had to apologise, and that one of them was always Bec.

'Hi, Bec,' Kate said, pleasantly. Bless her, at least she never sulked.

'Sorry about the other day,' Bec said.

'No. I'm sorry.'

'I didn't mean you know nothing about marriage,' Bec said. 'And I'm sorry I called Adam a dick.'

'I didn't mean you're bad at blow jobs,' Kate replied, apparently with a straight face. 'I'm sure you perform to your usual high-achieving standards in that department. At least I hope so.'

They laughed. Bec didn't want to say it – not even to Kate – but if she was completely honest, she was mildly proud of her oral-sex skills. So after the laughter finished, there was a silence. They never talked about the other thing.

'How are you?' Kate said.

'Things are quite difficult. Really crap, in fact.' They mustn't argue again. 'I'm not sure what Mum's told you? But Stuart's basically lost his job. There's hardly any money coming in. We weren't that far ahead on our mortgage and we're using up the re-draw at a rate of knots. Even the interest is just . . . and he's being hopeless. Just sort of defeated and wafty and *hopeless*.' It was good to open up, actually. 'You know how he was always so capable. He used to make me feel like a bit of a ditz, even. And then the other day I walked into the laundry because the dryer'd been beeping for ages, and he was just standing there, staring into space. The kids'll talk to him, tell him an excited story or ask him a riddle or something, and he just *blinks*.' She had only just realised she was furious with Stuart, and if Kate *fucking* defended him again, she'd get furious with her, too.

Luckily, Kate said, 'I bet. Poor old Stuart. This is probably the first major setback he's had in his whole charmed life.'

'I know! That's exactly what I've been thinking.' She had been, and right that minute Bec realised she saw that as a character flaw. 'Not that I've had a difficult life,' she added, humbly. 'This is one of the hardest things for me, too.'

'Well, you only have to look at his parents,' Kate said. And then they had a comforting talk about Stuart's family, Essie's new haircut (a cute little fringe; she'd send Kate a photo straight away), their dad's hip, their mum's Earl Grey tea cake (Adam had tried it and used too much bicarb; Kate hadn't finished her piece), the pile of essays Kate had to mark, Lachlan's sore gums, Mathilda's rolled ankle, and Kate's friend Juliet who was, as they spoke, on a date with a freelance graphic designer who had once been in jail for some sort of protesting. (Perhaps the Melbourne dating scene was rife with creative single people who had slightly shady personal histories. Maybe, Bec thought, Adamdick was the best of a bad bunch.)

'Well,' Bec said, when they were wrapping up. 'Maybe you could come down soon? And Adam, too, of course.' Obviously, she hadn't mentioned to Kate that straight after Adam's visit, she'd ordered a true-crime book about a woman who was defrauded by a lover. It was taking ages to come, actually.

'All right,' Kate said. 'He said something or other about Tassie rock-climbing, anyway.'

'Lovely,' said Bec.

She hung up. She took a cauliflower out of the fridge.

If Adam was lying, she thought, it was probably just because he was married. That had to be more likely than a financial scam. Maybe Kate even sort of knew. Maybe Kate *properly* knew.

Bec peeled off the leaves, and found herself reflecting that it was possible that Adam's wife also knew. It might just be one of those *understandings*. They were apparently very common.

Bec put the leaves in the bin, and walked back over to the bench. She began to chop the stalk off. Maybe understandings like that could work, she thought. People might even be happier. Maybe long-term monogamy was just impossible. Maybe infidelity wasn't always wrong.

Bec paused, with her hand still on the knife. She stood motionless, in her quiet kitchen, for almost a minute. Then she started chopping again.

She saw she was already sliding down a very slippery slope. Maybe there was still time to stop.

Chapter Nine

Kate

Bec would never actually ask for my help, in case anyone got the impression she wasn't perfect, but it was clear she needed a bit of company down in Hobart. This time Adam and I both seemed to take it for granted that he was coming with me.

We decided without properly talking about it to stay somewhere more modest this trip. He'd paid the last time, but I'd somehow been able to tell that the beautiful hotel room with its view over the wharf and its extensive supply of mohair throws had been meant as a special treat. So I found a teeny-weeny bungalow on Airbnb, halfway between the mountain (handy for his dolerite bouldering, whatever that may be) and Bec's house.

'It'll be warm, anyway,' I said. There were multiple forms of heating: I had been very careful about that. 'Freaking freezing Hobart. Even in autumn.'

In the end though, that Saturday was one of those blue-and-golden days where the frost melts by eight in the morning and a sprinkle of early snow gleams white on the mountain. The sun warms your back and the river sparkles in the still, cold air and all the tourists wonder why anyone ever complains about Tasmanian weather. (The locals wear shorts and down jackets, and grunt in a superior way about last week's horizontal rain and vitamin D deficiency.)

As promised, Adam went climbing in the morning – he left while it was still dark – and came back just as I was finishing up some yoga. My phone pinged as he walked in, so that for a second I thought our shabby-chic accommodation must be equipped with some sort of sensor alarm. He was glowing from his 'bouldering' and carrying two coffees and a loaf wrapped in paper. I checked my phone. (Juliet texting to ask if I thought the 'b' in 'obviously' was silent; she was settling a bet with her jailbird, she said.) Adam started cutting bread.

'How was it?' I said, walking the four paces into the kitchen.

'Unbelievable,' he said. 'Amazing. Stellar morning.' Then, like he hadn't thought about it, he added, 'And how's my beautiful girlfriend?'

'Oh, is that what I am now?' Same bantering tone. I was just *feeling* bantery, though. 'You take quite a lot for granted, Adam.'

'Shut up,' he said, happily, smiling down at the chopping board.

I became aware that I was wearing only a singlet on top, and that the room was bright daylight. I felt a bit self-conscious, but I made a valiant attempt to put body-hating thoughts aside and walked over to the fridge.

When I passed Adam, he caught me around my waist with one arm. He pushed me against the cupboards and started kissing me and we sort of tottered to the bed, and he kept saying my name. I was kneeling over him, he was tangling his hands in my hair, I wanted to be naked, I wanted him to be naked, we were kissing, scrabbling, a condom, finally, and I thought, *now or never*, and then I was sitting astride him, and he was holding my hips down hard onto him and staring, staring up at my face.

I had a really amazing orgasm at the same time he did. I lay down next to him, and then gently, and most unexpectedly, I slid into very soft tears. He tightened his arms around me, and stayed quiet, and stayed still, and stayed awake. As soon as I stopped crying he kissed my head and stroked my hair, and our bodies curled in toward each other, and I was thinking, we mustn't fall asleep and be late for lunch, because that would be rude, but in that skippy, twisty way thoughts go when you're going to sleep I also was thinking that I must stay awake, awake, awake or I would fall in love with him.

Lunch was lasagne at Bec's house. Mum and Dad came. No one was horrible to Adam. I had already told Bec about the not-a-photographer-but-a-data-analyst thing, and she chatted perkily about stone fruit and Spotify, and refrained from mentioning anything about his occupation. Stuart barely spoke. Mum said, 'Now tell me, Adam, what are your views on Extinction Rebellion?'

After lunch, Mum and BFG went home to plant out some broccoli seedlings, Stuart took Mathilda to her friend's house and Lachlan went mountain-bike riding with Tom From Soccer. Bec accosted me in the butler's pantry to ask if the two of us could have A Talk. The way she said it, I thought she was going to tell me either that a second woman had come forward with an accusation, or that someone we loved had a life-threatening illness but they'd decided to wait until after the banana cake to tell me.

'All right,' I said. I went back into the dining room and said, 'Adam. Essie! Want to go and practise kicking goals?'

'Nah, it'd just be mean,' Adam said. 'There's no way Essie could get any past me.'

Essie looked a bit abashed.

'And, Kate, if I raced her down to the tennis court, there is absolutely *no* way she would win,' he added.

'He has four nephews and a niece,' I told Bec, proudly, as we watched their departing backs. 'So? What's wrong?'

She gestured for me to come and sit down at the dining table. 'I think we're going to have to switch the girls' school,' she said.

'Oh! School.' I was very relieved. I said something about how I didn't think changing schools was that big a deal. The two of us both went to state schools, after all. (Well, until she was fifteen and got her scholarship.)

'I know.' Her tone made me remember how there's nothing much useful you can say when people are very sad. I offered to pay the fees, but Bec said she didn't think Stuart would be 'comfortable' with that.

'He doesn't have to be comfortable,' I said. 'You just have to let me.'

'Oh, Kate,' she said, so miserably that I kept quiet. 'Thank you for the offer. But it's too big a commitment. Even for you.' She added that Lachlan's school had some sort of different system, and they'd already paid his fees until the end of the year. 'Back in January,' she said. I could tell from the way she moved her jaw that her throat was all squeezy and tight. 'Before any of this.'

I said surely they had enough equity in the house to get them through for a bit, and she said their mortgage was enormous and they'd paid too much for their new kitchen and their cars were leased and Stuart wouldn't 'let' her sell her jewellery and she, Bec, was about to start a part-time job as a receptionist.

'Wow,' I said. For some reason, the thought of Bec going to work seemed ridiculous, like a school principal dancing on a podium, or a fancy interior decorator getting into a brawl at the football and telling someone to go shove a Chiko roll where the sun don't shine.

'Can't you ask his parents?' I said.

She shook her head. Tears were in her eyes and she was holding her face still.

'Pride,' she said, as if that single word was an iron-clad reason for whatever irrational, alpha-male bullshit Stuart had talked her into. Sometimes I really think she's more stupid than she once was.

130

'Well. The offer's there. From me. Whatever you two are comfortable with.'

I was as inoffensive and appropriate as an example out of a modern etiquette guide. In fact, I sounded like the sort of person I would definitely hate. (Or, as an etiquette guide might put it, the sort of person I may find rather challenging.)

Adam ended up spending nearly two hours defending the space between two potted bonsai trees against Essie's goal kicks, and then we stayed for dinner. We had pizza (my treat, which Adam accepted for once; he was probably too exhausted to argue). After the kids were in bed, Bec seemed keen for us to stay, and we sat around drinking a lot of wine. Probably not a very smart move.

When Stuart went to their wine-cellar to bring out some more bottles of riesling I said, 'He seems pretty down, doesn't he, Bec?' He had hardly opened his mouth all day.

She nodded.

'Reminds me of last summer,' I said.

'Summer before,' she corrected. 'But yeah.' She looked at Adam. 'Stuart was involved in a case where a baby died,' she said. That was when I realised Bec had had more to drink than usual, because neither of them usually talks about the specifics of his work. 'An unborn baby, I mean. He'd operated on the mother.' She drew a round belly in the air above her own tummy, which is something else she'd never usually do in front of me.

Without warning, Adam and I looked at each other for the tiniest could-you-possibly-be-thinking-what-I-think-we're-thinking-about-babies? millisecond. Fortunately, because of course Way Too Soon, Bec talked on, so we both looked back towards her with very great interest. Her neck was flushed with alcohol and emotion. She spoke as if it was important that Adam got the right picture of her upstanding husband – 'everyone knew it wasn't his fault' – and of what he'd been going through two summers ago, when he'd been so crushed by unwarranted guilt – 'even the coroner said so, in the end' – that we'd all left Hobart Food Festival early, even though Mum and BFG had the kids.

'Leaving early suited me,' I told Adam. 'We kept running into people I knew from school, and it wasn't very fun. I was a total bitch in high school.'

'Surely not,' said Adam, drily. To Bec he said, 'She would have made my life miserable in high school.'

Bec nodded, in a Very Strongly Agree way.

'Yep, I would've.' I was only half joking. 'So anyway, I kept wanting to apologise, but not knowing how, and at the same time I felt like telling them not to look so *forgiving* and self-righteous, because lots of people are bitches in high school.'

Adam laughed, Bec not so much. 'Sorry for all the times I was mean to you, Bec,' I said. I was still just mucking around.

To my surprise, Bec put down her glass, and said, in a hostile voice, 'Oh it was excellent being constantly undermined, Kate.' She used an offended fingertip to rub a tiny splodge of something off the table. Then she looked at Adam and said, 'Nothing like a beautiful big sister to make you feel fab about yourself when you're sixteen.'

She put 'beautiful' in air quotes. To imply two things: first of all, that everyone *thought* I was beautiful, which was pretty much true. (Actually, it was completely true, because I was. I never went through the gawky, too-tall, ugly-duckling thing that many models, usually untruthfully, complain about.) Bec's air quotes also implied that my beauty was only skin-deep. Also true.

'God. Bec,' I said. I felt sort of breath-taken, and Adam got a wary, big-cat-standing-in-long-grass-near-some-zebras look about him.

'I know. I was horrible, Becky. I was a total, *total* bitch at that really important and sensitive time. I'm so sorry.'

Bec kept her hands clasped in front of her, with her fingers all twisted like a ball of wool that was going to be impossible to unravel. She looked as if she was about to say something more, but Stuart came back with another two bottles and she turned her head to peer up at him. He was at least opening the wine with a convivial air, and she visibly relaxed. Her attention was always tethered to his pain at the moment. It was really nice, how they just loved each other so much.

As Stuart got on with the wine, Bec made eye contact with me. She shrugged and mouthed, "S'alright,' and shook her head rapidly, as if she was silly to be so upset. There was a little silence.

Adam said, 'Kate tells me you're starting a job, Bec?'

'Ugh, let's not talk about that tonight,' she replied, flicking her eyes up at Stuart. I could see her casting around for something else to say, but she'd had a little bit too much wine to come up with anything fast enough.

'I just thank God I was born with these legs and never had to work in a real job,' I said. I did a theatrical shudder, and Bec smiled a grateful smile at me.

'God, yeah,' she said.

'Yeah. Here's to Kate's legs,' Adam put in, right on cue.

Stuart had finished pouring the wine, and we all picked up our glasses and said, 'To Kate's legs' and the whole thing became kind of jovial. Bec smiled at me again. But Adam was sitting opposite me, and as he put down his glass, he shot me a look that was so loaded with private memories it made me nearly forget what I was even doing. He very much likes my legs.

Then Stuart chucked his arm across my shoulders, and said, 'Sensational legs,' and Bec laughed her secure-wife-being-pretend-horrified laugh, and Adam's posture changed a tiny bit. I gave him a don't-worry-about-it-this-is-just-family-stuff look, and we all slurped more wine.

On the way home in the Uber, I leaned rather drunkenly against Adam, and thought about how nice it was to be actually going home with a man.

A long time ago I had formed the habit of implying to Bec that I was dating multiple men and that I was having a lot of casual sex. It was pretty easy, because I actually *had* had quite a lot of semi-casual sex when I was modelling. This was in my early twenties, when I was living in London.

I used to tell Bec about most of those escapades. We'd email and talk on the phone. Back then, she was deeply in love with a Canadian boy called James. They were both medical students, and they met volunteering in Nepal, which would have to be the most nerdily romantic setting in the sweep of the universe. They painted a clinic, distributed antibiotics, had lots of (no doubt very safe) sex, and then went home. Though well aware that 23-year-old men adore passionate correspondence, neither Mum nor I were all that flabbergasted when, about eight months later, James met a Canadian girl. But Bec was devastated. For ages – nearly two years – she went all self-denyingly, primly single. Mum was getting a tiny bit worried, but then Bec met Stuart.

So the upshot was, whenever we chatted about sex, it was me who did most of the talking. It's difficult to ask saucy questions about your sister's boyfriend when he's in Canada, especially considering sexting hadn't been invented then, and we'd never heard of Skype.

A couple of times, Bec talked to me when she and Stuart were first dating. We probably spent way too much time giggling over terms like 'surgical strike' and 'smooth operator' and making lewd comments about his extensive knowledge of anatomy. But then they got engaged. You can't giggle about someone's fiancé. You just can't.

Anyway. Around the time of surgical-strike-hilarity, Bec and I went to buy underwear in Hobart. That was obviously the first mistake. It was about five months after my amputation.

Bec called in from her cubicle that she'd finished with whatever slinky thing she was planning to prance around Stuart in. I was trying on a lemon-and-white Elle Macpherson bra. It was too small, and therefore looked as if it had been designed around someone's milk-maid fantasy. There were no staff (obviously), so Bec said she'd grab me a different size.

I was just minding my own business, thinking about how nice my breasts were, when someone knocked once and opened my cubicle door. Is there anything more annoying than a single knock when someone's on their way in? There are few things more annoying.

I jumped, because I didn't realise it was Bec. She never used to do that weird knock thing. When I jumped, my stump flapped up. Your stump flaps up faster and higher than your arm when you flinch. It's to do with weight and muscle strength. (Before the Tudors, I went through a stage of obsessively studying arm anatomy, as though that would help.)

'Oops! Sorry!' Bec said. Apart from the ridiculous knocking, Bec had never before apologised if she caught me in my underwear. But that day she averted her eyes and turned her face away to Give Me My Privacy. She closed the door most of the way, and stuck in her arm with the bra dangling on its hanger.

But I'd already seen her expression.

'Thanks!' I said. I took the hanger from between her thumb and fingers and she went away. It took me ages to take the 10B off.

There was no one to help. Trying on the 10C felt way too hard all of a sudden, so I sat down on the floor. I thought of Bec in her sexy new slip, with her sexy new boyfriend, and I felt a twist of something unfamiliar and horrible that I would later identify as jealousy. I didn't buy anything that day.

On the way home – we were in a taxi, for some reason – I decided I was going to move to Melbourne. I thought Bec would say, 'Don't be stupid, stay here!' or 'But what will you do there?' or even 'Maybe I'll come too. Time for me to get back into my medicine.' But she turned to me with tears in her eyes and said, 'That might be a good idea.' I still don't know why she said that.

Soon after that day I started, not exactly lying, more alluding. Like, if she said, 'Things are going pretty well with Stuart,' I'd say, 'And you're not bored yet?' Or when she started saying, 'Well, Stuart and I have been together forever,' I'd sigh and say, 'It must be kind of nice to be with the same person for a long time, though. What you'd miss out on in excitement, might be made up for in intimacy.' Once she talked about a fight that they'd had and I said, 'But isn't make-up sex *so* great?' A few times I told her (truthfully) that I'd been in bed all weekend, and let her think it was with a man.

Whenever she asked if I wanted to bring someone to Christmas, I would pretend to think about it and then say, no there's no one special, or no it's just a sex thing, or no he'd argue with Mum about politics. Once I almost paid someone, an escort, but it was too unbearable and I cancelled at the last minute. Another time – Dad's sixtieth – I did actually pay an escort. He had goggly eyes and a tiny head, and he kept saying things were 'unbiloiver-bull, mate'. When Stuart took all of us to a fancy Melbourne restaurant for Bec's thirty-fifth, I asked the brother of a girl from my book club.

'I need a favour,' I said to Tara, as if I was inconveniently between boyfriends *just* when an important function was coming up. The brother's name was Troy; he had a serene look, like a patient in a brochure about leukemia research. I told Bec I'd known him for a while. Not exactly a lie. He was pretty good company after a beer, although he did say 'upliftment' twice. At the end of the night, he saw me to a taxi.

I said, 'Thank you, that was really fun,' and put my hand on his arm. I was wearing a tight lace dress that I'd bought especially. He laid his hand on my *stump* and said, 'I'm really glad, Kate. I hope everything works out for you.' Afterwards, I found out that Tara had cooked him osso bucco as a thank you.

I stopped going to book club a bit after that.

Maybe I could have tried harder. There are even special dating apps for disabled people. But I just couldn't seem to do it. I didn't want to be part of that, which maybe was my loss, but that's how I *felt*.

In high school I had two boyfriends. At university I met Horrible Hayden, who for some reason I thought I was in love with, even though when I look back, all I remember is the way he used to act as if he was doing me a favour by letting me stay the night before he had a big game.

And then, after Hayden, things changed. It got different, once I started modelling and became, if not exactly famous, then at least well-known. And after I lost my arm, it got different again.

'Hey, Kate?' Adam touched my hand. 'Are you asleep?' It was dark and cosy in the back of the Uber, and a song I liked was playing quietly. 'We're nearly there.'

'I'm awake.' I sat up and looked at him, and I tried as hard as I could to focus. I thought about the photographer lie. I thought about the way he'd called me his girlfriend. I thought about how lovely he was with my family, and the late-night texts he sent occasionally, and the way he'd held me that morning.

'Why do you like me?' I said. I watched him, as if by straining my eyes enough I would be able to properly see the man next to me. 'Do you like me?'

I heard him breathe out. 'Don't even get me started,' he said. He cradled my face with both his hands. 'Beautiful, beautiful mean girl.'

He kissed me, and the song whirled, and I let myself go, go deep, into the music and the kiss and the emotion. It felt wonderful. The relief. The surrender. The way my misgivings seemed like nothing, and I was pulled, down and in, down and in, down and in.

Chapter Ten

Bec

Bec woke up with an actual hangover. It took her a while to work out what the nausea was. In fact, as her aching head scooped her up out of sleep, she was thinking that surely she couldn't be pregnant, because she had a Mirena in, and Mirenas were 99.9 per cent effective.

Ah, wait. It was just all that wine.

And then, oh goodness, the dread. Because if Saturday night was finished then now it was already Sunday, and so there were only two more sleeps until Tuesday, when she had to go to work. She knew she was carrying on like a spoilt princess, but she honestly felt as if she was going to jail. It had been such a long time – more than a decade – since she'd had to be *accountable*, to strangers, for things she did. And she just knew she wouldn't have a natural ability to slot in behind a reception desk. She'd been considered a good intern, because she knew a lot and she cared about her patients, but she'd never been one of those terse, practical women, full of quick decisions and with a knack for applying protocols and enforcing policies. She knew that she'd forget names and have to ask stupid questions, and then she'd try to make up for it by being extra nice, and then she'd get so busy being nice that she'd forget to do basic things such as turning on the answering machine or putting an important piece of correspondence in the correct pigeon hole. And if someone said to her, casually, 'You might just want to check on the . . .' she wouldn't realise that that was actually an instruction at first, and then she'd have to go back later and ask in humiliating detail exactly how to do it.

She rolled over, and thought of Ryan. *Glad we finally got around to that.* It was now more than a week since she'd seen him. *Very, very pretty though.* Maybe she should call him. *Come back soon.*

'Hi,' Stuart said. He was already standing up, looking out of the window and rubbing the back of his neck. He was wearing a grey T-shirt and the blue pyjama bottoms they'd given him for Christmas.

'Morning,' she mumbled.

Stuart came and sat on the bed. 'Hey, Bec. Do you know what's going on with Kate and this Adamdick guy?'

She said Kate hadn't really told her much, but it seemed as if they were getting along *very* well. It was habitual, to use that inflection when they discussed Kate's romantic life, and she hoped she didn't really sound like a repressed teenager. 'Why?' she said.

Stuart looked more alert than he had in weeks. 'I overheard him on the phone last night,' he said. 'I'm concerned.'

Oh, what now? she thought, unforgivably.

Stuart told her what he'd heard, and Bec sighed. Once upon a time she would have snapped into horrified action, all bustling Google searches and serious phone calls. To her mother (Should we intervene?) To Allie (What would you do?) To Kate herself (I think you need to know). But that morning, she just wanted a cup of coffee. She wanted to be doing the laundry and tutting about the grass stains on Essie's tunic and wondering in a comfortable sort of way about whether she'd make Anzacs or bliss balls for the school lunches that week. Not thinking about school fees or *work* or horrible comments on Facebook or whether it was possible that her husband was a sexual harasser who fancied teenagers. And definitely not involving herself in Kate's colourful love life. For one thing, Bec had more than enough on her own plate. For another, she and Kate would more than likely just end up in another fight where Kate would make her feel as if she, Bec, was too staid and too stilted to grasp even the basics of properly sexy sex. And for a third, if a third reason was even needed, Kate was quite experienced enough to look after herself.

'Look, Stu, maybe you could talk to her,' she said.

'Seriously?' He leaned his head back on his neck in a way that reminded her of a turkey.

'Well, you're the one who heard it.'

'Me?' He was still doing the turkey look.

'She respects you, darling. And maybe it's the kind of thing that's better coming from a man.' That seemed a reasonable thing to say. 'Sometimes stuff like that can be weird between sisters.'

'Nah,' he said. He gave his head a little shake and looked towards the windows, 'It'd . . .' then back at her. 'Can't you, Bec?'

'Stuart.' She felt like screaming. For heaven's sake, she hadn't even been awake for five minutes. 'I just cannot take this *on* right now.' She was dimly aware that she sounded like a hysterical person off a teledrama. A hysterical Californian person. And she'd shared an adulterous kiss with a handsome man who made chai. Dear Lord.

'Just think about it,' said Stuart. He looked at her face. 'And yes. All right. I will as well.'

The rest of Sunday was not too bad a day. She left her phone on its charger in the cupboard, Stuart pottered around in the garden, and she made toasted sandwiches for lunch. Kate and Adam popped around to say goodbye, and once they'd gone, the five of them watched *Despicable Me*. After they'd had Bec's pumpkin soup for dinner and the kids were in bed, she sat down in the lounge room across from Stuart.

'Sweetheart?' she said.

'I didn't talk to her.' He looked up from his phone. His legs were extended on the coffee table.

'Not that.' Heavens, they had more going on than Adamdick. 'Listen. We need to think about the girls' school fees,' she said. 'Kate offered, yesterday, to pay, and I really think we should accept. I know you don't want to ask your mum and dad, and I can understand that, but—'

'Bec.' He closed his eyes briefly. 'We cannot, I will not, accept money from my parents or from Kate or from anyone. The kids are our responsibility, the fees are my responsibility, and that's all there is to it. I will not bring our children up to think that you can allow other people to bail you out.'

'She's their aunty! And it'd just be for a term, or two at most, and . . . and how can you let their little worlds be so ruined? What's responsible about that?'

'You're being melodramatic, Bec,' he said, calmly. He moved his feet off the coffee table, set them on the floor in front of his chair.

'And I notice, Lachy, the firstborn son, isn't going to suffer.' Her voice was shrill and ugly.

'Bec,' he said, like a school headmaster. 'Really. Bec.' He was always so measured and *right* in arguments. It drove her insane. (And in fairness, Stuart adored all three of his kids. In fact, she teased him that *Essie* was his favourite, but even that was only ever a joke. He said Mathilda had the makings of an excellent surgeon, but Lachlan was likely never going to be 'driven' enough, which was fine, because surgery certainly wasn't the career for everyone and Lachlan would find his niche.)

'All right. Sorry.' She took a breath. 'But the girls. You know how happy they are. And this, the poor little things, it isn't their fault.' She was ranting again, by the end, but maybe he should just ask himself where the fault actually lay. Not that she didn't believe him. Not really.

'Bec, please don't put me in this situation,' he said. He leaned forward. 'Please. Please don't.'

'I'm not putting you in any situation!' She was leaning forward too. 'They're my kids, she's my sister, no one's asking you to do anything. We're all just supporting you – I'm going out to work, Stuart. I'm . . . cleaning and cooking and trying to find Mathilda a second-hand blazer and lying awake thinking about the electricity bill while you faff around with the camellias and then snore your head off.'

'I'm not going to change my mind.' His voice was still level, but she could tell she'd hurt his feelings. She was glad. Just to get some cut-through.

'Well then,' she said. She raised her eyebrows, as if it was a challenge. 'I suppose I'm going to have to meet with Briarwood.'

'I suppose so,' he said. But sadly. There was a silence. He nodded a tiny bit. 'All right. Thank you, Bec. Thank you so much. For all you're doing.'

He reached his hand across the coffee table towards her. She stared at it for a couple of seconds.

'I love you so much,' he said.

Maybe it was just a few kisses, she thought. Maybe her marriage was solid.

She wrapped her fingers around his.

On Monday, which she kept thinking of as her Last Day, she dropped the kids off at Briarwood – 'Bye, darlings! Have a lovely day!' – and then semi-snuck into the Staff Only toilet. She checked her make-up, and told her reflection there were much worse things going on in the world. Then she went to the office and asked if she could please make an appointment to see the Business Manager.

Mary from the Office said, 'Why, of course, Mrs Henderson,' in a compassionate way. Bec got the feeling that Mary from the Office knew exactly what meeting the Business Manager meant. Mary from the Office must have seen this all before. 'How about three o'clock tomorrow? Just before pick-up.'

But Bec was due to finish *work* at three. 'Actually, Mary,' she said. 'I won't need to take up too much time. Could we make it 3.15?' The kids finished at 3.30.

'Certainly,' said Mary, writing the time down on a little card. 'There. Save you making two trips.' She handed over the card with an air of immense satisfaction.

Bec smiled in a way that conveyed that pick-up was a *nightmare*, and also that Mary from the Office had made her week – nuanced, eyeroll-y smiles were Bec's forte – and walked to her car.

She sat in it for several minutes. Then she locked the door.

'Hi, Ryan. It's Bec Henderson here.'

It was amazing, really, how easy it was. Like jumping into the swimming pool: it wasn't the actual jump, it was all the thinking about it beforehand. Once you were doing it, it just seemed inevitable. The Briarwood car park was going on as usual. A maintenance man was wheeling a barrow of agapanthus along the side path.

'Bec.' Ryan's voice was warm and familiar. He sounded so pleased to hear from her: pleased and surprised, she thought. 'Whatcha up to?'

'I've just dropped the kids at school.' She glanced at her own face in the visor mirror. 'I'm on my way home now.'

She was think-hoping he might tell her to pop by his place. (*Popping by* being so much more casual, and so much less like infidelity, than *arranging a tryst* in advance.)

That is simply illogical, you adulterer, said Stern Voice. Bec was beginning to feel that Stern Voice was an old-fashioned, slut-shaming woman. Stern Voice was probably deeply repressed and in need of scream-therapy or something.

Ryan said, 'I'm heading up the mountain in a little while. Want to come? I need a bushwalking buddy.' He left a short pause. 'And I reckon we'd have it all to ourselves, Bec.'

Bec thought of all the things she needed to do before she picked the children up. She had to vacuum the bedrooms, drink at least one cup of tea with Stuart, do the online shopping for the week, go out to K-mart and buy some navy-blue pants to wear to work the next day, make sure three suitable tops (Tuesday, Wednesday, Thursday) were ironed, go over *exactly* what Adamdick had said, negotiate dinner, clean at least the kids' bathroom, do the washing, speak to her mum, maybe talk to Kate – of course *she* should be the one to tell Kate, what had she been *thinking*? – and (just as bad) review the bank accounts and then draft a list of dot points to discuss with Briarwood.

'A walk sounds so nice, Ryan,' she said. 'But I'm actually starting a new job tomorrow. I need to, you know, get organised.' She laughed, as if she started new jobs all the time and this was just a bit of a drag because it interrupted her usual nature-appreciation-with-handsome-young-men routine.

'Or later in the week,' he said. 'What if I scout it out today, and then we go another time? On Friday? Reckon the weather's gonna be better then, anyway.'

'All right,' she said. 'That sounds really nice.'

'It's a date,' he said. 'Well.' She heard him swallow. 'Not exactly a date, I guess, Mrs Henderson.'

Bec chortled merrily, as if Ryan was just the darnedest li'l thing in the world, and then, as they talked about where and when to meet, she kept her voice straightforward, like she was booking a restaurant. She sounded pretty convincing, actually.

All her years in Sandy Bay were paying off.

On Tuesday morning, she woke at five-forty. She had less than four hours, now, until she was due at the clinic of Dr Daniel Gilbert and Associates.

Daniel Gilbert was an acquaintance of Stuart's; he was a dermatologist. He thought the situation with Stuart was ridiculous, and that the whole 'culture of complaint' was 'out of hand.' Bec was going to be working as his medical receptionist.

Bec had known Daniel Gilbert since medical school. He had been the kind of guy about whom Kate would have said, 'As *if*,' and Bec would have replied, 'Don't be mean. He's *nice*,' even though, in truth, she had never known him well enough to tell whether he was nice or not.

Anyway, Bec could work school hours on Tuesdays and Thursdays and a full day on Wednesdays. It would be, she knew, a dream job for many women with school-age kids, and she tried to feel more grateful. Her terror was shameful, really. She tried to feel less ashamed. Then she tried to accept herself without judgement even though she did feel ashamed. Then she sighed and wondered if she should see Ryan on Friday. After a while, she got up.

Just before nine, she arrived *at work*, and stood near a chair in the waiting room. The receptionist behind the counter gave Bec a be-with-you-in-a-minute nod and then said, 'Thank you for holding,' into a headset. She had exactly the capable, distant air Bec knew she herself lacked, and also a lot of hairspray. Bec wondered what to do. Surely no one would expect her to go around to the other side of the counter and start reception-ing?

A door opened, and Dr Daniel Gilbert appeared.

'Bec! Or should I say, Dr Henderson! Looking well!' Quick flick of his nimble little eyes. 'Now, I trust you're not going to be bored out of your brain.' Bec could only hope the hair-sprayed receptionist was too busy in her headset to hear him. 'Come along with me,' he said, merrily.

He led Bec very briskly along a short corridor – she'd forgotten all about the I'm-so-important doctor-y pace – and into an office. A woman sat with her back to them.

'Michelle's a gem, Bec,' he said. 'She keeps us all on track.' Michelle was the practice manager. Bec's *boss*.

'Yes. Dr Gilbert said you'd be coming in.' Michelle turned around and closed her eyes briefly. She sighed and stood up. 'We'll start you on scanning.' Bec followed her around a corner to a fluorescent-lit alcove, where Michelle rattled off instructions as if she was being forced to go over things Bec should already know. Bec stared at the scanner and the tottering pile of documents. It would be ridiculous to cry.

Turned out, boring was the last thing being a medical receptionist was. It was really hard. The phone rang constantly, and the doctors roamed about requesting appointments or photocopies or to know the whereabouts of spare batteries or envelopes or nursing staff, and all the while patients waited at the counter, and no one except Michelle and Sandra (the hairsprayed receptionist, who luckily was *lovely*) seemed to realise that it was Bec's first day and she hadn't had any training.

By three o'clock, when she said her tentative goodbye and thank you, she was exhausted. And she still had the Briarwood meeting.

It was beyond gruelling. All the politeness ('Oh, well yes, of course I'm biased but I'd have to say Mathilda's always been bright!') and the ruthlessness ('And you're aware the term two fees fall due, in full, on May fifteen?') and, underneath, her own barely contained panic. The fifteenth of May was only two weeks away, and unless something drastic changed, there was no way they would have the $7,000 for term two by then.

But she nodded ('Just one of those little hiccups!') and smiled ('Such a lovely school community, isn't it?') and hoped ('I can't see that being too big a problem').

She was halfway through that sentence when she realised she was lying.

As she drove home, with the kids in the back, she remembered she had to work again the *very next day*. In less than seventeen hours, she had to be back there, dressed in the navy-blue trousers and a different boring top. And in the meantime, she had to cook dinner and check soccer gear and make lunches and change Mathilda's dentist appointment and find an old family photo for Essie's show-and-tell and get everyone to bed. That was the bare minimum. It was crushing. And she was only one day in.

No wonder people cared so much about money, she thought, as the traffic lights changed. They weren't being greedy. It was simply to survive.

'Shepherd's pie,' said Stuart, on Wednesday. 'Your mum emailed me the recipe.'

Bec had just arrived home from work. She was thirsty. School bags were all over the dining-room floor. Lunch boxes would be inside, their congealed hummus and slimy cheese waiting. And screwed-up jumpers that would need ironing.

Stuart was peeling potatoes, even though it was almost six o'clock. Of course, he was already an expert on potato varieties. He'd only been helping with the cooking for a week, and knew more about Desirees and Kennebecs than Bec ever had. Too bad he couldn't empty a school bag. Or have dinner on the table at a reasonable hour.

The children trailed out of the lounge room and gave Bec dragging, sticky hugs.

'Why don't you go and get your jammies on?' she said. 'Dinner's a while off.' There was a chorus of dissent.

'Nope!' Bec stood up straight so Essie was forced to get off her. 'I do not want to hear it.' It felt like a burn, a literal, physical burn, to talk to them like that. She'd been missing them all afternoon. But she was so *tired*. 'Showers. Pyjamas. Right now.'

They drifted off. Essie and Lachy just looked mutinous, but Mathilda was bravely holding back tears. Bec would give her a big fix-everything hug, just as soon as she'd had a glass of water and at least half a cup of tea.

'How did you go with the locum thing?' she said, walking past Stuart to the sink. She turned on the tap, and hoped she sounded rational rather than desperate. After the Briarwood meeting, Bec had suggested he go and earn some money by working somewhere rural for a few weeks. Somewhere surgeons were in very, very short supply.

'No go.' His tone was flat. 'I'd have to sign something that says I haven't had any issues with a hospital, that I'm not aware of any complaints against me.' He was still chopping potatoes. 'I kind of knew that, anyway.'

'Well, how many did you check with?'

'I rang three agencies.' He sounded heavy and sorry, rather than terse and defensive, but at the same time, she could tell that he didn't care that much. 'But it'd be standard.'

Bec drank some water, then rinsed out a cloth. She tapped over to the dining table and started wiping it. Those crumbs were from breakfast, for heaven's sake.

'OK.' She didn't look at him.

'What?' He sounded mystified.

'Well, we need money.' She used her most patient voice, but made self-righteous swipes with her cloth.

'Right,' Stuart said, cautiously.

'You weren't aware of that?' Now she sounded like a silky prosecutor going in for the kill.

'I was. Yes.' His voice was tentative.

'So?' She scooped up the cloth with a flourish, and straightened her back. 'What do you suggest we do, Stuart?' Why was she being so horrible? And worse, why wasn't he telling her to *stop* being horrible? When she was moody and mean, he usually said, 'Bec. I am absolutely not having this conversation with you now,' or something like that, and left the room. Where was his fighting spirit today?

She went back to the sink and made a big show of wringing out the wiper. He turned to watch her.

'Did Essie eat much of her lunch?' she said, with her back to him.

'Sorry, Bec, but I'm not sure.' He sounded so humble that she felt, if possible, worse. She wanted the old Stuart back. ('Bec, you can see I haven't got to the school bags,' he would have said, casually. Or – in an edge-less voice – 'What's wrong, Bec? Can you just say it, please?')

'Well.' She let the cloth flop into the crumb-ridden sink, turned, and spoke more softly. 'Looks like the girls change schools. Won't be the end of the world.' She was bluffing, though. She thought he'd tell her to stop being ridiculous, that there was no way they'd cause such disruption to their daughters, that yes, she was right, this *was* actually an emergency, they should speak to Kate immediately.

'These Dutch Creams are perfect for mashing,' he said. His desperate little smile took away the comforting anger and replaced it with something worse. Pity, maybe. Or terror. Or scorn.

'Lovely.' She patted his back as she crossed the kitchen. She prepared her own cup of tea, and remembered all the times he'd come home from work exhausted, and dinner was done and the kitchen was clean and the school lunches for the next day were made and the washing was folded and put away, and the showered, pyjama-ed kids were waiting charmingly in bed so he could swan in and kiss them goodnight while she made him a drink.

She sat down at the kitchen table with a sigh, and shucked off her shoes. Only two days in and she was sighing just like Michelle.

'Stu?' she said. 'Do you think you need to see someone? You know, to talk things through?' When he didn't answer, she made a patient-slash-impatient '*well?*' gesture – palms to the ceiling, hands apart.

'Bec.' He looked at her with such an expression of dismay and disbelief that she turned her eyes down.

'All right,' she said. 'But you know. Kate did say. About the fees. And we *could* ask your parents.' Her voice was hard again, by the end. Because, $7,000. Even ten. It was so little, in the scheme of things. He could earn that in a *week*.

Stuart's head snapped up from its contemplation of creamy root vegetables.

'Absolutely not,' he said. 'On both counts. It is out of the question.'

Once upon a time, she would have given him a serve about his macho pig-headedness and his I'm-in-charge attitude. ('Stuart, this is a conversation. I'm not your registrar! And I certainly hope you don't take that tone even with him. No doubt it's a him!') But that

Wednesday she honestly didn't have it in her. In fact, it was sort of a relief to hear him sounding more like his usual self.

In the night, she lay awake, and thought about the mean way she'd spoken to the children and how Stuart had left wet washing in the machine for hours and she'd forgotten to fill in Michelle's 'Wednesday Closing Reception Tasks' check-list and had she turned off the treatment-room heater? God. *Had* she? And should she go with Ryan on Friday and Kate was seeing some sort of scammer and Briarwood and Bec should certainly be the one to talk to her and they only had six weeks of re-draw left on their mortgage and she'd have to sort Essie's sports gear in the morning and Kate might say she was uptight and Stuart was probably depressed and should she go on Friday and she must get Mathilda's iron level checked and what if he never worked again and $7,000 was hardly anything, really, when it came to the girls, and should she go on Friday, not that she begrudged Lachy anything, and she needed to finish his swimming registration, and had anyone been feeding the fish?

Then she did what she often did, which was summon up every single one of her memories of Ryan. The way he'd looked at her, as if he was restraining himself, but only just. That first, flirty – of *course* it had been flirty – text message. The 'come back soon', the 'glad we finally got around to that'. And his fingers against her neck: so assured, so insinuating, so much about *possibility*. And the kisses. Her very own ridiculous-chemistry kisses. She saved them up until last.

She replayed every Ryan-thought in her mind, over and over, as if she was doing a spiritual practice. Every time a scary, angry, painful thought came, she swept it aside with a Ryan-thought. The Ryan-thoughts started off keeping her awake, but after a while, they acted like Valium. Eventually she fell asleep.

*

After work, Lachlan and Bec made it to the pool.

A lifetime ago, back when they'd been so cheery together in the Briarwood car park, Allie had said that she'd scored big by getting both her kids into swimming lessons at the same time as Lachlan. 'We can drink that revolting coffee together. That'll numb the pain of swimming,' Allie had said. 'So foul, isn't it, taking them swimming this time of year?' Bec had nodded, although privately thought that there was nothing particularly foul about swimming lessons in autumn, and that she'd quite like to just sit alone and watch. She loved the earnest look on Lachlan's face when he completed a lap. He was a particularly good swimmer, actually.

But by the time Thursday afternoon rolled around, she really felt like chatting to Allie. It would be sort of fun to tell her about the scanning and Michelle. ('You're doing something to help the sick. Living your values!' Allie might say, admiringly.) And if she told Allie about the way Daniel Gilbert's eyes had dawdled over her in the tea-room that morning, Allie would call him a sleaze and make vomiting noises. She'd look him up on her phone within seconds and say, 'In his dreams! Ooooh, that is *rank*, you poor thing!' And Bec would giggle and things would take on the proper perspective, and seem silly and funny and not soul-destroying and grim. It might become easier, then, to text Ryan and cancel their 'date'.

But.

She hadn't seen much of Allie around Briarwood, which of course could be coincidence. She'd also sent Allie two texts that hadn't been answered, but maybe Allie was just really busy. Because after all, Bec was busy too. With one thing and another, poor Lachy had missed almost all of his swimming lessons, and Essie had barely been to ballet. So, maybe. Maybe she still had her friend. Maybe she should stop her paranoid, negative self-talk, and instead choose a positive mental attitude. Wasn't that what you were meant to do?

Or were you supposed to see things as they were, de-clutter, and prune from your life those people who didn't make you feel good?

Anyway, there Allie was, marching Henry and Olivia down to the shallow end. Bec moved to the kiosk. She bought two coffees – nearly ten dollars – and went and sat on one of the bleachers beside the pool, and waved. Allie waggled her fingers back. After a few minutes, Bec took the first sip of her coffee. She really needed it, and perhaps Allie was going to be stuck down there for a bit. Maybe Olivia was being clingy: that happened sometimes. Allie had been at her wits' end last year about Olivia's lack of independence. 'She *is* only nine,' Bec had said, on the third conversation. 'Maybe she's simply not ready for sleep-overs yet? Maybe she just needs a bit more down-time?' Allie had looked at Bec as if Bec had just suggested a radical plan to deliver cheap, clean electricity. 'Really?' she'd said, intrigued and hopeful. 'Do you think?' In the end, Allie had cancelled Olivia's gymnastics and instituted Mum Time once a week.

She never thanked me for that advice, Bec thought, taking a short, emotional slurp of her latte.

After a while, Bec held up the second coffee and tried to wave again. But Allie had started chatting to one of the other swimming mums, a woman they had both previously agreed was way too neurotic and competitive. Allie didn't meet Bec's eyes.

Bec looked down at her own knees. She lowered the pathetic second cup – with its fifty-cent glug of hazelnut syrup, the way Allie liked – and tucked it down by her feet.

Then she concentrated on looking enthralled by Lachlan. Not that she needed to, really. She wasn't, after all, actually conspicuous. When the lesson had four minutes to go, she threw Allie's coffee into the bin. She'd stacked it inside her own empty cup, so it wouldn't be all that obvious that there had been two. So it would not seem – to anyone – as if she'd had the audacity to expect anything.

'You missed out on your coffee!' she said, very cheerfully. Both Allie and Bec were down at the poolside now, wrapping the kids in bright-coloured towels.

'Oh well,' said Allie. 'You know how it is.' Allie turned away, and started chivvying her children about warm clothes, changing quickly and listening to their swimming coach. Bec smiled and looked at Lachlan.

'What's wrong with you, Mum?' he said.

'Chlorine stings my eyes. Now will you *please* just pick your shoes up.'

'OK,' said Lachlan, looking stung himself.

'Sorry. Darling. Sorry. How about you go and quickly get changed? I'll meet you by the doors.'

'All right, Mum,' he said. 'I won't talk to any strangers.'

Bec turned to say goodbye to Allie, but she had already gone.

It was Friday.

The road up to the summit seemed to go on for ages, a narrow, winding pathway that was far riskier than she remembered. In Ryan's old ute, she supposed she was much less safe than in her own four-wheel drive. She leaned back in her seat, watching the feather that hung from the rear-view mirror swing back and forth as they rounded yet another blind corner. Ryan's tanned hand cradled the gear stick; every now and then he looked over at her with a smile.

'All right?' he asked.

'Fine,' she said. Then, 'I'm a bit tired.' Essie had been awake in the night, apart from everything else.

He gave her another smile, as if he wouldn't mind at all if she fell asleep. Stuart would never have let her snooze, she thought, disloyally. He'd start talking about the view or the fresh air so that she'd stay awake and 'enjoy the experience' with him. She watched the feather again. At first it just looked brown, but when the light caught it a certain way it gleamed iridescent blue.

'This though?' he said. He made a back-and-forth, you-and-me gesture with his hand. He had a very gentle voice. 'This all right?'

''Course,' she said, as if she was twenty-three, and a bushwalk during the week with a new-to-Hobart person she'd kissed once or twice was just something she did between Physiology tutorials.

'You tell Stuart you were coming?' he said, knowingly.

She shrugged. She hadn't, but she wasn't quite faithless enough to admit it.

The weather still wasn't that great, and hardly any cars were parked at the summit. There was a light, misting rain, and the view over Hobart was obscured by cloud.

'Let's go,' he said. An easy grin, as if this was an innocent, youthful adventure. As if they really were just two casual acquaintances who both liked walking in the wilderness. Or maybe, she thought, maybe as far as he was concerned, that was the reality. There still hadn't been any more kissing.

He slid out of the car and grabbed a small pack off the back seat. She adjusted her beanie in the feather-adorned rear-view mirror (there was no mirror on the visor) and looked at herself for a second over the top of her sunglasses. They were sort of a disguise, which she knew was ridiculous.

'This way,' he said, as if he was the local. He didn't lock the ute, but led her quickly across the car park and onto the plateau. The greens and browns of the foliage were deep and smooth under their veil of mist, and there was little wind. 'You go first,' he said, at the start of the path. The track snaked towards the horizon; the sky was low and white; the grey mountains of the south-west were just visible in the distance.

So she went in front. It had been years since she'd done this walk. Simply zipping up her goose-down jacket felt exhilarating, and even under the layers of gear, her body felt loose and powerful, as if she could run to the edge of the world. They walked in silence.

After a while, she realised she was thinking about her twenties. University and Laura and free cups of instant coffee in the student cafeteria and Nepal and shaving her head for charity and James the Canadian – when she was getting over him, she used to go tramping alone on this very mountain, feeling tragic and spirited and fairly beautiful – and blackcurrant vodka and Thai beef salad and day trips to the Hartz mountains and exams and echinacea and graduation. That long line of students, all of them so unquestioning. So *obedient*. Then her internship.

And Kate.

And Stuart. He was working in Sydney at first, but he would come down at the weekends whenever he wasn't on call. At the time, those dates felt like chocolate chips in a dreary muffin. In hindsight, they'd been an orderly, predictable progression from dinner to dinner plus kissing to dinner plus kissing plus (a whole three-and-a-bit visits in) sex. It had been very nice sex, if you were going to be blunt about it. Lovely, in all fairness.

Bec recalled the time she and Stuart went to the resort in the Whitsundays; the personalised, luxury dolphin cruise, the expression on the guide's make-up-free face when she'd looked at Bec's engagement ring, as if it was a mildly interesting artefact from another, not particularly desirable, civilisation. 'Oh, I'm not really *that* sort of woman,' Bec had wanted to say to her. 'I'm honestly so much more like you.'

She stopped for a moment and tilted up her face to the sky. Rain was still gentle on the air.

'It's so wild up here, isn't it?' she said. Ryan had stopped just behind her.

'Yeah.' She imagined she felt the trace of his breath on her cheek. Probably it was the wind.

She started walking again, a bit faster this time, enjoying the way she had to pull the clean, cool air deep into her chest. There was not another soul in sight. The car park was no longer visible. Pristine wilderness unfurled in every direction. She took off her beanie. The breeze was cool against her scalp, and she felt her shoulders and face relax – blessedly, needfully – under its touch. Her cheeks were damp with mizzle. The Botox she'd had seemed suddenly ridiculous. And had she really been contemplating filler?

In the far distance, the sun broke through. Its rays slanted down onto the grey landscape; there was a gleam of silver like faraway water. 'Be lovely to swim,' she said. 'Imagine just ... immersing yourself in a mountain lake.'

'Yeah?' She sensed he was grinning. 'Pretty cold.'

'I just like the thought of it.'

He put his hand on her waist. She stopped, and turned towards him.

'You're very surprising,' he said. 'And I'd love us to go swimming in a mountain lake one day.' She didn't bother to hide her smile. Love. What a word to use. He was still looking at her.

'Hey, Bec, out of interest,' a little ironic eyebrow-raise, 'my first real love was an older woman.' He still had one hand on her waist. More her hip, actually.

'Is that so?'

He grinned. 'Yeah. Long time ago now.' He dropped his hand. After a second where nothing much happened, she thought she'd better turn away.

But ... love. The word lingered. Standing off to the side, but undeniably there. Love was a presence suddenly. Like an exquisite birthday cake, with its candles ready to be lit.

They walked quietly for a while. Thank goodness she had agreed to this. She felt as if the mountain air was recharging every cell in her body; she felt radiant. This was life. In all its imperfection and naturalness, with all its wonder and unpredictability. She had forgotten how good it was just to walk, with no one pointing out features or asking to have their shoelaces tied. She wanted to lie down on one of the ancient boulders, let its strength and solidity permeate her unsettled mind, her fragile, indecisive bones. She wanted the vast quiet to soothe her tangled emotions.

'Bec,' he said, after a while. 'Let's stop.' He jerked his head, indicated a smooth, flat rock at the side of the path. 'I'll make tea.'

As he busied himself with a little gas cylinder and a jar of milk, she rested back on her palms and closed her eyes. (Stuart – the old Stuart, at least – would have insisted on going all the way to the lookout, would have talked about how they'd have to return when the weather was clear, would have cajoled her into photos that would all come out perfectly focused and flattering.) The rock was grainy, the basalt not as cold as she'd expected. Her body was warm. Only the air was very cold.

'You should lie down,' he said. She opened her eyes. His look was tender and unwavering. 'Go on. Just give yourself over to nature for a bit.'

She lay down on her back and stretched her arms above her head and breathed in. As she exhaled, it felt as if the very earth was accepting her, as if it understood her apologetic, conflicted self. And, too, as if the earth was reminding her that all the mess in her life was just ephemera, just stuff that would pass. How long had it been since she'd really thought about her place in the universe?

'Thank you for suggesting this,' she said, with her eyes closed.

'I knew we'd love it.' The only sound was the lilt of the wind and the clinking of the tea things.

After a while, he touched her leg. Her thigh. 'Tea,' he said.

She sat up. He handed her a metal cup of scalding English Breakfast. They didn't talk. When the tea was gone, he said, 'Let's watch the sky.'

She lay down again, and he lay beside her under the restless grey. They weren't touching though. Well after she'd started to feel cold, she said, 'Probably we should be getting back, shouldn't we?'

He turned his head towards her. 'Guess so.' He watched her face for a moment. 'It'd feel so right to go home to bed for a bit, wouldn't it, Bec?' It was clear he meant bed together.

She didn't reply straight away. What could she possibly say? Yes? Do you mean to actually have sex, Ryan, or just to kiss some more, but lying down? Is that even an option, at our age? In this internet-driven-sex-everywhere society? Ryan, maybe if you could just kiss me now? At least as a start?

'I didn't have to go see a garden, the other day,' he said. He turned away, so he was looking at the sky again. 'I just needed you to leave.' But he put his hand on hers, and after a moment, he turned back to look at her. Their faces were close together.

'I'm not offering you anything, Bec. I don't know if I'll be here long-term, or even if I am, how I see my future. But this is how I feel, right now.' He was moving his thumb. 'Sometimes these things are just mysterious, right?'

'I thought maybe I was imagining things,' said Bec.

He did a tiny snort which meant, *That's sort of cute, but no, you most definitely were not.*

'I know what I'm asking you,' he said, after a moment. 'And I know you can't.'

Bec didn't squawk and cover her mouth like a teenager. She didn't laugh. She didn't chirp, 'My goodness, yes! *Such* a shame that it's all so difficult, isn't it?' She didn't say anything that made her sound like a flight attendant or a cheerleader.

She let her whole body exhale into the rock.

She said, 'Maybe I could.'

Chapter Eleven

Kate

My happy mood lasted until we were back in Melbourne. I was happily at my desk, happily contemplating fleece transport in fifteen-hundred-and-something, when Stuart rang me and I happily answered. He was sounding a little bit more like his usual natural-leadership-skills self.

'Kate,' he said. 'I need to talk to you about this Adam fellow.' (Were we in a costume drama? I asked myself.)

'Pray, speak on, dear chap,' I replied.

He didn't laugh. Seemed I'd misjudged the mood.

'I overheard him take a phone call, last Saturday night,' he said. 'When you were here. Bec said to tell you. I've been slow to get around to it.'

'Yes?' A sick, cold feeling washed over me. Stuart was doing his surgeon-y tone, the way he does when he's presenting facts, all black-and-white and *certain*.

'The second time I went to get more wine, he was in the corridor when I was on my way back. Just opposite the playroom. He said, "We absolutely cannot talk now," and then the person said something else, and then Adam said, "Do not call me on this number. I'll text you later."'

'Right,' I said. I could feel sweat come under my arms.

'He sounded agitated, Kate. Angry, even. I came back to the dining room. I don't think he heard me.'

'OK.' I said. 'Are you sure, Stuart?'

'Yes.' Of course, he was sure. Stuart was always sure. There was nothing much else to talk about, so I said to tell Bec I'd call her soon, and to hug those beautiful kids, and thank you very much for your concern, and goodbye.

Then I got up from my desk and looked down from my window for I don't know how long. It was the afternoon. There was a mild smoggy haze at the horizon. The buildings jostled the coastline.

I thought of all the pain – all the unemployment and infertility and custody battles and bereavement and cancer and homelessness – even in the relatively nice bit of world that I could see. Then I thought of Syria and Afghanistan and the poor Great Barrier Reef.

I remembered Adam taking that phone call.

He'd told Bec and me it was the nursing home.

When he'd come back, I'd said, 'Is everything all right with your nonna?' and he'd smiled a sweet, affectionate smile and said, 'All's well. Need a top-up?'

He hadn't seemed at all angry or agitated. He'd looked so believable. I'd *believed* him.

I sat back down at my desk and looked at my thesis. I couldn't think about fleece transport anymore though. I just thought: in 500 years, my life won't matter at all.

That was a little bit comforting.

I was supposed to be having dinner with Adam that night. Obviously, I picked up my phone at least thirty times, and drafted many curt cancelling texts. My favourites were:

It's been nice getting to know you, but I don't want to see you tonight, or ever again.

Or:

Never contact me, liar.

I didn't send them though, and not because I wanted to do things in a mature, face-to-face manner, or to hear his side of the story, or to confront him and pour a creamy blue cocktail over his head and thus obtain 'closure'. It was just because I wanted to see him one more time. I wanted to be *near* him. And a not-very-tiny part of me was thinking that I'd like to have sex with him. 'It would be on my own terms,' I kept telling myself. Of course, that 'my own terms' business means absolutely nothing and is definitely the stupidest saying ever invented.

We had a booking at some Thai restaurant that some friend of his had said was good, and that night, he managed not to cancel. In fact, any data-analysing crises must have been under control, because he arrived before me. He watched me, as I walked towards our table. I knew he'd be noticing that other people were looking at me, too, and I really wished I didn't have an amputated arm, because then the looks would be different, and Adam would feel so jealous and so possessive and so proud that he'd immediately stop sleeping around and actually fall in love with me. This is me! I thought, in my most obstacle-overcoming, life-affirming manner. Then, in my most honest, non-pop-psychology manner: Alas.

'Hey, babe,' he said. He half stood up, as if to give me a hug.

'Hello.' I sat down. I was wearing a tight white top he hadn't seen before.

He sat down too.

I resisted the urge to say, 'No spreadsheets requiring your urgent attention?' Or, better still, 'What was wrong with Nonna, the other night at Bec's?'

'Are you OK?' he said. He put his hand on his pretentiously casual water glass, but he didn't raise it to his mouth. 'What's up?'

'So, Adam.' Conversationally. 'What was wrong with Nonna, the other night at Bec's?' Turns out I just couldn't resist the urge.

'Ah,' he said. He picked up his glass. 'Some new worker needed to check something on the file. To do with a medication.' He watched my face as he sipped his water.

'And they check with you, do they?'

He returned his glass to the table. He shrugged. Fake modest.

'I would have thought her doctor would be the appropriate person, for a query regarding medication.' You only had to watch television to know that.

'What are you asking me, Kate?'

'You know it wasn't the nursing home who called you.'

A waitress was suddenly standing next to me. You could just tell she had stickers all over her MacBook and that she pretended to enjoy kombucha. She asked, in what I considered an overly aloof manner, if we would like drinks to start. 'No, thank you,' I said. She actually took a step backwards. You beautiful mean girl, I thought. But I am so much more beautiful and so much more mean, and I am so very far from being afraid of you.

'Perhaps in a minute,' Adam told her. She looked at Adam as if he were a hero, for some reason.

'Adam, what is actually going on with you?' I said. Not at all gently. 'Really? What are we even doing?'

He did an infuriating little scan of the restaurant, as if the most important thing was that we didn't make a scene.

'Because you stroll around acting as if you know oh-so-much about me, and say I'm your girlfriend and, and *do things* – other things like that – and five seconds later you'll be postponing lunch' – he'd done that the day before – 'or taking weird phone calls or making up more lies about your work or your nonna.'

'I—' His face moved in a funny, closed way that told me everything.

'I never asked you for any of it.' Tears came into my eyes, because that was almost the most heartbreaking thing. 'Look, just be a man, be honest, buy me dinner, screw me and go home. You don't need to pretend we're an item or meet my family or act like you care about me or my ... *psychology.*' I stood up. 'Just – you know – go and—' I was crying, I was half yelling, '– go and shag whoever you want. Or whomever. Whatever.' It really wasn't my best moment.

'Kate. I told you I'm not seeing anyone else, and that's true.' Credit to him, he was looking up at me and speaking in a clear voice, even though other people were definitely looking. A young woman in a nice floral vintage dress had turned right around in her seat to stare.

'Fine.' I took a deep breath in, and I drew myself up to my full height, and I pulled the slurry of agony that was gushing out all over the restaurant back inside my body. I breathed out. 'Well, Adam.' I managed a little shrug. 'If you think I'm dumb enough that you will ever get your hands on any of my money, then you are delusional. So you can give up now.' The floral-dress girl was still staring. Let her, I thought. I don't care.

He was silent for a moment.

'That's really what you think, is it?'

I made an angry, flapping gesture with my one and only palm. 'Of course, that's what I think.'

No heroic, don't-be-ridiculous-Kate response was forthcoming, apparently.

'It's been nice getting to know you, but I never want to see you again,' I said. 'Never contact me, liar.' Then I added, slightly irrationally, and very loudly, 'My family love me, Adam.'

Vintage-dress girl looked concerned, but in a thrilled way. 'You're welcome to him,' I told her. Hopefully she looked mortified. I didn't see.

Because it was like a scene in a movie, and the only possible ending was for the heroine to walk out, so I did.

*

In a movie the next scene would be the heroine looking out of her window, and it would be raining, but I couldn't bear to go home alone. I walked around the busier, lighter streets and ended up in a McDonald's. Quite a diverse bunch of people. A very handsome businessman type, expensive suit, was buying two large take-away fries. Odd. A group of uncool teenage girls – their bad skin plastered with pale make-up, their eyebrows a sad riff on current catwalk styles – sat in a booth. Their voices were unattractively loud.

When I walked past, one of them went to get up and nearly bumped into me. 'Courtney!' yelled her friend, as if Courtney was about to fall over a precipice. Then they all proceeded to shriek with pretend-stifled, scandalised laughter, as if accidentally almost bumping into a grown-up was the funniest, most embarrassing thing that had ever happened in the whole history of the universe.

I ate an apple pie. It was the first time I'd been in a McDonald's since they started admitting to the kilojoule count. Apple pies have a lot of kilojoules. Maybe, I thought, I should just let myself go. Have an apple pie every day. Nothing stopping me. I felt an urge to go and sit down with the teenage girls and give them make-up tips. One of them had beautiful lips. One of them had auburn hair that would be gorgeous if she stopped ironing it and stopped having cheap yellow foils. I wanted to take them all shopping and buy them MAC primer and Chanel loose powder and Covergirl mascara. I would take the one with the worst acne to a dermatologist. I would demand proper treatment, whatever the cost.

I will never have a teenage daughter, I thought.

Whatever women choose is fine and you don't have to be married and life can be very rewarding without kids and blah-de-fucking-non-judgemental-blah. I will celebrate my fortieth birthday with Heaps of Fantastic Friends and my beautiful sister, her lovely husband, my wonderful parents, my adorable nieces and fabulous nephew to whom, yes, I Am Very Close. They will be a consolation. Because I wanted a husband. I wanted a few normal (yes! normal!) kids of my own. I wanted to stand up at my party and say, '*We* are so happy you could all be here.'

That's what I wanted. But this was my lot. I licked the inside of the apple-pie wrapper before I threw it in the bin.

When I got home, Adam was sitting next to my front door.

'Kate.' He stood up as I approached.

'How did you get in?' I said, crossly.

'That red-haired lady from downstairs.'

'Elizabeth.' I said it as if his failure to remember her name made him pretty much an axe-murderer.

'Can I come in?'

I shrugged, like it was an idiotic question, and opened the door. On my own terms, I said to myself, uselessly.

When we went inside, we started kissing straight away. Very, very enthusiastically. I grabbed one of his hands and shoved it inside my top and up under my bra. He took my skirt in his fist, rumpled it up around my waist, clinked his belt open, rustled a condom. I was against the wall, and I said some embarrassing-in-hindsight thing along the lines of *harder* and he groaned and then he finished really quickly.

'I'll make us some tea,' he said, and then he did up his jeans and off he went. I leaned against the wall and thought: That was really, really amazing, but also, I feel sick at myself.

After a bit, I followed him into the kitchen, and stood near the bench. He put tea in front of me, swivelling the cup – *almost* undetectably – to make it easy for me to pick up. Acting all grave, as if he was about to announce the family business had to close because of an economic downturn.

'Kate, babe. I need to tell you something.'

'I've heard that line already, Adam.' I didn't touch my tea. 'I just want you to go.'

The thing is, even though he was pretending to be so humble and serious, I could tell from the light way he was cradling *my* teacup, and the poised way he was leaning against *my* bench, that he assumed that after he'd told me some more lies, we'd be going to bed. He thought he'd be kissing my hair and telling me I smelt gorgeous and cuddling me to sleep. He thought I was going to allow him to keep occupying the space he'd been chiselling out for himself – so easily, actually – in what had been a perfectly fine life.

'Kate, what I—'

'Just don't, Adam. You've fucked me, well done, you've salvaged your evening, it wasn't that great for me—' I just said that to insult him, obviously '– but whatever, you can go now, and if you want to have sex again some time, fine, I'll maybe be free, I'm not exactly, you know, the hottest girl in the world anymore, so just text me.'

He looked so gutted that I felt guilty for the three seconds it took me to remember how manipulative men like him work. Even then, I considered saying, 'But actually don't worry about all that. Let's just snuggle up on the couch and drink our tea, and the good news is that this morning, before Stuart rang and ruined my life, I bought us chocolate biscuits.'

'I asked you to leave,' I said.

'Kate—'

'I am telling you to please get out.' It occurred to me to consider my safety. I took my phone out of my pocket, and stepped backwards, away from him, so I was closer to the door.

'If we could just—'

'Adam! I said I want you to go.' I held up my phone, thumb poised.

He stepped back and put both his hands up, fingers spread, palms angled towards the floor. 'OK. It's all right, Kate. I'm going.'

When he got to the door, he said, 'I'll text you. I mean, not for . . . just, in the morning. Or call you. Bye.'

'Liar.'

I stayed sitting at the bench. My apartment was silent except for the fridge, and when it stopped whirring, I felt, bizarrely, very alone. As if the fridge was my friend. I looked over at Philomena, and she helped the tears to stop.

After a while, I did something I hadn't done for a very long time, which was to take some of my favourite pictures out of their box in my wardrobe. There's a perfume ad that used to be on a billboard near Covent Garden. I'm wearing a short, light-blue slip. There's my only *Vogue* cover: my face, close up, and a mauve caption reading NEW MILLENNIUM PRETTY, as if my beauty was more real and wonderful than the sort that had been around in the mediocre Old Millennium. There were quite a few other photos. To do with skin cream and clothes, mainly. I looked at them all for maybe an hour. Then I went and put on my favourite white silk chemise and pouted around in front of the bathroom mirror for a bit. Then my favourite black chemise. More pouting. After a bit more pretend-modelling, I went to bed.

I had a big cry, and I tried to masturbate, but it seemed that it wasn't my night on that front either. So I just lay there and thought about everything.

I wondered if he'd have bothered even trying it, if I still looked like that girl in the photos. I thought probably not. I didn't really know what he wanted, or why, but I knew that men like him prey on the vulnerable, and I supposed that was how he saw me.

It was very hard to accept somehow. Another loss.

And I wondered if I would have been with him, if I still had my arm. I lay and thought about that for a long time. I didn't know, but at least I could see that it wasn't as simple as that, because if I still had my arm, I wouldn't be the person I am now. I'm not saying having an amputation is character-building (as I am not a cretin) and I'd always told myself that I would refuse to let it define me. Everyone seemed to believe that the it-doesn't-define-me view was the correct one.

But losing my arm *had* shaped me, the same way that being born 'beautiful' shaped me, the same way that becoming a businesswoman or a mother would have shaped me, the same way that being born smart shaped Bec into the person she was, the person who always had the answer.

In the end, so much of it all was just what was in our genes.

Chapter Twelve

Bec

Essie didn't eat on the morning of the first day at Ashton Heights Primary, even though Bec made waffles and (in desperation) offered maple syrup.

'Go on, Essie. Breakfast will make you run fast,' said Mathilda, with a quick glance at Bec. When Essie shook her head 'no', Mathilda doggedly ate on, even though her own little face was like a cracked dinner plate. She took her breakfast things to the dishwasher without being asked, and when it was time to go, shouldered her backpack in a quiet, responsible way that made Bec want to sit down on the floor and howl.

'Shouldn't we go and say bye to Dad?' Lachlan asked, at the front door.

'Let's not,' said Bec. 'Dad's not feeling very well. He needs to have a good sleep-in.' Stuart, she knew, had taken three temazepams at two o'clock that morning. And to be honest, it was easier without him.

No one spoke on the way to school. It was the middle of May. The autumn leaves along their street were brown and wet and unattractive. When they dropped Lachlan off, Essie said, 'Mummy, since Briarwood's near here, maybe you could just let me out and I could have a play with Mrs Wilkinson just for today? Because it's Monday and—'

'I'm afraid not, Essie darling,' said Bec. 'But you'll get to see your Briarwood friends at Isabel's party on the weekend, so that'll be good, won't it?'

The new school was pleasant enough. Red-brick single-storey buildings, aluminium windows, a covered walkway near the oval, a basketball ring over a large square of concrete, a cluster of demountables.

'Please don't go yet, please, Mummy,' Essie whispered, into Bec's thighs, as the two of them stood uncertainly just inside the new classroom door, next to a display titled OUR TRIP TO THE MUSEUM. A girl in a navy-blue polo shirt with toothpaste on the front stared at them with apparent hostility as she passed. In the far corner, two boys were hitting each other with some large, soft puppets.

Bec knelt in front of Essie and said, 'I do need to go now, darling, but I'll be back at half-past three to pick you up.' Essie bowed her head to hide her silent tears in Bec's shoulder, and the teacher finally came over.

'Right. Essie Henderson, isn't it? I'm Ms Goldbold. Got your bag on its shelf? Good. Time to say bye-bye to Mummy and sit on the mat, please.'

She didn't make eye contact with Bec, who could only stand for an agonised moment looking after the tiny, golden-and-navy little girl who was being led briskly away.

On Tuesday, eleven sleeps had passed since their bushwalk and she hadn't heard from Ryan. She hadn't contacted him, either. Maybe he was right. Maybe she actually *couldn't*. Maybe they needed to let it go, let the feelings pass, let things be.

Mathilda seemed to take all right to Ashton Heights. Her teacher was smiling and efficient, and, at pick-up on the second day, told

Bec that she'd sat Mathilda with some of the quieter kids. 'Gives her a chance to find her feet,' she said. She touched Bec's arm. 'Don't worry. It's harder on you than them.' The teacher gave Bec a quick smile before turning away.

But for Essie, things seemed to get worse instead of better. 'When can we visit Mrs Wilkinson?' she kept asking, as if it would be possible to just drop into her old school for morning tea under the oak trees. 'How many sleeps till Isabel's party?'

There were tears every morning at drop-off. Ms Goldbold was the sort of woman who you could just tell had a messy car and teenage children with no boundaries. She always had a half-full cup of cold instant coffee on her desk and had called Essie 'Mia' at least once.

'Can't you home-school her or something?' Kate said on the phone on Thursday. She sounded anguished, more so than Bec would have thought. 'The poor little kid.'

'You've changed your tune,' said Bec, trying for light-hearted. 'I thought you were all for diversity and equality and down-with-private-school-elitism.'

'Yes, well this is Essie,' Kate said, and Bec could hear her impatient shrug down the phone. 'And let me say that I can't believe Briarwood wouldn't let them finish the term. Sorry. Don't cry, Becky. Should I come down at the weekend? We'll take them for ice cream. It fixes everything with Essie.' Kate sounded close to tears herself.

'She's got a birthday party,' said Bec. 'Maybe come soon, though?' She really wanted to talk to Kate about Ryan, apart from everything else. 'And hey, Stuart told me he called you about Adam. What happened?' She should have asked sooner, really. 'Sorry I didn't call myself. I should have. It's just . . . crazy here at the moment. Are you OK?'

But Kate sounded as offhand as ever. 'Oh, you know me,' she said. 'I just told him, better we keep things casual. Or not see each other. Whatever, I'm not taking his calls.'

'As long as you're happy.' Bec kept her voice very neutral. 'That's all we want.'

Kate said she'd better go.

On Friday after school – still no Ryan, and it was now a fortnight since their bushwalk – Bec left the older kids with Stuart and took Essie shopping for a present for Isabel. Essie's little hand was warm in Bec's as they caught the escalator all the way up to the third-floor toy department at Myer. They spent nine minutes at the Beanie Boo stand, deciding which of the fluffy toys to buy. 'Isabel likes unicorns and narwhals, but not butterflies or ladybirds,' said Essie, with authority.

'And is this for you?' said the man behind the counter, as he handed over the booty.

'No, it's for my friend Isabel,' said Essie chattily. 'It's her party tomorrow.'

'Aren't you lucky!' said the man, with an isn't-she-sweet? glance at Bec. 'You have fun.' Essie swung the bag in a merchandise-threatening arc all the way to the elevator.

The next morning, for the first time all week, Essie got dressed without help from Bec.

'Is this smart enough, Mummy?' she asked. She was wearing a flamingo-spattered dress that had been a Christmas present. 'And can you please braid my hair?'

They arrived at the play centre at one minute past ten, the Beanie Boo wrapped up in pink paper with a pink sparkly ribbon, and a card made by Essie sticky-taped to the top. There was a smell of coffee and plastic, a chrome-and-Perspex barrier with a sign saying

175

SOCKS MUST BE WORN AT ALL TIMES, and, beyond the barrier, a dazzling buffet of twirly slides and trampolines and huge, squashy mats.

'You're here for the Campbell party?' said the attendant, a young woman with thick foundation that was entirely the wrong tone. She had to raise her voice above the hubbub from the play area. 'I just need your name.'

'Yes,' said Bec. 'This is Essie Henderson.'

'*Isabel* Campbell,' piped up Essie, who knew the drill and was already removing her shoes.

'I'm afraid Essie's not on the list. Hang on.' The girl appeared to be counting. 'They've got twenty girls booked, twenty names on the list, but no Essie Henderson here.' Her face was bland.

'Well, I've got an invitation,' said Bec, feeling something like panic.

'Mummy, there's Isabel!' said Essie, waving to some girls who were ascending an enormous plastic climbing frame. 'There's Madeline S! And Madeline G!'

Bec rifled in her handbag. The pink postcard-sized piece of cardboard, with its printed details and Essie's name written near the top in silver pen, was in the side pocket. Bec had been carrying it around for weeks; she'd kept forgetting to put it on the fridge. She was proffering the invitation to the girl behind the counter when Isabel's mum appeared on the other side of the barrier.

'Oh, Lydia, hi!' said Bec, more relieved than was really necessary. 'Major drama! I thought we weren't going to be allowed in!'

'Bec, I'm sorry. There's obviously been a mix-up,' said Lydia. 'We went ahead and invited the new prep girl in Essie's place.'

'Oh,' said Bec.

'It's, you know, this is a whole-class party for the Briarwood preps.'

'But. Oh.' Bec took a deep breath in. 'Well, I mean, Essie's here, and she's been so excited. Maybe I could ... maybe I could pay and she could just come in and have a play and see Isabel and the girls?'

'It's not about the money,' Lydia said, loftily. 'I mean, I haven't got a party bag or anything for Essie. I haven't set her a place at the party table. There are only twenty helium-filled balloons.'

'You didn't maybe want to let me know?' said Bec. 'She's been . . . I'm sorry.' Bec pressed two fingertips against the tip of her own nose. 'She's been really very much looking forward to seeing everyone.'

'I think it's probably better for everyone if Essie focuses on making new friends at her new school,' said Lydia. 'It gets a bit confusing for all the girls otherwise.'

'Could she maybe just come in and give Isabel her present?' said Bec. Essie was holding Bec's hand now; her shoes were unbuckled but still on; she was staring at a point in front of her on the white linoleum floor. 'We chose it especially. It's a unicorn Beanie Boo,' Bec added, pathetically.

'I'll take it for you,' said Lydia. 'We're not opening anything here anyway.' She extended her hand over the barrier. Essie relinquished the gift as if it was her baby. 'Thank you. I'll pop it on the table with the other presents.' Lydia looked at Essie for the first time. 'Isabel will open it at home. Now. You have a great weekend, Essie! Enjoy your new school, won't you? Bye, Bec!'

'Come on darling,' said Bec, swiping at her cheeks. It was all she could do to keep her voice steady. 'I'm afraid Mummy got a bit mixed up and it's not Isabel's party after all. Let's go and have a big ice cream instead!' She couldn't even look at Essie's face.

They turned for the doors.

'Would she want a free jelly snake?' called the bad make-up girl, and Bec derived a crumb of comfort from the fact that she looked utterly appalled. 'Would you – maybe want a tissue?'

'Oh no, that's fine,' said Bec. 'Thank you, though—' she checked the girl's name badge '– Tegan.'

They turned and walked out through the sliding doors, hand squeezing hand. Bec thought about how, to a casual observer, it would have looked as if nothing very much had happened.

'That absolute bitch.' You could always rely on Kate. 'That absolute *fucking* bitch.' They were on the phone later that night.

'I know.'

'I'd like to kill her,' said Kate, who had never met Lydia. 'I'd like to get a lethal injection and stab her through her new-season bulge-disguising knit.' It had been a long time since Bec had heard Kate be so catty. She sounded more like her twenty-something self. 'Or else I'd do it while she slept. I could creep up and strangle her. With a silk scarf. I'd leave it there, as if I was some sort of glamorous serial killer.' She paused. 'Actually, you'll probably have to help me if we go for the strangling option.'

Bec laughed sadly. This was very comforting. When they'd arrived home – Essie with ice cream and tears all over her face; she'd started sobbing in the car, of course – Stuart had said, 'What's wrong with Essie?' and when Bec told him he'd said, 'Sheesh. Poor kid,' and gone back to trimming the hydrangeas.

'Darling little Essie,' Bec said, now. 'She'd even put on her favourite undies.' Bec had intended to say that with a laugh, but she lost control of her voice halfway through and it came out more like a gasp. 'Oh Kate. Why would anyone be so *awful*?'

'Because they're an absolute fucking bitch,' said Kate, and there was not a shred of laughter in her voice. 'I'll be down next weekend.'

*

'Well, there's one plus about this whole state of affairs,' said Kate, between sips of her coffee-van long black. 'State school dads are hotter, apparently.'

It was the next Saturday, and Kate had arrived as promised. Unbelievably, only a week had passed since Isabel's party. Bec had been to work (three times), cooked dinner (five and a half times), organised lunch boxes (four times), and had sex with Stuart (one time).

Also, quite a few other things.

She sipped her own coffee and scanned the soccer field boundary line. They were watching Mathilda's first match for her new school. Clusters of unfamiliar parents stood in snug groups; their breath was visible in the freezing morning air as they chatted and called out, 'Go, Ashton Heights!' and, 'Good effort, Ruby!' and (to an adventurous toddler), 'Come back here, Ada, love; it's only for the big girls!'

'Actually, you're right,' said Bec. Most of the dads had that sort of lean, windswept, stubbly look. They were wearing outdoorsy clothes: all well-worn down jackets and scrubby polar fleeces, as if they were just about to go mountain-bike riding or kayaking or something. Bec thought of the Briarwood dads: their suits and bellies and darting, kid-tracking eyes. Their phones and lanyards and terse instructions. They weren't *all* like that, she reminded herself.

A tall man with a shaved head yelled, 'You can do it, Esther!' and then clapped with his hands over his head as a spindly girl kicked the ball a long way up the field.

'And nicer,' said Kate.

'Who knew?' Bec took another sip of her cofffee.

'Yeah, some of those Briarwood dads,' said Kate. 'Remember that tosser in the car park last year?' Bec nodded. Kate was referring to a time when Bec had come close to scraping someone's shiny four-wheel drive with her own. (The school was old; its driveway hadn't been designed for cars that big.) There had been an altercation, and Kate, who had been in Bec's passenger seat, had ended up getting out and telling the other driver, who'd turned out to be a grade-six dad, to go and relieve himself manually.

'Ordinarily I'd suggest you get fucked,' she said. She was leaning into his window and speaking sweetly and quietly so that none of the children would hear. 'But clearly it'd be impossible for you to get a fuck under any circumstances.'

'I don't even know who he was,' Bec told Stuart later, when the kids were in bed and the three of them were drinking wine. Kate had been staying with them for the Regatta Day long weekend.

'Some penis in an Audi,' Kate supplied.

'Well, that narrows it down,' Stuart said, grinning and clinking Kate's glass. Bec had been stranded between mortification ('Was that *your* sister?' people would ask her at drop-off on Monday) and pride (Kate was so cool. Stuart was so relaxed. Even if both he and Bec did drive enormous Audis).

'So,' Kate said, as Ada-the-toddler made another dash towards the goals, 'how are you guys holding up?'

'Um,' said Bec. Of course, Kate would assume that the complaint against Stuart was the most pressing thing in her life. 'I actually said to Stu he should see a doctor, but . . .' She shrugged. Kate made a spluttering noise.

'Oh, as *if*,' she said. 'He needs a better lawyer, not a doctor. It's outrageous, this reputational damage. What does Rodney say about that? And what's happening with MPRA? Did Rodney send that letter in the end?'

'He sent it. We're waiting. I don't know.' She told Kate that she had deleted both Twitter and Facebook from her phone.

'Don't blame you. I saw some of it,' Kate said, in a flat tone.

They watched the soccer for a while. Mathilda was doing a lot of running up and down the wing. Someone called Imogen seemed like an extremely good kicker.

'Heard from that Adam guy?' said Bec, after a decent interval. It was the best segue she could think of.

'Oh,' said Kate. 'I blocked him. As you do.' She waved a dismissive coffee cup. 'It's not as if we were, you know, serious, or anything, Bec.'

Bec barely heard.

'Kate. I have to tell you something.' There was no one anywhere near them, but she lowered her voice anyway, and cast a quick look over her shoulder. Kate would be horrified. Kate would say things. Kate would know how to make her *stop*.

'What?' said Kate. 'God, what now?'

There was a little moment when the world seemed very quiet. Then Bec touched her sister's wrist and said, 'I'm sleeping with someone else.'

Because that week, she had also had sex with Ryan. (At least three times. Possibly more, depending on how you defined sex.)

Last Monday morning he'd called her. Not a text. An actual phone call. 'I need to see you. Today. Please?' he'd said, as soon as she answered. She'd walked so much more slowly, that morning, down his path.

'You sure about this?' he said, in his hallway. But he was already kissing her, properly this time. His hands were already moving from her shoulders to her hips; he was already breathing hard and fast, already walking her backwards into his bedroom, angling her mauve jumper up over her head, muttering things like *so soft* and *your beautiful skin* and *oh God, Bec, finally*.

'Pardon?' Kate turned towards Bec, and peered at Bec's mouth, as if she honestly thought she had misheard.

'You heard me.'

'What, Bec? Just, what?'

'With the fire-eater,' said Bec, penitently. But she was loving talking about it. In fact, she felt like giggling, a bit like when the slightly famous rugby player had winked at her in the Qantas lounge. (When she'd had Lachlan in her arms!)

'You've *slept* with someone?' Kate's voice took all the giggle out of Bec. 'Once?'

'No.' Two visits to his house. More than two actual . . . what would you call it? Episodes? Intercourses? The man was twenty-seven, for heaven's sake.

'Bec, are you seriously telling me that you're having an affair?'

'No. Yes.' Twenty-seven; seventh heaven.

'With *what* fire-eater?'

'From Stuart's party? You thought he was sexy.' Kate was so deeply and disapprovingly silent that Bec's voice trailed off. Really, how did Kate *do* that?

'*Why?* Bec. Are you and Stuart having, like, problems? Bec. Bec! Just what exactly do you expect me to say?'

'I don't know,' Bec said. 'I want you to talk me out of it.' But I didn't know, Kate, she wanted to add. I didn't know it could be like this. Did you know? Is this what it's always been like for you?

'Well, stop cheating and stop lying and stop . . . *doing it.*' Kate's voice reminded Bec of a smashed window. 'How you could do this to the kids is absolutely beyond me.'

'That's the sort of thing! I know. I know. This is just what I've been needing you to tell me.'

'What makes you think I won't tell Stuart? God, Bec, the way you take your life for granted – it makes me . . . it is *breathtaking.*'

'Please don't tell him. Kate. You're my sister.'

'Oh, just shut up,' said Kate. 'You're going to ruin everything. Did you think about that?'

'Yes,' said Bec. 'It's all I can think about. I know it's terrible. Of course I do. I keep saying I'll stop, and then I just – Kate, it's just so – so—'

'Yeah, yeah, the fire-eater sex is great, I get it. No doubt he *understands* you more than anyone ever has.' She sounded furious. 'Who else knows? You told Mum?'

'No one else knows,' said Bec. Thank goodness she hadn't mentioned the way Ryan seemed to get her almost completely. 'I've been really careful. He's never met the kids; we never go anywhere near our house.'

'Oh, shut up,' Kate said again. Astonishingly, Kate looked as if she were about to cry. 'You don't get prizes for that, you know.'

'I know.' Of course, you didn't. 'I know.'

'I had an affair once,' said Kate, as if that was an extra reason *Bec* should be ashamed. 'In London. And I barely thought about the wife. I barely considered her. Because *I* was twenty-two and a selfish little cow.'

'What happened?' How had Bec never known about this?

'What do you think? Beautiful girl. Rich man. Fancy hotels. He seriously wanted me to go to Paris with him. Perfume. Lingerie. Boxes full of clichés.'

'Who was he?' Bec said.

'Well, he didn't have little kids,' hissed Kate. 'Even me, even at twenty-two, I wouldn't have stooped that low. Go, Ashton Heights,' she added, loudly. A girl with a headband had scored a goal.

Kate was very much more upset than Bec had anticipated, but Bec was also surprised – concerned, even – by how Kate's words were just sliding off her. In fact, she was mainly wondering what would have been wrong with going to Paris.

'What I'm saying is that – look at what you've got, Bec. Look at it. Really. It's – I promise – it's so not worth it.'

'Did he stay with his wife, in the end?'

'We are talking about you.' Kate's words sounded the way Lachy's metronome would if it ever got angry. So paced and deliberate and unyielding.

'Yes, of course.' Bec made her tone meek, but she was thinking that there was surely no need for quite this amount of distress. It wasn't *Kate's* marriage.

'You can't have both, Bec. You just cannot have every single thing you want.'

'I know that.' Of *course* she knew that. And maybe Kate shouldn't be so bloody judgemental, all things considered.

'Everyone wants both. You're not special.' Kate often talked as if she had a degree in Psychology, which she absolutely did not. 'And Bec, sometimes you need to stop and think, think properly, about what the consequences are, before you just rush in. What you do, choices you make, they affect other people, you know.'

'I realise that, Kate!' For God's sake. Her whole life was one long series of choices made with other people in mind. She breathed in through her nose and out through her mouth. 'But to be honest, this ... whatever it is, with Ryan, it doesn't seem to be something I've chosen.' That was entirely true.

'You must be insane,' said Kate. 'Just. Bec. You ... *Stuart.* You have absolutely no idea.'

The two women sipped their coffee. When Bec glanced over, she saw that there were tears on Kate's face.

'Hi,' said Ryan. 'I've been waiting for you.'

It was just before 9 a.m. the next Monday. Her car was parked around the corner. She'd pulled over on her way home from dropping the kids at school, as if she was nipping into the dry-cleaner. His front door clicked shut behind her; his arm was already like a band around her waist.

'You look gorgeous,' he said. He kissed her, firmly, edging her back against the wall. He had one hand on her shoulder; he pressed against her black shirt dress.

'This thing you're wearing is so sexy,' he breathed, running his hands along her body. 'Clingy. Thin.'

She could only kiss back. He pushed her into his bedroom, sat on his bed. She stood in front of him.

'Take it off for me,' he said. She smiled, and shook her head.

'Bec,' he said. His voice was business-like. 'Take it off.'

Her hands moved to her belt. She unlaced it. Then she began to undo the buttons.

'That's it,' he breathed. 'Keep going.'

Another button. Bec swallowed. The dress fell open. She was wearing new underwear. Cheap, but nice. Pale-blue lace. She'd bought it the week before, on her lunch break. Unforgivable. But it was less unforgivable than wearing any of the underwear – the expensive, sexy-in-a-classy-way underwear – that Stuart tended to give her.

Ryan looked her up and down, slowly.

'Really gorgeous,' he said. 'Take your dress off properly.'

Bec allowed her dress – freshly ironed! – to fall off her shoulders, to the floor.

'Sexy,' he said. He pulled her hip so that she was standing between his knees. He ran his fingertips over the straps of her bra, flipped them down, onto her upper arms.

'Very pretty,' he said. 'Take it off now.'

She could hear her breath coming faster as she unhooked her bra, slipped it off. He immediately reached for her breasts, bounced them gently in his cupped hands. She whimpered.

'Yeah,' he said, in response. 'Nice, aren't they? You've got such beautiful tits.'

Tits! Who *said* that? It was really quite distasteful. But also, surprisingly nice. Sexy.

'Turn around,' he said. She did, wondering what was going to happen next. He stood up, behind her. In his little mirror, they could see their own faces. He started playing with her nipples. Pressing himself against her bottom. He was watching her.

'Your pussy,' he breathed, trailing a hand down, gentling his fingers under the blue lacy triangle. 'Soft.'

It didn't even occur to her to laugh, which is what she'd always thought she'd do if someone started using words like *tits* and *pussy* in real life. This was the kind of sex she'd always imagined Kate had. Overwhelming and practised. She sank back towards him, closed her eyes.

She heard his breath. It was fast and deep. Goodness. He wasn't stopping. He was just playing with her, with her breasts and her . . . pussy, as if he was really, really enjoying it.

'Ryan,' she said. She opened her eyes, which met his in the mirror. 'I think I'm going to come.'

'I'd reckon,' he said, giving her a slow grin. He did something else with his hand, pushing her a bit harder and then she did actually come, leaning back against him, half falling. After a moment he turned her around to him again and kissed her.

'You feel amazing,' he said. 'Lie down, Bec.'

His bed was neatly made, like always. She lay on top of the doona cover, on her back, propped up on her elbows. Her body actually was quite nice, she thought, dreamily. He took off his shorts.

'Take those off,' he said. She slithered her underwear down her legs, and he made a little groaning sound. 'I always forget just how beautiful you are,' he said. Imagine if she had never done this. Never had this. What a tragedy that would have been.

'I like ... this,' she said. It was becoming easier to say that kind of thing.

'Yeah,' he said, caressingly. 'I know.' He moved over her, one palm on each side of her head. He began to kiss her again. 'This,' he breathed, as he slid into her. 'Is this what you like?'

She nodded against his neck.

'Me too, Bec,' he said. His voice was urgent, low. 'Since the moment I woke up the only thing I've been wanting to do is to fuck you.'

Chapter Thirteen

Kate

I was eating muesli – contemporary-era grain; I'd run out of ancient – and reminding myself that today was simply another day of writing my thesis and living a Full and Independent Life. (Not full and independent in a differently-abled-look-at-me-go! way. Full and independent in a single-no-children-loving-life! way.)

At that time of day, the thing I missed most was the morning messaging. We'd been in the habit of sending each other one or two morning texts, even on mornings when we'd woken up together. Just sweet little messages, like an observation about something we saw on the way to work (*Adam, why are there ads for milk? Isn't it well known enough already?*) (*K8! I just saw* INCWINC *on an Alfa Romeo Spider. Not too bad, eh?*) or a song to listen to or a recipe to try or a movie to see. He thought I didn't know enough about Australian music. He thought we should cook dinner together more often. He thought *Good Will Hunting* was one of the best movies Hollywood ever made.

Except, of course, the man who thought all those things didn't really exist.

I put my forehead on the nice cold bench. Isn't it funny, how when someone has hurt you, you still yearn to see them? Isn't it hard, to accept that in real life when a man seems not to like a woman very much, it's probably because he doesn't like her very much? Why didn't he *like* me enough? I kept asking myself. As if that was the main and most important consideration. As if, had I been just a bit better, then the Adam I loved would have been real.

After a while, I lifted my forehead up and realised that I hadn't finished my muesli. I'd been there for ages, doing nothing, except thinking. I blinked at my bowl. I stared at my phone. I remembered another message. In a different flat, in a different city, in a different decade, in a different life.

In London. More than fourteen years before.

'This is a message for Kate Leicester.'

The voice on my answering machine had been plummy and well-educated, like a butler out of a film. (Although butlers, surely, would not have been particularly well-educated.) 'Kate, this is Mr Michael Cartwright. Please call my rooms as soon as you're able.'

Maybe if I'd listened more carefully, I might have noticed Mr Cartwright sounded slightly less pompous than usual. Maybe if I'd been savvier, I would have been surprised that the great man had picked up a telephone himself.

I'd been away for a few days for British *Vogue*, shooting something that was about how – even though it was the new millennium – traditional tartan was timeless and therefore still a goer. We'd been in stony Edinburgh: lots of thin, beautiful men in kilts blurring up the background, and me in the foreground wearing a succession of tartan-accessorised evening dresses and many, many pearls. Anyway, I had a lot of messages, so I didn't call Mr Cartwright back straight away.

'Is that Kate Leicester?' he said, the following day, when he got through. 'Mr Cartwright, your surgeon, here. I've been leaving you messages.'

One message, actually, I thought. Peremptory git. I said nothing.

'Now, Miss Leicester, I have some unfortunate news.' He was speaking in a slow, interested voice, the sort you'd use to draw children into a story. 'The histology – the laboratory report – is back on your right arm procedure. And it appears the lump we removed is, most unusually, not a benign lesion.'

'Right?'

'It's important I see you as soon as possible to arrange further surgery.' His tone definitely did not sound as if he was giving me life-changing news.

'Well, I could come in towards the end of next week?'

'Sooner is better in this case. I've popped you in at the end of my clinic today. Half past five or so.'

It was a day off; I'd been planning to eat my monthly Mars bar and start the new *Harry Potter*.

'All right,' I said.

I wore jeans and trainers and a tight lemon singlet top with shoe-string straps. Even though my right elbow was a bit painful and stiff, it took me less than a minute to twist my hair into a loose bun at the nape of my neck. I wore fuchsia lipstick. As I was running down the stairs, I tied a filmy pale-pink cardigan around my waist, because although it was August it was late August, and it was London. I can't remember what underwear I wore. I caught the Tube.

Mr Cartwright – who I'd met the week before, for my first ever 'procedure' – looked like someone who'd grown up in a house that had grandfather clocks and more than one staircase. I imagined that he'd turned to his receptionist after I'd left and said, 'Pretty thing, isn't she?' or else, 'Good Lord, what an accent!'

I sat down opposite him, his desk between us.

'As I said on the telephone, we are no longer dealing with a benign lesion. Last week, as you know, we took that little lump off your right arm. It seems we resected a rare malignant tumour called a leiomyosarcoma. It is possible not all of it has been removed, so we will need to go back and operate again.' He looked at me, then frowned at his computer as if it was an impertinent medical student.

'All right,' I said. I touched the healing wound on the inside of my right arm. It was still swollen. With commendable presence of mind, I said, 'Do you mean I've got cancer?'

'It's possible there might be some malignant cells left, yes.' He looked down at my arm, reached out, pressed at the swollen bit, and then frown-nodded. 'After re-excision I'm going to refer you to an oncologist for an opinion.'

His tone was so reassuring. He made it sound as if this was a natural, if inconvenient, course of events, something that happened from time to time that he knew how to deal with. Like when a pilot announces there's too much fog to take off, so everyone back to the terminal, please.

A few months before, a girl I'd known through work (Hortense Maloney) had been told she had cancerous cells on her cervix. The way she carried on (wailing about how she was being cut down in her prime, wondering aloud about *why*) it had seemed very serious, as if she (literally) would die. But then she had a (much wailed-about) day procedure, a dose of laser or something, and it turned out she was as good as gold. Well. Certainly I was not going to be like Hortense Maloney.

'What's an oncologist?' I would be assertive and rational.

'A cancer specialist. I propose I operate again on Friday.'

'Friday. So . . . how serious is this?'

'Very serious if left untreated. I realise this might come as a shock.'

I remember thinking that if Mr Cartwright wasn't worried, then there mustn't be anything to worry about. Naïve, yes, appallingly so. The thing is – quite apart from Hortense Maloney's cervix – I was used to fashion editors. They were often young and terrified and would completely drop their bundles if someone's hair wasn't going right or the shoes were the wrong type of burgundy. Grown adults would pant things like, 'That absolutely is not bronze, that is 90 per cent fucking MUSTARD!'

Mr Cartwright was not panting or running, no one was shouting, 'Clear!': there was obviously no emergency.

'I am a bit shocked,' I said. 'But I'll re-arrange my schedule. I suppose I'll need a few weeks off work?'

'Yes. Start with that,' Mr Cartwright said, approvingly.

Then he added, 'At this stage we're very hopeful that a limb salvage procedure will be possible.'

For reasons hardly anyone understands, I told no one.

I went home, rang Alison (my agent) and told her I had to have an operation – I'm sure she thought it was an abortion; she didn't sound anywhere near sympathetic enough. I spent long periods of time looking at my beautiful right arm, pressing along various bits of it, reassuring myself that it looked virtually back to normal and was not even all that sore. I went running further than usual in Kensington Gardens, all the time thinking that surely if I had proper cancer then I wouldn't be feeling anywhere near so energetic.

Only the two-inch long, almost-healed, whitish-pink line just below my elbow – where Mr Cartwright had done the first procedure – showed that anything at all was amiss. He'd removed the little lump that had started off like a grape, and then grown almost to the size of a golf ball, in his office. I'd been wide awake, wincing at the sting of the local anaesthetic and hoping he wasn't going to try to make conversation. I needn't have worried. 'Bound to be a lipoma,' was all he'd said. 'Very common. Completely harmless.'

On the Wednesday, I had a (pretty much compulsory) lunch with Alison. 'There's some problem with the muscles of my arm,' I told her, entirely truthfully. She narrowed her eyes, and recommended glucosamine and Nurofen. I thanked her and said I'd probably be OK for Fashion Week, a whole month away. 'Gracious, Kate, we'd certainly hope so,' she said.

I went to a shoot about age-defying face cream on the Thursday. That night I went out for upmarket hamburgers with a few work friends. I told them I was going away for a week or two. Maybe they thought it was to do with an eating disorder or a cosmetic procedure or (perhaps if they'd talked to Alison) an abortion. In any case they didn't ask even a single question. Not one.

On Friday I got up very early and took a black taxi to Fulham and Kings Road Hospital. A thin young man in a dressing gown was loitering out the front, holding a metal wheelie stand with a bag of liquid attached to it. I thought he probably had AIDS, and I'm ashamed to say that that comforted me. Made me feel less alone.

The hospital was pretty new then. There was lots of glass and metal and natural light and a foyer like a department store's, except that the signs said things like SPINAL UNIT instead of HOMEWARES. Also, the staff were not well-groomed enough to be working in a shop in that part of London. (It's a very fancy part. Hugh Grant had a place nearby.)

I didn't see Mr Cartwright that morning. In a cubicle with green curtains and a sign that said KATHERINE JANE LEICESTER – CARTWRIGHT – NIL BY MOUTH, I got changed into a white paper gown. A nice young woman called Nicola Devitt came in, carrying a blue plastic folder with my name on it.

'I'll be your anaesthetist, Kate,' she said.

I answered *no* to her every question (Regular medications? Allergies? Smoker? Recreational drugs? Other medical conditions? Pregnant?)

'Well, you'll be nice and easy, then,' she said, shutting my folder with a casual clap. I thought that she meant my operation was bound to be a success.

Later that day I woke up feeling very happy. There were no beeping machines or worried faces or bright lights or choke-y tubes down my throat.

A nurse with a number of silver studs in both his ears said, 'Ah! Kate Leicester! You're back with us! Welcome. Now, you're in Recovery, darl. Just let me pop this back on your finger. Got to make sure you're breathing for me. Terrible look if you stop. Ruins my day, the paperwork. Your oxygen's on ninety-eight. Bo*nus*. Now, how are you?'

'Fine,' I said. 'Great, actually.'

'Good drugs, aren't they, darl?' He winked, but in a reasonably enjoyable way. 'So, no pain?'

'No.'

He put a little plastic thing on a cord into my left hand, like an electric blanket control except smaller. 'Press this when it starts to hurt, Kate, darl,' he said.

Only after he'd walked off did I look over at my arm. It was still there (bo*nus*) and it had its own little table thing that it rested on, so it was up a bit higher than my shoulder. Not at all like last time, when I'd just had a modest little bandage below my elbow. This time white crêpe was wound from my shoulder to below my wrist, and there must have been a lot of padding underneath it because my arm was much wider than usual. Like a python. Also there were two plastic tubes poking out from inside the bandages, disappearing down towards the floor. Some sort of reddish fluid was inside them.

The tips of all five of my fingers were visible though. I wiggled them a tiny bit. The little finger didn't move at all, and the ring finger was a bit numb, which was disconcerting but not unbearable.

And the drugs really were making me feel very happy.

Is there anything more annoying than false hope?

No. There is nothing more annoying.

Nothing.

Mr Cartwright turned up a bit later, after I'd been moved to the ward. I was groggier then and in no mood for him. I wanted Nicola Devitt, with her cheery blue folder. I really, *really* wanted Mum.

I wished that I'd told someone where I was. My friends, who could have crowded around my bed and brought flowers and magazines and made jokes about putting vodka into my drip or stealing my morphine. Or Bec. She would have arrived straight from Heathrow, with just-brushed, terrible hair, a shiny nose and a backpack full of medical textbooks with Post-it notes sticking out of them, as if knowledge about cancer would give us power over it. I wanted my dad. He would have turned up, sat next to my bed for hours, said almost nothing and then, when it was time to go, pulled on one of his enormous ears and murmured, 'And as if that Cartwright character's not bad enough, they expect you to *drink* that tea, Kate-o.'

'Kate,' said Mr Cartwright. His nose that day reminded me of a big earplug. 'Things went well. The tissues came together beautifully. The lab is checking the specimen. Making sure we've got it all. We'll get you to have some scans before you go home. As a precaution.' He said things about a physiotherapist, the elbow joint, the ulnar nerve, the flexor muscles. Someone who looked and sounded exactly like a 25-year-old Prince William stood next to him, scribbling in my cheery blue folder and then bending down to inspect the tubes that poked out of my arm. 'Thirty mills,' he said, as if that was a compliment.

I felt very hopeful. Not even hopeful. I assumed that everything was as fine as everyone seemed to think.

My scans were all clear. I had a spectacularly normal torso, apparently. My little finger started moving, first of all when I tried really hard, then when I tried only a bit hard. The antibiotics were stopped. A nurse took out my drip. Another one took out my 'drains'. I was allowed to walk to the toilet. The new bruises on my arm shrank, so that they looked like a purple archipelago instead of the whole of Europe.

I was very glad I'd told no one. Unnecessary fuss and fretting and flights; I would have looked like a drama queen. No Hortense Maloney-style carry-on for me, the down-to-earth Australian with my sultry pout and my to-die-for curves.

My right arm, now partly exposed, was like a new lover. At physiotherapy I gripped a squash ball over and over. I dealt cards. I touched my thumb to each finger, many times. Back on the ward, I rubbed my hands together and scratched my nose and wiped my bottom (in the bathroom, obviously) and turned page after page of books. I undid little paper sachets of sugar for the horrible tea and I thought, wouldn't it be *awful* to lose your hand.

I felt the way you feel when you hear about a shooting in America: genuinely sorry for those involved, but also, not *really* disturbed, because losing a limb was clearly something that happened to others, such as people in the First World War. I, on the other hand (as they say) was lucky enough to have the British National Health Service and CT scans and sterile equipment and Mr Cartwright.

See, everyone was so upbeat. My temperature was normal – 'Good work!' said the intern. My pain was well controlled – 'Sterling,' said the pain doctor. I was eating and drinking and my bowels were working – 'Keep it up, do,' said the nurse. I was making great progress at squash-ball squashing and card-dealing; there were no signs of infection; I had commendably avoided acquiring a blood clot in either one of my legs.

The way they all – even Mr Cartwright: 'Those wounds are healing beautifully, aren't they?' – acted, it was as if there was nothing at all to worry about. At no point did anyone sit me down and say, 'Kate, you're not out of the woods yet. All this is just trivia, because your amazingly healed skin and your fabulously rehabilitated muscles and the fact you're young and fit and have a perfectly functional bowel won't matter *at all* if there's any cancer in there still.' But no one said any of that, so it seemed to me that I'd shrugged off a leiomyosarcoma with my trademark fucking insouciance.

That's why it was quite a shock when, six days after the operation, the laboratory report came back.

Chapter Fourteen

Bec

Bec had been working for just over a month.

She made it through her shifts in a sort of chirpy, dazed fog, looking forward to morning tea, then lunch, then finishing up and driving home and seeing her kids and changing into her round-the-house clothes and having a cup of tea. And then doing all the other stuff. How people worked this way for years on end honestly perplexed her. If ever she needed to be financially independent, she'd definitely need to do something easier and better paid than medical reception.

She looked down at the rings on her left hand as she waited for a fax to go through.

The first time Bec's mum had seen Bec's engagement ring, she'd laughed and said, 'Excellent service at Gloss coming your way, I predict.' Gloss was a ritzy boutique that had – back then – seemed slightly intimidating.

'Yes, I'll be able to buy pant with ease,' Bec had giggled. Stuart proposed to Bec around the time the word 'pant' was storming the fashion world, leaving 'pants' and 'trousers' for dead.

What's happened to me? Bec asked herself, as the third page disappeared. She used the term 'pant' without irony now. Even 'short'. And what had she even been thinking, buying fifty-dollar shorts (yes, from now on she was calling them shorts, like a normal

198

person) for her children, who would have them grass-stained or tomato-sauce-spattered within hours?

Ryan thought children didn't need a lot of expensive stuff. He thought the current obsession with gadgets and social media and photographing every single moment was a tragedy. His poor-but-happy childhood in Western Australia sounded idyllic. His mother – the potter – would send all five kids down to the beach so she could work. He always wore hand-me-downs and they drove an old Ford Falcon station wagon. He and his brothers slept on a covered veranda in the summer. ('Didn't your parents worry about you running off?' Bec had said. 'Getting abducted?' Ryan had laughed and said, 'Nah, of course not,' as if she'd asked about a zombie attack.) His dad was a chef, and they went surfing together and caught fish off the rocks, and his younger brother played violin in a folk band, and his sister won the junior triathlon every year. Once they'd entered a family team; he'd done the swimming leg.

'What about your family?' he said.

'I grew up just round the corner. One of those draughty old houses that looks charming from the street.'

'I know the sort of place. High ceilings. Amazing floorboards. Bathroom the size of this bed.' They exchanged a sexy look. It was two in the afternoon on a Monday. 'Bit different to your house nowadays,' he said.

There was a silence. They'd been facing each other; now she turned to lie on her back.

'Bec?' He put a hand on her cheek. 'Sorry. Sorry. I totally understand you'd want to keep that part of your life separate.'

'It's all right.' She shrugged. 'I feel so worried about it but at the same time . . .' she trailed off, indicated them, their naked, delighted bodies, all the irresistible, perilous, intoxicating pleasure. Under the sheet, they knitted themselves together again. It felt as natural and easy and wonderful as coffee in the morning, as sweet tea when you'd had a shock.

'I know.' He sounded upset too. He tilted her face up to him, traced her mouth with his thumb.

'These lips,' he said.

It was remarkable, how, when he was actually kissing her, she didn't even have to try to put the guilt to one side. It evaporated, as naturally as spilt water on sunshiny concrete. As if she wasn't even doing anything wrong.

Driving home that day, Bec thought about her parents' house, and her childhood room, and then, because thoughts skirt and circle before they finally land where they were going all along, she got to her sister.

It had been just after 7 a.m. on a Saturday, and Dr Bec Leicester had been in bed, drowsing under a patchwork quilt that her grandmother had made. Her mum was in the shower; her dad was out getting the paper. When the phone rang in the hallway, Bec knew straight away it was Kate. Who else would ring that early? Bec wished she'd go away. She'd started work at the hospital before eight every morning that week; today was supposed to be a sleep-in. The phone would ring out in a minute. It did. But then it started again.

Bec moaned and sat up. She put her feet on the Persian rug. Kate's childhood bed was still on the other side of the room. Bec threw it an annoyed look as she stomped into the hallway.

'Hello, Bec here,' she said, into the phone. Brisk international-call pips cut in. 'Hi, Kate,' she sighed.

That was the first time she heard Kate's stringy, see-through voice.

'Bec?' she said. 'Are you sitting down? Is Mum there?'

'What?' Bec said. 'And yes, I'm sitting down.' She sat on the hall chair, the peach velvet seat firm against her pyjamas. The wooden back dug into her spine in an uncomfortable-comfortable way.

'Don't let Mum hear,' said Kate.

'She's in the shower.' Bec listened. 'Yep, definitely. What? God, are you pregnant?'

'No.' Kate's voice was full of what sounded like scorn.

'Fine. What then?'

Silence down the phone. Bec twisted the cord of the receiver round her fingers.

'Kate?'

'I'm coming home. I've been in hospital. I – I had to have a bit of surgery, but I need more. It'll be better if I have it in Australia. At home. Insurance and support and rehab and blah-blah-blah.'

'What are you talking about?' said Bec. Kate was twenty-five.

'I . . . there . . . Bec, I had . . . it was such a little lump. On my arm. It . . . turns out it's not benign.' Bec sat forward and put her head between her knees. 'It's a—' There was a rustle of paper and Kate said something unintelligible that sounded like Leo-Moss-Are-Coma.

'Spell it out,' Bec said, very quietly. After Kate got to the sixth letter, Bec interrupted.

'Leiomyosarcoma,' she said. Lie-oh-my-oh-sar-coma.

'That's right.'

'But . . .' Bec sat up. Her mouth was dry. 'They got it all?' she asked.

She was a bit hazy about leiomyosarcoma. It was extremely rare: what her Pathology lecturer had called the small-print stuff. Unless, of course – the dry, sorrowful half-chuckle he reserved for particularly dreadful illnesses – you were the one with it.

'Well,' said Kate. 'I think no? They have ... to cut more away. Bec. That's why I have to come home. They said they might have to cut away quite a bit of my arm.'

That was the first time bad news made Bec vomit.

It was winter now, and there was no morning sun on the path to his bungalow. She'd been seeing – well, sleeping with – Ryan for what the calendar said was three weeks. It felt like months.

In the beginning, she used to hurry home to regroup. She'd shower and do cleaning or shopping so that when it was time for school pick-up she'd feel nearly back to normal. 'I did lots of washing today,' she could say truthfully, to the children. 'I went to four different shops to find the right size leggings.'

Nowadays she tended to stay in his bed. He would make them tea. He liked trying different types of organic, spicy things. 'Elderberry is used to awaken creativity,' he'd tell her. 'Fennel's for your inner fire.' She could almost believe him.

Stuart never asked where she'd been. Even when he was up and about, if she just put milk or bread on the counter, he seemed to assume they had taken her hours to buy.

'What are you doing now?' Ryan finished his tea and set the empty cup on the floor. The arc of his arm through the air reminded her of a sea bird swooping. 'Just checking my plans for you are realistic.'

'I see,' she said, flirtily. She was wearing only a white cardigan. 'Well, I'm all yours till two. Nothing much on today.'

'Glad you're free.' He looked like a kid who was being a good sport about the grand final he'd just lost. He curled closer around her legs, with his face near her hip. She tangled her fingers in his hair, and waited for him to speak. His voice was a bit muffled as he said, 'Bec, it's just that you've got this whole other life that I can't ever be part of.'

She said something about how difficult she'd find it if things were the other way around.

'I think of you. You in your kitchen, all calm and earth-motherish.' She made a pleased sort of scoffing sound. 'Or lying on your couch reading one of your parenting books.' Had anyone ever listened so well to her? 'And if you come over and you seem a bit grumpy or a bit down or really joyous – like you were last week, I could tell – then it's weird to even ask why.'

'Surely I'm never grumpy,' she deflected. Last Friday she'd been in a particularly good mood because one of the new school mums had invited Essie for a play date.

'Oh, I know how to read you, Rebecca Anne Henderson.' He squeezed her feet and smiled a pleased smile.

'I know,' she said. 'It's part of why I like you.'

'Not just the epic sex, then?' He was still smiling.

'God, of course not. Sex schmex. It's all about how perceptive you are,' she said, and they both laughed. She pulled his head a little bit, so that it was on her thighs.

'Tell me some stuff,' he said. His hair tickled her tummy as he nestled into her lap. 'Stuff about your life.'

'Well . . .'

'Go on.' He opened his eyes and looked up at her. 'Probably got about four minutes till I do something about that cardigan.'

So she told him about Essie and Lachlan and Mathilda. About the ridiculous love and the relentless work of motherhood, and how it felt as if – when you did it right – you were taken for granted. She told him about Allie. She told him about Daniel Gilbert.

'You look after everyone,' he said, softly. It had been much longer than four minutes, but he said, 'Tell me more.'

'Well, then of course, there's my husband.' She stopped. She hadn't meant to talk about Stuart.

'Sorry,' she said. 'I really – I have no idea what the boundaries are here.'

'No boundaries,' he said. He sat up all of a sudden, and straddled her legs. He put his hands around her waist, and her cardigan fell right open. 'Tell me anything. Everything. Whatever you want.' She lowered her head. When she looked back up, he was still looking at her face.

'He's had a complaint made against him,' she said. 'My husband. To do with, like, sexual harassment. He lost his job, basically. And so, things have been pretty strained. That's why I've been working, and the kids are that bit more challenging, and life's just – well, you know, much harder than it once was. Not that – Ryan, sorry, I didn't mean – that's not what *this* – between us – is about, I honestly don't think.'

'S'all right.' He waved away her apology. 'Serves me right. Carrying on with a married woman.'

'And everyone in the family all think he's perfect and that there's no way, but I think that he'd been drinking and that people can surprise you.'

He made a face. Understanding. She got the feeling he was remembering Stuart. 'It's not my business, but – speaking as a man – it can be so easy to fall into the trap of thinking you have the right to whatever you want.'

Bec had heard all that before, she honestly had, and she'd always thought it was just a big excuse. She'd certainly never thought of Stuart as that type of man. She was *sure* he wasn't.

Almost sure.

She leaned back, and shrugged a let's-change-the-subject shrug. He nodded.

'Hey, Bec. D'you ever think about our first kiss?' His voice was like glitter. Warm fingers tapped a little rhythm on her waist

She nodded. Of course she did. 'It was very gentlemanly,' she said.

'I know.' He smiled. 'It nearly killed me.'

She thought for sure he'd kiss her (in an ungentlemanly way) right then, but he just looked at her. No one spoke. Outside, a car sounded a friendly, farewelling sort of bip-bip.

'Bec?' he said, in the end. 'Do you ever think this is more than just a fling?'

She picked up his hands from where they lay on her skin, and held them in both of hers. They sat like that for quite a while.

'Sometimes,' she said, finally, to their hands.

It was almost as if she was holding a ticket to a whole new life.

Chapter Fifteen

Kate

They told me to go home to Australia for the next lot of surgery.

'The rehabilitation process will be more arduous, next time around,' Mr Cartwright said. 'You'll certainly need family support. Certainly.'

It turned out the Hobart doctors said I needed to go to Melbourne. They said I needed something called an oncological orthopaedic surgeon which, apparently, didn't exist in Hobart. I imagined David Attenborough talking about oncological ortho-paedic surgeons. He'd call them OOSes. A rare breed, he'd intone. Fussy about their habitat. Only ever sighted in enormous city hospitals. And – the punchline; he'd use an awed voice – in a miracle of biology, virtually always male.

So, Mum and Dad and I went to Melbourne. Bec stayed home to work – she'd almost finished her internship then. She wrote down a list of questions for me, in blue ballpoint pen on lined A4 paper. She underlined some of them – What about bone grafting? What about radiotherapy? – in red.

The Melbourne OOS's name was David Rowe. He asked me all the questions Mr Cartwright had asked, plus a whole lot more. Questions about my 'living arrangements', and whether I had a partner, wanted children, followed a spiritual faith. When he got to the part about what I did for a living, I told him I was a 'fashion model'.

'Full time? That's your main source of income?'

'Yes.'

'Do you have income protection insurance?'

'Yes.'

For some reason, he glanced at my parents as he said, 'You'd be astounded how many people don't.' I waited for BFG to nod at me, as if to say, 'See? What did I tell you, Kate-o?' but he didn't.

David Rowe flicked on a light-box and looked at the brand-new lot of scans I'd had; he skimmed the reports I'd brought with me from England. He seemed particularly interested in the fact I'd already had two surgeries and in how far along my arm the scars extended.

Then, David Rowe laid it out for me.

'There's good news and bad news, Kate.' He didn't look away from me. 'Your tumour, as you know, is of a very aggressive type.' I had not known this. 'Chemotherapy offers no hope of cure. Radiotherapy might help, but again would not be curative.'

I kept my face still, but I had only just realised that – since David Rowe was an oncological surgeon and he had said the word chemotherapy – I must have proper, non-Hortense-Maloney style cancer. Denial, eh? My personal super-power.

'Very fortunately, the tumour does not seem to have spread beyond your arm. So, at least in my view, a cure is still possible. That's the good news.' He looked out of the window. I got the distinct impression that he was calculating how much to say.

'However. When the original malignancy was resected, there was, very unfortunately, a great deal of bleeding. You probably noticed it as swelling. That bleeding gave the tumour a chance to seed cells through your arm's tissue, including, it appears, into your elbow joint.'

He seemed to be waiting for me to say something, so I said, 'Yes?'

'The tumour was seeded so extensively that its complete removal – although attempted in your second operation – was in my view never likely to be possible.'

'Right.'

'In my view, the initial lump removal and your second operation were ill-advised.'

'I see.'

'Most ill-advised. In my practice, such a lump would always be biopsied – needled and then tested – before being removed.' He made a face so compassionate I felt terrified. 'Having said that, given it was fairly large – and deep – when you first came to medical attention, it might not have made any difference anyway.'

I nodded. I thought of Bec. Then I thought of my parents. I decided to say nothing.

'So – and this is the bad news – we are unfortunately now at the stage where amputation is our only curative option.'

'I don't understand.' Amputation. What? What? What?

He gave me such a tender look. Tender as a father, as a lover, as a best friend.

'Kate, my advice is that the best chance of your long-term survival lies in amputating your right arm above the elbow joint. But I would advise you to seek a second expert opinion before we proceed, and I will refer you for that today.'

'To cut off my arm?' I said. The rest of the room had gone dark. It was only me and David Rowe. He nodded into our quiet.

'Yes.'

I sat for a bit. The next thing I remember is that he talked to my parents. He knew their names.

Mum said, 'Could the tumour have already spread into her body but just not showed up on the scans yet?' She'd obviously been talking to Bec, because that was one of the blue-ballpoint questions.

David Rowe told her that 'micrometastases' were a possibility and said that I'd need a scan of my body every six months for eight years. We'd all need to cross our fingers, he said, without any irony at all. But he crossed all eight of his own fingers and looked at me, and he made a face as if he really was hoping for the best.

Dad spoke. 'If it spreads, then what would be done?'

'If this tumour spreads beyond Kate's arm, then we would certainly be dealing with a terminal illness.'

'So, you'd want to do it soon? Get it out of Kate before it spreads?' I could tell Mum was upset, but only because she had used the word 'get' to a virtual stranger. Mum believes there is always an alternative to 'get'. ('Remove it from Kate,' for example.)

David Rowe said, 'That's right.'

Maybe he made eye contact with me first. I can't remember. I just remember the way he looked at my mum, and how gentle his voice was as he said, 'I would propose we operate as soon as possible. Certainly within the fortnight.'

Mum reached out and took my hand in hers. BFG put his arm across Mum's back. David Rowe said something about a referral letter and began to type.

I squeezed Mum's hand, very, very hard. What with all that squash-ball training, I could do it without even thinking.

I woke up in Recovery again. I felt remarkably happy again. Even though, this time, I knew that on the edge of the happiness, there was something very bad. I kept with the happy feeling, and pushed the bad thing away.

Animated voices came. I opened my eyes. Quiet, efficient people were doing things. I was, apparently, breathing like a trooper. My blood pressure was good. The intravenous line was functioning really well. Blood-clot-preventer stockings were in place. I knew none of that really mattered though. And, this time, I could tell by how nice everyone was being that no one else thought that stuff was what really mattered, either.

Bec and Mum were waiting when I got back to the ward. I had a private room at the end of the corridor. The orderlies heaved me off the metal wheelie trolley onto my bed. A nurse plugged me in to a new drip and said more things about pain control. Finally, everyone went away except Bec and Mum. Even though I'd wanted all the staff to go away, I suddenly wanted them to come back. I didn't want Bec and Mum to see me. I so very much didn't want them to see me.

'How are you?' said Bec.

'I'm all right.'

'Are you allowed to eat?' said Mum.

'Yes,' said Bec and I together. 'But I'm not hungry,' I added.

My arm – stump – such a horrible, horrible word – was under a baggy hospital gown thing. I didn't want to look at it, but at the same time, I wanted to be alone with it, to inspect it, to look at my new self in a full-length mirror. To see the worst. But I wasn't allowed out of bed yet.

'I'm pretty tired,' I said. 'Can you just stay here while I sleep?'

'Of course!' they said, in exactly the same voice.

When I woke up, after I don't know how long, they were, of course, still there.

This is what I remember about the week after:

A kind resident who made me a cup of tea and moved the box of tissues to where I could reach it easily.

A mean nurse who said, 'It shouldn't hurt *that* much!' when she was changing my dressings. We called her Mean Mandy after that, even Mum, who doesn't believe in 'labelling' people.

David Rowe – David, I seemed to be allowed to call him, but everyone else, even Mum and Bec, and especially all the junior doctors, called him Mr Rowe – coming to see me every day. Sometimes he even came without his retinue. He'd pull a plastic chair alongside my bed and sit down. 'Everything's tracking along as well as we could have hoped,' he'd say, as if he knew that that wasn't particularly great.

Bec coming to say goodbye, on her way to the airport. She had to get back to work. I pretended to be asleep, for a whole hour. I just couldn't face it.

The first time I saw it in the mirror. I didn't cry, or vomit, or faint, or do any of the things I thought I might do. I just stood there, with my remaining hand holding onto the edge of the sink. I looked at my face. Even under the hospital fluorescent, there was not a blemish, not a wrinkle, not a visible pore, not the tiniest imperfection.

I stayed in the Melbourne hospital for eleven days. Mum stayed at a hotel thing nearby. Apart from Mean Mandy, the main nurses were Blonde Mandy, Nice Cindy and – I was much meaner about people's looks in those days – Fatso Liz. (Fatso Liz was also very nice. She was not at all pretty, though. If she'd lost weight, she would still have been, in fact, remarkably ugly. She also didn't have any sense of humour. Few natural gifts, to be honest, apart from her kindness, which I was then too young and too stupid and – somehow, even at that point – too *unscathed* to appreciate.)

At one point, we decided Mum should learn how to do a dressing change. I turned my head away so I wouldn't see her face when Blonde Mandy unveiled the remnants of my right arm.

'I see,' said Mum, to Blonde Mandy. 'And is it OK to use plain tap water when we need to clean it?' She managed to make her voice so matter-of-fact that I was able to look over at her while Blonde Mandy explained about tap water (fine), itchiness (normal), pus (a cause for concern) and disinfectant (to be avoided at all costs; it would impair healing.)

'Pay attention, won't you, Kate, darling,' Mum said. 'In case I forget something. You know what my memory can be like.' Mum has a memory like a steel trap. (I mean it's sharp and accurate, and never lets anything go. Not rusty or harmful to native animals.)

'I'll try, Mum,' I managed to say, in the same business-like tone.

That was the first time I looked at it uncovered. It was very swollen and red, and the stitches were sort of straining across the closure. It was just so ugly that I found it hard to believe that it was part of me, to be honest.

Shortly after, BFG came to visit for the weekend. Bec had planned to come, but at the last minute she'd gone to New South Wales. She had an interview at Northmead Hospital on the Monday morning. It was for a paediatrics residency and apparently a very big deal.

'How's my beautiful girl?' BFG said, when he bent down and hugged me. I started crying, because it was Dad, and because that was the first time since I was about thirteen that either of my parents had called me beautiful. (I think they decided early on it would be better not to praise me for something out of my control. Or that enough people were calling me pretty and I should be developing other aspects of myself. Something like that.)

My dad hugged me tighter for a moment, then kissed my forehead.

'Chin up, Kate-o,' he murmured, as he pulled away.

I said, 'There's shortbread here.' Nice Cindy had brought it in for me. 'Want some?'

Later that week, the agency had flowers delivered. ('Bloody hell, they're gorgeous!' the kind tea-and-tissues resident said, and then apologised for her language.)

And a few days after that, Alison sent a letter saying Prance wished me all the very best but would 'of course' no longer be 'in a position' to represent me. It was the 'of course' that upset me the most. (I guess things would be different nowadays. Maybe Alison would've negotiated me all sorts of contracts to do with everybody-is-beautiful activewear, and I'd have an Instagram account about resilience and organic smoothies and overcoming obstacles by meditating on the beach. Maybe if I was twenty-something again, I could even model normal stuff; maybe my lack of arm would simply be my unique selling point. But anyway, back then it definitely wasn't. Back then, it was just the end of my career.)

A little while after Alison's letter, David Rowe told me it was almost time to go home, and that he'd see me in four weeks at his rooms. 'And you'll be all healed up and well into your rehab by then, fingers crossed,' he said. Still no irony on the finger-crossing thing, but no one's perfect.

I could tell he thought I'd be glad to see the back of him, but actually it felt as if I was losing a friend. It's possible that I fell a little bit in love with David Rowe, in hindsight. There's probably a name for that – some syndrome for being attracted to the person who amputates your limb. Or maybe it's just that if we'd met in other circumstances, we would have hit it off. He was attractive, smart, nice. He wouldn't have been the first surgeon in history to take up with a good-looking younger woman. But it was very obvious that he felt nothing but compassion for me.

Mum and BFG both came to take me home on the day I was discharged. We went straight from the hospital to the airport. People noticed me, which, in a way, I was used to. But that day was the first time there was the different kind of noticing. Not a kind I liked.

At first, I thought I'd do anything to look normal. At first, I believed it would be possible.

'That sounds so great, Kate,' Bec said. We were back at Mum and Dad's, lying on our childhood beds. 'Won't it be good when it's all fitted? Not saying you'll be able to magically move on, or anything, I don't mean it'll be like a miracle, but it'll help, won't it?'

'Of course it will!' I said. A prosthesis was the answer, and prostheses, as I told Bec, were getting better all the time. I could afford the best, what with my fashionista earnings and my yet-to-be-finalised settlement. (There was an almighty brouhaha between my lawyers, my income protection insurance company's lawyers, and Mr Cartwright's medical indemnity insurance company's lawyers. In the end, I came out of it well, but only because my lawyers were like the shark in *Jaws*.)

In any case, I could have a fantastic new kind of prosthesis from America. I could choose a cosmetic one or a functional one. I could have a special sort – with fixed grippy fingers – that was especially for bike riding, just in case I ever wanted to take up cycling. I could have several! One for every occasion. It was really just like buying bras!

'And I think I'm moving on already. Christine says I'm doing really well.' Christine was my occupational therapist. She had told me that virtually all activities of daily living could be mastered with practice, but that it was just a matter of prioritising what was important to me. Christine always emphasised that it was all my choice, as if I was a visitor to some sort of exclusive spa instead of a day patient at a pale-orange-brick rehabilitation centre that smelled of rancid oil. I remember its frosted windows all had heavy mesh over them, perhaps to protect the walking frames, fit-balls and parallel bars from roaming gangs of disabled master criminals who just couldn't get enough physiotherapy during normal working hours.

At one point Christine and I talked about getting dressed. 'Well. *I* don't do *tights*. I wear stockings,' I said. Christine's greying, unshaped eyebrows spasmed up in a way that made me think of a high school boy having his first orgasm. Then she gazed into the middle distance and said, 'Well, Kate. We could probably get some suspender belts adapted. Velcro.' I said I'd rather eat my own head, but that turned out to be a good idea.

In addition to organising my Velcro'd suspender belts, Christine was helping me get a special knob put on my new car's steering wheel so I'd be able to drive again. I was learning to chop apples and carrots and cheese on a special chopping board that had a little fence around one corner and a spike on the other end. I had a squeezer thing for my teabags and a series of balance exercises so I didn't list to my left, like a boat that was heavier on one side.

When it was time to see about the prosthesis, Bec waited outside while I had my appointment. I had just turned twenty-six.

'When?' I demanded of the rehab doctor. His name was Dr Flannery, and he had chapped lips and very red hair.

'Well, there are a number of factors to consider—'

'Yes, you said. But when do you think? Best guess.'

'Six weeks.'

'Six *weeks*.' That would be summer.

'Minimum.'

'Oh.'

'It's just, as I said, if we go too early, before the swelling's settled . . .' and then he said a whole lot of stuff about irritation and skin breakdown and infection and pain. He looked at me properly, the whole time, with his pale eyelashes and inflamed-looking eyelids.

'Darling, just do remember what Dr Flannery said,' Mum reminded me, six weeks later. We were on the way to what I thought was going to be the final fitting. I was convinced I was going to sail out of the Prosthetics Centre that very afternoon with a right arm that was pretty much as good as new. Maybe just a bit hard and stiff, but basically fine.

'Sure, it'll take a bit of getting used to. I'm prepared for that,' I said. I looked behind me at Bec, who was in the back seat, in an isn't-Mum-neurotic? way. Bec gave me a tight, encouraging nod.

'Meeeeessh,' said the prosthetist. His name was Rufus and his job was to fit fake limbs to people's dismembered bodies. He had eyes like a seagull. 'I'm not altogether happy, Kate. It's OK if I call you Kate?'

I nodded.

'Not entirely happy. See how it's not quite hugging your stump there? You don't want skin abrasion.'

I nodded again. The use of the word stump in connection with my arm – I wasn't used to that.

'Could lead to infection and you don't want that. Stump infections, they can be nasty.'

That time I couldn't even nod.

'We'll need to do another cast,' he said. It would be another chunk of weeks.

On the way home in the car I shouted at Mum and Bec to put the fucking windows up. It was one of those chilly, sunny days that make parked cars unexpectedly warm.

Bec immediately started rolling up her window, but Mum said, briskly, 'Stop throwing your weight around, Kate, darling.' She wound her own window down even further. 'I know you're very disappointed, but you're not the only one in the world with problems.'

'Fuck off,' I said. Mum put on the brakes and pulled over in a no-standing zone.

'If you speak to me like that again, then you will need to get out and make your own way home,' she said. Very calmly. When I didn't say anything, she drove us back to our house, still very calmly, and made everyone tea. She brought out home-made muffins, which I realised later she would have woken up early to make. They were banana and cinnamon, with no horrible sultanas, currants or dates: my favourite.

Dear Mum. She is an absolute force of nature. I would be dead without her, no doubt.

At a later fitting I went to, I met a doctor called Dr Darcy who apparently hadn't reviewed my file. He happened to be quite attractive, so I kept thinking about *Pride and Prejudice*. (The BBC series. I had not, at that point, read the book.)

'What did psych say?' he said. I can't remember now why I was even seeing him, only that it was almost autumn by then and it was late in the afternoon on a Friday and I still didn't have my prosthesis.

'Pardon?'

'Have you seen a psychiatrist?' As if I was an imbecile.

'Yes. Once.' David Rowe had organised it, while I was still in the Melbourne hospital. 'For what it's worth,' David said. He shrugged, a bit apologetic. 'It's routine in cases like yours.'

(The psychiatrist wore an egregious maroon sarong-skirt. David Rowe told me later that she pronounced me to have an 'intact personality'. 'Whatever that means,' he said. He'd rolled his eyes in a way that had cheered me up enormously.)

'And . . . ?' Dr Darcy pressed, that warm Friday afternoon. I was wearing a low-necked T-shirt and I sat forward so as to show him my *Sports Illustrated*-worthy cleavage. He kept on twiddling his ballpoint between his thumb and index finger, like he was itching to record my response.

It was as if I hadn't even moved.

'And what?' I switched to my best imperious voice, the sort I used to use on shoots when I suspected anyone thought I was an airhead blonde. But to be honest, I was gutted that he hadn't cared to look at my breasts.

He sighed. 'Did the psychiatrist recommend follow-up?'

'She did not.'

'You're not thinking of trying something? That's what I'm getting at.' He looked at me – through his long eyelashes and the sort of trendy tortoiseshell glasses men of his demographic wore then – as if suicide would be just the sort of thing a tiresome girl like me might attempt.

'Trying what?' Innocent as an ice cube.

He glanced down at the folder in front of him, to remind himself of my name.

'Kate,' he said. He was still twiddling his pen. 'You're not thinking of hurting yourself, are you? Cutting or anything?'

'No, Doctor,' I said, very sweetly. 'If I was to decide to commit suicide, I'd do it sensibly and put a gun in my mouth.'

This unfortunately triggered an avalanche of questions that sounded as if they were designed to cover his no doubt attractively muscled butt in the event of my shooting myself. Eventually I said, 'I have no intention of self-harming at the present time, Dr Darcy.'

When I got to the door he spoke again.

'Kate,' he said. He rapped the tip of his pen on the desk in front of him. 'Regarding your mental health. Sorry if you took offence.'

'Not very competent, are you?' I had learned by then that doctors hate being called incompetent. It's medical professional kryptonite, the same as telling a bogan man that he punches like a girl.

Mean, very mean. But also justified. Very, very justified.

Even though Dr Darcy had managed to strut his long-eyelashed way to a place where he wasn't, actually, all that far off the mark. 'Trying something' was not completely out of the question, at that point. Not out of the question at all.

There are several problems with prostheses, apart, obviously, from waiting months to get one. The first problem is that it's harder to do things with them, because – even still, more than a decade after that very first fitting, and despite iPhones and 3D printers and driverless cars – no one has actually worked out a way that your brain can make prostheses move very well. So they tend to get in the way, whereas you can use your stump to hold things down relatively easily.

The second problem is that prostheses can irritate your stump, even break the skin, and thereby usher you into a nightmare world of 14-year-old doctors and swabs and antibiotics and thrush.

The third thing is that you have to slot a prosthesis into a really gross harness sort of thing, like a weight-lifter's truss except on the upper body, and it totally wrecked my underwear look and gave me back pain.

The fourth thing – which should be the least important, but which (yes, superficial, yes, vain) became by far the most important – is that if you're going to have sex – or even just go swimming – with someone then that person is pretty much going to have to see you without it.

Now, just to be clear, I think there's almost nothing more annoying than men who criticise women for wearing push-up bras. If my breasts were smaller, I would probably be first in line for the most cleavage-enhancing contraption on the market. God knows my face has had enough fine-line-removing laser to sink a ship.

However, given my 'enviable' (fashion-writer speak) body, I never felt any pressure to don a Wonderbra. In my youth, many a man had made comments along the lines of 'I can't believe these are real/they're amazing/you're so wonderful/natural/genuine etc.', as if my exceptionally lovely breasts in their non-padded bras meant I was a superior person. And, even more annoyingly, as if the poor man had spent an unreasonable portion of his life being duped by cunning, padded bra-d women who'd had the temerity to bow to lifelong, society-wide pressure to look a certain way. The way *he* wanted them to.

Anyway. Wearing a prosthesis and long sleeves felt different to wearing a padded bra in a way I couldn't really explain. More like concealing herpes or bankruptcy or a husband than just pretending to have bigger boobs for the first date or two.

So what would happen – this was back in my late twenties, before the Tudors – was that I'd spend ages feeling bad about wearing the prosthesis, and then men would see my hand was fake straight away anyway. (Prostheses appear to be much less convincing than Wonderbras.) At a certain point, maybe on the second or third date, when we'd both had a wine or two, whomever I was dating would awkwardly ask me about it. Then I usually wouldn't hear from him again, perhaps because at that stage I tended to become emotional during such conversations, but perhaps also because he just didn't fancy me anymore.

Around that time, there were two men – both called Dave, rather oddly – who said they didn't mind, because they liked me just as I was, and they therefore wanted to 'get to know me better'. They both used the same phrases, too, as if they'd looked up the same guidebook on euphemisms to seduce women.

With the Dave-the-First, I said no-it-just-wouldn't-work and then I cried for about a week (pretty much literally). Not because I liked

Dave-the-First that much – I didn't, to be honest – but because of what it meant for my future if I couldn't even risk being naked with someone like him. (The reason I didn't like him that much was because he said he was philosophically opposed to tipping waiting staff. Also, he worked in health insurance, which seemed likely to be deceitful and also was somehow *girly*.)

With Dave-the-Second, after about six dates, I agreed we should – as he put it – 'take our connection to the next level'. We went to his house, which was in a suburb quite a long way out – Dave-the-Second had been married previously – and into his bedroom. The house had been built in the 1980s. There was a lot of exposed brick, and his built-in-wardrobe handles were spheres of exceedingly shiny wood.

We were both a little bit drunk, and I had a sick sort of feeling. There was some jerky, non-rhythmic kissing. He was feeling around my dress, trying to work out how to remove me from it, presumably. It had a left-sided concealed zip, the sort I find fairly easy to deal with.

'I'll just go and . . .' I indicated his bathroom. I went in, unzipped my dress, slipped my left arm out, used it to pull the dress over my prosthesis, and then pushed the dress onto the floor. I unbuckled the prosthesis and laid it carefully in Dave-the-Second's corner spa. Then I inspected myself in the mirror.

My underwear look was not well-developed at that stage, but I was at least wearing a matching lacy bra and knickers set. I had bare legs. Some of the sick feeling went away, because, to be honest, I thought I looked really beautiful and extremely sexy. My hair was all rumpled and was falling down over my shoulders. My skin was hairless and had, in a pre-sex grooming frenzy, been exfoliated and moisturised to a strikingly lustrous sheen. In that instant, I realised that I'd been making far too big a deal of the arm thing in my head, and that Dave-the-Second was bound to like what he saw. I marched straight back out towards the bedroom, high heels still on.

'Just coming,' I called. It was partly a warning, in case he was picking his nose or something, and partly . . . I don't know, partly, I was trying to both make an entrance and to sound *humble*.

He was sitting on the edge of his bed, and was wearing boxers and a T-shirt.

He stood up and said, 'Wow! Kate!' But he used the tone a mum would when her kid plays a tune on the recorder. (Assuming her kid is an ordinary child of recorder-bearing age, not a grown-up who plays recorder for the Melbourne Symphony Orchestra.)

We started kissing again, standing up, and I could feel that he didn't have an erection, but I knew (although not from personal experience) that that happened sometimes. So, at first I didn't worry. After a while he stopped kissing me and took off my bra (both hands). He looked at my boobs and felt them for bit. I closed my eyes and tried to enjoy it, but then I opened them at the exact moment he glanced up at me. His face was tense, like a game-show contestant who is pretty sure he's going to lose.

'Sorry, I don't think this is going to work after all,' said Dave-the-Second. He still had his hands on my breasts when he started speaking, but he stopped squeezing them on the word 'think' and politely removed them as he said the word 'work'.

Then he turned his back, so I could pick up my bra and depart. I went into the bathroom and put on my dress. I shoved my (tiny, eighty-dollar) bra into my handbag, heaved up my (enormous, many-thousand-dollar) prosthesis and telephoned a taxi. I said, 'OK, Dave, I'm going to wait outside.'

He said, 'Oh, no, you don't have to do that, Kate. Why don't you wait in the kitchen?'

I waited outside, and the taxi came after about thirty-five freezing minutes – it was a Saturday night in a pre-Uber world – and I held my prosthesis all the way home.

I vowed never to wear it on a date again. It is a vow I have kept. Also: Dave-the-Second was my last kiss until Adam.

Chapter Sixteen

Bec

There was no way Bec wanted to see a psychologist in Hobart. 'What was your car doing parked on Macquarie Street?' someone would say. Not that there was anything wrong with seeing a psychologist, but Stuart would wonder.

Kate said she'd pay for everything, and Bec booked an appointment with someone in Melbourne called Glenda O'Malley. Glenda's internet photo had been professionally taken (unlike some, that looked as if they'd been cropped from holiday snaps) and her profile said she had eight years of accredited training and thirty years of experience. Hundreds of clients whose life-disruption had been significantly reduced while their priority-management had been positively impacted. Well. Bec needed Glenda to make her understand why she was being so *unreasonable* as to be having this affair, to say something like 'it sounds as if this is all coming from your deep-seated fear of abandonment'. Then, in a flash Bec would realise what the problem was. All her ridiculous feelings would be reduced to easily understood products of her own flawed psychology. It would be possible – painless even – to go back to normal.

'I think Kate could do with a bit of company, after that Adam guy,' she told Stuart, as she was setting the table. She said something about cocktails and pampering. 'What do you think? Girls' weekend away. I'd go the Thursday night, be back Sunday arvo.'

(Kate seemed perfectly fine, in actual fact. When Bec had checked in about Adam, Kate had snorted and said something about stop fussing and just a bit of fun and emotional distance. Her tone had implied that Bec was overthinking the Adam situation, and Bec had wondered, yet again, if she would ever understand sex as well as Kate did.)

'Of course, you should go,' Stuart said, looking in random drawers for the tongs. 'Spend time with your sister. You both deserve a treat.' Then he added, 'Your mum and dad can help out with the kids, can't they?'

Bec wasn't sure why he'd need help, but she was in no position to take the high moral ground. In fact, she had to just not think about what she was doing. She had to slam the door shut on the feelings. She had to . . . what was that thing? Compartmentalise.

Because. Stuart's *face*. It was the face that had creased with delight when he surprised her with that party on her thirtieth, that had looked up at her with such tense, unexpected vulnerability when he asked her to marry him, that had barely been able to hide his pride and relief when he passed his final exam, that had been next to hers, tearful, when each of their children was born. She could read his face; for her it had always seemed like a map of his whole mind. And she'd always been able to look back at him and show him everything she was feeling too. She'd barely hidden anything from Stuart. Only the normal stuff. Only things like ingrown hairs and body-shaping underwear and tiny barely-worth-mentioning bits of Botox.

But now. He'd made chops and vegetables, and dinner was on time, and he'd managed the lunch boxes, and when the kids started complaining that she'd be gone for a whole three nights, he told them that their amazing mother needed a break, she'd been working so hard, they should all just give it a rest because they were going to have a great time with him. And he looked across at her with an expression of such understanding and apology and gratitude that she had to hide her own eyes. She had to concentrate on the water jug.

Of *course* he hadn't said it to that waitress. This was *Stuart*.

'Yeah, you'll have a great time with your dad,' she told the kids.

She looked around the table at all of them, and felt, for a brief, blissful moment, that nothing with Ryan was worth it. And yet. Melbourne was all arranged already, so she said, 'Thanks, my darlings,' and got on with eating her dinner.

'The thing is,' said Bec, 'that before the complaint, I honestly believed there was nothing wrong with my marriage.'

Glenda O'Malley nodded her head. She was wearing one of those necklaces with beads made out of bright-coloured felted wool, and a shapeless black linen dress. Her shoes were chunky and expensive and mauve. Bec felt mildly surprised that a psychologist would care to think so hard about accessorising.

'I love my husband. Truly. I always thought we were really great together.'

'In what ways?' asked Glenda. She had a soft voice.

'Um—' In what ways, exactly? She could hardly say he was rich and handsome. It made her sound so superficial. And that wasn't it, anyway. She'd fallen in love with Stuart – and she really had – precisely because he could have gotten away with just being rich and handsome, but he made the effort to be more than that. When one of his receptionists was widowed at thirty-four, he gave her six weeks of paid leave. He stopped to let people out of side-streets when the traffic was bad. He once said, 'That's enough, mate, you're well out of order,' to a man who was yelling abuse at a checkout operator. One time last year, when Bec was out to dinner with some of the school mums, a tipsy woman from a few tables over had squatted down next to Bec's chair and raved about what a fantastic surgeon Stuart was. ('So smart. And so lovely! We all absolutely adore him! I'm Ruth, by the way.') Bec thought she must be a patient – perhaps one with alcohol-related health issues – but it turned out Ruth was a theatre nurse. ('We saw you one time? Dropping off his laptop? We'd all been wondering about his wife. We knew you'd be gorgeous!') Ruth was really very drunk. Bec had wondered if she was going to be working in theatre the next morning, hung-over, rushing out between laparotomies to vomit in the staff toilets. Surely not.

'He's very kind. Good manners,' Bec said. 'He's a great father.'

'In what ways?' asked Glenda, again. What on earth were people taught in a psychology doctorate?

'Well – he's – he really loves the kids. And me. He's very respectful of me, in front of them. And when we're alone too, obviously. And he – he plays with them – when he has free time – which is not often, because he's always worked very hard. And then lately he's been, I guess, understandably, pretty down.'

'He works very hard?'

'Yes,' said Bec. 'He was – is, a surgeon.'

Glenda nodded, as if Bec had said Stuart was a mid-level manager in a mid-tier corporation.

'And he generally worked very hard?'

'Well. Yes.' Shouldn't that be obvious?

'Did that bother you?'

'Yes. No. I mean, that's part of his job. It's what I signed up for.' Twenty-six. So young to marry.

'You knew, when you married him, that he would be extremely busy?'

'Yes. Of course.'

'But now you find it bothers you, maybe?'

'Well, not *now*.' Had the woman even been listening? 'Now I wish he was working *more*.'

'I see.'

Glenda left a pause. Bec declined to fill it. Of course Stuart working so hard had bothered her. She'd been tired. It was *lonely*. Every evening she'd wished she had a husband who came home at 5.30 p.m. and took the children rowing or cycling or even to play a computer game for an hour before dinner. Even twice a week! It wasn't that much to ask. But he just *wouldn't*.

'So. Stuart is great in that he's a respectful man and a loving father to your children, despite his having had a heavy workload.'

Another pause. In fairness, Bec herself had always sort of liked the fact he was a surgeon. When Stuart couldn't come to things because Stuart Was Working or Stuart Was On-Call, most people said 'Oh of course', in a deferential sort of tone, as if to suggest that her husband was above school fairs or neighbourhood Christmas drinks. 'He'll only be taking out gall bladders,' Bec sometimes wanted to reply. 'How hard can it really be when you've had eleven years of training?' But she was proud of him, she supposed. His profession was altruistic and a bit glamorous and, let's be honest, very lucrative.

'Yes, he's a fantastic father,' she said, firmly. 'He loves the children very much.' How weak did that sound? Even fathers in jail for armed robbery or domestic violence probably loved their children. 'And he always *had* to work very hard. That's what his profession demands.'

Glenda raised her eyebrows. 'And aside from being a good father?' she asked. There was a silence.

'Well,' said Bec. 'He – we generally can talk. We laugh together sometimes. I always trusted him. But I guess just with this complaint, it's made me wonder a bit about whether I actually *should* trust him.'

'I see.'

'He's—' Bec smiled, in a woman-to-woman way. 'He's very handsome.' Maybe she should extract her phone from her bag, show Glenda a photo.

'And his being handsome. That's important to you?' Glenda asked.

'Yes,' Bec replied, neutrally. She would not apologise. It wasn't as if Kate was the only woman in the world allowed to have a handsome man. 'I realise that makes me sound very superficial.'

'There are no wrong answers, Bec.' Oh, for God's sake. Of course there were wrong answers. For one thing, that she was falling in love with someone else. For another, that sex with Stuart was perfectly good, but not as good as it was with Ryan. And that no one, surely, could expect her to give *that* up. There you had it. A wrong answer, if ever she'd heard one.

'He's very smart. My family adore him.'

Glenda sat back in her seat and recrossed her ankles.

Bec thought about the $300 Kate was paying for this appointment, and, so very much more importantly, how much she needed resolution. She may as well be completely honest.

'I'm having an affair with a younger man,' she said. She sounded poised and self-aware, she thought. 'He's very gorgeous and sexy, and the chemistry is ridiculous' – she wished Kate could hear her – 'and of course I know that that is just how affairs always feel. From what I've heard.'

Glenda nodded, but in a non-committal manner, as if she declined to give away any insights into how affairs in general felt. The woman was really very exasperating.

'But also, it feels as if – and he's said this to me, Ryan, the other man – that perhaps it's more than just a fling. Maybe it's . . . proper love. But I don't know, whether I'm sort of – straying, just because of the complaint, the trust issues, and the stress that that's brought up, because I think if that's the case then I should – could – be working through that. With Stuart.'

Glenda tilted her head to the left.

'But then, maybe there's something fundamentally wrong with my marriage. And I'd like to figure that out, so that I know what to do, because it's crossed my mind' – it was almost unbearable to say it out loud – 'that perhaps I should even leave. Leave Stuart.'

Glenda O'Malley nodded. She glanced at the elegant taupe clock on her desk, as if she'd had a private bet with herself as to how long it would take Bec to tell her about the Other Man. (Seven minutes, it turned out.)

Then Glenda said, 'So, what was happening for you, Bec? When you first met Stuart?'

Ha, thought Bec, as Kate's smiling, gorgeous, twenty-something face and breasts and legs flashed in front of her eyes. *That's more like it, Glenda O'Malley.*

Chapter Seventeen

Kate

Adam. Adam. Adam. Adam. Adam. Mada. Mad-A.
Ad-am. A-dam. A dam man. Adam. ADAM. Adamadamadam. Madam.
A Madam. Madam Kate.
Kate and Adam. Adam. Adam Adam Adam.

I was still thinking about him at least 98 per cent of the time, which was annoying. I had hoped by now to be down to, say, 72 per cent, because it was June, a whole new season, and weeks since I'd purged him from my devices and told Juliet never to mention his name.

That day I was varying the activity during which I would be thinking about him, because I was seeing Bec. She had come all the way to Melbourne to go and talk to a psychologist about whether or not it would be sensible for her to leave her faithful, normal, trustworthy husband. After the appointment, Bec and I were going to have lunch at a somewhat fancy restaurant. We'd probably text Stuart a photo of our desserts or something, to make it seem as if we'd been having all manner of frivolous, girls'-getaway-type frolics.

When Bec walked into the restaurant, her face was like a kitten's, the way it used to go in high school, before she had an exam. She sat down, and I poured her some of the twelve-dollar fizzy water. I was more upset than I let on, partly because I loved being, in a way, part of their family. But also, less selfishly, because it seemed to me that Bec had everything – a love-filled, sweet, precious life – and she was about to flick it away as if she was changing a television channel. It made me want to shake her.

'Was the psychologist helpful?' I said, in my most open and considerate tone. I had, obviously, decided to do that I-support-your-choices-even-though-you-are-freaking-insane thing.

'Yes,' she said. Then, 'Kate, do you think I *ever* really loved him? Because it's not just this complaint – even though, you know, I can't be sure, Kate, I'm sorry, I know how you feel, but I can't – and now I'm thinking that it isn't even about Ryan. What if I – maybe I married Stuart just because . . . he was a surgeon or good-looking or rich or something?'

There was so much wrong with that little speech that I had to take a very big sip of water, probably at least two dollars' worth. Then I said, carefully, 'Well, Bec, those things – his profession and so on – were part of who Stuart was. And is. But I don't think you were someone who prioritised those things too much, when you first met him.' The words were out of my mouth before I realised, but she didn't even notice. 'You certainly acted like you really loved him. I remember. That first time you guys visited me in Melbourne and you stayed really late?'

That was the second time I met Stuart. It was just after I'd moved away, maybe six months or so after my amputation. We all drank lots of red wine; it was before it started giving Bec migraines. At one point – Bec was out of the room and I was a bit teary – he said, 'God, Kate, I would never presume to tell you how to handle it.' He realised what he'd said, and instead of apologising or looking awkward he put his arm across my shoulders and said, 'That must happen all the time. Hands come into everything.' Another time – a year or so later, when Bec was on a Kate-you-so-need-to-see-someone-and-get-some-help mission and going on about cognitive behavioural therapy and grief

232

counselling – he snorted and said, 'I'm with you, Madam Kate. All the CBT in the world won't bring your right arm back.' He started calling me Madam Kate early on. I hadn't realised until recently that it even meant anything to me.

Anyway, I thought Bec would have fond memories of that first wine-soaked evening, because she and Stuart did seem really in love that night – they got a taxi back to their hotel at 3 a.m., even though I had a spare room, and they both laughed like mad whenever anything even slightly funny happened, and it was obvious from how *kind* he was to me that he completely adored her.

But now she got tears in her eyes.

'I felt so guilty about you,' she said. She actually shrugged. 'Maybe he just seemed like someone who could keep life safe.'

Well.

Here I am, about four decades in, and I find life – safe or otherwise – can still astound me. I couldn't believe that Bec would, after all these years, bring the whole thing up so ... casually. At a restaurant. In the context of her own dilemma about whether or not to disband her perfect family.

'You were feeling guilty about me?' I said, quite calmly. The waiter approached and I waved him away without making eye contact, which was something I hadn't done in years.

'And he was so solid. You know. Safe pair of hands.'

Oh, for God's sake.

'And where did I come into it?' Self-focused, I know, but surely no one could blame me.

'Well.'

There was no drum roll, oddly. She just spoke in a normal way. Not even a deep breath before she said it. 'I felt that I gave you bad advice, and that if I had given you better advice then maybe you would have had a better outcome. With your arm.'

'You were feeling guilty?' That time I didn't sound calm. I sounded how I felt, which was devastated all over again, incredulous and above all very, very angry. (*You* were feeling *guilty*?)

'Yes. Because. Kate. Remember, you asked me what I thought and I said—'

'I remember,' I said. Of course I remembered. I remembered it as if it had happened that very morning. She'd been wearing a hideous mauve cowl-neck jumper and I was in low-slung tan pants, a tight dark brown sweater and a turquoise-and-coral-beaded belt thing.

'That time at the pub?' she said, just to make sure I had it right. 'In England. In that little village.'

'It was The Miners Arms, in Cobham, and of course I *fucking* remember.'

'Oh.' Her eyes went like two dessert spoons. She'd finally realised that the conversation was not about her, her guilt, her affair or her marriage.

I had nothing to say. I'd always expected that when we finally talked about it – and I had imagined the conversation taking place on one of our deathbeds – there would be drama and tears and catharsis and abject apology (her) followed by magnanimous comforting (me). *We don't know for sure it made any difference*, the deathbed me would say, all serene and Buddhist-y. My face would be lined in an adorable way, like a very old rural woman from a developing country and the room would be high-ceilinged and sunshiny and would smell of apples like an old-fashioned convalescent home. *It was a series of errors, not just yours.* But, of course, we would both know it was mainly her fault and that I was the big-hearted one.

'I need to order,' I said. Then I did something else I hadn't done for years, which was lean forward and use my stump to drag the menu over the table towards me. It made a loud clattering noise – it was one of those parchment-clipped-to-a-wooden-rectangle jobs – and she had to hurry to move the bottle of water out of my way.

'Kate?' said Bec. 'Are you mad at me?'

I looked up. My face, while not exactly Botox-free, still has quite a degree of movement in it – of course, in exchange for my right arm I got so much money I can afford the best dermatologists in the known universe – so I decided I'd leave it to her to work out how I was feeling. Her being the smart one, after all.

I used my stump to run down the list of menu items, like it was a forefinger.

'I've never forgiven myself, Kate. Never.' As if this was *The Young and the Restless*.

'Right,' I said, with my eyes on the menu. 'We could share a side salad? Actually, no. Just order your own meal.' I put my menu down. Shoved it away (with my stump).

She reached way across the table and took hold of Left-over. I didn't move Left-over. I let it be limp as a daffodil.

'Kate? I'm so sorry, Kate. I'm so, so sorry.' Hint: using people's names a lot does not make your apology more effective. I thought of saying this but couldn't be bothered.

The waiter came over again, and that time I looked at him and ordered.

Bec said, 'I'll have what she's having,' without taking her eyes off me. She was still holding my hand in both of hers; the waiter probably thought we were a gay and 'diversely abled' couple, which would have been quite unusual in that not-particularly-minority-friendly postcode.

I took Left-over away and looked around.

I thought about how everyone except me had been surprised at Bec's family-only beach wedding. Bec had always been so social.

At uni, she was surrounded by girlfriends: she used to email me in London about their fundraising-for-wells trivia nights and their scarf-knitting nights and their *Sex and the City*-and-cheesecake TV nights. I'd never asked what became of all those bouncy, fizzy, pretty girls.

I refused to be a bridesmaid. All the dress fittings. All the eyes.

I guess she felt she couldn't have anyone.

I never asked Bec to quit medicine. Never. Not exactly.

My arm actually was a series of errors. Not just hers. But hers was the first. It was the necessary if not sufficient one. And she was my sister, which made it both more and less forgivable.

This is what happened.

She'd recently graduated. She was twenty-four and doing her internship at the hospital in Hobart, and I was twenty-five and flitting about Europe letting my mild and meaningless fame go to my head. Bec had come to England to see me for a fortnight, and on her very first day we went out to a little village pub for lunch. It was a Thursday, so all the men who lived in the village had gone. Bit like the war, except they were in banks in London instead of off at Dunkirk or somewhere, and the women left behind were at the hairdresser or Tae-Bo rather than slaving away in munitions factories. (I'm not being sexist. It's how it was. Maybe even still is, except these days the women would be getting their filler refreshed or having a crack at mindfulness meditation while the men are off developing software.)

That Thursday.

I'd reached across the wooden table at which we were sitting and said, 'Check this out,' and I showed her the lump on my right arm, just a bit below the elbow. It was little then. 'I call it Grape,' I said.

She pressed it. Even though she'd only just become a doctor, there was a sort of professional authority in her fingers that was nothing like the squeamish, amused little pokes my friends had given it, and her face was thoughtful and serious.

'What do you think?' I said.

'That'll just be a lipoma,' she said. She sounded so sure. 'Nothing to worry about.'

'I'm going to the doctor tomorrow.'

'Tomorrow?' Her voice went up a notch with every syllable. 'Kate! We've only got ten full days.' You see, it was back when she could say what she wanted. 'Look, you'll need an ultrasound. Then they'll either leave it there or take it out, it'll be up to you. It's nothing. And I have literally come halfway around the world to spend time with you and to have a break from thinking about ultrasounds.' She tried to make the last bit sound like a joke, but she was very obviously hurt that I'd scheduled an appointment during her visit. She would've been thinking about priorities and caring and making the effort. It was just a big-sister/little-sister thing.

'OK,' I said. 'If you think it can wait.'

And she nodded. She waved a confident, dismissive hand and said, 'It could wait a year.' She sipped her lager.

And so I'd thought it didn't matter if I waited a few weeks, and they turned into two months, and the lump got bigger but I didn't realise that mattered, and I didn't ask Mr Cartwright any of the right questions or demand an oncologist early or do any of the things that could have – so very easily, in hindsight, if she'd said something even a little bit different, if I'd known just a little bit more – saved my arm.

But Bec had wanted to be a paediatrician from the time she was four. In every single primary school Book Week parade, she dressed up as Dr Craven (from *The Secret Garden*; he was the only doctor-in-literature character anyone could think of).

I remembered how, when Lachlan was born, she said, 'Kate, just wait till you hold him!' and – when I got to the hospital – she put her firstborn into my arm in such a trusting, delighted way, even though neither of us could remember me holding a baby even when I'd had two arms. He was so little. His head was so floppy, in its yellow towelling hat.

I started thinking about Adam, and how I'd screamed at him that my family loved me. I thought, randomly, about the sort of mother I would want to be, if ever I magically had a baby.

Bec's hand was still on the table. I reached out and tapped the back of her knuckles with the pads of my fingers.

She looked up, right into my eyes, and for the first time I properly faced where my indomitable little sister – with her zippy bike-riding and her messy hair and her bubbly chatter about fair trade and poverty and Doctors Without Borders – had gone. It wasn't Sandy Bay or Briarwood or the kids or even Stuart. She'd evaporated because of me, not on purpose, and not all at once, but gradually, because when a part of you is destroyed you prop yourself up with whatever is going.

And I had watched, and I had known, and I had not intervened.

When Mum said, once, 'What do you think's going on with Bec and medicine?' I said, 'She seems to like the shoe shop. I think maybe she didn't love her internship that much.' It was one of those lies that at the time you tell yourself is not really a lie. But it was. A terrible lie, an enormous lie, a deliberate, life-changing, irrevocable lie.

'It was just a mistake,' I said. I thought she'd reach into her handbag for a pristine packet of tissues, but she didn't. She put her elbows on the table and her face into her hands.

'Oh Bec. Becky.' I got out of my chair and came around next to her and put my arm across her shoulders and my face near to hers. Quietly, I said, 'Please. Becky. Could we please, please just not worry about it anymore?'

My face was red and wet, and so was hers, and the waiter sort of spoiled things by putting down the main courses while we were in the middle of our very long hug, but, on the whole, it was as Buddhist-y and heart-warming a moment as you could wish for.

There wasn't really anything to say afterwards, though. I went back to my seat. We ate our identical lamb tagines and I figured we'd have to talk about her marriage issues another time.

Chapter Eighteen

Bec

Four days later, Bec arrived home from work to find Stuart sitting next to Essie at the kitchen bench. Essie's ankle was coiled around the leg of Stuart's stool. Their heads were almost touching over a plate of hummus and rice crackers.

'Bec!' he said, looking up. 'My work. It's going to be fine.'

'Hear that, Mummy?' Essie said, so knowledgeably that Bec felt terrible.

'Bec? It's going to be all right.' Stuart was standing, with his arms open, waiting for a hug. He was smiling like a kid who'd just bought his first car. It occurred to her to say, 'Would you just let me get in the door before you start?'

But she smiled back, as excitedly as possible. It was awful, but the way he patted her back as they hugged reminded her of a frantic, flapping fish. Bec left her arms around Stuart, and reminded Essie about their look-after-your-pets-if-you-ever-want-a-puppy deal and Essie hustled off to feed the guinea pigs.

''Atta girl,' said Stuart, looking after Essie as if she was on the way to collect her third Nobel prize. Bec withdrew a bit from the hug and looked up at his face.

'What's happened?' she said.

'MPRA emailed Rodney an hour ago. No further action required.' He left his hands on her waist, and started talking fast, about assessment phase and Rodney raising hackles and senate references committee and time-frame recommendations. She let his words wash over her.

Her first thought – her main thought – was that now she really was going to have to decide what to do. Affairs might be acceptable during a crisis – it was a bit like having sex with a soldier during the war – but if things were going to settle down, then it was a different matter. So did she, actually, *want* things to get back to normal?

Her second thought was that it would be lovely, for all the horrible stuff to go away.

And her third thought was that it probably wouldn't go away. Didn't he realise that people still talked? People still knew? Last week Laura had told Bec that the Tas Medico Mums' Club Facebook page had a thread where female GPs were musing about whether it was fair to refer their patients to him, or whether it was unfair *not* to. 'I think his private clinic's closed,' one of them had written. 'He always seemed like one of the more approachable surgeons,' wrote someone else. 'Shows you never can tell.'

When Stuart eventually stopped talking – he always liked to make sure everyone was across the salient points – she got a word in.

'That's really exciting, and obviously a huge relief,' she said carefully. 'But still . . . as far as your public image goes . . .'

'We reckon that'll all blow over now,' he said. 'Rodney said to get PR involved. I spoke to someone called Suzette just a minute ago.' And he was off again. A letter to his referral base enclosing a short factual statement that emphasised the MPRA finding, testimonials on his website that would 'play well' with the general community, a meeting – the very next day – with the hospital, at which Rodney would be present. 'There's no point counter-suing,' he said. 'Time. Money. Gives the whole thing oxygen.'

Bec's mind went straight to Suzette, for some reason. She'd have on-trend lipstick and patent high heels and an office with a big window. She'd be the outrage-dampening female who was paid enormous sums to help men like Stuart get on with their lives.

'Where's Suzette?' she asked.

'Sydney.' No surprises there, then. 'I'm flying up Thursday. Hopefully within a couple of weeks, things'll start getting back to normal.'

Bec extracted herself, and crossed the room to turn on the kettle. She remembered the time – they'd just got engaged – that she'd been squatting down in the supermarket looking at five-kilo-bags of rice, and a man had come and stood right next to her. 'Like it down there, sweetie?' he said, with his hand on a packet of arborio. She said something inaudible, and stood up, and walked away. She didn't stop to take the basmati, which was annoying, because she needed it. When she told Stuart he said, 'Do you think maybe he was just being friendly?' And she, pathetically, had thought, Well, it's possible. Maybe I got it wrong.

'So. Do you think it's the right outcome?' she said. He'd sat back on his stool. She stayed standing, and faced him across the bench.

'What?' Incredulous.

'Did you say it? Did you ask for that blow job?' It just burst out. Loud and unexpected, like when the sound system goes wrong at a school assembly.

'No!'

'Then why, Stuart? Why would she complain?'

'Christ, I have no idea, Bec.' He kept his voice quiet, because of the children upstairs. 'Maybe she was hoping for money. Maybe she's delusional. Shit, how would I know?'

'And you think there's no chance that you and your "mates" got a bit carried away?' Her throat was closing over, so that her voice sounded jagged and uncontrolled. 'No chance at all that you had a few drinks and decided it was your big night and you'd just have a bit of friendly banter with a pretty young thing?'

'You can't be serious.'

'Those men make me sick.' She spat the sentence out. He'd always *known* she didn't like them, but he'd gone along with the whole thing anyway, with having them over, with going to their 'functions'. 'The way they talked about Miranda. The way they look at me, even.'

'I'm not them, Bec.'

'Yes, but you invited them. You stand there and ... *guffaw* with them. You ... *enable* them.' 'Enable' was the kind of word Stuart hated, and she took great pleasure in using it against him.

He didn't speak. He got up from his stool, but stood there, his hands on the bench, looking at her.

After a moment, the kettle clicked off. She fumbled with the tea bags and slopped some water into a cup, and reminded herself that she was sleeping with – yes, screwing! – another man, and that maybe Stuart *hadn't* said it. And he'd been so excited, and so relieved, and so happy to share the good news with her.

'Want some tea?' she asked, in a semblance of her normal, friendly-wife voice. 'And why didn't you call me straight away? When you heard from MPRA? You could have called me at work, darling.'

'I did,' he said. 'I left you a voice message.'

'Oh.'

'Bec? I thought ... Bec, didn't you believe me?'

She stretched her eyes open wider and smiled and nodded. 'Of course I did. I do. I just ... Sorry. I didn't mean. Of course. Of *course*. I'm really ... It's great, Stuart. Absolutely fantastic. We should celebrate. Vodka and tonic? Or Champagne?' She was already heading towards the cabinet where they kept the drinks.

But he held up a hand to make her stop. Every line on his face deepened at once.

'Sweetheart,' she said. She walked back to where he was standing, and hugged him, tenderly this time. She put one hand on the back of his neck, and the other on his back, between his shoulder blades. His head sagged, piteous, on her shoulder.

'I didn't say it,' he said. 'I promise I didn't. I promise.'

'All right,' she said. 'It's all right.'

'Work's one thing, but if you didn't believe me then that would be – the worst outcome imaginable. Bec. You do, don't you? Believe me?'

'Yes,' she said. Either way, there was no point arguing.

After a bit longer, she turned her head, and rested one cheek on his chest, and looked over at the sink. There was nothing in it. She decided not to say, 'Well done on the dishes!' She hugged him tighter. In a minute, she'd let go. Then she'd sort out the school bags while he finished making dinner.

Soon she'd be doing it all herself. He'd be at work until seven most nights, the windows would be un-smeary and she'd cook the dinner and very often eat with the kids.

Life would be getting back to normal.

The day Stuart went to Sydney to plot the rehabilitation of his public image, Bec came home from work and made sausages and mashed potatoes for everyone. She stirred horseradish through some of the potatoes and left the rest plain. (Lachlan and Mathilda did not like horseradish. Essie did sometimes. Stuart did not like mashed potatoes without horseradish. Bec liked whatever.)

At just before five, Stuart rang. His plane had been delayed; he was only just boarding; he wouldn't be back until the children were in bed. Could she please save him some dinner, because the airport food was not particularly appetising, and maybe the two of them could eat together?

244

'Lovely!' she said.

Fine then, she thought.

She went back to planning what to wear for Ryan the next day.

'I've been thinking about your thing at Daniel's,' Stuart said, a few hours later, when they were sitting eating dinner in the quiet (tidy) house. He meant her job. 'Tomorrow you could give four weeks' notice. I presume that'd work for all concerned.' He looked up from his horseradish mash. 'With the hospital wanting me back straight away. You're all right with that, aren't you?'

'Sure,' she said. It wasn't as if she enjoyed her work. If she felt like getting out of the house, then she certainly had better things to do than hear about Michelle's gluten intolerance – 'Not pleasant to be around today! I've had Nutri-Grain! Nightmare!'

'Yes. If you think. That's totally fine.'

'How is Daniel?' Stuart said. It was the first time he'd asked. 'Think he'll manage without you?' Oh, the *condescension* of these men. She'd like to see them put in a day behind that reception desk. They would honestly not last ten minutes.

'Same as ever. He was always sort of . . .' she paused, trying to think of an accurate but not-too-inflammatory description, 'unpleasant.'

'Daniel? You serious?'

'One of those people you just don't warm to. Unlikeable.' She put a small forkful of dinner into her mouth, and remembered the looks Daniel had given her, and the three times he'd left his hand on her arm just a split second too long.

'I understood you were enjoying working there,' said Stuart.

'Really?' Her mouth was still full; the word came out all mangled. Through her broccoli, she managed a jokey you've-got-to-be-kidding-me face and sat back in her chair. She swallowed. 'No. Not really.' It was the most gracious response she could think of. ('How can you be so dense? Don't you know me at all?' would have been more real.)

'So why did you work there?'

'Because I *had* to work there, Stuart. So we could buy food and electricity and petrol and keep living here.' (Enjoying the ridiculous marble splashbacks you wanted, she added, silently. Those ostentatious, look-at-how-much-money-I-make-because-I'm-so-brilliant splashbacks that cost a *semester* of my little girls' school fees.)

'All right, all right. Settle down.'

'Don't you *dare* tell me to settle down!' He really did act as if it was 1950. He probably *had* said it.

'Bec, can we just enjoy our meals, please?'

'I don't like it when you tell me to settle down.' Her voice was steady, bitter and serious.

'I apologise. And about your job. You're quite right. Entirely.'

She nodded. She *knew* she was right. He didn't have to inform her of that, as if he was the arbiter of rightness.

'Now, about the school situation.' Stuart's tone was serious. 'What do you think?'

At least he cared about the kids.

'Yes,' she said. 'I've been wondering because—'

'Would the disruption of changing back outweigh the benefits of Briarwood?'

She, of course, hadn't been wondering in such a neat, PowerPoint-presentation sort of way. She'd been thinking about how weird it would be to go back to Briarwood. All the questions and glances. Allie. The feelings. The feelings that Stuart never seemed to know, notice or care about.

'Um . . .' Bec folded her arms.

There was something else too. It was that she didn't *like* Briarwood as much, for some reason.

Bec had noticed that, compared with Briarwood days, she now presented herself differently at pick-up. If she wasn't in her work clothes, she'd go get the kids in jeans she hadn't ironed and a round-the-house shirt; she'd started letting her hair stay frizzy. She liked it. It reminded her of university. It reminded her of James the Canadian and how they used to lie in bed and listen to Oasis and talk about nothing much. The other day, she'd even listened to Oasis while she cooked dinner. 'Are you trying to do the floss dance, Mummy?' Essie had asked, earnestly.

She liked the way the Ashton Heights mums talked to each other, even though they didn't, yet, talk much to her. And she liked how the P & F hosted a mid-year pizza night instead of a silent auction, and how lots of the kids rode their bikes to school. Ashton Heights wasn't exactly disadvantaged: the kids all lived in a fancy suburb, most of them would go on to private secondary schools and university. But Briarwood had its own indoor swimming pool, and Ashton Heights felt somehow more like *her*. The kids there had stopped seeming raucous and hostile and had started seeming spirited and scrappy and authentic. She found that she wanted her kids to be Ashton Heights sort of kids.

'I don't think Briarwood would have places right now,' she said. This was almost certainly true. 'And cash flow might take a while to, you know, get back to normal. How about we just leave it for a bit? I'll call Briarwood soon and see what their availability's like for next year. If we're not happy, we can look at changing them back then.'

'Sounds very reasonable,' Stuart said.

She smiled over at him – a we've-been-through-a-hard-thing-but-look-at-us-working-it-out-together sort of smile – but he was busy placing gourmet sausage and horseradish mash onto his fork.

*

'I made you a dream-catcher,' Ryan said, the next morning. 'Or at least, my version of one.' She'd just arrived, and he'd ambled the two of them into his bedroom. He pointed up at a mobile, hanging from a newly installed hook on the ceiling.

'It's made from willow. Willow is the tree of emotion and love.' He met her gaze very directly. 'And then, that's a rose quartz, amethyst, crystal quartz for clarity, that feather is from a black swan, for strength and beauty and taking flight.' He smiled, and said something about it just being a little hippy offering from a penniless surfer boy. 'But from my heart,' he added, not even shyly.

'So how does it work?'

'Well, it's supposed to channel good dreams down to you, and protect you from bad dreams. Or if you don't want to think about it like that, then it can just be something nice for you to watch when we're lying in bed.'

Of course, she didn't say the obvious. She just thanked him, and said she should have a proper look. She took off her coat, and they lay down, chastely, on their backs. It was just like that day on the mountain, except now she was looking up at her dream-catcher. 'That really is beautiful,' she said. 'Thank you.'

They kissed and he said, teasingly, 'You don't bring me chocolate biscuits anymore.'

'Well, we barely talk anymore,' she answered, between kisses. 'And your kissing has got so ungentlemanly.'

'Oh yeah. Conversation. That thing. How are you, then, Mrs Henderson?' She didn't really like him calling her that, but it seemed churlish to tell him, especially right now, and when he always said it so affectionately.

'Let me see.' She could flirt perfectly well, actually, whatever Kate may think. 'I'm seeing this really gorgeous younger man, and the sex is OK, but the conversation is amazing, so I can't complain.'

He stopped kissing her. He looked kind of sad.

'Well, actually, I think I'm going to quit my job,' she said, in her normal voice. 'It looks like the complaint against my husband's not going to go anywhere, so his work'll be coming in again, we think.'

Ryan appeared to put aside his hurt feelings. He watched her face for a moment.

'So, you think he didn't say it? Or just, you're not sure, but . . .' He spoke with so much sympathy. Not pretending that anyone could be certain, but realising that even if Stuart had said it, Bec might choose to ignore it, or to forgive him, just so her life could go on.

Bec shrugged. 'I think he probably didn't,' she said. That was the honest answer.

She rolled onto her back, and looked up at the black feather rotating slowly above her head. Ryan kept his hands on her, in an undemanding way she liked. 'It's just,' her voice became very quiet, 'I'm more thinking about, well, you.'

'Oh.'

'I went – I want to tell you – I went and saw a *psychologist*, to try to work out what to do, and I think, well, what came out of it for me is that maybe my marriage is founded on – on – not on healthy foundations. But I—'

Ryan put his fingertips across her lips. 'I know I said we could talk, Bec. But turns out, I don't reckon I can. I might pressure you, because of what I want. Not fair on you.' He kissed her collarbone. 'And, y'know, it hurts a bit much.'

He stroked her mouth, firm and slow, and then got to his feet. She rolled onto her side to watch him. He wasn't angry, but his movements, as he straightened his clothes, were less deft than usual; there was a subtle haste to his gait. At the doorway, he turned around.

'I don't really see myself as your gorgeous young man to – have sex with,' Ryan said.

'I don't think I can leave him,' she replied.

Tears filled his eyes. He looked wretched. *Your decisions, they have consequences*, said Kate's voice, in her head. Oh, yes. Yes, they did.

They were still for a moment. The man over the back fence was calling his dog.

Ryan turned away and went into the kitchen.

That time, she didn't wait for him to make up an excuse. She just said she had to go. He helped her on with her coat, and kissed her goodbye at the door. The kiss became more and more passionate, and he put his hands up under her skirt. She wasn't wearing underwear.

Ryan swore. He was almost panting. She thought maybe they'd have sex right there in the hallway. But he swore again, and stepped back.

'So that was a proper kiss,' he murmured. 'Not the gentlemanly sort.' He opened the door for her. 'Bec? Reckon you could do that some more? With your underwear?' Sometimes he sounded so young and so . . . easily delighted. 'And you could think of me? 'Cause I'll be imagining you. Like that. All the time. All the time, Bec. Till I get to see you again.'

That night, she and Stuart were drinking peppermint tea after dinner.

'I wanted to apologise properly for last night,' he said.

She made an effort to look receptive and pleased. He always did this kind of thing, as if apologising – or saying goodbye, or choosing a present – were challenging techniques and he was committed to continuous quality improvement.

'It was great you took that job. I'm sure it wasn't easy. I've seen how hard it is in reception.'

'Thank you.'

'I know people can be awful, and it's not – not as if it was ever your dream job. And so much of the load here, you were still carrying, but you just got on with it.'

'Thanks, darling.'

'You've always done so much for us all. And I took care of the financial side of things.' He leaned forward slightly, so he could meet her gaze. 'So it was very difficult, to be in a position where I wasn't able to do that. That's why I was being unreasonable yesterday.'

'Oh well,' she said. She touched his thigh.

'You're the glue for all of us, Bec.' He reached out and rested his fingers on her wrist. She smiled at him. They both had tears in their eyes.

She looked down at his hand. She looked up at his face.

She thought of her kids.

She thought of Ryan, and of the dream-catcher, and of strength and beauty and taking flight.

What was she going to do?

When Bec was at university, she would sometimes dream that she was sitting at an old-fashioned wooden school desk, the kind with an inkwell in the top right corner. She would be in a big room – one the size of a football oval – with countless rows of other students, all sitting in stern silence at their own desks. The invigilator would say, 'You may begin,' or there would be a bell, or Bec would realise with a jolt that she was supposed to start – it varied – and she would turn over a pale-blue examination paper. Then she would find the exam was in a subject she hadn't taken, and didn't know anything about. Eventually, after failing to make anyone understand, she would wake up. She hadn't thought about it in years. But all day Bec had felt the sick kind of terror that she remembered from that dream.

By the time Stuart arrived home, the children were in bed and the kitchen was clean. Bec was sitting on the couch in the lounge room, doing nothing. Reading was impossible. The washing was already folded. Looking at a screen felt disrespectful; leaving her phone in her bag seemed a small but important penance. She was definitely wearing underwear.

'What are you doing in here?' Stuart asked. He switched on another lamp. 'Everything all right?' But it was a casual question.

'I'm fine,' she said. 'Want some dinner?' He said he'd had a sandwich at the hospital. It was after nine. Astounding, how quickly, how entirely, his job had reclaimed him.

'I've got something to say,' she said. She was sitting still and very upright; her feet were together on the floor, her hands in her lap.

'What's up?' Stuart sat down on the edge of the coffee table, so he was facing her. He leaned forward and put his hands on the sides of her knees, his fingers spread, the way an Aussie Rules footballer holds the ball.

'What?' he said. He looked so *innocent*. It was as if he thought she was going to say that she'd accidentally scraped the car, or that one of the kids had been naughty and she hadn't handled it very well.

She examined the grey weave of her jeans. She didn't have to put them through this. If she rang Ryan – no, saw Ryan, she'd definitely have to see him – in the morning she could tell him that their affair was over. They would just have one last time together. Then life could go on as usual. No one else need ever know. Bec lifted her eyes to Stuart's.

'I've been seeing someone else,' she said.

'Right,' said Stuart. His face stayed even. He sat back on the coffee table, removed his hands from her legs. Bec imagined all the times Stuart had delivered bad news to patients. 'I'm sorry, but your cancer is inoperable.' 'I'm sorry, but her blood loss was overwhelming.' He used to talk about all that to her: not so much, the last few years. Had the terrible things he saw at work just become routine? Had they both been too busy? Had he forgotten she was once a doctor too, someone with whom he could not gossip but *debrief*, someone who might be expected to understand?

'I'm sorry,' she said, because what else could she say? Stuart stood up and put his hand over his mouth. It was a gesture she had never seen him make before. He was close to her, standing as he was right in front of the couch. His crotch was almost level with her face. She turned her head to the side.

He sat back down again.

'Bec? What do you mean? Seeing?'

She hadn't rehearsed anything. She hadn't even been sure she was going to be able to go through with it. This was Stuart! She loved him. She did. What was she doing?

'*Bec?*'

'Yes. Yes, seeing. I've been unfaithful to you.' Unfaithful. She lighted on the word with relief. It was such an old-fashioned term. But so useful, in the circumstances. It allowed her to confess without giving details that would be hurtful and tasteless and which, to be blunt, were really none of Stuart's business.

'Unfaithful,' said Stuart, as if it was a weird millennial word. He gave a little shake of his head. 'I'm going to get a drink.'

He walked into the kitchen; she heard the fridge being opened, the ice-cube dispenser, liquid being poured. A clink when the glass was drained, more pouring. Then silence. Was he not going to come back?

She stood up and went into the kitchen. It was almost dark in there: the only light came from the globe over the stove. Stuart was standing at the breakfast bar. She stood across from him.

'What is this about, Bec?' he said. 'Is it because of all the . . . all the recent stress?'

'No. I don't think so.'

'Then what? You never said you'd been unhappy.'

'I'm not unhappy. I love you. I don't even know what I want. I just couldn't bear to lie to you anymore.'

'Who is it?' he said. Extracting all the facts.

'The fire-eater. Ryan. From your birthday.' It took a startling amount of effort to keep a proud smile off her face.

'The fire-eater.' For the first time Stuart looked appalled. 'How old is he?'

'Twenty-seven, and I knew you'd say that!'

'Who else knows?'

Bec hesitated.

'Kate,' she said.

'Right,' he said again. He looked as if he might cry.

She watched as he took a swallow of his drink. He set it down, and touched the rim of his glass. It held ice cubes, which had already started melting, and the remnants of lemonade.

Without looking at her he said, 'A year or so ago there was this physiotherapist on the ward. Graduate. She would have been about twenty-four. Sophie.' He met her eyes. 'She was gorgeous. The medical students were apoplectic whenever she was on the ward. All these poor 19-year-old boys.' It was as if he was recounting an amusing story about a normal day at work. 'At least one in ten of the girls too, I guess.'

'Indeed,' said Bec. They exchanged a brief, smiling glance.

'Yeah,' he said. He took another swallow of lemonade. When he looked at her again, he'd stopped smiling.

'She and I got this little flirty thing going.' He shrugged. 'Nothing much. At all. I was just being a 39-year-old idiot and she was – well, God knows what she was getting out of it. And then one day there was a spare coffee – you know how I take in coffees on a Friday? The registrar was off with appendicitis, and Sophie asked if she could have it, so of course I said yes.'

(She vaguely remembered him talking about the registrar with appendicitis. 'He's making a bit of a meal out of it,' Stuart had commented, when the registrar returned to work, forty-eight hours after his operation.)

'The next week she invited me out for coffee. Just the two of us. To say thanks.' He put air quotes around 'say thanks'. Bec could just picture her, her lip gloss and her 24-year-old neck and the predatory, intoxicating swish of her ponytail.

'This girl was beautiful, Bec. Sweet. Sexy. *Smart.*' He was suddenly vehement, like a four-year-old wrongly accused of some misdemeanour. 'I told her no. I told her *of course not.* I hurt her feelings on purpose, so she'd stay out of my way.'

'Well, thanks,' she said. 'And there was me, bringing up your children, failing to realise that you were making this enormous sacrifice.'

'You have got to be kidding,' he said, for some reason.

'Fine. But if you're saying you were miserable because you gave up the opportunity to sleep with some gorgeous twenty-something so I should stay miserable too, then I'm sorry but I . . .' There was no need to finish the sentence.

'I'm not saying I was miserable, Bec.' He sounded angry now. 'I'm saying I was happy with you. I am happy with you. That's why I didn't let myself get *tempted.*'

'Well, congratulations,' she said.

'Bec,' he said. 'Stop implying that I'm the one who's done something wrong.'

'OK,' she said. In a sombre voice she acknowledged she was the one who'd done the wrong thing.

'Did you just say you were *miserable*?' The thing about Stuart in an argument, was that he never forgot what you said in the heat of the moment. He was so bloody logical. But now he also sounded devastated. Worse than devastated. He sounded *confused*.

'I'm not miserable,' she said. 'But I've been through so much. I never even had my own career. I was never *free*.' He wouldn't understand, but she said it anyway. 'And then it was marriage and kids and you know what it's like. And with Ryan I feel so – I feel like the self I never got a chance to be.' Stuart was the kind of man to whom you just could not use words like wild or authentic or healing. You couldn't use phrases like impossible beauty, or excruciating agony, or the relentless lap of yearning that would just keep on and on and on until it utterly eroded you.

'Wow,' he said. 'You realise you're having a mid-life crisis, don't you?' He sounded as if he couldn't believe it had taken him so long to make such an obvious diagnosis.

'Don't be nasty,' she said.

He opened his hands, as if waiting for her to answer a perfectly simple question. After a moment he said, 'I'm going to go now. You'll need to tell the kids I've gone to a conference or something. I'll call them tomorrow evening.' They were certainly used to that kind of thing, she could have pointed out. 'When I come back, we'll talk. You decide what you want; I'll decide what I want.' He could have been discussing an appliance purchase, except for the way he blinked when he said 'I want'.

'All right,' she said. It was the only possible response. He picked up his phone and keys off the bench, his backpack from the kitchen floor. The sensor light flicked on, then off, as he crossed the porch.

It was quite a few minutes before she heard the sound of his car reversing. She could tell he was driving briskly but not too fast, efficiently negotiating the curves of the driveway, his behind-the-wheel bloodstream alcohol-free, just like always.

Stuart ended their marriage the following morning, on a Friday so blue and calm it felt like an accusation. Bec arrived home from dropping off the kids at school, to find him sitting at the dining table.

'Hi,' she said. He was supposed to be at his clinic. She was due at Ryan's at eleven, to tell him, face to face, that Stuart knew the truth.

'Hello,' he said. He looked so normal. Blue shirt ironed; hair clean. There was not a bloodshot eye or an unshaven jaw or a trembling hand in sight.

'Kids are at school,' she said, for something to say.

He told her he was aware of that. 'You'll need to fix the shelf before they get back.' He waved his hand at the lounge room. 'I've taken some books.' She noticed the box next to him. 'My clothes and a few other things are in my car.'

'So you're . . . going?' she said. She sat down opposite him.

'Yes. Of course.' He looked at the wall next to them and said, 'Jesus fucking Christ, Bec, of course I am.'

'You're leaving me?'

It took him less than five seconds to regain his composure. 'I haven't taken any of the photo albums. I'd like you to have them copied for me please.' He was so businesslike. There was not even the slightest sarcastic inflection on the 'please'.

'What . . . what?'

'I'm going to organise my workload, going forward, so that I can have the children at least 40 per cent of the time. You can stay here with them, for now. We'll need to put the house on the market, in the medium term. I intend to rent a flat in town. I'll pay child support as per regulations. I suggest I see them every second weekend and one or two evenings a week, initially, then increasing when, as I say, my work schedule is settled. I think we should tell them tomorrow morning, here, at ten. Rodney has recommended someone who'll act for me should you dispute any of this,' he added. 'And as you've probably already made yourself aware, we would need to have dispute resolution counselling first, as a formality.'

She was, for honestly the first time in her life, finding it impossible to get air into her lungs. She had always thought people who had those kinds of panic attacks must be sort of neurotic.

'But . . .' She wanted to say: What about us? What about *me*? Don't you care about what's happened? Are we going to even try to work it out? Aren't you going to *fight* for me?

But she knew, that if she said any of those things, then he would say something that made perfect sense. Something about decisions and outcomes and the time for that sort of discussion being over. Which would, she had to admit, be fair enough. Or at least, he'd make it sound fair enough.

He didn't speak. He didn't touch her. He just waited until she was breathing properly again. Then he stood and picked up his tidy cardboard box.

'Stuart?' she said, when he reached the door. He turned back to look at her. 'I'm sorry.'

'Not as sorry as you will be,' he said, as if it was a simple truth that gave him no pleasure.

And *that*, right there, was precisely what drove her crazy about Stuart, and exactly why things were at this point. The way he was always so calm and *rational* and definite.

But also, very often, he was right.

She turned on the kettle and then wandered into the lounge and sat down on the couch. She regarded the ruin of the bookshelf, feeling a bit like a teenager who had disobeyed, and was now out of her depth and terrified.

Her rebellious thoughts – about freedom and guilt and releasing the patterns of the past – seemed withered and immature. Or maybe not. But at the very least, those issues were much harder to care about, now she was alone in her punctured house. Without him.

She heard the kettle flick off, but she didn't move.

'Your plan is extraordinarily selfless and commendable, Rebecca,' Dr Nightingale, her boss, had said. She was twenty-four, and had almost finished her internship, and Kate had recently come back from London.

Dr Nightingale had looked down towards his thumbnail and then at her. 'I'm sure you've thought it through.' He adjusted the stethoscope around his neck and seemed to come to a decision.

Yes, Bec realised. He was going to *cross boundaries*. He was going to *offer personal advice*. And him a cardiologist! He must feel very strongly.

'But this opportunity in Sydney – the paediatrics residency. Well. Sometimes you do have to put yourself first.' He gave a sad nod. 'You must seize this chance, Rebecca.'

'Yes,' said Bec. Everyone she knew had already told her either that taking the job in the shoe shop was a tremendous waste (her father, her mother, her grandma) or that she'd be bored to death (Laura, Brent, several other tentatively helpful colleagues) or that it was extremely selfless and commendable, but also most unwise of her (Professor Wyatt of Northmead Paediatric Department via email, and now Dr Nightingale after a ward round). Bec had already cried into her pillow and decided that the right decisions were not always easy. She was not going to be the sort of person who believed that caring for others was only for those without another option.

'You've been an excellent intern, Rebecca,' Dr Nightingale said. 'It's clear you could make a very substantial contribution, should you pursue a career in paediatrics. Perhaps even' – he permitted himself a small smile – 'paediatric cardiology.'

She looked down at Dr Nightingale's shoes. My sister is having six-monthly scans! she wanted to scream. My sister cannot drive a car. My sister asked me to stay in Hobart! His shoes were black and extremely shiny. Presumably his wife polished them. She wondered what would happen if she gripped Dr Nightingale's immaculate white shirt and yelled, 'Northmead Hospital doesn't know about my *sister*!' into his kind, avuncular face.

'Thank you, Dr Nightingale,' she said, as if she were a polite little girl who'd been given a type of lolly that she didn't really like.

That was her last week of being a doctor.

It was a warm December day, less than two weeks after the Dr Nightingale conversation, when Bec first presented for work at Toot Sweet. She wore a mauve knit top with a flowing black skirt and pair of dark purple suede heels that Kate had loaned her.

'You look like you're going as a witch,' said Kate, nicely enough, as Bec was getting ready. 'Put your hair up. With your two hands.' The last sentence was a wrecking ball. Demolishing.

They were both living with their parents at that stage. Kate had just come back from Melbourne after the amputation. Bec was in the twin room that she and Kate had shared as girls. Kate had been allocated a proper double bed in the study, but in the night, she often came and got into her old bed in Bec's room. 'Are you awake?' she'd ask Bec. 'Yes,' Bec would say, as brightly as possible.

Even on Saturdays, their busiest day, Toot Sweet had the muted, serene sort of quality that went with very expensive merchandise and sales assistants who had been to private schools. Bec didn't usually work Saturdays, but on the Labour Day long weekend one of the other girls had a wedding to go to. Bec didn't mind at all. Toot Sweet was so orderly, with its tidy racks of boxes in the storeroom, and its dust-free shelves. 'I'll just cram my foot in!' girls would giggle. 'I'll just tell him they cost $230, and then say *each* in a very quiet voice,' ladies would intone, cheerily. And if you made a mistake, well, it didn't matter that much. No one was going to die because the plum patent brogue didn't quite match the dress.

Bec had been thinking about lunch when she saw Stuart through the window. The self-assured surgeon who had once asked her out. The girl she'd been that day seemed like a different person, someone she'd met on a holiday once, someone she'd liked but had never properly got to know. He had a woman with him. Bec could tell straight away that she was the sort who blow-dried her hair even when she didn't have anything much on. When Immaculate Woman saw the window display, she touched Stuart's arm as if they were tourists who'd spotted a koala in the wild.

'Can I help you?' Bec asked, when she had finished serving a lady in a spotless white drapey top who was the only other customer.

'Hi,' said Immaculate Woman. 'Can I please try on those grey pumps you've got in the window?' (He, meanwhile, gave no sign he recognised Bec. So predictable.)

'Sure,' said Bec. In a little while she was kneeling in front of Immaculate Woman, adjusting the straps. Stuart stood well off to the side, opening and shutting his phone.

'Done,' said Bec.

'These'll do, won't they?' Immaculate Woman peered into the mirror. 'We've got a family lunch this afternoon,' she added, to Bec.

'Lovely,' said Stuart, firmly. Still no sign of recognition.

'I hope you enjoy them,' Bec said, a little while later, as she handed over the maroon paper bag. It smelled of sticky-tape and synthetic flowers and had the shop's phone number printed in pale pink on its side. Immaculate Woman slipped her well-moisturised hand under the satiny loops that made the bag's handle and walked off towards the belts.

'Thank you very much,' Stuart said to Bec.

'My pleasure.' Sometimes Bec wished she was the sort of person who could sleep with someone random, just so she could tell Kate about it. Even if it was really bad – in fact, especially if it was really bad – it would be all right. It might make Kate laugh, if Bec could tell the story right.

'Didn't you used to work at the hospital?' Stuart asked.

'Yes,' she said. 'But my sister has been very unwell, and so I'm taking an extremely early career break.' She'd honed that line, used it so many times it rolled off her tongue lightly, amusingly even. Bec waited for surprise – or concern, or horror (A Fellow *Doc*tor! Working In A *Shoe* Shop!) – to show on his face, but it didn't.

'I'm sorry to hear that,' he said. 'I hope she makes a good recovery.' Men like him! They might be entitled, but they had such excellent manners. And they were so conscientious, with their well-kept shoes and de-pilled jumpers and ironed scarves and impeccable teeth. Immaculate Woman was on her way back towards them.

'Thank you,' said Bec. She was wearing a soft, buttercup-yellow sweater that day, with a pair of tight-ish black pants. Then she added, 'That's very kind of you.'

Stuart smiled at her. Bec smiled back. When she told Kate about her day, she'd make Stuart extra handsome – he was pretty handsome, anyway – and really, really arrogant. She'd make Immaculate Woman mean and jealous and way too thin. All in a good cause.

'Stu?' said Immaculate Woman, coming over. Stuart's head turned toward her but he kept looking at Bec.

'Bec here is a doctor,' he said. His eyes didn't leave Bec's face. 'She used to work at the hospital. We met when I was down here last year, while she was doing her orthopaedic term.' He ran a hand – briefly – over the back of his own neck. 'Her sister's been unwell.'

'Oh. I'm sorry,' Immaculate Woman said to Bec. Bec could tell immediately from the grave way Stuart said 'unwell' and the tender way Immaculate Woman said 'sorry' that Immaculate Woman must be a doctor too. 'Unwell' – when said in that particular way – was practically medical code for either severe mental illness or cancer.

Bec thought they would leave, but Dr Immaculate Woman jerked her head at Stuart and said, 'He wasn't too annoying to work with, was he?'

'Just – you know – the standard amount of surgical insufferableness,' said Bec. 'Only kidding. I couldn't tell you, to be honest. We didn't really work together much.'

'This is my sister Phoebe,' Stuart said, rather hastily. 'We've all come down for Dad's birthday. She forgot her shoes.'

Phoebe said something about how her parents often came to Hobart for a long weekend, how they loved Tasmania, how they might even retire here one day.

'Anyway, we'd better let you get on with your work,' she said. 'And we have to do the impossible and find Dad a present. Nice to meet you, Bec.'

'Bye now,' said Stuart. At the doorway he turned and glanced back. Bec was still looking at him. They smiled at each other again.

She'd flipped back her hair and leaned very slightly forward and been glad she'd decided on the flattering yellow angora.

The gappy bookshelf stared down at her.

Sometimes, she thought, you don't know in advance. You plan and think, but until things actually happen, you can't know how they'll make you feel; you can't see, beforehand, what you can see so plainly, even a short time afterwards.

A number of things were suddenly clear.

One was that she hadn't been free, back then. She really hadn't. But she also realised that it wasn't how she'd been *then* that mattered. Because the long-ago decision to end her career was irrevocable, and despite it, she'd ended up pretty happy.

The other thing was that she had, deeply and definitely, loved him.

In the end she texted Kate. Talking was impossible; they'd both get all upset, and Bec had to go and see Ryan soon. Best to keep it short. Less unbearable.

Stuart left, she texted. Almost immediately, she sent a second text that said, *He left me, I mean.*

Predictably, her phone rang straight away.

'What?' said Kate, without preamble.

'I told him, last night.' Bec made a small sound of both sorrow and contempt. 'He didn't even want to talk about it. He left this morning.'

'What about the kids?'

'Tomorrow.' Bec put both her hands on her phone, and winced. Then she voiced what she'd been thinking for the last hour. 'Actually, Kate. Maybe. I really hate to ask, but is there any chance you could come down, straight away, to sort of, you know, support them? And . . . me?'

'Since when do we call it support?' snapped Kate. 'You're an idiot, Bec, and I'm your sister, not your social worker, and of course I'm coming.'

Bec had a second shower and then drove to Ryan's house while her hair was still wet, combed back from her face, the way he liked.

Walking along the nicely swept path, she took a deep, cleansing breath. She didn't need to decide whether to act casual or vulnerable or decisive, for goodness' sake. He had *wanted* her to tell Stuart.

'I did it,' she said, as soon as Ryan opened the door. She wasn't prepared for the exultant smile that formed around his white teeth. He threw back his head.

'Whoo-hoo!' he said, to the ceiling. Then, 'Come in!' He stood back as she entered, and shut the door behind them.

He flicked on the kettle. She had bought it for him a week ago: the very cheapest one she could find, white plastic, so that he wouldn't feel like a toy-boy. ('What says toy-boy louder than a mid-range kettle?' Kate had snorted, when Bec mentioned it. 'It's Stuart's money you spent, anyway,' she'd added, brutally and unfairly, considering how she'd always gone on about couples being economic units.)

Last week, he'd leaned against the bench and she'd stood between his legs while the kettle boiled. Today he was busy with teabags. After only a microsecond of hesitation she sat down on one of the stools.

'How are you?' Ryan said, over the puff of the kettle. Did he sound shocked? Excited? 'How did it go?'

'As well as can be expected. He left.'

'To . . . just think about what to do?'

'No.' She was conscious of how her lips were pressed together.

'Well,' he said, turning around properly. 'Main thing's how you are.'

'I'm OK. Just. The kids.'

He emptied his hands and walked across the kitchen to put his arms around her. His chest smelled like a health food shop.

'It'll be all right,' he said. 'Least everything's out in the open.'

She could hear the lub-dub of his heartbeat. Fast and hard. So his system, too, was flooded with adrenaline. She looked up at him, and prepared to make her pitch.

'Ryan, I just want to say that this doesn't have to change anything between us. I'm not expecting anything from you.'

'OK,' he said, thoughtfully. He put a hand on her cheek. 'But maybe you can stay over sometimes? When the kids are with Stuart?'

'Of course,' she said. He was so young. She put her face back on his chest and heaved an enormous sigh.

He was silent.

'Maybe I could meet them?' he said, eventually.

'Um,' she said. Only really irresponsible people let their children meet new partners too early. It would be very confusing, send all the wrong kind of messages to her daughters. Not to mention Lachlan. She looked up at him. 'We probably have to be very careful about the children.'

'OK,' he said. He dropped his arms and moved away, back to the tea. 'Just let me know when you're ready.'

'Is that all right?' she asked his back. 'It's not that I don't want you to meet them. But we have to see what happens, how they take the news, and then give them time to sort of adjust and to explain things.'

'Sure,' he said, as the smell of lemongrass filled the room. 'I just want us to be authentic with them. We don't give kids enough credit.' He reached for the honey, then turned around and said, 'You know, probably most children have more EI than adults.' ('Emotional intelligence,' Stuart would have scoffed. 'Surely that was only invented to make dummies feel better.')

'I know what you mean,' she said. She rubbed her face. Lying and concealing didn't exactly send good messages either. 'Let's just see.'

'Just saying, we want to let this thing between us come together naturally.' He gave her the sweetest glance when he said 'this thing'. 'And your kids are part of your life.'

'Yep,' she said. 'I know.'

She remembered she had no underwear on. For some reason, that made her start to cry.

Chapter Nineteen

Kate

I'd been in Tasmania for six days. I was staying at Bec's house, and thinking about Adam only 92 per cent or so of the time. It probably would have been 97 per cent, except the kids were quite demanding, Bec was a bit up and down, and my PhD proposal was needing attention.

Luckily, Bec had stopped asking me about 'that Adam guy'. I didn't mention him, and I only cried in bed. No humble pie in front of my little sister. Not even when her marriage was rubble.

On Thursday, Bec took the older kids to the dentist on the way home from school. In true being-supportive-while-simultaneously-keeping-myself-busy fashion, I took Essie to a park nearby, and pushed her on the swing.

NO CALLER ID, said my phone, when it rang. I don't know why I answered. Actually, I do know. I wanted so much to hear his voice. It was cold, in the park. I was tired. He caught me at a low ebb.

'Yes?' It was difficult to wedge the phone under my ear and push the swing.

'I need to talk to you.' He sounded the way he always had. Calm and friendly and pleased to hear me.

'No.' To his credit, he didn't say, 'Why did you answer then? And I'm already talking to you, so hahahaha.'

'Please?' It did sound like a plea, too. 'Not on the phone. Can we meet?'

'I'm in Tasmania.' I was already hating myself for even answering the phone. And what was even worse than the fact I'd answered, was that there was this little part of me which was thinking that maybe all the lies didn't matter. Maybe we could just pretend everything was all right and I'd take us on a lot of nice holidays or buy him a house or a Ferrari or something. It would be like one of those 1950s marriages where the wife knows the husband's gay, but she just goes along with it. At least I'd get to have lots of nice sex. At least I'd get to say I had a boyfriend and have someone to go to dinners with.

'Can I come there, then?'

'It's a free country.' It may have been better if I'd got that retort out of my system during high school.

'Where are you staying, babe?'

'Don't you fucking "babe" me.' Essie twisted her neck so far around to look at me that I thought she was going to fall off the swing. She looked delighted and horrified. I did an oops-but-this-is-a-*very*-naughty-person expression, and she giggled.

'Sorry. Kate. Can we maybe meet somewhere?'

'No. Go away.' I hung up.

Of course, I know that no means no, but at the same time, I also knew I was only pretending to myself. I actually didn't really want him to leave me alone.

Sometimes that kind of thing is very confusing.

Bec and the other kids arrived back at the park while I was still pushing the swing, because Essie could stay on a swing for hours and of course we were all being extra nice to the children. In order to forestall any revelations, I said, 'Sorry, Bec. I accidentally said the eff word in front of Essie.'

Bec smiled at me and spoke for Essie's benefit. 'Oh well. Even grown-ups make mistakes. The main thing's to say sorry afterwards.'

We exchanged a nice little look.

'Time for a go on the slide, Essie,' I said. Essie will usually do pretty much whatever I suggest so she only said, 'Awwww,' once, and then ran off. Bec and I wandered over to a seat.

'That Adam guy rang,' I said. And I said it as an explanation. I just couldn't keep pretending. Low ebb.

She stared at me. 'Are you all right, Kate?' We watched Essie make it to the top of the slide's ladder.

'Oh, you know. No. Not really.' I shrugged in the way that means 'I'm very, very far from all right, but I suppose eventually it'll pass'. Bec curved one of her nice little hands onto my leg.

'Sorry,' she said. 'I hope you meet someone properly nice one day. I mean, if that's what you want.'

'Yeah. Me too.' I didn't even bother trying to sound casual. I just sounded how I felt, which was humiliated and hopeful and despairing.

'That fucking fucker,' she said, as a joke, and we both laughed.

'Adam was—' I wanted to tell her that Adam was treasured and beloved. That he was my first lover – my sole and so-long-yearned-for lover – since I lost my arm. I wanted to tell her that I had lied. I'd weaved stories and twisted words and created an image. I'd pretended because I didn't want her to feel sorry for me, and because, also, and perhaps especially, I didn't want Stuart to feel sorry for me.

The effortless, easy way Stuart flirted with me, as if I was a maiden aunt from the olden days, it just *mortified* me. The 'sensational legs' and the 'torturing Melbourne men' and – last Christmas – 'you're looking far too hot to be allowed, Madam Kate' – it was all so very much worse than if he'd screeched and pointed and called me Armless. Because he wouldn't have said those nice things, if I had my arm, you see. That was just the reality. He couldn't have. He would have felt too shy; he would have been much too aware of the line that the two of us must never, ever cross. And Bec would not have liked any flirtiness, then, either. She wouldn't have laughed her secure-wife laugh. She would have hidden her hurt face.

'Adam was the—' But it turned out, I just couldn't find the words. I looked at her, and shrugged, and settled on, 'I really liked him. So much.'

Then I swivelled towards her a bit, and said, 'And how are things with Ryan?'

'He's great,' she said. And I swear, she got this expression on her face: this terrible, bewildered, child-like expression, as if we were schoolgirls and someone had said something mean to her on the bus. I was about to ask her what was wrong, but she took a breath in and said, 'We seem to have something very precious. And very' – she gave me a shy, proud little smile, which reminded me, somehow, that she was the younger sister – 'very passionate, I suppose. And, you know, it's not something we feel we need to view in terms of either future plans or our physical ages.'

For God's sake, I thought. She's been drinking too much elder-flower cordial or something. But also, I saw that she was wondering whether she'd done the right thing. It was not as if I didn't understand what that sort of torture was like.

'I really hope it works out for you all,' I said, meaninglessly. But sincerely.

I still hadn't told her the truth, though. I still hadn't told her that I'd lied about my fabulous sexy life. That I'd invented my fabulous sexy self. That in reality, I'd so often been lonely and jealous and struggling to make the best of it.

I felt my face go into a frown; I licked my upper lip with the effort of forming the words that would say, 'Bec. About Adam . . .' because

I knew I shouldn't let her go on believing my lies. I knew I should tell her. I *knew* I should.

'We better get these kids home for dinner,' she said.

'Yes.' I stood up. 'It's nearly five.'

But I knew I was making a mistake. Maybe if I'd told her, things would have worked out differently.

Adam found me the next morning.

I was running along the beach in front of Bec's. I saw him from a long way away, but acted as if I hadn't, so I had about forty seconds to compose myself. You know the feelings, when you see a person you unfortunately love despite the fact you know they don't love you. The impossible, overwhelming, body-wide rush of whatever chemical it is, and you know that you're not going to be able to do or say or be all the things that you wish you could, because the person doesn't love you back, and so the way you want to be doesn't make any sense. There is simply no place in the world for the way you want to be.

He walked towards me and stood in my path. Not creepily so. A few metres away. So I wouldn't have to go out of my way to greet him.

I stopped. I wasn't in the least out of breath, because I have excellent cardiovascular fitness. 'Yes?' I said, in a tone that would have made Catherine of Aragon proud.

He had a small black wallet in his hand, and before he started speaking, he held it out towards me.

'I'm a police officer,' he said. 'I work in organised crime.'

We both took a small step forward. He flipped open the wallet in an impressively dextrous gesture. Fitted inside were a metallic badge on one side, and a photo ID on the other. The photo was definitely him. The writing said: ADAM CINCOTTA. Then a short series of numbers, and the words CRIME COMMAND. There was also the Victoria Police logo.

I took another step towards him. I reached out and touched the badge. It was all I saw for quite a few seconds. I heard nothing. Then a healthy-looking older man ran past, and a young woman with a bouncy pedigree dog on an aqua leash. I withdrew my finger. He flipped the wallet shut and put it away. Neither of us said anything for a moment.

'I couldn't tell you. For your safety. And mine.'

It was such a dramatic *CSI*-type sentence that I laughed automatically.

'Really?' I said. I looked at him. For one thing, it seemed such a bizarre conversation to be having. Especially at that particular Sandy Bay beach. Discussions about anything other than outdoor-space refurbishments and school fees were practically forbidden there; God alone knew when it had last seen any sort of emotionally charged confrontation. *'Really?'*

As if he was answering my question, he said, 'The first night we went out to dinner, I took my firearm. Just in case.' His voice was quiet, level and serious.

'In case I was a baddie? Or . . .'

'Just.' He shrugged in a way that indicated he wasn't going to say anything more. 'In case.'

'Oh.' I stood silent for a moment.

'Wanna walk?' he said. I nodded. I felt as if I'd just drunk about ten caffeine-containing energy drinks. We fell into rather brisk step. 'Morning,' he remarked, jauntily, to a middle-aged couple in matching spray jackets. He sounded for all the world as if the two of us had just been discussing our new patio furniture.

'Did you not trust me?' I said.

'At first I couldn't tell you. And then, when we – when it became obvious that I *needed* to tell you – I was concerned for your safety and also about compromising the operation I was involved in. With the data-analyst thing – I do actually analyse a lot of data. It's a thing we say, sometimes. My colleagues and I. To keep what we do on the down low.'

I nodded. I was speechless for quite a few seconds. (Rare event.)

'Believe me, Kate, when I tell you that the people I spend my days thinking about are the dregs of humanity. Just horrific human beings. I was very, very mindful of your safety.' He shot me an imploring look and said, 'Melbourne's really not that big a place. When we met, I was in the middle of a big op, it was crap timing, actually, and it was just better if you knew nothing, not even that I was involved in a police matter.'

'What were you doing on Tinder, then?' I said, a bit indignantly.

He made an I-am-merely-a-hopeless-red-blooded-man-so-what-do-you-reckon-I-was-doing? gesture with his hands. We laughed a little bit.

'But like I said. I took a gun to that first dinner.' He looked at me, very seriously. 'Probably just as well you changed your mind about me coming upstairs with you.'

It was nice. That he knew that, and that he remembered.

I thought of something else. 'So, what was all that photographer stuff?'

'Just what I said. Honestly. We'd been taking photos that day. And, you know, when you asked me, I – Jesus, Kate, you were there.' He was smiling. 'You know how it was. I just misspoke.'

I said that really made me worry about community safety, and he said fair enough, but that he was very rarely as overwhelmed as he had been that evening. Of course, that made me start smiling too.

'Kate.' He'd stopped smiling. 'I was in an impossible position. That last night – when you chucked me out – I so nearly told you then. But you were really angry, understandably, and I was concerned you might lose it and . . . I don't know, send a tweet saying, "Look at this prick I'm dating who reckons he's a detective in the middle of a major op" and a photo of me with your windows in the back-ground. Or something. You know?'

'I would never have done that.'

'Well, maybe not exactly that. But you threw me out before I could tell you, anyway. And then I thought, what am I doing? And I've been trying. You wouldn't answer my calls. Which was fair enough.'

'And you're telling me now because?'

'If I want to be with you, then you have to know. And I want to be with you, Kate. So here I am.'

'Right.'

I hugged his words into me, as if they were my lost kittens or children or something.

'Look, that night. At Bec's? One of the targets moved. We hadn't planned on it. I was kicking myself for being out of the state. I shouldn't have been. That's why I had to take that call.'

'Why didn't you just tell me?'

'What I said.'

'All right.' But I had to laugh again. It sounded so dramatic. There was a man up ahead with his butt crack showing as he tried to restrain his labradoodle, for heaven's sake.

'Kate, I have to go back tomorrow. You have to keep this to yourself. You have to use the data-analyst line; you have to be very circumspect when you're communicating about me, and I will never be able to tell you anything – nothing – about what I do. That kind of thing – the target moving – it's exactly what I'm talking about. I shouldn't even have said that much.'

'I understand,' I said, soberly. The whole thing was quite exciting, to be honest. And, oh my God, so very much sexier than data analysis, even if I couldn't tell anyone.

'So, are you an *agent*?' I said. 'Like, undercover?'

He laughed. 'Only the AFP call themselves agents.' From his tone, I could tell he thought the Australian Federal Police were a bunch of dills. 'And nah. Not undercover. This is me. My only mates are work mates. I genuinely have no life apart from my job and my family and, you know, you.'

'Pretty tragic, really, aren't you?' I said. But in a friendly way.

We walked on a bit, in an elated sort of silence. After a while, he gave me a little look. Long look. Sweet look. I started to worry we might trip over a small dog or something. Then, looking ahead again, he said, very softly, 'Lovely Kate.' We walked a bit further, until he said, 'I know you probably need time to process all this.'

'Nah. I don't.' I didn't need any time *at all* to 'process' anything. My biggest concern was the fact he'd just used the word 'process' to refer to thinking things over. Next minute there'd be talk of getting into the zone, learnings or stepping up. But other than that, I was exuberantly happy. I was thrilled and disbelieving, and to be honest, all I could think of was how very much I wanted to be alone with him. I felt like I wanted to see and touch and kiss all his skin, all of this Adam, who was, miraculously, the Adam I loved.

I stopped walking, and he stopped too. 'Can we please go somewhere?' I said. 'You do have, like, a hotel, or something, right?'

He smiled his smile – and can I also say, that when some men, such as health food store attendants or naturopaths, get the tiny beginnings of tears in their eyes, it is beyond repulsive, but when Adam does, it's absolutely gorgeous – and then he nodded.

I said, 'Because I'm just so really glad it's you.' The sentence didn't even make any sense, and I started crying a tiny bit at the end of it. Only in an eye-welling, romantic-heroine sort of way, though. There was no snot, which I suppose made a nice change, especially for Adam.

It was the best feeling in the world.

Outside was grey and rainy, and I was alone with Adam, in his lovely bed, in his lovely hotel room, with his lovely hands in my hair, and both of us naked and intertwined and warm and drowsy. And, I have to say, satiated. It was a very, very good feeling.

'You were pretty confident.' I indicated the large bed and fancy room. 'What would you have done with all this if I'd turned you down?'

'Seduced someone else.' Impossible to tell if he was serious.

'Really?'

He made a funny, wincey face. 'Maybe.' Bit of a sigh. 'But you know. Those drunk and horrible things. Only enjoyable for about fifty seconds.' He obviously felt that full disclosure of all non-work-related aspects of life was required. 'Not even fifty, really.'

'Adam? You can just exercise a normal level of truthfulness, in general, you know.'

He grinned as he ran his hand down my side, then brought it back up and rested it on my cheek. 'Jesus, Kate. It's so good to see you again.'

We lay there a bit longer, and I managed to extract that he was the *head* of a drug-lord-fighting *task force,* that his 'squad' had eight men and no women (drug-lord fighting is still very male-dominated, apparently) and that there was such a thing as the Organised Crime Management Committee, the name of which I obviously found very amusing.

I filled him in on Bec and Stuart and the fire-eater and the kids and my PhD proposal. I asked if his family knew what he did, and he said they knew a bit, and that when it came to talking about his work situation to my family, I should be extremely discreet, use my own judgement, and check with him if I needed. I could see that it was a very big deal for him, and I promised to be sensible, even though I was of course most disappointed that I couldn't tell every single person I knew that Adam went on stake-outs.

After all that, we decided it would be excellent fun to have hot drinks for afternoon tea. It took some time to disentangle ourselves, but eventually he got up and pulled on garments and started working out how to fill the teeny-tiny kettle. I put on his T-shirt, and leaned back on two of the many very comfortable pillows.

'Did you bring *Milo*?' I'd only just noticed it, standing near the mini bar.

'Yep.'

'Way over-confident.'

'I wouldn't get too big for your boots,' he said, not looking around from the cups. But he said it in such a way that it was obvious he was delighted we were both there.

'Adam?' I said, to his back. 'Just, you know, just confirming . . . you know. You know that night we had the fight, and you said you hadn't been seeing anyone else? That . . . was that – is that still true? Because, I just, you know, I know what I said, about you could see other people, but I was furious, as you know, and actually the thought of you, you know, dating anyone else, it upsets me.' I possibly deserved an award for using the phrase 'you know' the most times ever in a single speech, at least in the over-35s category.

He put down whatever bit of the coffee-and-tea making facilities he was using, and turned right around to face me. He was standing a few feet from the foot of the bed.

'Well. *Yeah.* I'd certainly hope so.' He looked down at the doona and said, quietly, 'Of course that was true, Kate. I'm – I am so much in love with you.' Then he looked at me.

'Oh.'

'I assumed you knew that,' he said.

I shook my head. I'd thought it was only me, the poor, sex-starved, Tudor-fixating, lingerie-obsessed amputee. Fully aware I sounded like someone with lamentably low self-esteem, but unable to resist, I said, 'Why?'

''Cos you've got really nice breasts.' We both laughed, perhaps a bit more than was strictly necessary, but when we stopped, he could tell from my face that I wanted a proper answer.

'Look, being honest, it was—' He rubbed his hands over his scalp as if he was giving himself a quick head massage, and then flopped his palms onto the bench behind him. 'It was pretty much one of those at-first-sight things.' He was looking at me properly now. 'Never happened to me before.'

I made some sort of sound, a bit like, 'Oh,' except not quite.

'Kate. That first dinner. After all the pasta and chocolate stuff, you didn't hold in your tummy. It stuck out a little bit, and you let it. You didn't press me about what I did.' He did a little nod – an *admiring* nod – and his quick smile. 'And when I walked you home you were so poised. Gentle.' He was looking down at the bedclothes again. 'Then when I somehow managed to get myself through your door, and I complimented your place, you were so excited when you said how much you *loved* it. It was really nice. And obviously . . . when we're together it's just very, very good indeed.' He cleared his throat and looked at me. 'You're really, of course, smart and, you know, funny, and we have, I think, similar values, very family-oriented, I'd say, and, and, a good work ethic and, um. And obviously your beauty can't *not* come into it, but I've been with a

279

lot of really very pretty women over the years—' a horrified all-right-what-the fuckety-*fuck*-am-I-even-saying-now? look crossed his face 'and, anyway, what I mean is that it's always been completely different with you, and not just because of your beauty. Right from that first night at the restaurant, you looked up at me and you didn't really smile, and then you said you were giving very serious consideration to the gnocchi, and you were so . . . well, you were the only person in the place, Kate. I've been totally, totally gone, ever since.'

'Well, I've got to say, I hope you're more concise and, frankly, a bit more diplomatic when you present things to your Crime Committee.'

'Yes. Me too. Fuck.' Smiling.

'Apart from that, that's all really nice, Adam,' I said. 'Lovely, in fact.' Of course, it was all so very, very lovely and wonderful that I couldn't even begin to compose a proper reply. I also couldn't look at him. But I heard him smile before he went back to the kettle.

'Adam?' I said.

Because if we didn't talk about it now, then would we ever? Because what about when the glorious sex and the nice hotels and the let's-lie-around-chatting-because-I-want-to-know-every-single-thing-about-you wore off? When my only wrist got sore, yet again, and I *cried*, or when it was forty degrees and I didn't want to go to the beach because I just couldn't face it that particular time? Did he know that one evening some man in a restaurant would look at him with a certain sort of scornful pity and then, the next day, or the next week, or the next month, a pretty, ordinary girl in a café or at work or at the gym would smile at him, and he'd feel, at the very least, a pang of something that would make him hate himself? Had he considered any or all of that?

He turned to face me. I couldn't say anything, but I held up my stump. It was a part wave, part challenge, part plea.

He met my eyes, properly. He nodded in a resolute, discreet way, like a movie US president. Then he put down the teaspoon and sat on the side of the bed. Not compassionately, though. Not like I was sick. Just as if he wanted to be close to me. We stayed silent, and I watched his face, as all the responses he'd already considered and discarded flitted again through his mind.

'Babe, I'd be lying if I told you I never noticed,' he finally said. 'Or even if I said I hadn't thought much about it. But . . .' And he reached out his hand and laid it on my stump. Held it. It was the first time anyone had done that. He looked at my eyes and gave a what-are-you-gonna-do? shrug. I did a weird gulp thing, and he lifted his hand to my face.

There was a moment, and he leaned forward and kissed my mouth. It started off extremely tender and sweet, but, after not very long *at all*, turned into something else entirely.

'Jesus, Kate,' he said. The side of his thumb was right near my lips, and his other hand was moving along my waist in a slow and purposeful skate. 'Felt like so long away from you.'

'No drinks.'

'Really, babe?' Firmer pressure on my waist, leaning on top of me, gently pushing me backwards. 'No tea? Milo? Maybe just a peppermint or something?'

I didn't even answer. We kissed for quite a long time before anything else happened, and oh, the weight of him. The pressure of his hands, and the feeling of his skin under mine, and the way I could make his breath change, and the short, murmured words. All that.

Afterwards, I wondered if I was meant to say, 'I love you, Adam,' or 'I'm in love with you, as well,' or something like that, and I did want to, but surprisingly, I couldn't quite find the words.

*

At some point that evening, we checked our phones. Adam showed me a photo of him, his parents (now looking older, but still beaming), his sister (younger than him, cool clothes, also beaming) and a number of others, at Nonna's ninety-second birthday (in a depressing nursing-home room, but with a cake and candles). Then he spent a bit of time firing off texts (presumably about sexy detective stuff).

I had two texts from Bec wondering where I was (oops), a text from Juliet asking whether I thought gluten-free tiramisu would be passable, and a missed call from Stuart.

I sent a text to Bec saying that I was just spending a bit of time with non-effing Adam and would explain later, and to Juliet saying of course not, that should be obvious. Then I rang Stuart.

'It's Kate Leicester returning your call,' I said. It hurt to say my surname. I was the first person Stuart called when Lachlan was born, before his parents, even. But it had occurred to me that he might have accidentally rung me while in the process of deleting my number from his phone.

'Madam Kate,' he said, actually sounding almost normal. 'How are you?'

'I'm fine.' (Obviously, I could have said, 'Oh my *God*, my boyfriend is the Sexy Head of a Drug-Lord-Fighting Task Force, we totally misjudged him, especially you, and now I'm the one in a great relationship hahahaha.' But, I didn't.) 'How are you?'

An uncharacteristic pause. I had never known Stuart to spend any time choosing his words.

'Have you met this man Bec's seeing?' he said.

'At your fortieth.' My voice was very small.

Stuart didn't react. He just said, as if the question was being dragged out of him, 'How do you think she is?'

'I think she's . . .' I wanted to say: 'I think she's sad, but also all loved-up, because almost anyone would be if they were sleeping with that man, and the no-doubt-amazing sex is clouding her judgement.'

'To be honest, Stuart, I reckon she'll eventually come around.'

'Huh. What about my kids?'

'Well, the main thing I'd be concerned about is just, you know, the impact of the separation, and keeping things as civil as you can.' I was having none of this don't-involve-yourself-in-other-people's-relationships malarkey. Who even made that up?

'Yeah.' Very, very drily.

'You and Bec, you need to find a way to be nice to each other. And I've said that to her as well.' I had, a number of times.

'Yeah.' Even drier. Then, not drily at all, but sadly, 'Yeah.'

'Stuart?'

'Kate?'

'You all right?'

'Yeah. Thanks. Can you – Kate, I'm sorry to ask, but can you keep me posted? With . . . things? The kids? I'm seeing them, twice a week, but I'm losing sleep. It's affecting my work, even.'

'Of course I can. I saw them all this morning, and, you know, they were doing fine.' I didn't add, 'Children are very resilient,' because I am sick of hearing it, and who really knows if they are or not?

He said he hadn't 'appreciated' that I was still in Hobart, and that maybe we could meet the next morning. I said what about the day after, and Stuart said no he'd be working, which was supposed to be my cue to reshuffle my own plans.

'Might not be possible, then,' I said. Then I decided the man's life had pretty much ended, and I should not be such a selfish cow. 'Actually, all right. How about tomorrow morning? And Adam could join us?'

Stuart is very polite, so even though he definitely still thought Adam was a dick, he said, 'Good. Eleven at Redman's?' (He is also a more concise communicator than some others I could mention.)

'Lovely. We'll see you then.' Apparently, I was back in the 'we' swing of things already.

I wondered if I should text Bec to tell her, and decided not to.

I wasn't being deliberately disloyal. I truly wasn't. I just thought that when the fire-eater sex wore off, and she came to her senses, she'd see that it was for the best.

The next morning, we had room-service toast for breakfast and then I called Bec. I told her that Adam and I were going out for a sweet treat and then I was taking him to the airport.

'I'll fill you in later,' I said, even though I still hadn't worked out what I'd say. Not only about seeing Stuart, but about Adam's job.

'All right,' Bec replied. 'It sounds like you two need some couple time.' I had often wondered why Bec felt compelled to give all forms of activity a label. (Me Time. Family Time. Couple Time. Quality Time. One-On-One Time. What would be wrong with just doing things?)

'We'll have to sit down the back,' I told Adam, when I hung up. 'It's like an undercover operation.'

'Yes, Kate. This is exactly what they're like.' His tone was tinder dry. He and Stuart could start an acerbic comments club.

Stuart was already there when we got to Redman's. It is a very nice café in a very picturesque, ye-olde-convict-would-be-surprised-to-find-the-dim-sandstone-cottage-where-she-once-scrubbed-hearths-is-now-worth-two-point-three-million-dollars sort of area. Of course, the place was chockers with tourists, and the three of us clustered (down the back) around a table about the size of a tennis racquet. Stuart and I ordered long blacks. Adam asked for a flat white and a lemon-curd tart. I really don't know how he stays so lean. Perhaps 'dolerite bouldering' and so on are very kilojoule-burning.

'On second thoughts,' I told the waiter, who looked as if he had either hayfever or a rotten hangover, 'I'll have a hot chocolate and one of those custard donut things.'

'A Berliner?'

'Yes.'

During this exchange, Adam rested his hand on my arm. He is not really the type for public displays of affection, and after a second I realised that he wanted the waiter to know that he – not Stuart – was the one 'dating' me. (Dating here meaning: seeing me exclusively, and getting on a plane purely to tell me he wanted to be with me, due to his being 'so much in love with' me.) (Just saying.)

Anyway, the little arm touch – the *pride* behind it – was unexpectedly moving. I gave him a smile – gentle, understanding, intimate, like a 1990s ad for decaffeinated instant coffee – and shifted in my chair, so that I was closer to him. Poor Stuart probably now felt as if he was doing a panel interview. Something like *Oprah*, where she lets the audience ask sympathetic questions until the guest – usually a 'survivor' of something horrible – cries. (I went through a stage of watching a lot of daytime television. *Oprah* was actually one of the better shows.)

'So, how are you?' I said to Stuart. 'And by the way, Mum and BFG are totally on your side.' Of course, they hadn't said that out loud, because Mum doesn't believe in taking sides and the BFG hardly ever talks, but I could tell.

'Well, things are rubbish,' he said. 'Totally crap. But life goes on.' He didn't look crap. He looked shiny-haired and even-keeled and, maybe, just a tiny bit tired.

'He's not coming to the house. He hasn't met the kids,' I said.

'Are you sure? I mean she said that, but . . .'

'I'm positive. She wouldn't lie to you. You know that.'

He didn't even have to raise his eyebrows.

'About things with the kids. I meant. Sorry.'

Stuart looked at the table in a way that made everything feel awkward. Adam, excellent man that he is, said something about being back in a minute and walked off.

I turned back to Stuart.

'Look. I'm so sorry. I told her to *stop it*. We were never . . . I'd hate you to think that we were sort of giggling about it or something.'

'Kate, I've known you nearly fifteen years.' To show he believed me.

'Really? God, we're old.'

'Yes,' he said, and I could tell he was working hard to avoid 'becoming emotional'. I affected interest in the mascarpone-and-berry items being delivered to the next table until Stuart said, 'So how are things with Adam?' He'd gone all surgeon-y; it was as if his next question would be about my blood pressure.

'Going well,' I said. I stopped talking while the drinks were delivered. When the waiter had gone, I started to say something else non-committal, but I changed my mind. Own judgement, I thought.

'Hey, listen. Adam? He's a police officer. Senior. Organised crime. He keeps his job quiet. And you have to keep it a secret. Seriously, Stuart. I'm not even telling Bec or Mum or BFG yet. But' – I was turning into a woman who cried in public – 'you've always looked out for me. Since I've known you, you've been like a brother to me. An older brother, obviously.' Shaky laugh. 'And I want you to know.'

Stuart stared at me for a second and then looked away. His forefinger made a slow half-circle around the rim of his water glass.

'And you're sure that's true?' He looked up. 'He's not trying to – impress you?' Dear, lovely, tactful Stuart. I knew he thought Adam was after my money.

'I've seen his badge.' It already felt like ages ago.

'And you're sure?'

'Yep.'

'A badge?'

'Yep.'

'Well.' He made a face that said life just kept surprising him, but at least this time it was in a nice way. 'Well, it's very good to see you happy, then, Madam Kate.'

'Thanks,' I said. 'And seriously, no one else knows. No one in our family, I mean.' I may have been first to hear that his wife was shagging the fire-eater, but by God, he was the one with the scoop on my boyfriend's occupation. 'So. Secret. All right?'

He nodded his competent nod, and we started our drinks.

When Adam came back, Stuart stood up and shook his hand.

'I told him about your badge,' I said, by way of explanation. 'He won't tell anyone.'

I had a split-second fear that Adam might be cross, but he returned Stuart's handshake in a grave, we've-got-a-lot-of-testosterone-but-we're-modest-about-it-aren't-we? way and then sat down and began his coffee.

They both looked enormously relieved, actually.

Chapter Twenty

Bec

'It'd be good,' Ryan said. It was less than a month since Stuart had moved out, Kate had gone home, and they were eating Sunday brunch at – for the first time – Bec's house. The kids were with Stuart, but Lachlan and Essie were due back by one o'clock. (Mathilda had a swimming intensive that afternoon.) 'Be good for them. Good for' – he waved his toast in a back-and-forth gesture – 'them and me.'

'Hey! Want to go boogy-boarding?' she asked Lachlan, when he got home.

'With you?'

'With me and Ryan.'

'Whatever,' Lachlan said.

'How about you, Essie?'

'Everwhat,' Essie said.

Bec looked at Ryan for an isn't-she-adorable? glance, but Ryan hadn't noticed.

'Well, your choice.' Bec's tone was brisker than Essie was used to.

But a little while later, Lachlan appeared in his rashy – it was suddenly a bit too small for him – and said, 'So, are we going? Or what?'

The beach was white and long and exposed; the water grey under a huge, shifting sky. Bec stood on the sand, taking deep releasing breaths and then looking at her watch.

Stuart had agreed that Ryan could 'meet' the children. (He'd agreed reluctantly, and because he knew he didn't really have any choice. No doubt he'd calculated that it would be a waste of energy and poor strategy to argue.) And there they were – Lachlan and Essie and Ryan – in the surge and swell of water that was shallow but which seemed to Bec to be as turbulent as a washing machine. She was pretty sure Stuart would not have agreed to *that*.

Well, she thought, it's not as if Stuart ever took them boogy-boarding on weekends. This sort of thing was so much lovelier than the relentless swimming lessons he'd insisted on. (She imagined Mathilda at her lesson now. Stuart would be checking his emails as she trundled up and down her tepid chlorine lane. Maybe Bec should talk to her about how it was possible to be too much of a good girl.)

Bec chewed the inside of her cheek, then smiled when she saw Lachlan. He was coasting into shore, trying to hide how delighted he was. Bec gave him a discreet thumbs-up sign, which he returned in a professional, manly sort of way. On the wave behind him was Essie. Her eyes were fixed on her big brother's back, her chin was jutting out of her life jacket like a too-short driver at the wheel of a big car. She looked somewhere between astonished and elated as the unspooling roll of white foam delivered her back to the beach.

Ryan stood some distance behind her, his hair full of water and sunlight. He was laughing.

'I won't go in the water today,' announced Essie, the very next Saturday. Lachlan had spent the week subjecting them all to a relentless please-boogy-boarding-this-weekend-please campaign.

'Really?' Bec left the wiper on the dining table and got down to Essie's level. 'How come, darling?'

'Just ... don't want to.' Essie looked over at Ryan, who was washing the morning-tea plates, as if she was worried about hurting his feelings.

'Not in the right mood today, hey?' Bec kept her voice soft.

'Don't want to,' Essie said.

'Sometimes the idea of something seems a bit scary, but then when you—'

'I don't WANT to. I don't LIKE that beach! And stop SAYING things to me!'

'All right, darling.'

Essie stomped off into the lounge room, where – in breach of former rules about the lounge room being grown-up space – her Sylvanian Families house had been set up. Bec straightened and went over to the sink.

'I'll do that,' she said, indicating Ryan could step aside.

Ryan kept washing for a moment, then put a damp hand on her back.

'Reckon she's just a five-year-old being five,' he said.

'I suppose so,' said Bec. 'You and Lachlan can go. I'll ... I'll stay here with her and Mathilda and we'll make a cake or something.'

'Think he'll be OK with that?'

'Who? Lachlan? Or Stuart?' said Bec.

He winced. 'Both. Last thing I'd want to do is—'

'Lachlan's been ready since dawn,' said Bec. 'And Stuart will just have to deal with it.'

'Hello. I was busy.'

She'd waited until Monday evening, when she was pretty sure he wouldn't be operating, but it hadn't helped. No matter when she called, his tone was terse and clipped. And she was no better. It was as if they were in a competition about mean politeness.

'Thank you for finding time to take my call. It's about one of your children.'

'What do you need, Bec?' That was his new way of saying her name. In place of an exasperated tut at the end of sentences.

'I want to discuss Essie.'

'Yes?'

'How does she seem to you?'

'What's your concern?'

'Well.' She left a deliberately long pause. She wasn't, after all, his intern. She didn't have to prepare a concise list of dot points for his consideration. 'Essie just seems very clingy. Very. At school she's very withdrawn, apparently. And still being really tearful, at drop-off. I mean, she has a new teacher, so maybe ... But wanting to sleep in my bed. There's an excursion in a few days and she's saying she doesn't want to go. And when she's home she ... she just doesn't seem all that happy.'

'And why is this bothering you today, in particular?'

'I thought I should see if you, her father, had a view. If you think she's just going through a normal sort of adjustment, or if we – by which, of course, I'd mean *I* – should look into getting her some professional help.'

'I find it very difficult to believe there's any form of help, as you put it, that will make our children happy. Of course she's "adjusting". All of them are.'

'That's your view?'

'Yes, at this juncture, Bec.'

'Fine. Thank you for your support.'

They both hung up.

*

291

The Friday of the excursion started well enough.

Essie's class was going to Clifton – way over the river! – to see what a real surf beach was like. It was part of their 'Exploring Where We Live' project. Ms Goldbold was on long-service leave, providentially, and Essie's new teacher was a youngish man called Michael Castilano, who wore shorts in all weathers and encouraged the children to call him Mr C. Of course, they weren't going swimming. For one thing it was July, and for another, even Mr C wasn't up for supervising twenty-six kids in that sort of water.

'Be brave!' Bec said, as she kissed Essie's cheek. Bec wasn't going along to do 'parent help'. She had plans to see Ryan, and to be honest, she'd done so much parent help over the years that it felt as if it would be fair enough to leave it to someone else once in a while.

By eight-thirty the children – excited, mostly – had been installed on the bus in their pairs. Essie waved through her tinted window, turning her head all the way around to Bec. She was sitting next to Mr C. Not a good sign, Bec felt.

Bec waved with one hand and rubbed her forehead with the other. There it was: that unambiguous sensation between her eyebrows, as if the skin there was being unpicked from the muscle beneath it. She knew it would soon be much worse. The headache would kill every thought; the nausea would be as inescapable as the sky. Well, it was entirely her own fault: she should have known better than to let Ryan talk her into red wine, especially with the kids in the house. She needed to be stronger with him. He was too young, and too *childless*, to be expected to understand. ('It'll make us all slow. And you'll go all gorgeous and soft.') She needed to get her act together. She should have more self-control.

With a sinking heart, she texted Ryan to say she was sick, drove home, took two Nurofen and got into bed.

*

Her phone woke her up.

'It's Michael Castilano, Bec,' said the teacher. He had that enthusiastic excellence with using names. 'I'm afraid you're going to need to collect Essie. She's all right. It's just the same sort of thing, and we've tried a few strategies but no luck today. Pretty distressed. I wouldn't be surprised if she's coming down with something, even.'

'OK,' said Bec. She got the details of Essie's whereabouts and stood up. Her chest seemed to fall down into her legs and the urge to vomit overwhelmed her. She sat on the bed to collect herself, and had to lie straight back down again. Four minutes passed; she watched them on the little silver clock beside her bed.

There were two other options. She forced her mind to circle each of them, tried to stand up for a second time, and retched. In the end, she picked up her phone again and dialled.

'Hello. I'm between cases.' Stuart called back a few minutes later.

'Fine. It's sorted.' She couldn't even lift her head off the pillow.

'What's sorted?'

'Essie's on an excursion. They were having trouble calming her down. Wanted me to go.'

'And?'

'I have a migraine. You know how I—'

'Right. So what's happening?' He knew her parents were on Bruny Island that week.

'It's fine.'

'What's happening?'

'You can get back to your case.'

'What. Is. Happening. Bec?'

'Ryan is getting her.'

'What!'

293

'Look, I'm unwell. You were too busy to answer my call. He was near there anyway.'

'Where is Essie?'

'You'll have the email from the school, Stuart, same as me.'

'Where is Essie, Bec?'

'Clifton Beach. Stuart.'

'When did you send him to get our daughter?'

'I don't know. A little while ago.'

'Bec!'

'One point three minutes ago, Stuart. Maybe one point four.'

He hung up.

'It was a simple misunderstanding,' she said, for the second time. She was digging her thumb, hard, into the bone under her eyebrow.

'They happen,' said the police officer. He was young and uniformed, and had something earnest about his demeanour that suggested he might be a Christian. 'Are you sure you don't need to see a doctor about your headache, Mrs Henderson?' He glanced at Stuart as he spoke. Stuart met his gaze in a level, why-are-you-asking-me-mate? way.

They were in a small, linoleumed room off to the side of the police station reception. On the wall was a poster showing an old-fashioned, aerial-bearing mobile phone with a red line through it. When she first sat down, Bec had, for a confused moment, thought it meant that people should upgrade their phones. Migraines always made her mind go a bit funny.

Stuart, in what was clearly a major over-reaction, had brought Essie here when he'd found her paddling alone on a quiet beach near Clifton. Essie was now sitting off to the side, earpieces in, delighted to be watching a *Frozen*-related YouTube clip on Bec's phone. Ryan had gone back to his place.

'That man left my child alone on a beach. A beach that is well known to be dangerous,' said Stuart. 'It is pure coincidence I arrived before she took herself into the water.'

'I accept that, sir. But I understand your daughter's whole class was on a school excursion at a beach nearby?'

'Well, they certainly weren't swimming. She had no lifejacket. No wetsuit. She wasn't being supervised.'

'Oh, for goodness' sake, Stuart! She wanted to have a paddle. He'd gone to the car park – like, thirty steps away – to get her a towel. I would have thought you'd be pleased she was enjoying herself.'

Stuart's eyes remained fixed on the wall, near where the skirting board would have been if the room had had one. He sat next to Bec, with his knees apart, his feet pointing straight ahead, his forearms on his thighs.

'So there's nothing you need to do, Officer? No immediate steps I can take to ensure my children's safety?' he said.

'No crime has been committed today,' the officer said, again. 'You'll obviously need to take your own legal advice about long-term custodial arrangements and so on.'

Bec felt the way Stuart went even more still. She could still feel things like that. You couldn't just cut yourself off from someone, whatever you decided. There were links, no matter what you believed, and your body reacted whether you wanted it to or not.

'Thank you for your help today, Officer,' Stuart said. He stood up and walked out. Essie looked after him, then at Bec. Then she went back to her screen.

Chapter Twenty-One

Kate

It was wintery Sunday morning, and in the correct and traditional manner of newish couples, we were at home reading the papers. Adam had gone out to buy actual newsprint – 'May as well do the thing properly' – and now he was sitting on my couch, lower lip stretched, reading an article about American politics.

I was making us both more coffee. The moment he heard me pouring beans into the machine, he looked up and said, 'Want me to do that, babe?'

''S OK.' I kept looking at him as he turned back to his paper. The weekend bristle, and the angle of his jaw, and the little frown of concentration, and the stretched, vulnerable neckline of his blue T-shirt.

The words were proving impossible to say. I meant them. They just wouldn't come out. I was like the opposite of those insincere people who constantly talk about how much they 'love' (or, more annoyingly, 'are loving') other people. (Oh! Her! I just *love* her! Oh! Him! I am just *loving* him!)

I got on with the coffee.

After a while, Adam picked up another bit of newspaper. He looked up again, ran a finger around the edge of his neckline, and said, 'D'you think you'll always want to live in an apartment?'

'Not necessarily.' I put the milk jug on the bench, and explained why I bought my apartment, which was because I wanted to be

296

somewhere where I could always see people, and life. 'It was partly just so I stayed, you know, in it. In life. And' – I picked up the milk and began pouring it – more carefully than usual – into our cups – 'I know this sounds odd, but sometimes I would kind of, look out at everyone, and I'd think: lots of people have it worse and we all suffer, so I should toughen up.'

He nodded, as if he understood, and as if that was entirely reasonable.

He was so great.

After we were settled with the coffees and our papers again, I said, 'When I was younger, I always thought I'd like to live in a little old-fashioned cottage, but near the city. And the water.'

'Like Albert Park or somewhere?'

'Yes! Exactly.' I mentioned a particular Albert Park street and a particular Albert Park café, and he looked at me so – I don't know – *condescendingly* – that I said, 'But public transport's not very good to Albert Park,' and went back to my article about crypto-currency. Obviously, that only lasted for about five seconds.

'Adam,' I said, 'if you don't want to move in together, that's fine, I'm not even the one who brought it up, you'll notice, and you are actually here in my house, from which you're free to go. I'm not cramping your space or invading your territory or hinting about wedding rings or doing whatever it is men apparently get so worried women are going to do. God! Is this because I'm nearly forty? Have you just read some terrifying article about female nesting instinct or something?'

'Kate, I'm totally up for moving in together.' His voice was a tiny bit different from usual when he added, 'If you are.'

'Oh. OK.' I looked down at cryptocurrency, fought a brief and unsuccessful battle against my no-doubt-beaming face, looked up again, and said, 'Just not in Albert Park?'

'Well.' He shut his paper. 'Albert Park's astro*nom*ically expensive.'

'I know that.' I shut my own paper, and there was a slight edge to my voice, because I knew a lot about real estate, probably more than he did, and I did not appreciate his superior, I'm-so-working-class-and-down-to-earth tone. 'But Adam, this apartment is worth a lot of money. You know, I have quite a lot of money.' We hadn't actually had this conversation. 'Literally millions, four or five million dollars, invested. And I own a unit in Cheltenham, and a couple of other places.' I bought in good areas ages ago, before the market went crazy. I am actually extremely good at money. 'So. If we seriously were looking for a nice little house, together, well, that'd be lovely. And Albert Park wouldn't be a problem.'

'Yeeaaahhh.'

I knew men could be funny about income and bread-winning and all that, so I breathed in and out and resolved to be sensitive and patient. 'Would you feel awkward about living in a house, if I'd paid for more than half of it?'

'Yeah. Nah. I don't know. I wouldn't want – remember what you said, in the restaurant that time?' He nudged my leg with his foot, and smiled. 'Actually "said" is probably not right. "Hissed" would be more the word. About your money.'

'I remember exactly what I hissed, and that was a totally different situation.' More deep breathing. Clear, direct, honest, patient, forgiving, et cetera. 'I realise now that you were not trying to defraud me, which was my concern, at the time.'

'Babe, I just don't want that possibility even being in your mind.'

'Do you think I'd be here now if that possibility was "in my mind"?' My voice was rising. 'You'd *lied* to me, repeatedly, if you remember.' Then I collected myself and said, 'For which I have magnanimously forgiven you, due to the Sexy Head of a Drug-Lord-Fighting Task Force situation. But it was different then.' (In addition to his badge, I had now seen his firearm safe. And his *gun*. And, once, when we'd been at Victoria Market, a pair of uniformed police officers had nodded at him, all respectful. They'd then nodded at me, even more respectfully. In fact, their gazes had been so glued to my face, it'd seemed as if someone inside their heads was bawling, 'Eyes UP, lads!')

'It's—' he began.

'Oh, just stop being so stupid.' Actually, there's no point being with someone you have to tiptoe around. 'I don't – God, we don't have to live on a policeman's salary, do we? I want to *share* with you.'

He made an amused face, as if I was cute. He's so *great*.

'Well. It's a big thing, Kate. Let's both think it over.'

'I know. All right. Yes, of course, that's fine.' Gentle, sensitive, understanding. I could run workshops. 'Anyway, Albert Park was just an idea.'

He nodded. After a moment he added, 'It's nice you want to, Kate. Move in together.'

''Course I do.' Then I added, '*Obviously*. You were there last night, right?'

He did an ironic, macho wink, and we both went back to our papers. He looked really pleased.

But I knew I was meant to say the love stuff too.

The next day, PPP and I took a long and unauthorised lunch break to celebrate the end of the semester, and also the fact that I had officially decided to do a PhD.

'It'll be great,' said PPP. 'I'm excited about your thesis already.'

We had two glasses of wine each and shared a piece of really yummy chocolate-and-coconut cake for dessert, and she said, 'This is lovely. I'm so glad you've been getting me out of my eyrie.'

It wasn't until I was on my way home – at 3.17 p.m. – that I saw I had missed a call from Stuart. He picked up straight away.

'Kate, sorry to bother you, but I'm very concerned about the children. Especially since this episode with Essie.'

'What episode?'

'He left her alone at Clifton on Friday. She was about to head in. By herself.' There was no need for him to tell me who 'he' was.

'No way!' The fire-eater probably thought Essie could commune with the waves, allowing her child-spirit to connect with nature's rhythms or something.

'Well, exactly.'

'Have you talked to Bec?' I asked, even though I knew the two of them were spitting emails at each other.

'Not productively,' he said.

I thought for a minute. Adam and I were due to head down to Hobart that very weekend. We were going to Hobart's Dark Festival, which was an extremely fashionable thing to do, and also fun if you enjoy listening to electronic music, guzzling warm mulled alcohol, freezing, and eating artisan food off organic biodegradable plates all at the same time. Adam was keen – he'd booked a different nice hotel for us – and I was quite looking forward to it. The only snag was that Bec wanted us to go out for dinner so we could meet the fire-eater 'properly'.

I didn't say all that to Stuart though. I just said, 'We're heading down this weekend. I'll, you know, suss things out with her, and keep you in the loop.' Now I understand why people use such ridiculous turns of phrase. It's to avoid saying things like: 'I will spy on my little sister and her lover, and then secretly report to you, her ex-husband.'

'Thanks. Sorry to involve you.'

'Don't be stupid. I *am* involved. In fact, Stuart?' I thought some more. 'I might go down early. Uni's on holiday and—' I'd been about to say that Adam had a very busy week coming up at work but decided not to as a) had life of my own and b) must be 'circumspect' about his detective-ing. 'So if Bec wants me to stay again, I'll just fly down in a day or so.'

He said something about appreciating that and family support and the kids loved me and he 'very much valued' me. Then he added, 'Maybe we could catch up on the Sunday? With Adam, I mean. The three of us?'

He wouldn't be used to the weekends, I realised.

'All right,' I said. 'Let's go to Redman's again.'

That evening, while Adam was off fighting baddies, I called Bec.

'Oh, Kate, I'd love that,' she said, and I could tell she really meant it. 'Stay as long as you like. The kids'll love it too.'

So I spent a tedious eleven minutes changing my flight to Hobart. I texted Juliet to postpone lunch, and called Adam. I explained I was going to head to Tassie early, the next morning in fact, and he said he'd come around straight after work.

I was in bed, half asleep when he arrived. He came over to me, and I reached up and put my arm around his neck, and he leaned down so I could let my head rest in that place under his jaw for a while. Then I snuggled down into bed again. I heard him go into the bathroom, the shower go on, and then off. Finally, he slid into bed, and took my hand in both of his. I explained about Bec and Stuart and we talked a bit about our days, and then he adjusted his body behind me, his chest against my back, his hand on my waist. We said goodnight.

'God, Kate.' His voice was soft in the darkness.

'Sorry?' I half thought he was talking in his sleep.

'You.' He was speaking very quietly, but his voice was fervent, and he put his arm tighter around me. 'Just. You.'

I felt so soft, and so lucky, and so safe, and so in love.

And I still couldn't say it.

I arrived in Hobart early Tuesday morning. It'd now been over a month since Stuart and Bec separated, and the situation seemed to have settled as follows: Mum and BFG called her 'Dear Bec', as if her leaving her lovely husband for an incompetent fire-eater was a sort of heartbreaking accident.

They called Stuart 'Poor Stuart'.

Mum had christened Ryan 'That Fire-eater Man', even though she had never before in living memory identified anyone by their occupation. ('She's not a cleaner; she's a *person* who cleans,' and so on.)

Also, we all called them the 'Darling Children'. Like in *Peter Pan*.

Poor Stuart, who was renting a tiny flat near the hospital, had the Darling Children after school once a week (on Wednesdays) and every second weekend. The plan was that this would continue while he reorganised his workload and they sold the house and he got a bigger place and blah-blah-medieval-calibre-bloodletting-blah.

As far as I could see, Dear Bec spent most of her time ringing child psychologists with huge waiting lists and meeting revoltingly jaunty real estate agents and having 'passionate' sex with That Fire-eater Person and terse, fake-level-voice conversations with Poor Stuart. Also, of course, completing her usual programme of washing and cleaning and driving and cooking.

I sat at her kitchen table and worked on my thesis, and, after school, played with the kids and helped with dinner and tidied up and sponged school uniforms and said as many supportive, stable-environment-providing things as possible.

I told everyone 'My Boyfriend Adam' and I had worked through 'Our Issues'. I used a solemn, fragile tone, so no one, not even Dear Bec, would dare ask any questions.

I was still generally known as 'Aunty Kate'.

The week was good. On Tuesday after school, Bec and I took the kids to a very noisy trampoline centre. We drank surprisingly delicious hot chocolates while the kids played. On Wednesday, I worked on my thesis and then did origami with Essie. The kids went to Stuart for the evening: he picked them up. When I heard the tight, adult voices from the hall I said, 'Hey Essie, want to show me your cartwheels?'

I couldn't talk loudly enough, though. We heard Stuart say, 'You'll find it's because I have your mortgage and my rent to pay,' and Bec said, 'Well, thank you so much for meeting your legal obligations, Stuart,' and Mathilda's face went like a spilt drink.

I went out to the hall, and made a the-children-can-hear-you-you-*idiots* face. Then I handed Stuart two of the surprisingly heavy Smiggle backpacks. He smiled at me, all clunky and sincere. As if we were at the funeral of someone we loved.

Once the children were out the door, Bec prepared to 'visit' the fire-eater.

'Probably best if we stay at his place tonight, I guess,' she said, when she was ready to go. She was wearing a fitted cream jumper and black legging things. Her hair was artfully messed-up, and she'd obviously spent quite a bit of time on her natural-looking make-up.

'Guess so,' I replied, as if I'd barely thought about it. Lachlan had let slip that the fire-eater stayed at their house sometimes. I was shocked, to be honest. In fact, I was making judgements galore and not even feeling bad about doing so.

'Will you be all right here by yourself? Sure you don't want to go to Mum and Dad's?'

'I'll be fine,' I said, firmly.

Bec and the fire-eater arrived back very early the next morning. Most unfortunately, they came into the kitchen, where I was trying to drink coffee in peace.

'Heya, Kate,' he said, all humble and intimate, as if I was a princess he'd just rescued from a dragon.

I have to say, he was as gorgeous as I remembered from the party. In fact, he looked like a younger, cooler, slightly more handsome version of Brad Pitt. (Apart from denial, my other personal superpower is immunity to good looks, though, so I still found him annoying.)

'Good morning, Ryan,' I replied, as if I was a whip-smart, cut-throat, prime-time television interviewer and he was a politician in the middle of a scandal.

He said something husky and pretentious about 'gathering' some garden cuttings, and, mercifully, left.

By the time that evening rolled around, I was tired and happy and looking forward to seeing Adam the next night, and at the same time keen to spend my last evening at Bec's house sitting around chatting. I was hoping she might tell me a bit more about the fire-eater, to be honest. I was a bit curious, obviously, and so far, she hadn't really gone beyond 'passionate'. And I was also wondering if I might tell her about what a big deal the thing with Adam was. Maybe even about all the dating that hadn't really existed.

'Want a wine?' I said. The children were finally asleep and she'd just reappeared in her lounge room. I'd been reading a high-end fashion magazine and noticing that nowadays they use a sprinkling of models over forty.

'Umm . . .' She looked as if she was wondering what to say.

'Or a tea? I'm having one.'

'Kate, if you don't mind, I'm thinking of just turning in early.' (*Turning in*, I thought to myself. Are we on a prairie, here?)

'No worries,' I said. But my surprise must have shown on my face, because she said, 'Sorry. I just seem to be really tired.'

'Exhausted from your night of passion?' I thought she'd probably blush and giggle and – if she was feeling particularly indelicate – use a word like 'virile', but she didn't.

She looked at me and said, 'And would that really be so surprising?' There was a decent level of bite in her voice, actually.

'No! Of course not, Bec.' I flipped a page as if I was really interested in the ridiculous platform shoes a certain very-annoying-on-many-levels designer still seemed to think we should all be wearing. 'No worries at all. I'll see you in the morning then.' My voice sounded hurt, despite my best efforts, but I managed to look up and do a small smile.

She walked towards the lounge-room door, and when she got there, she turned back to me and said, 'I'm sorry, Kate. I didn't mean to be nasty. I just get a bit sick of always being the boring, *smart* sister.' She shrugged, as if that was all very obvious, as if she really thought I had spent the last decade feeling sorry for her while I cavorted my merry, single-girl way around Melbourne. 'You know,' she said. 'The un-sexy one.'

'I never thought of you like that.' I shut the magazine. That time, I made no effort to keep the hurt off my face. 'I've always envied you, Bec. You know that. You *know* that. I've envied you the children. I envied you Stuart.'

God. I had finally said the unsayable. Because even though Stuart and I had always had the we-know-it's-never-going-to-happen-so-we-can-flirt-a-bit thing going on, and even though, of course, it has never, and could never, and would never happen, and even though I'd meant it, when I'd said he was like a brother – that wasn't all of it. Because it would also, somehow, be untrue to say that I had never thought that he and I might have been good together, too. It would be untrue to say that I had never lain awake, in the long years before Adam, and thought about what the two of them were doing when they were alone together, and about the way he would have been with her. And with me. 'I've always thought you had a really great life with what you had.'

She nodded. I could tell she was genuinely surprised.

Then she gave a small, private smile. 'I actually am pretty tired,' she said. And she turned away and went upstairs.

Bec appeared her usual well-rested self at breakfast. She teased me about my life-long insistence on runny egg yolk, and said how much she was going to miss having multiple cups of coffee with me in the mornings. Then she said that after she'd dropped the kids at school she was going to go and see Ryan.

'Have fun,' I said. But I said it the way you'd say it to a co-worker who's leaving early to go have her Pap smear. A co-worker you don't like that much. Because I was already dreading that night's dinner at the Festival. What would I talk about with a 27-year-old fire-eater, for God's sake? What would *Adam* talk about with him?

I focused on my PhD proposal until my phone rang. It was Stuart.

'They're at school,' I said. 'Essie seemed fairly good today.' I talked for less than a minute about Lachlan being excited about practising his assembly and Mathilda spilling an entire glass of orange juice down her school dress that morning.

'Dilimical disaster,' he said. 'Dilimical disaster' is a family phrase for things Mathilda thinks are disastrous but that actually aren't. 'And how are you?'

I said good thanks, a PhD, I must be crazy. 'And how are you?' I added, as if it was the answer to a trivia question. The penny had finally dropped that he wanted to chat.

'Fine. Busy.' Or maybe not. 'I'll see you and Adam for coffee Sunday morning, right?'

I'd actually forgotten we were supposed to be meeting him, and I really would have preferred to be alone with Adam on Sunday morning.

But I was not twenty anymore, so I said, 'Yep. Great. See you at ten.'

'Aunty Kate?'

'Yes, Essie.' It was after school, and we were making banana muffins. There were blobs of mixture on the shiny floorboards.

'What is chocolate actually made of?'

I started to say something about cocoa beans, but before I got to the end, Bec snipped into the room.

'Kate!' she said. She was carrying secateurs and some dead roses. 'The pool gate.'

'Yes?' It's hard for me to open the pool gate from the outside, and once – *once* – when it was summer and everyone – including Mum and Dad – *was in the pool anyway*, I propped it ajar when I went inside to the loo. Later that day, Bec had asked me quietly not to do that again. She'd explained it might give the children ideas – they were younger then – which I'd thought was fair enough.

'Look, can you just, please, can you just *ask*? I'm more than happy to open it for you as many times as you need. Or Lachlan. He can manage it.' She was doing a patient-slash-compassionate voice that

307

made me want to tip the muffin mix over her head. Poor smart boring sister, my *arse*, I thought.

'I haven't been in there,' I said. I indicated my blameless dry hair. 'Although, we sailed our origami boats the other day, didn't we, Essie?' I covered my mouth and raised my eyebrows at Essie in an uh-oh-we-are-in-mega-big-trouble-now gesture. 'Do you think maybe we didn't quite shut it behind us?'

'Well, it was open.' There was no laughter in Bec's voice. 'So, can we all please keep it shut?'

'Certainly,' I said. 'Sorry.'

'And can you maybe go easy on the choc chips? It'd be good if those were even slightly nutritious.'

'Certainly,' I said again. She was looking at me, so I picked up the muffin spoon, licked it and then put it back into the mixture. Turns out I'm only understanding and supportive up to a certain point.

'And I just mopped that floor, Essie,' said Bec. 'You'll have to help your Aunty Kate clean it up before I take you kids' – her voice changed gear, she found her usual steady, gentle lilt – 'to Grandma and BFG's house.'

Dear Bec, I thought. She always tries so hard to be good.

'Sorry about the floor,' I said, sincerely. 'We'll take care of it before I go.'

I was going to meet Adam at our hotel and then go back out for the dinner with Bec and Ryan. I sighed.

Bec went off, and after a bit, Essie said, 'I'm a good swimmer now, Aunty Kate. I don't even need a life jacket anymore.'

'Really?' I said. I tipped a bit more milk in. We were doubling quantities and I was pretty sure I'd made a critical miscalculation. 'Well, you know it's very important to do whatever Mummy or Daddy say about water, right?'

'I'm a pretty good little swimmer. And also, why do sharks like yellow?'

'Do they?'

'Yes! They love yellow!'

'Did you also know that elephants do one tonne of poo per week?' I research fun facts for the kids. It's mainly Mathilda who's into them. 'Which is, like, nearly enough to fill this whole house.' I was improvising, no doubt incorrectly. 'Now, one more choc chip each, then let's get these into the pan.'

As I mopped the floor, I wondered if I could get out of the dinner. I don't like electronic music or biodegradable plates, and I'm not even that mad on gin or performance art, and most of all, I was very unimpressed by the fire-eater. I thought Bec must be mad. I thought I'd rather eat a fold-out map of Canada. I thought he was a beautiful idiot.

But I was distracted. I should have paid more attention. To him. To Essie. To everything.

'I'm late,' I said.

We'd checked in to our hotel, and I hadn't meant to tell him. But he was shaving, and I was warm from my shower, and the words felt so wonderful in my head that they show-offily pranced right out into the informal luxury of our craftsperson-approved bathroom.

Adam wiped his jaw on a folded white towel. Didn't even rinse his face first. Smiled.

'Really?' He laid his razor carefully on the edge of the sink and looked back at me.

'Yep.'

He stood behind me. He undid my hotel dressing gown and put his warm hands on my tummy. We both looked down, at his middle

309

fingers touching just above my belly button. 'Be great, wouldn't it?' he said. His eyes met mine in the mirror, and he looked so pleased I wished I was twenty-six and could give him five babies. 'Should we . . . do a test thing?' His hands were still on my tummy. 'I could go to the chemist?'

No. No no no no no. Hate tests. Hate false hope.

'Nah.' I put my hand on his. 'It's only since about yesterday. Let's just wait till we get home, and then see. Probably it's nothing – probably just the travel or something.' I'd definitely been due the day before, though. And I was usually pretty regular. I was usually like clockwork, in fact.

He was watching my face in the mirror. ''Course.' He moved his hands and did a tactful little shrug that would definitely have made me fall in love with him, had I not been already.

I busied myself with my make-up bag.

'Maybe I won't drink tonight, though,' I said, to my blusher. 'Just, you know. In case. I'll have lemonade or soda water or something. And pretend it's vodka.'

'Sure,' he said. Very nonchalantly. Already shaving again.

We hadn't really talked about it. And I hadn't even let myself think about it. But weeks before – on the morning after I'd told him I didn't want him to see other people and he'd said that he loved me – Adam had muttered something about having been tested recently. We were sitting up in a muddle of doona, drinking coffee and eating room-service toast.

'Well, you're safe as houses, with me,' I'd said. Between bites, I somehow ended up telling him about Dave-the-Second and my prolonged period of celibacy. I tried to do it in a way that made me sound as little like a loser as possible, so I didn't mention the escort, Tara's brother and the osso bucco, or the golden-skinned lawyer who'd had to be elsewhere. I mean, I'm all for honesty, but there are limits.

'He seriously took you to his marital home? In bloody *Edithvale*?' Adam said, as if that was the main point of the Dave-the-Second story.

I nodded. 'Maybe he wanted to impress me with the goldy tapware in his en suite?'

Adam quirked his mouth. 'Sounds like he wasn't over his wife.'

'Oh,' I said. I had never even considered that angle. I looked at my toast and thought about the sixteen dates, and then I thought: plenty of four-limbed people have bad experiences when they try to meet nice men.

'Well, maybe,' I said. 'Anyway, I very much have a clean bill of health. But I'm not – you know, I'm not on the Pill or anything. So . . .' I chanced a quick look into his eyes.

We both had toast and peanut butter in our mouths. We stared at each other, with our lips closed, chewing and chewing and chewing, and not looking away, not looking away, not looking away and neither of us saying anything. Finally, I had absolutely no alternative but to swallow.

Adam swallowed too.

'Well,' he said, when his mouth was empty. 'I'm game if you are.'

And after that we'd stopped using condoms.

Chapter Twenty-Two

Bec

So this is Dark Festival, Bec thought. She liked it even better, this year. In fact, it was really rather wonderful.

Ryan was sitting next to her, in a dim and crowded marquee. When she leaned forward to speak to him, or angled her ear towards his mouth to hear him, her hair grazed his forearm. Outside, red lights glowed in bare plane trees; people in beanies clustered around food stalls and pop-up bars. A candle on their table shone in a little glass; its light bounced off Ryan's eyes, the jug of warm cider in front of them, her silver bangle.

'It's well past eight,' Ryan said, easily. He poured the last of the cider into her glass.

'Not like Kate,' said Bec. 'To be late.' She was pleasantly tipsy. 'Maybe I should text . . .'

But just then they arrived. She gave Kate a hug and Adam a big smile. Kate had said he'd redeemed himself. And who was she to judge, really?

'G'day mate.' Adam offered Ryan his hand. Ryan took a second to realise he was supposed to stand up and shake it, and then shot Bec a sorry-I'm-a-juvenile-dufus grin. Bec giggled, and the men were despatched to get drinks.

The sisters sat quietly. In one corner, a woman with a red crew cut started playing a violin. Several silent teenagers made their carefully dressed way past the table. Two children in thermal leggings danced near a fire-pit.

Bec thought of Stuart, alone in his little flat. She had to work quite hard to put the image out of her mind.

'I'm loving that violin,' said Ryan, twenty minutes later. He was pouring mulled gin out of a jug. Star anise and dried berries floated in it. 'I queued for ages to get this,' he told Bec. 'Next time you can have vodka like your big sister; the place Adam went to served him in about three seconds.' But the way he said it, Bec knew there was nothing on earth he'd rather do than bring her things she liked. Things like dream-catchers and mint-and-ginger tea and silver bangles and lovely, warm, intoxicating drinks. 'Cheers.'

'Cheers.' Adam sipped his beer. 'So, ah, where in New South Wales did you live? Before you came to Hobart?' he asked Ryan.

'Nowhere with forest like Tassie,' Ryan said. He talked about their weekend plans. They were going to Mount Dobson, to take the kids bushwalking. Ryan was keen to walk to Lake Themis on Saturday, and they were planning a technology break.

'When you heading down?' Kate said. 'I thought the weather was meant to be terrible?'

'We'll go tonight,' said Ryan.

'What about the kids?' Kate spoke to Bec, apparently confused. 'Aren't they asleep?'

'Oh, we'll carry them to the car. They're at Mum's now. They'll sleep on the way.' She tried to sound authoritative. She was a tiny bit *drunk*, actually. 'Although maybe,' she added, to Ryan, 'we could leave them at Mum's overnight and drive in the morning?' She really only felt like going to bed. With him. They could go to his place;

she liked it better there. She put her hand on his leg. He held it. He looked at her as he spoke.

'Long way,' he said. 'Boring for them, if they're awake.'

'And we're having all these drinks . . .' she thought to say. Best to be responsible. Responsible service of alcohol. 'Better not drive.'

'I've only had two.' Ryan grinned at her.

Bec put her own drink, very carefully, down on the table. Difficult. The table was on a tiny slant. 'It's really raining, isn't it?' It really was. 'Wowey wow.'

Ryan looked at Adam in a what-do-you-suggest-I-do-with-this-delightful-woman? way. She *was* actually sort of delightful. And no one seemed to need her to do anything right now. Maybe it didn't matter when they went, actually. Maybe she'd just sleep in the car on the way, and so would the kids, and when they got there Ryan could carry everyone into bed, even her, he always said he could carry her as easy as a seashell, and then she could just sleep and sleep.

'Wow. Isn't it just like so, *so* rainy?' Had she already said that?

'Aren't you just like so, *so* drunk?' Kate said, smiling.

Ryan said, 'Reckon it's better we go tonight. Then we can walk in the morning.'

'All right.' Whatever. Ryan smiled at her. She smiled back at him. Then she smiled at Kate, who was smiling at Adam.

It was lovely. They were lovely. She was lovely.

She remembered the day Stuart left. His crisp cardboard box. His neatly flipped cuffs. He'd said she'd be sorry, but she was having a lovely time. She was definitely not sorry. Not at all. Certainly not.

Poor Stuart, she thought. He was wrong. Very unusual.

Chapter Twenty-Three

Kate

The Festival dinner was over and we were back in our excellent hotel room. Someone had been in and lit lamps and turned down covers and left chocolate fudge on our pillows. (Wrapped, of course. No actual confectionary on the Egyptian cotton.) I was sitting on a chair in my dressing gown, eating my chocolate, wriggling my bare toes and thinking maybe I should stop wearing high heels, even though it would be a wrench.

'Hey, Kate.' Adam was casting the numerous bed cushions onto the floor. He had his fudge in his mouth. 'Something's niggling.'

'Have you got a "hunch", Detective Senior Sergeant?'

He didn't properly smile. He came and sat down next to me. We swallowed our chocolates.

'What?' I said.

'I reckon that guy is scamming her. The fire-eater. Scamming Bec, I mean.'

'What? Really? Why?'

'I'm not sure she's his type. No offence to your sister.' He looked extremely apologetic.

'Too old, you mean?' (Is being older really an offensive thing? I asked myself, severely.)

'Too old. Not pretty enough. A mother.'

'Bec's very pretty!' I said. Apparently *that* was the offensive thing. (Bec is actually very pretty. In fact, at risk of sounding unbelievably

315

up myself, in just about any other family, she would have been the Pretty And Also Smart One.)

'Yes. She is,' said Adam. 'Very pretty. And lovely. And, you know, a 38-year-old mother of three.' He frowned. 'It's just unusual, is all I'm saying.'

'Right.' Of course now he'd said it, it seemed obvious.

Adam told me that earlier, in the very long queue for their mulled gin, he'd sipped his own beer and nursed my 'vodka' and asked the fire-eater a few chatty questions about what he'd done before coming to Hobart, and exactly where his Airbnb property was, and the fire-eater had been 'evasive'.

'And later, too. But pretty clever about it,' Adam said.

'Wow. You really think?' I didn't feel particularly concerned. It felt more like we were in a Nancy Drew-style adventure. (A modern one, with an inclusive feel.) 'But why would anyone want to scam Bec?'

'Money. It's money, sex or drugs that get people into trouble. Almost always.'

'Or revenge,' I said, dramatically. I was in Nancy Drew-mode.

'Revenge is rare as a cause of crime,' he said. 'In the general community. Pretty rare, anyway.' He likes me to know he's good at his job, I've noticed. It's very sweet.

'Well, she's not that well off,' I told him. 'They have practically no equity in that house.'

'He mightn't know that, though,' said Adam, reasonably. 'And there's another thing. He says his full name's Ryan John Abbott. What hippy parents gave their kid a middle name like John twenty-odd years ago?'

I wondered briefly how on earth Adam had managed to ask Ryan his middle name while in a queue for drinks at an arts festival. Presumably he'd sounded extremely socially challenged.

'Maybe it's sex.' I felt I was being very sensible. And providing an emotionally intelligent, feminine-type perspective. 'But not in a bad way. You know, maybe they just have, like, intense physical attraction.'

'Hmm.' Still frowning. He rubbed the back of his head.

'The sex thing's possible, Adam,' I said. 'Sometimes there is just chemistry.' I looked at him (eloquent, sultry, even insouciant) and we both *chortled* in a self-satisfied way that I would have found intensely annoying if anyone else had done it. (We were being so unbearable because we had very recently finished enjoying Chemistry.) (For *ages*.)

'Should we check?' I said, when we managed to stop our chortling. 'Have you got some special detective-y database we can use?'

He shook his head once. Very definitely. 'Wrong jurisdiction. Risk of corrupting evidence. My computer's not here. I'd rather not get fired.' He paused. 'It's your sister, babe. Of course I'd do it, if it'd be best.'

'But maybe I should talk to her about it?' I reached for my phone, then hesitated. It was very late. 'Tomorrow? Or whenever she's finished her "technology break" and he's not there?' It would be a freaking marvellous conversation, obviously: 'Hey, Bec, Adam and I think the fire-eater is way too hot to actually like you. He's probably after your money, even though you hardly have any! And no, we're not just getting you back for thinking pretty much that about us!'

Adam nodded. 'He'll be playing the long game.'

And then he said I must be tired, and was I all right, and could he get me anything, and I said don't be so silly I'm probably not even pregnant. We sorted out the complicated hotel bed covers and cuddled up.

I settled my back against his chest. He rested his hand on my tummy, which he didn't usually do, and I weaved my fingers through his. I closed my eyes. He made a little tired-and-very-happy-to-be-here noise, and so did I.

But I didn't feel quite right. It wasn't just what Adam had said about the fire-eater. It wasn't to do with maybe being pregnant. There was something else. Something weird. It was trickling, deep and subtle under all the lovely feelings, but definitely there.

Adam's breath became slow and rhythmic. I lay awake.

From outside, despite our billionfold-glazed windows, I could hear the dull throb of a bass beat. A siren, and occasional shouts – angry, or gleeful, or possibly even frightened; it was hard to tell – penetrated our bubble. We'd left our blinds partly open, and a spotlight was candling into the sky like some biblical column of pale fire. It made the heavy clouds glow a dull yellow-white. I could see silvery pellets of rain against the windows.

My face creased as I tried to figure out what was wrong.

Then sleep began its inexorable creep.

When I woke, I thought the time on the hotel clock-radio must be wrong. Adam's arm was lolling near my pillow, so I looked at his watch. It really was almost midday. We were apparently leading a dissolute life. Goodness me.

The market would have started hours ago. People in merino wool fingerless gloves would be buying lovely cheeses and apples that still had leaves on and whisky-and-apricot jam. There would be buskers, and kids in soccer uniforms, and tourists ordering lunch. But I still felt funny. Perhaps I believed I didn't deserve happiness: that sounded like a sound, therapy-approved sort of reason for emotional disturbance.

I wriggled around a bit and wondered when Adam would wake up. I recalled the talk we'd had about contraception, if you could actually call it that. I thought about when we met, and about the first time we slept together. I remembered the night back in autumn, when Bec told her sad story about Stuart's work, and the tiny, enormous look Adam and I exchanged when she said the word 'baby'. It was amazing, I was thinking, how much we said in that single, silent instant. I turned my body towards his. I was thinking I wanted to drink coffee and eat brunch and then maybe even go and buy a pregnancy test.

But instead I suddenly said, 'Oh!'

I scrambled up. I threw on Adam's jumper and ran to my handbag and grabbed my phone.

I'd worked out what was wrong.

'*Bec!*' I said, to the still room.

Chapter Twenty-Four

Bec

Bec was washing the lunch dishes. Mathilda was reading, and Lachlan was doing an old Rubik's cube that he'd found in the lounge room of Mount Dobson Nature View Cottage. Ryan was standing by a closed aluminium window. The vertical drapes had been rickety-racked open, and he was looking out at forested hills and turbulent sky.

'Weather's clearing,' he announced. They'd been cooped up inside all day, the rain relentless and dense.

Bec turned from the sink. 'It's getting late,' she said.

'It's not even three.'

'You're further south than you once were, Byron boy. It'll be pretty much dark by four.'

'Five-ten is sunset.' He held up his phone to clinch the argument. 'Sorry, Bec. I bailed on the technology break about thirty-seven minutes ago.'

'I noticed about thirty-six minutes ago.' They shrugged silly pretend-guilty/pretend-cross shrugs. But he switched his phone off again.

'Come on, Bec. We've driven all this way. It'll be fun. Bit of an adventure.'

'I'm not sure.'

'You'd want to come for a walk, kids, wouldn't you?' said Ryan. 'To a secret lake? And have ice cream on the way back?'

'Yep,' said Lachlan, looking up from his Rubik's cube.

'Yes!' said Essie. 'Because there's *sharks*, in the sea, but not in lakes, and also I'm a good little swim—'

'What about you, Mathilda?' said Ryan.

'Thank you, but that's not my cup of tea today,' recited Mathilda, who was perhaps the only child in the world who didn't really like ice cream. She looked towards Bec, as if she was wondering whether that was the right answer. Bec gave her an affirming nod. Little girls must be taught they can say 'no'.

'The three of us could go?' Ryan said. 'And you and Mathilda could stay here, Bec?'

'Well—' Bec said. Stuart would find out, and he would hit the *roof*. And, to be honest, she didn't feel very comfortable with Ryan taking Lachlan and Essie off into the forest at this hour. Especially in the cold. It just didn't seem that sensible.

It felt a bit irresponsible. A bit reckless. Even a little bit . . . odd.

Or maybe she was just getting old.

Chapter Twenty-Five

Kate

'I'll drive, mate, you won't be able to concentrate,' Adam said, when Stuart picked us up from the hotel. It was almost three o'clock, nearly three hours since I'd first woken up, and we were going to Mount Dobson to look for my precious, trusting little sister.

Stuart nodded. He was white-faced and terrified in a way I had never seen before. I sat in the back. We travelled right on the speed limit, and Adam overtook whenever it was safe.

Mount Dobson is both a village and a mountain, a couple of hours' drive out of Hobart. The bottom slopes have nice waterfalls and are very touristy, but the higher bits have ancient trees and alpine lakes and earnest-looking bushwalkers. People used to make jokes about locals with a lack of teeth, but they don't anymore. Now it's all about the world-class mountain-bike tracks and the farm-to-plate cooking schools and the rejuvenating experience of the 'landscape'.

As Adam steered the car out of the city, Hobart's biggest bridge was a distant leap across the blue-grey. Usually I thought that bridge looked beautiful, but that afternoon I remembered the terrible things that had happened there.

'Stuart? Adam and I think we should call the police.' I spoke as soon as we were on the open road. 'Is that all right?'

Adam said, 'We wanted to check with you. Because my worry is Child Protection might get involved. Believe me, it can be a total shit-show if you get the wrong worker.'

Stuart said, 'I think we have to call them.'

Adam said, 'Yep. Good.'

I made the phone call, and as we sailed past a hardware store and a car wash and a defunct dog-grooming business, the officer in the radio room asked me lots of questions.

He used telecommunications data (with unexpected promptness) to look for Bec, but her phone was off so it didn't work. He said things like 'concerns for welfare', 'crime car', 'manage resources'. It seemed the police stationed in the Mount Dobson area were taking a suspected drugged driver to hospital in Hobart for testing. After that, those police would come. In the meantime, he'd see who could head to Mount Dobson from New Norfolk, but the officers there had their hands full with a domestic matter. And there was a two-vehicle collision on the Lyell Highway.

I should stay in touch, he said. I should call back immediately if anything changed.

It was a very busy weekend, he said. Everywhere. With Dark Festival and all.

We drove for a long time. No one spoke. I looked out of the window. Most of the river was in shadow, and there were black swans drifting near the reeds. Their feathers were puffed up against the bitter air.

'All right back there, babe?' said Adam.

'Sort of.'

The sky was changing. Soon it would start to get dark.

*

It was a look Ryan had given me.

The night before. He'd been standing with a jug of mulled gin in one hand and two glasses in the other. Adam had passed me my lemonade – 'Yay, vodka,' I'd said.

I am adept at deception, and Adam was almost unsettlingly natural. But still. Ryan glanced at us.

He saw. He observed. He *knew*. Because he was more alert, and more sober, and much, much cleverer than he was pretending to be.

And then his face moved. I had almost not noticed, because straight afterwards, he'd been really sweet. He'd grinned at me, affectionately, all hippy sensitivity and easy-going warmth. With a mixture of pleasure and humour and understanding. Enough to make me believe he was a gorgeous, eager-to-please rainbow child. Enough to make me forget, so nearly forget, about what I'd seen on his face.

Which was hatred. That single unguarded moment. That silent instant, tiny and enormous, when everything was said.

That morning, when I'd jumped out of bed and run to my handbag, I still hadn't known who he was, or why he hated us. But I knew he had my sister, in a forest, without her phone. And with the children.

We passed a tiny shop with lacy curtains closed over its windows. Outside stood a single petrol pump and a hand-lettered sign that read LAST MAJOR FUEL STOP. The road became bendy, narrow, and slick with recent rain.

I rang Bec, again, and once more it went straight to voicemail. I'd already called her eleven times.

The first time was straight after I'd got up. She hadn't answered then, either, so I'd texted.

Call me as soon as you get this, it's urgent. Xoxoxoxoxo

Adam had been stirring in his sleep as I called Mum. No answer. I imagined her scrabbling around inside her handbag, saying, 'Where are you? Oh, don't stop ringing, you stupid thing!'

I left Mum a message, and then I rang Allie. She said (rather coldly) that she had no idea where on earth Bec might be staying. So I called BFG. I love my dad, but he is not a phone person in the same way that the Queen is not a vinyl minidress person.

'Hello?' he answered, as if he was talking down a tunnel.

'Dad! Hi! Do you know where Bec is?'

'Is that you, Kate-o?'

'Yes.' How many daughters did the man have? 'You spoken to Bec today?'

'No, love. She's gone off with that fire-eater of hers. Mount Dobson. Went last night.'

'Yep. Do you know where they're staying?'

'No. But I don't think she's quite herself, your sister,' he added, unexpectedly.

'Really?' But BFG only ever proffers information when it's correct.

'Not herself. This business, taking the kids off so late. Not like her,' he said.

'I know.' I'd thought it was weird, too. 'Get her to call me straight away. If you hear from her.'

'All right, Kate-o.'

'Love you, Dad,' I'd said, finally. We'd hung up without saying goodbye.

I'd stared at the hotel-room window, seeing none of our expensive view.

*

Near a tight bend, a home-made wooden cross had JOANNA written on it in white paint. The cross was old, but bunches of fresh flowers in plastic wrap were stacked at its base.

'You OK, Stuart?' Hopeless question, but I thought I'd better ask it.

'Yes, thanks,' Stuart said. He turned right around in his seat to look at me. He'd mastered himself, which was typical. 'I'm fine. But, Kate, would you step me through it again? Maybe there's a detail that will help.' It was not the time for criticism, obviously, but sometimes Bec must have felt that she was married to a computer.

'Adam thought the fire-eater was dodgy,' I said. I sounded upset, and I made no effort to hide it. God's sake. 'And then I worked out he was very smart, and that he was only pretending to be all lovey-dovey. That he was full of *hate*.'

'I see,' said Stuart. He was still looking at me. I moved into the middle of the back seat, so we could talk more easily.

'I rang Bec, and my parents, and Allie and you, and I got a text back from someone that you were operating. And then I started thinking about your work, and how sometimes things must go wrong.'

'You just had an inkling?'

'I knew he was full of *hate*,' I corrected Stuart. 'And your job, I mean, it was all I could think of. Revenge for something he thought you'd done wrong.'

It sounded methodical, but I'd been frantic. By the time I'd considered Stuart's job, I'd already trawled through fruitless pages of Google entries. There was a Scottish Formula One driver called Ryan Abbott. There was a Perth recruitment specialist called Ryan Abbot. Pages and pages. Time had passed. I'd woken Adam.

'I use the coroner's website in tutorials sometimes,' I told Stuart. 'That's why I thought of it.' I talk to the students about sources of data, about archives and reporting. I talk about individual privacy versus community interest; personal welfare and public wellbeing; records of workplace accidents and traffic fatalities and health system errors.

Those reports are pretty gruelling reading, to be honest. They're chronicles of deaths that were unexpected or violent, or both. Some are so sad you can't believe everybody doesn't know about them. The dodgy smoke alarm, the sleeping family. The icy road, the young driver. All those stories, just sitting there, minding their own poignant business in their obscure little corner of the internet.

Adam had been sitting next to me when I opened the coroner's website. He'd been trying to call Bec. Talking to Mum and BFG, pressing them for details. When he saw how scared I was, and how certain, he called a mate on the police force in New South Wales to see if he could check the fire-eater's background in Byron. The mate said he'd see what he could do.

I scrolled down the 'Name Of Deceased' column. Next to each name was a cluster of keywords, like macabre hashtags. Boating accident. Drugs and Alcohol. Safety Gear. Or: Nursing Home. Infection Control. Communicable Disease.

My heart was beating, hard, as if I'd done something wrong.

'I can't find anything,' I said. 'There's nobody with the surname Abbott. Why don't we just get a car and go to Mount Dobson?'

'Maybe Ryan's his surname. Crims do that sometimes. Try that.'

'OK,' I said.

And there it was.

Our car slowed. Just ahead was an old ute, with firewood piled high on its tray. Adam put on his indicator, pressed the accelerator hard, and we crossed double white lines to overtake.

'Anyway,' I said to Stuart. 'That's when I found the report on Danika.' Danika Janelle Ryan.

Stuart nodded.

He already knew a lot about Danika. He'd known about her for a long time. He'd known Danika arrived at the Royal Tasmania Hospital early in the afternoon on an ordinary Thursday, two summers ago. She was 28 years old, and twenty weeks pregnant; she was very ill. Stuart had operated on her. He'd saved her life, but afterwards, her baby's heart had stopped beating.

We'd all known about her, in a way.

Bec had told me and Adam, while we were drinking wine. *Stuart was involved in a case where a baby died. An unborn baby, I mean ...*

Stuart had also known that Danika died by suicide last winter.

The suicide was made public ... Stuart certainly takes things to heart.

But none of us had known who Danika Ryan was.

Chapter Twenty-Six

Bec

'Please, Mum!' said Lachlan.

'Please, Mummy,' said Essie. 'Ryan could carry me on his shoulders.'

'Come on, Bec.' Ryan smiled his most affectionate smile. 'Rain's stopped. Resilience. Risk-taking.' He winked, man-to-man, at Lachlan. 'And ice cream.'

'Give it a rest, all of you!' Bec said. Everyone looked at her. A surprised-hurt look crossed Ryan's face, the way it did whenever he was reminded there were limits to how involved he could be with the children.

For some reason, she was thinking of Stuart. Stuart, who hardly ever came on day trips, but who, when he did, made everything easy. As if he thought bad weather or complaints about long drives were inevitable – as if dealing with all that was just part of being a dad – and who never would have suggested ice cream right before dinner. She missed him, suddenly. She missed her kids' father.

'Look, I just need to think,' she said.

'Ma-ar-umm!' Lachlan stretched the word out to three syllables. They were laced with a subtle scorn, in a way Stuart would never have allowed. ('Where'd you get the idea it's OK to use that tone to your mum?' he would have asked Lachlan. 'Not on, mate. Absolutely not on.')

'Course it's up to you, Bec,' Ryan said, after a moment. ''Course it is. Only if you're comfy.' He looked at Essie. 'Your mummy loves you, and she knows best.' But he added, in a loud whisper, 'I'll carry you on my shoulders, and we'll beat Lachy.'

Essie nodded, vigorously. 'Now, Mummy. You please have your think,' she said, very politely.

Three pairs of eyes implored Bec from across the beige room. She sighed.

Chapter Twenty-Seven

Kate

For the last ten minutes there had been headlights coming fast towards us. The day-trippers were heading back to Hobart.

'You got the coroner's report there?' Stuart said.

It was on my phone. I passed it to him. He read, quietly, but aloud. I listened as he said, '"Danika Ryan's background. Estranged from her parents ... family violence ... chronic ulcerative colitis ... anxiety ... moved to Tasmania from Margaret River in the early stages of her first pregnancy."'

Then, '"She arrived at the Royal Tasmania Hospital on 14 January ... very unwell ... assessed in a timely fashion ... twenty weeks pregnant ... untreated ulcerative colitis ... in septic shock ... urgent surgical procedure ... deemed necessary to preserve Danika's life, despite threat to pregnancy ... recent medical evidence concurs with this view."'

'I remember her so well,' Stuart said. 'Poor young woman.' He hesitated, and then said, 'She'd stopped her medications for the ulcerative colitis. Saving for a good car-seat for the baby.'

I thought of her, Danika. The young woman who'd had more, and also, so very much less than me.

We passed a small, freshly painted fire station.

Stuart started reading again. '"On 15 January, obstetric ultrasound scan performed on Danika in the intensive care unit found that all foetal heart activity had ceased. This foetal-death-in-utero was not reported to the coroner, and I make no comment about it, other than to say that it was not unexpected, and in any case would not generally be reportable.

"'Danika made an uneventful recovery. She received assistance from the Royal Tasmania Hospital psychiatric and social work teams and was discharged. When seen in the surgical outpatients' clinic four weeks later, her wound was healing well. According to the medical record, she reported that she was taking medication for long-term ulcerative colitis as prescribed, and that she had no concerns. She was duly discharged into the care of local services."

'That was the last I had to do with her,' Stuart said. 'I honestly thought she was fine.'

No, Dr Darcy. I have no intention of harming myself at the present time.

Then Stuart read a whole lot of stuff about how Danika didn't turn up for her psychology appointments, and who rang who and when and whether they all should have assessed her risk of 'self-harm' better. But I knew Danika wouldn't have 'attended for mental health follow-up' because she wouldn't have been able to plan her days, or have a shower, or get out of bed. Takes one to know one, let's just say, because I have never lost a baby but I know about grief, and I couldn't go and talk to strangers either. There was a time – after the arm anatomy and Dave-the-Second, but before the Tudors and the underwear – when I couldn't really go out at all. When I just wanted someone to lie down next to me and hold me. Bec rang me almost every day. Mum rang me every single day for more than a year.

Anyway.

After all the how-can-this-sort-of-thing-be-avoided-in-future?-slash-let's-find-someone-to-blame part, it said that the following August, about seven months after her baby died, Danika left two letters under her pillow.

Stuart read, "'The letters were addressed to a family member and a local friend, and were in their nature farewell messages. One contained a discursive reflection on the unfortunate loss of her pregnancy.'"

It said that Danika bought a bottle of Kahlua. She drove for almost three hours to a beach on the Tasman Peninsula.

"'Danika Ryan's car was found in a beach car park near Eaglehawk Neck by police on 20 August, under a sign that read, BEWARE THE RIP.'"

There was quiet in the car for a moment. Then Adam said, 'We didn't know about her connection with him yet. But we thought we should look.'

I hadn't been able to think of anything else to do. And it all seemed to be taking so much time. Adam's mate hadn't got back to him.

We'd googled *Danika Janelle Ryan*. Nothing much we didn't already know.

Then: *Danika Ryan mental health Margaret River*. On the third page, we found the little article. From the *Bunbury Telegraph*. There was a quote from a local politician about unprecedented funding. There was an announcement about a new helpline. And a photo of Danika Ryan, the well-liked and vivacious bartender, who had died by suicide, thousands of miles away, at a Tasmanian beach with a well-known rip. There was a photo of her from the 'good times' alongside her 'much-loved brother'. She was an angular-looking girl in a tight green dress, with an awkward smile and both her arms around a very handsome man, as if he was a wonderful prize she'd won.

It was the fire-eater.

Chapter Twenty-Eight

Bec

'All right then,' said Bec. 'Let's go. Essie, time to pop your coat on. You too, Mathilda, up you get.'

Lachlan put down his Rubik's cube. He'd finished the green side.

Mathilda said, 'Can I bring my book?'

Ryan put his hand on the back of Bec's neck as she locked the front door behind them.

Chapter Twenty-Nine

Kate

It was properly dark now. Steep rocky walls ran alongside the road; up ahead, the wind made the trees look puny.

Two hours earlier, Ryan's face, and Danika's, had been staring out from my phone when Stuart rang.

'Madam Kate, I've got a couple of missed calls from you. We still on for coffee tomorrow?' He'd sounded so unbelievably normal.

I'd told him what I knew. I hadn't bothered trying not to alarm him.

'Adam's here. We're going to go and find them,' I'd said. I'd looked at Adam. 'And we're thinking we should call the police?'

But Stuart hadn't answered the question.

'I'll come right now,' he'd said. 'We can go in my car.'

In the darkness, a watch-for-wildlife sign flashed bright under our headlights, yellow with a black kangaroo silhouetted on it. Something else started to turn in my memory.

The little girl with melting choc chips in both hands and muffin mix all round her mouth who said, 'Why do sharks like yellow?' and 'I don't need a life jacket anymore,' and, 'I'm a pretty good little swimmer, now.'

'Stuart?' I said. 'Is Essie allowed to go swimming by herself? Or without a life jacket?'

'No way,' he said. 'Struggles a bit with swimming, Essie does. Not like the other two.' After a moment he said, 'She should have been nowhere near those waves unsupervised, not even for a paddle.'

Stuart had again turned around to look at me. His eyes moved, as he read me, then stopped as he understood. We both knew, at the same moment, but I was the one who spoke.

'He wanted her to go in, that day. That school excursion at Clifton.' My voice was fraying. 'I think he *tried*. I think he opened the pool gate on Thursday. I think he'll encourage a swim this weekend.'

Adam said, 'It's rained nearly all day, and now it's late. Surely they wouldn't . . .' He didn't take his eyes off the road. 'But we better head straight to the lake. Just in case. And let's call the police again.'

I dialled. I held my phone towards him.

It was after five o'clock.

'Are we nearly there?' I said, stupidly.

'Five minutes,' Adam said, looking at the GPS. 'Four.'

Adam had talked to the police. He'd said things like single member, Vic Pol, constables. Two police cars were less than ten minutes behind us.

WELCOME TO MOUNT DOBSON, THE APEX OF ATTRACTION, said the sign. It was white and green. To our right, the mountain itself was grey-black and huge. Cloud covered its summit. I tilted my head to look up at it. I remembered now, from childhood trips. The entrance to the Visitors' Centre, and the track towards the lake, was just a couple of minutes up ahead.

We passed some holiday cottages. Mountain Retreat. Leafy Nook. Nature View.

'Nearly there,' Stuart said. I nodded. More headlights came towards us. Stuart and I sat up straighter, then turned and squinted after the vehicle. But it wasn't them.

Adam slowed down as we passed a brick, cream-painted building. A pub. On the roof was a satellite dish and a big green beer sign that had a corner missing. In the gravelly car park, there were a few impressively safe-looking four-wheel drives with huge bike racks against their back windows and some dodgy old utes.

And Bec's white Audi.

'Stop!' Stuart and I said together, but Adam was already pulling in. He'd even remembered to indicate. He said he'd call the police again. When he lowered the phone, he told us that the officers were less than five minutes away.

Stuart and I looked at each other. He'd held himself together so tightly, but still. Tears of relief were in his eyes as well as mine.

We walked fast, almost running, along a dark, uneven concrete path at the front of the building. There was a door that said BAR. Two men stood under the eaves, smoking. They were in their fifties, with flannel shirts and beer guts and noses like mushrooms, and they looked at me in a way that made me glad both Adam and Stuart were present. I went in front and put my hand on the door's sticky handle.

'Give it a nice hard pull, darlin',' said one of the men.

Adam turned his head very quickly and said, 'I'd shut my face if I were you.' The man stepped back, holding up his hands as if *he* didn't want any trouble. As if Adam was over-reacting. Adam had barely broken his stride.

I opened the door, which – unsurprisingly – required just a normal-strength pull, and we went inside.

There was a billiard table and a huge L-shaped bar. Behind the bar stood a lady with bright hair and a nice smile. To one side, men roosted on little black stools. In unison, they turned and glanced at us, as if we were all in a Western. A wooden sign above a doorway in the corner read THRU TO DINING ROOM. We walked, without speaking, towards that.

As we passed, one of the stool-men muttered, 'Farken typical.'

Even though my body was full of apprehension, I couldn't help but wonder if he really thought that one-armed former up-and-coming supermodels were all that typical of anywhere. Even the big smoke.

Stuart went into the dining room first, then me, then Adam.

They were there. I heard Stuart make a soft sound when he saw them.

The five of them were sitting at a little wooden table near the middle of the room. It was noisier, and – to be honest – much nicer, than I'd expected. Ochre walls and an electric fire and lovely old wooden tables, and lots of mountain-bike-y-looking men. Very few women. Clearly this was where you sat if you were Not From Around Here. It was a huge relief to be somewhere so public – and sort of more familiar, in a way – and I managed a deep breath.

Essie was next to Bec, slumped in an unappealing way against her, because by that time of day she was always exhausted. Bec's plate appeared virtually untouched; her arms were on Essie. On Bec's other side, at the head of the table, was the fire-eater, lolling back in his seat with his legs extended. He had a beer in one hand and a fork in the other. Mathilda and Lachlan had their backs to us, but looked to be eating chips with their heads down.

As soon as we walked in, a few things happened.

Bec saw us straight away. She heaved Essie off her lap and stood up. A woman in black jeans came out of the kitchen, carrying two enormous plates of chicken parmigiana. Some of the mountain-bikers glanced our way.

Essie ran towards Stuart as if she'd just been given a fairly large dose of amphetamines, and he scooped her up. Lachlan and Mathilda trotted over too, their faces confused and delighted, as if they'd just been told they could watch television and eat chocolate until midnight.

Ryan looked up at Bec and said something. She made an I-am-constantly-mystified-by-my-bizarre-ex-what-will-the-idiot-do-next? expression.

'Lachlan!' she called, sharply. He either didn't hear her, or pretended not to. He was already next to Stuart.

'I'm taking you guys home,' I heard Stuart say. He was clearly making a huge effort to keep his voice level.

'But we're going for a bushwalk tomorrow.' Lachlan sounded puzzled. 'To this lake? Mum wouldn't let us go today, and we're going to race—'

'No can do, mate,' said Stuart. He was already steering them out. There was another door off to the side, marked EXIT. I presumed it led directly outside, rather than back through the bar and along the dark, drunk-man-ridden path. Stuart obviously thought the same, because he started to move towards it.

'What about Mummy?' said Mathilda.

'Aunty Kate and Adam will bring your mum home,' Stuart said, firmly. The kids seemed to sense that it was not the time for arguments, or maybe they wanted to go with him, because there were no further protests. Stuart gathered up Mathilda, so he was carrying her too, and somehow managed to put a hand on Lachlan's shoulder as well. He took a path well away from the fire-eater and Bec. The black-jeaned waitress – having delivered the parmigianas to a table of mountain-bikey men – stood aside for him.

People were watching them idly; they were the only children there. The bright-haired woman from behind the bar appeared with a paper order pad in her hands. She smiled after Stuart in an approving way, the way women her age often do when they see a nice man doing anything with his kids.

A song about having the time of your life was playing as Adam and I approached Bec and the fire-eater.

'What exactly is going on?' said Bec, still standing up in her seat. She was doing her I'm-clearly-in-the-right-here-but-look-at-me-being-the-bigger-and-more-reasonable-person voice. My body felt barely mine as I glanced to my left, to make sure Stuart still had the children.

Adam moved so that the fire-eater was right in front of him. The fire-eater was still sprawled at the head of the table, the cool kid down the back of the bus. Adam was next to me; he angled his body ever so slightly in front of mine. Protectively. Bec was across from me; the table – holding an enormous quantity of half-eaten pub food – steaks on skillets, an almost-empty basket of garlic bread, Essie's kids-menu spaghetti bolognese – was between the two of us.

'I asked you what's going on, Kate?' Bec said. She was only just managing to use her restaurant-voice, and she kept turning her head to look at Stuart and the kids. They were almost at the exit by then. Essie's little face was examining us over Stuart's shoulder.

'Becky, you have to come with us,' I said. 'He's trying to hurt you.' I didn't look at the fire-eater.

Her face wrinkled – confused, appalled – as if I'd made a racist joke. 'What are you even *doing* here?' she said. 'Stuart!' she called, and that time she did raise her voice. She sounded very angry. '*Stuart!* Lachlan! Mathilda! Essie!'

'Mummy!' Essie called. She started wriggling in Stuart's arms. I could see she was tired and confused, and the novelty of it all was wearing off. 'I want my *mummy!*' Stuart still had both girls in his arms, one hand on the door handle, the other on Lachlan's shoulder. He turned.

Ryan had his back to them, but he turned around and stared in Stuart's direction. He draped a languid hand along Bec's hip, and Stuart's face changed.

'I want my MUMMY!'

And somehow Essie was on the floor. I saw her stand still for a split second. She had her feet apart, and her eyes on her mum. Her arms were pointing straight down, and the tip of her tongue was between her teeth in the invincible little way she'd always had.

It was as if Bec wasn't really thinking about it, because she probably wasn't. It would have been so much of a habit. But Bec half turned. She held her arms out for her girl, even though her mystified, angry eyes were still looking at me.

'Essie, stop!' yelled Stuart. He'd already dropped Mathilda. He reached both his hands towards his youngest child.

But Essie was running towards her mummy.

Adam grabbed the fire-eater's nearest arm. 'Stay there,' he said, and he began to twist the arm up Ryan's back, the way I'd only ever seen on television.

The fire-eater didn't even stand up. He grabbed a skillet with his free hand. Chips and bits of lettuce flew everywhere; a half-eaten steak fell with an ugly squelch onto the floor. The fire-eater's arm was an elegant arc through the air as he smashed the cast-iron skillet down, fast and hard, onto Essie's little golden head.

Chapter Thirty

Bec

The day after the pub, Bec sat in a room off to the side of intensive care. There were evil-looking dark-turquoise carpet tiles on the floor, and a vending machine against one wall. There was a squishy caramel-coloured couch and blue vinyl chairs with wooden arms. There was no smell, except of them. She could hear elevator doors opening and shutting down the corridor.

Lachlan and Mathilda were with her parents. Stuart had been on the phone to his father most of the morning, using phrases like 'midline shift' and 'mass effect' and looking as if he had just been told that everything he'd ever believed was a lie. Kate was next to her, always to her right, so that she could hold Bec's hand. Adam came and went, murmuring to Kate about cars and food and school uniforms for the older children. The second time, he nodded to Stuart. Stuart nodded back, ended his phone call and went and shook Adam's hand in a way that almost became an embrace. Adam had broken the fire-eater's swipe, just a little bit. But the fire-eater had weight and momentum.

Essie had a subdural and an extradural hematoma, clots of blood inside her head that were putting pressure on her brain. The night before, some of the blood had been drained by the neurosurgeon who'd been called in especially. When Bec met him in the emergency department, he was wearing ironed jeans. Bec nodded and heard little he said. Stuart heard everything. She could tell. Even though

Stuart stood with his shoulders turned away from her, even though his eyes didn't look at her, but slashed at the air near her head.

Afterwards, in the middle of the night, the same doctor arranged chairs on the turquoise carpet tiles and sat them down and told them that Essie's bleeding had stopped but there was still some swelling near her brain. They were going to wait for it to reduce and then try to take her off the ventilator.

'We'll see what happens,' he said.

'OK,' said Bec.

'Of course,' said Stuart.

Despite everything. Despite the efficient unfurling of the blue-green surgical drapes, despite the practised ballet of sterile tubes, despite the inimitable pop of the glass ampoules as the magical, terrible drugs were unleashed, despite the scans and the instruments and all the long years of training, everyone still had to wait and see what happened.

The doctor spoke again. It was difficult, he said, to predict the degree of 'neurological insult' should Essie survive. Bec wondered, randomly, inconsequentially, why the doctor didn't just call it brain damage. After he left, Bec sat on the couch. She held Kate's hand again.

She thought: why didn't I make that Peter Rabbit radish cake myself?

She thought: I should have let Kate pay for Briarwood. I should have *forced* Stuart to let Kate pay.

She thought: How is it that Stuart can stop having feelings for me? Just by deciding to?

Some time on the second or third day, the police came back.

Ryan – no, not Ryan, because the fire-eater's name was Jacob; in reality Ryan was his surname – had been charged with grievous bodily harm and his application for bail had been refused. If Essie died, he could be charged with murder. Or maybe they'd get him on attempted murder anyway. The police said they'd have to talk to the DPP.

Ryan had drug convictions in New South Wales. He'd made money selling marijuana and pills. His mum lived in Western Australia; she worked at a petrol station. Over the years, she'd taken out six Family Violence Restraining Orders against Ryan's dad, who had four convictions for assault. The fire-eater had no siblings apart from Danika, who had been three years older than him.

'He said he was from this big, happy family,' Bec said. 'He said his mum was an artist.' It felt as if the words didn't quite fill the whole room. Kate squeezed her hand. Stuart didn't react. Maybe the words didn't make it all the way over to his ears.

While a monitor beeped sedate time with Essie's heart, and a machine hissed breath into her perfect lungs, the police said they'd found a folder under the fire-eater's mattress. It was labelled COMPENSATION. On its inside was written, 'Eye for an eye, tooth for a tooth. I will restore the true balance of universal justice. I am a co-creator.'

Bec wondered how often the fire-eater thought of his folder, lurking tidily within his bed, while he had sex with Stuart's wife.

In the folder was a letter from the coroner's office, dated a couple of months after Stuart had operated on Danika. It thanked the fire-eater for his request, but said that the coroner would not be holding an inquest into the death of Danika's baby, because that kind of foetal loss was outside the purview of the coroner and anyway, the loss was neither unexpected nor violent. Someone had written BULLSHIT four times in green pen across the letter. At the bottom, in blue pen, was Stuart's clinic address, and then, in black, his home address. They thought the fire-eater probably followed

Stuart home one night. Followed her. Learned her local deli, learned her kids' schools.

There were also copies of fliers. Purple paper, professionally printed. Bec only vaguely remembered them: she always just threw that stuff in the bin. But it seemed he'd letterboxed at least part of her street, advertising gardening and then – on green paper, in a different font – kids' circus skills workshops and – yellow paper – children's party entertainment. He'd got himself a Tasmanian Working With Vulnerable People card. He'd applied for a job as a gardener at Briarwood. There was a copy of a cover letter and his CV; he'd sent them to Lachlan's school, too. Jane Payne, Stuart's practice manager, recalled he'd visited the clinic. He'd said his business supplied fair trade coffee beans to workplaces; he'd left a card, but she'd thrown it away. (Jane Payne would not believe in paying the extra for fair trade, Bec thought, irrelevantly.)

There were copies of receipts, pristine, from an online bookseller. Over weeks, he'd had four kids' books about the circus delivered to their home address. One of the books was *Five Have A Wonderful Time* by Enid Blyton. Mathilda had loved it. It featured a circus. It even featured a fire-eater. Stuart remembered that Mathilda was the one who'd suggested having a fire-eater at his party. (Not that Stuart told Bec that. She found out from Kate.) Bec hadn't properly questioned where that book had come from. Book parcels turned up all the time. She ordered them. Stuart's dad sent them. Kate did too.

It would have been a few weeks after the date on that receipt, that she saw his advertisement on the Briarwood website.

When Bec contacted him, he'd asked to friend her on Facebook. 'I don't use Facebook, but Messenger's best with my data plan,' he'd said, meaninglessly. She'd thought it was some young-person save-money thing.

She'd made it so easy for him. She'd *been* so easy.

'Your wife was the easiest bit,' he'd said to Stuart, from the floor of the pub. Adam had leaned down hard and said something that made the fire-eater stop talking.

He'd broken up their marriage, and then he'd set his sights on the children. He'd insisted on staying over. Manipulated her into letting him meet the kids. The night before Essie's beach excursion, he'd said that it was tension, not red wine, that gave her migraines. He'd said she should have some and then he'd give her a massage. Had she told Ryan the joke about Essie being Stuart's favourite? Is that why he'd targeted their youngest? Or maybe Lachy was just too good a swimmer, or the beach was too busy, on that boogy-boarding trip.

The police said they might be able to charge the fire-eater for the morning at Clifton Beach, but only with something like wilful negligence. The oldest officer said he'd bet his house that it'd be impossible to prove Jacob Ryan had intended to watch Essie drown, and that Essie herself, even if she recovered, would probably be too young to make a useful witness.

There was no way the police could prove anything about what he'd planned for Lake Themis, but they seemed to think he'd designed it for a weekend when emergency services would be busy. In the cold, dark month Danika died. 'Good you said no to the walk, love. I mean, Mrs Henderson, apologies,' said the oldest officer.

All the police were very kind.

Stuart looked at Bec, stonily, the whole time they were speaking. She didn't really care. Did he think him looking at her like that would make it worse for her? Did he think anything he could say or do or be could make it worse?

She knew all the stuff about victim blaming, and she never thought she'd be part of that. But she also knew that she was the one who'd let him in.

*

346

At some point, Kate went home to sleep for a few hours. Bec was alone with Stuart in the turquoise-floored room.

He was sitting on one of the vinyl chairs. His back was to her. She was slumped on the couch with her eyes closed. Every time she moved, the fake leather squeaked in a way that made her feel self-conscious. After a long time where nothing happened, he stood up and turned his chair around. Its wooden legs grated unpleasantly against the floor.

Stuart sat back down, facing her. Still a long way away, though. The vending machine, right over against the wall, was the third point of their equilateral triangle. She looked at the Fruit Jubes.

'Bec?' he said. It was the first time for ages that he'd made her name sound like something other than a stab. He cast a glance towards the door, as if to check that no one would interrupt them. 'I thought I had her tight enough, Bec.'

'Of course you did.' She saw the teenage boy he used to be flickering behind his face. Stuart's still here after all, she thought, illogically. At least that's something. 'Sweethear— Stuart. Of *course* you did.'

There was nothing else they could say, right then, but he didn't turn his chair around again. They sat. Someone clipped along the linoleumed corridor outside. The elevator doors dinged open and slid closed. Bec remembered her own enjoyably professional hurries along that very corridor. So long ago. She imagined all the times Stuart had walked along it since. Residents would nudge each other when he entered ICU, would murmur, 'Mr Henderson's here,' would make haste to find the right file.

Her world was going to be so bleak, now, without them. Without Essie. Without Stuart. Without, somehow, and inexcusably, Ryan. She let her head wilt onto her chest.

'I know I should have realised,' she whispered. 'I know I should.'

She sobbed for a few indulgent and relieving breaths, and then raised her face. He was still looking towards her. A few seconds passed before their eyes properly met. It felt like tuning a radio. Static, static, then, *there*. Stuart.

'We can't dwell on it,' he said. 'You can't. We have to look after them all. All right?' He didn't look away. 'They're going to need us. All three of them.' They nearly started crying, because he'd said that automatically and they both knew it might not be all three. 'Especially you. Especially you, Bec. So you have to . . . we both. We both have to just get on with it.'

Without thinking, she reached part of the way across the space between them.

He looked down at her hand, which hung in the empty hospital air. He wasn't cross, or contemptuous. Just sad. Just decisive. Just . . . aware that the two of them were finished. Sharp scalpel. Clean cut. Quicker to heal, in the long run.

She hauled her hand all the way back into her own lap, and nodded at him instead. Touch. She had only just realised she was never to touch him again. Impossible.

'Yep,' she said. She pulled her hair back behind her neck as if she was making a business-like ponytail. Then she let it sag. 'You're right, Stuart. I'll try.'

'Good,' he said. 'Me too.'

He nodded, just the once. He gave her a tiny smile. But only, she knew, because that was what had to be done.

Chapter Thirty-One

Kate

On the third morning, I drove Bec to Mum's so she could see Mathilda and Lachlan before school. Bec's car was as immaculate as ever. Adam had retrieved it from the police, and sorted it out. There was the blue bottle of water in the console. There was the handle on the steering wheel for me. There was the booster seat in the back, for Essie.

At some traffic lights, two young women crossed the road with hurried strides. It was a small, predictable shock, that people were going to work. And that, when we arrived at Mum's, the wattle in the front garden was starting to bloom.

Once the engine was off, I turned away to open my door. Bec spoke.

'Kate?' she said. I stopped immediately, and as soon as I looked at her, her face crumpled up. It was the first time I'd seen her cry since the pub.

I leaned across the car. I put my arm around her neck and my stump on her cheek. For a long time the only thing I could hear was her broken breath.

'I liked him so much,' she said, in the end. She looked up at me the way three-year-old Mathilda used to as she said something like, 'That big door hit into my head!' 'But you knew, Kate. You *saw*, straight away.' She started crying, harder, against me. 'I was ... you were ...' She couldn't properly talk.

349

'Oh, Becky,' I said. 'It's not your fault.'

After a while she sat up. I reached for her hand, but she shook her head, gave her cheeks three brisk little slaps with the flats of her fingers, and gestured to the clock on the dashboard. 'We have to get going.' She reached for the door handle.

'Hey, Bec, just a sec.' She turned to me. Tiny capillaries were visible in her eyes.

It almost seemed as if telling her didn't matter – because in one way nothing mattered except Essie – but also, I knew it mattered very much. I tapped my closed lips with my forefinger a few times.

'Bec, all the stuff about men I used to say,' I began. 'Before Adam. Adam's the first man I've been with since the amputation. That side of things got really, really difficult for me, and so I sort of lied. I lied. I couldn't handle you and Mum and Dad and' – the air made a noise when I breathed in – 'Stuart, all feeling sorry for me.'

Then I waited.

'Wow,' she said, but flatly. There was silence. 'And there I was.' She sort of laughed. 'Feeling like the boring one, all those years.'

We both sat and thought about that. But after just a little while, Bec smiled, sadly, and fluttered a tender little dove of a hand onto my cheek. 'I can see why you might've felt you had to, Kate,' she said.

Then she opened the car door and got out.

That night, I woke up in Bec's spare room. Adam was sitting in the dark, with his feet over the side of the bed.

'Adam?' I put my hand on his back. 'You all right?'

He didn't turn around, didn't speak.

'Adam?'

'I thought if he went for anything it'd be the steak knife.' He sounded very sad. 'I only saw the knife.' His voice barely stretched around the words.

I sat up, and knelt next to him. I stroked his hair and held him with both my arms, and after a moment he turned and let his face rest against my collarbone.

'I love you so much, Adam,' I said.

Of course it was easy, in the end.

She didn't die.

They pulled the tube out of her throat, and she coughed a lot, which Bec said was a good thing.

My period came that same afternoon. A whole six days late. I sat in the hospital toilets looking down at my underwear and, to be perfectly honest (yes shameful, yes ugly, yes vile, yes completely unforgivable), I had to push aside the thought that it's not fair, the way Bec always seems to get away with things, and I never do.

Chapter Thirty-Two

Stephanie

The week before Stuart's fortieth

I waited thirty-eight minutes for the doctor to call me in. Like usual, she smiled and said, 'Sorry to keep you, Stephanie.' No one except her and teachers call me Stephanie, and teachers would never say sorry to me.

'I've come about my pimples,' I said. 'Still pretty bad.' I'd put concealer on. You could still see them.

'Hmm,' she said. 'Yes.' She touched my chin with her fingertips, tilted my face to the side. 'Hmm,' she said again. It's only when you're right close up you can even tell she's wearing make-up. 'And you've been using the cream? And taking the tablets?'

I nodded. The cream costed thirty-two bucks. I nicked money out of Dad's wallet, and he spat it with my brother.

'You're going to need a specialist,' she said. I knew that. I'd looked it up. It said if your acne was severe and your GP couldn't help you then you should ask to see a skin specialist.

'Yeah.' I showed her my phone. I'd taken a screen shot of the site.

'That's right.' She was surprised. 'A dermatologist.' She looked at me like she was thinking I was poor. She wouldn't say 'poor', though. Reckon she'd say some other bullshit doctor word for it. 'I'm afraid they're rather expensive.'

'How much?'

'In the order of a couple of hundred dollars for the first consultation.'

'Two hundred?'

'Afraid so. Is that something you think you could manage? Could your parents perhaps help you out with that?' She had a picture of her kids on her desk. Two boys and a girl, all wearing school uniforms with jackets, and the girl had braces. None of them had any pimples.

'Um. I reckon,' I said.

'Lovely.' She smiled. She typed a letter and gave it to me in an envelope. She wrote a phone number on the front. 'Daniel's very good,' she said. 'Dr Gilbert. He'll sort you out.'

'Thanks,' I remembered to say. I stood up.

'Anything else today, Stephanie?' she said, standing up too. 'Everything all right at school and things? Year Eleven going well?'

'Pretty good,' I said. I took my letter and put it in the bin at the mall. I'd missed my bus. Dad kicked my arse.

The night of Stuart's fortieth

I got ready in the bathroom. I took ages. Dad said to get out, in the end, he reckoned he needed a shit.

I looked all right in the mirror except when I stepped back under the light and then my skin looked bad again, and we had to wear our hair in ponytails. I hoped the light wouldn't be too bright at this party. It was in Sandy Bay, near the Casino.

Even though I'd turned seventeen, I didn't have my licence. So it was two buses to get there and then I thought I could maybe get a lift back. I didn't know what time it'd finish but sometimes if things go late, I get twenty bucks extra. Dad says I'm a very lucky girl to have this job. Our next-door-neighbour's son gave it to me. Brody, he's called.

I reckon boys don't talk to you much when you're waitressing, cause you're working and that, but still, I thought there might be someone all right there, so that'd maybe be good.

*

There were three of us waitresses, plus Brody, plus this guy who knew how to make cocktails and shit. The other waitresses knew each other. Snobby bitches. Brody said they could take the trays around and I could stay in a little room next to the kitchen. I had to get stuff out the containers and put it on trays, and help Brody carry them to the oven. I had to pour all different kinds of sauce into bowls.

After that I did washing up in the little room. The others kept bringing plates and glasses and stuff in. I heard people singing 'Happy Birthday'. I heard people cheering. The other waitresses reckoned that the doctor whose party it was told them they could have some of his cake, but he hadn't offered me, so I thought better not in case Brody spat it.

Right before midnight, Brody said we could go home, even though there were still heaps of people there. He and the drinks guy were going to finish cleaning up.

I walked out with the other waitresses. They turned out not that bad. They were called Alyssa and Lauren and they were in Year Twelve. When we walked past the coffee van – like, a real coffee van but parked in the *garden* – these old guys in the queue for it said, 'It's the hard-working staff!' and 'Haven't you young ladies been fantastic!' and 'You heading out on the town? Stay and have a dance before you go!' and stuff like that. They were smashed as.

Alyssa said well could we all get a donut, and they laughed like she'd said something massively funny and started shouting at the man and lady in the van, 'Doughnuts! Immediately! Urgent doughnuts required!' and snorting their shiny bald heads off. One of them put his arm across my shoulders. 'What's your name?' he said, and when I told him he said, 'You look as if you need a donut, Steffy, and by God, a donut you shall have!' You could tell the couple in the van were like, 'Shut up, you pissed idiots,' but they had to just smile and give us heaps of their donuts and coffee for free. Pretty good.

The street was quiet. Alyssa and Lauren said did I want to share an Uber, but then this guy came over. He had bare feet, so I thought, Dickhead. But he started talking, mainly to me. I could tell Alyssa and Lauren wanted him to talk to them, because they kept asking him stuff about surfing. He surfed a lot, he reckoned. I kept quiet. Sometimes I reckon that's better.

He said he better go and did I want a lift, and I said all right. He didn't offer one to the others. Maybe he doesn't like real stuck-up girls like that, I thought. Good to know some guys aren't all about the looks.

On the way home he started saying it's not right, those doctors touching us like that. He said he was watching and they shouldn't have been giving us donuts either. He reckoned it's not allowed. He said maybe him and me could go to the movies. Before he dropped me off we did some stuff. He reckoned I was a good kisser.

I thought if he texted that'd be all right, and he did, the next morning.

After the movies, we went in his car to the beach. We did more kissing and he felt my tits a bit but nothing else. Then he started talking about the party. Said it pissed him off to see another man with his hands on me. He reckons doctors do whatever they want.

I told him how it cost two hundred bucks to go to a specialist. I didn't say skin specialist, because how embarrassing.

'That's the kind of thing. They do what they want. We should complain.'

'Yeah?' I said.

'They were only giving you donuts so they could put their hands all over you. Like you were hookers or something.'

'Not like all over,' I said.

'I saw them.' He was really cut. 'One of them pinched your friend's arse. One of them said he wanted a blow job.'

'Shit,' I said. 'That's no good.'

'It's practically like saying, if you want me to give you stuff, let me pinch your arse.'

'Yeah,' I said. I really just wanted to start kissing again.

'You should take them down. That one, whose party it was, I know him, it happened right in his garden, you should just make sure he doesn't let those guys do it to anyone else.' He nearly started kissing me, but then he said, 'Every time I touch you I think of their hands on you.'

He kept talking like that, so in the end I thought, well, all right, if it's that big a deal to him.

'Do it properly, Steffy,' he said. 'If you're gonna complain, make sure you do it properly.' This was a couple of days later. He said I should say about a blow job and a lap band. He said that'd be better. He said if I just complained about what happened, no one'd listen, and nothing would change.

I wasn't sure, but he said, well if I wanted to be his girlfriend, I wasn't going to be able to stand by and let strange men touch me however they wanted. I was going to have to step up.

He said he knew it was crazy hard. He said he'd help me. Which was nice, because I'm not much good with forms and Facebook and shit. He said someone from the government might ring me and he'd help me with that too, because we were a team. But when she rang I just quickly said I didn't know anything about it and hung up. Didn't tell him.

Anyway, he ghosted me after a bit, which was shit but in the end lucky, because some cops came and talked to me about him, and I had to sign a statement, and I'm not getting charged. But he was in the paper the other day, and looks like he went to jail. So I dodged a bullet there, I reckon.

Epilogue

Bec

Nowadays there was always feel-good music playing in the supermarket. Songs that made Bec think of the glitter-infused body lotion she used to wear to parties and of being squashed against her friends in the back of someone's old car. Market research probably indicated that middle-aged people would spend more on household items if they were reminded of their youth. She sighed.

The kids had been late to school. Mondays were almost always the worst for Essie. Bec had wanted to call Kate, had composed a text to her even (*Good time to chat? Hard morning!*). Then she'd deleted the exclamation mark. Then the *hard morning* bit. Then the whole text.

Kate was coming down this weekend.

'I think the kids need as much family around as possible,' she'd said. But Bec knew she was just being kind.

She looked up. Coming towards her past the tinned fruit was Allie.

'Hi!' said Bec.

'Hi,' Allie kept walking, manoeuvring her half-full trolley past Bec.

'I'm fine, thanks,' Bec muttered.

To her surprise, Allie whipped her head around and said, very angrily, 'I'm *sorry?*' She had taken one hand off her trolley and put it on her hip. The other hand still rested elegantly on the trolley's handle.

It was as if Allie was starring in some sort of reality-television-meets-classical-ballet theatrical event.

'I said, I'm fine. And thank you very much for asking,' Bec said.

'Glad to hear it,' said Allie. She must have been able to see the hurt on Bec's face but her gaze didn't soften at all. With a contemptuous little exhalation, Allie turned away.

'Guess I've found out who my friends are,' said Bec. But she was speaking to the back of Allie's immaculate powder-blue knitwear. Her words were not a retort. They were a plea for mercy.

Bec held onto her shopping trolley's green plastic handle with both fists, and put her head down. She hoped it would look like she was just checking the label on her eggs. After a few moments, a terrified-looking young man asked her if she was OK.

'Oh, fine! Thanks!' she said. She didn't make eye contact, but pushed her trolley onward, past the soy milk and around the corner. She looked at the clean, grey-flecked linoleum. She counted her breaths.

The next aisle was busier. A man was telling his daughter she needed to sit down or she'd have to get out of the trolley and walk. A young woman was contemplating her soy sauce options in a worried sort of way. And Allie was tinkling her tastefully gold-bangled arm up to the condensed coconut milk.

Bec kept her eyes down and walked at what she hoped was a normal pace. What did she even need in this aisle? Now Allie and her trolley were coming. Bec turned her face away, as if considering the taco kits. Allie walked with a straight-backed gait. She passed Bec without seeking eye contact, her trolley full of respectable married-woman things.

What even was a hard'n'soft taco? Bec wondered, brokenly. Was she supposed to magically know that too?

*

Forty minutes later Bec was unloading her bags into her car when her phone pinged. Now that the Aisle Confrontation Crisis was over, her head was a mixture of the cutting sort of lines she hadn't been able to come up with at the time – Sorry my family's not up to scratch. Silly me, I thought friends stood by each other – and Dalai-Lama-esque inspirational thoughts: I release all blame. I can only control my own responses, not the behaviour of other people.

The amount of delight she felt at the sound of an incoming text was humiliating. She shielded her phone from the sun so she could read. The text was from Allie.

Hello, I have been wishing to contact you for some time. I realise you would still be going through a difficult time currently, and we sincerely feel sad for your family and especially for poor innocent Essie, and Mathilda, Lachlan and Stuart.

Bec let out a weak, incredulous 'ha'. But Allie possibly wasn't intending to be especially bitchy.

The reason why I have not been engaging with you in recent months is because I heard you and your sister making judgemental comments about me. At Stuart's fortieth. I always knew you were so much smarter than me, but it is a real shame you had to be so nasty about it. You didn't act like a friend, Bec. You hurt my feelings very much, and that is why I don't want to spend time with you anymore. From, Allie Vincent.

Oh.

Bec shoved her phone in her back pocket and began heaving shopping bags. She seemed to have sudden, super-human strength. What, oh what, had they said? They'd been drinking. A tin of tomatoes rolled free, and she chucked it loose into the boot. Maybe she'd remarked on Allie's tendency to make every comment about clothing sound as if she was reporting breaking news from a war zone. It must have been well after the speeches because Allie had embraced Bec as soon as they'd finished and said – eyes brimming – 'You must be so very proud of your beautiful family and life! This is an amazing night!'

What had happened after the speeches? She could only remember walking Ryan to the door. Recalling any other specifics felt impossible, as if she was trying to lift a building. She banged her knee hard against the tow bar as she shoved a bag of potatoes to one side. The pain brought tears to her eyes.

And there it was, the memory, as intact and real as a coin in the bottom of a handbag. Bec put the last of the shopping into the boot, moving slowly now.

She and Kate had been in the butler's pantry. It was nearly three in the morning and almost everyone had left. They'd been talking about nothing much. Kate said something about Stuart's sister Phoebe. ('She's smart, but she's so busy and tense she makes me feel as if *I* can't breathe,' Kate said.)

Then Kate brought up That Allie Woman. Kate said Allie was sweet, but then she added, 'And what a beautiful life you lead, Bec dahling! It's just ... Gwyneth Paltrow-standard!'

And Bec imitated back, 'Kate dahling, I'm so inspired by your statement life I could almost eat a trans-fat!'

'Not the sharpest knife in the ... knife-rack,' said Kate.

'I think you mean not the sharpest tool in the box. Poor old Absolutely Vacuous,' said Bec, half-heartedly examining a dirty wine glass. 'Please God let everyone have gone already. Want some chamomile or something before bed?'

But apparently not everyone had gone already.

Bec imagined Allie. Her Briarwood-bestie, the one who would stay till last. Allie must have been at the half-open door to the butler's pantry, about to knock, or standing in the kitchen, waiting to gush her sweet, open thank yous and goodbyes. Bec imagined Allie's face, the way she must have had to hold back tears as she found her husband – he would have been twitching about the living room, wondering whether the paintings were worth anything – and they saw themselves out. She wouldn't have told Rich, Bec knew. Allie would have kept it all inside until she could get home, and into the shower, and cry.

Dear Allie, she texted back. *I am very sorry for what we said. It was mean, untrue and inexcusable, and I don't blame you for being angry. I really hope that Olivia, Henry and Rich, and you, are all going well. I am just so truly sorry. You were a wonderful friend, wonderful, and I really, really miss you. Sorry, again, for what it's worth. Love, Bec Henderson.*

Sometimes it seemed as if she would never get to stop being sorry.

'Is Daddy coming today?' asked Mathilda. It was the soccer presentation day.

'He sure is,' Bec said. 'That's exciting, isn't it?'

'Yes!' said Mathilda, so enthusiastically that Bec wondered for a moment whether she was being facetious. But no. Mathilda was doing a little dance, making a clatter with her soccer boots on the kitchen floor.

'And then, next weekend, you'll go to his place.' Bec corrected herself. 'You know, you'll go to your home at Daddy's house.' Obviously, she was very much on board with all the helping-your-children-come-to-terms-with-separation protocols.

'OK,' said Mathilda, as if she wasn't really listening. Everyone was going to receive a medal, she was telling Bec. Last year they had been purple, did Bec think they would be today? Because she'd missed out last year, she added, informatively, as if Bec could possibly have forgotten. Last year, the soccer presentation had happened while Essie was starting to walk again.

An hour later, Bec unlatched the child-proof gate that led into the school yard, and all three children scudded off towards the bright yellow plastic hats on the school oval. A herd of kids and two of the sportier mums were doing dribbling drills. The air smelled of cheap, delicious sausages and cold, sticky mud. The three kids were all enrolled at Ashton Heights now, and there had been no further talk of them changing back to their private schools.

('Well, they seem fine,' Stuart had said, six months back. 'The principal's been excellent really. And you're the one who's doing most of the school runs, so if you think . . .' His casual deference had made tears come into her eyes. He'd tapped his phone on the edge of their open front door – she still thought of it as *their* front door – and said, 'See you Saturday at ten.' He'd moved away so briskly she knew he'd seen her wet eyes. He wouldn't have wanted her to feel embarrassed, was the thing. Or maybe it hurt that he couldn't hug her. Or maybe he just wanted to get on with his day.)

She scanned the school ground. There he was. He was standing with his back to her, watching the field. He was wearing a new down jacket and Essie already had both her hands around one of his. Bec could see that the two of them were talking; Stuart's head was angled down; Essie was craning her face towards him as if her plait was being pulled backwards towards the ground.

Stuart's other hand was resting on Amelia-the-Architect's neck. Bec'd read somewhere that if you could just wait thirty seconds then most feelings would diminish. God. She decided to go and see if she could help on the sausage sizzle.

'Oh thanks, Bec, but I think we're pretty right,' said Fiona. (Fiona was Maddie in Grade Three Yellow's mum). Maybe she sensed Bec's desperation, because she added, 'But Nat needs help with the second-hand boots.' Fiona's voice rose to a bellow. '*NAT!*'

A grey-haired woman on the main hall veranda looked up.

Nat, it turned out, was younger than she looked from a distance. She was standing behind a trestle table that held muddy garbage bags and a row of old soccer boots. She introduced herself as the mother of Cooper in Grade Two Blue. 'I'm doing this to get away from him for a while. Although really, this has to be the worst job ever made. Would you smell those!' She thrust a pair of child-size orange boots towards Bec.

Bec said she was going to have to stay and sort out soccer boots all day because her ex-husband was around somewhere with his newish girlfriend.

'Ugh. Desperate,' said Nat. She grinned. 'Worse than my Cooper.'

'Well,' Bec said. 'I pretty much brought it on myself.'

'I did kind of hear about it,' said Nat. Her voice was very sympathetic, or maybe it was just that everything sounded that way when said in an Irish accent. 'And it's not my business, but I wouldn't be thinking you brought that on yourself.'

'Thanks,' Bec said. 'That's what my psychologist says.' The sentence – especially uttered to a virtual stranger – was so *odd* that she gave a small, genuine laugh.

After a while, Nat offered to make them both coffees in the staff room – 'I've done so much parent help; I do as I like around here' – and Bec sat down cross-legged on the cold concrete. She was frowning over a particularly savage set of knots when a voice said, 'Hi there, Bec.' Stuart was standing in front of the table.

'Hi!' She stood up much too rapidly. The worst part was that he knew her so well, he'd be able to tell she was flustered. And that she was trying to hide it. The whole thing was just impossible.

'So you drew the short straw today?' He indicated the boot in her hand.

'Yes. Sort of.' She could hardly say she'd been desperate to volunteer because scraping dried mud off pre-loved footwear was a million times better than standing watching him charm the children, their friends and a pretty part-Danish (for fuck's actual *sake*) architect.

'Can I help?' he said. 'Mathilda sent me over.'

If she said no, then it'd sound as if she didn't want to 'develop an amicable co-parenting relationship'. That was the first dot point he'd put on his 'Suggested Aims For Our Kids This Year' email. He'd sent it on the first of January. (The second dot point was that the children should have minimum upheaval, and that he thought they should leave the house off the market 'for the foreseeable future' and that the children and Bec should stay in it on 'an ongoing basis'. He could manage somewhere 'low-key' for himself, he said. When Bec read that email, she stood up and walked around the dining table twice. Then she sat back down and read it again and – since the children were very fortunately all in the lounge room rearranging the furniture and pretending to be the servants at Downton Abbey – cried with relief.)

So, it would be churlish to say no.

But if she said yes, then she'd have to be near him. She'd have to see the way the lines around his eyes were infinitesimally deeper, and how he was leaving his hair the tiniest bit longer, and that his hands were still so effective and somehow both conscious and casual. She'd have to smell him and smile at him and keep her voice steady, and the whole time she'd know that she'd remember every little gesture he made and every single word he said, and that, 'for the foreseeable future', she'd lie in her bed and examine them all for the smallest sign that he still, miraculously, loved her.

'OK,' she said. 'Maybe you want to knot the pairs together?' He said he'd give it a go, he'd just go see about the chair situation. He strolled into the empty assembly hall as if he had every right to. He was always like that.

Bec took a deep breath, and to steady herself further, did a three-point check of the school yard. Essie was scrambling up the littlest climbing frame, Mathilda was arm-in-arm in the sausage queue with her current BFF and Lachlan was playing handball. Bec was restraining herself from rushing over to make sure Essie didn't fall, when Stuart returned with a couple of black fold-out seats. He opened one up, and she sat down on it.

'Sorry!' she said, rocketing to her feet. 'Did you mean that for me?'

'Yeah.' Gently. Of course he'd meant it for her. The man's manners were impeccable.

They sat down, their heartbreakingly careful knees paralleling straight ahead.

'So, how's Amelia?' Bec had practised the question, just in case, and she forced herself to ask it fairly promptly.

'She's well, thanks,' he said. He handed her a pair of boots, their laces now neatly slip-knotted together. 'She's gone off to yoga.' Bec remembered how, whenever they used to see people going into the local Flow Balance studio, he would wonder aloud how anyone could possibly flow in such tight pants.

'That sounds . . . nice,' she said, as neutrally as possible.

'She's trying a new place,' he went on, unexpectedly. 'She says she's reached a point in her life where she point-blank refuses to pay for parking while she exercises.' His voice was at least as neutral as Bec's, but for all the world, he looked the way Lachlan did when Lachlan confessed to some mild misdemeanour.

'Oh, right.' Bec felt as if she was in a diplomacy grand final. Bland acceptance and mild, friendly interest were radiating from her every pore, even though she was thinking that yoga car parks were hardly a social justice issue, and so there was certainly no need to use the phrase 'point-blank refuse', and that Stuart would *definitely* agree with her on that.

But Stuart shrugged and smiled in a way that she couldn't read, and she thought about how he'd probably woken up next to Amelia that very morning and how Amelia hadn't had any children and that she no doubt had a non-stretch-marked tummy and would know about things like what was trending on Twitter. She wondered what sort of contraception Stuart and Amelia were using. If any. Suddenly, she stopped feeling proud of her diplomacy, and shook her head without meaning to. Luckily, he was concentrating on his knot.

'How about you? he asked, politely. Being Stuart, he sounded only a little bit uncertain. 'You seeing anyone?'

'Nope,' she said, lightly, looking at the boot in front of her. Then, with a quick glance at him, because, after all, he was still *Stuart*, she added, 'God, no.'

'Ah well.' All casual. He handed her a second pair of boots, and asked her what they were doing anyway. For a second she thought he meant the soon-to-be-finalised divorce, the 'amicable' emails and Amelia-the-Architect, but then she looked at his face. He just meant with the boots, so she hurled herself into an enthusiastic spiel about second-hand sale and fundraising and that he wouldn't believe how expensive brand-new boots were and how quickly children's feet grew and the importance of team sport in underprivileged lives. ('You sound as if your sole mission in life is to provide exercise

equipment to the needy,' Kate would have said. 'Just calm down.')
But her evangelical fervour carried them through until Nat came
back with the drinks and then they all started chatting about how
instant coffee wasn't that bad as long as you didn't expect it to taste
like real coffee, the value of guinea pigs as pets and the way they
really couldn't handle late nights anymore. Did that mean that he
and Amelia-the-Architect weren't having all night sex-a-thons? Or
that they were?

When it was time for the medals the three of them parted. Bec
got Nat's number, and said goodbye to Stuart in a textbook amicable
co-parent sort of way. When Essie and Lachlan materialised, she
led them down to the very front. She told them it was so that they
could all see Mathilda up close when she got her medal, but really
it was so that there was no danger of Stuart's undefeated shoulders
being in her line of sight. She didn't think she'd be able to bear it.

'Mum!' said Mathilda, charging into the kitchen. It was the next day.
'We've forgotten to make honey joys!'

'We haven't forgotten.' She was emptying the dishwasher. 'It's
only ten-thirty. There's still nearly the whole of Sunday.'

'Then why,' said Mathilda, sounding like an OHS inspector who'd
just discovered a non-compliant staircase, 'is Daddy's car coming
down the driveway?'

The children swamped him at the front door while she humbly
dried cutlery in the kitchen. She heard squealing (Essie's) and Lachlan
saying urgently, 'But you're still taking us to Fish Frenzy for dinner
tonight though?' Then everything went quiet. She should go and
see what was happening.

'Hi,' he said. She looked up. He was already standing on the deck,
and the sliding glass door had been left half open.

'Hi! Where are the kids?' She sounded as muddled as she felt, and found herself trying to smooth back her hair while holding a fistful of wet teaspoons. 'Sorry, did I mess up the times?'

'Nope,' he said. 'Kids're outside. I came to talk to you, actually. Can I come in?'

'Of course.' To be honest, it seemed incredible that he was even asking. Not because he paid the mortgage, but because this was their house.

He took a seat on one of the stools, and put his phone and keys on the bench. She chucked the spoons away wet in their drawer and moved a stool so she could sit down across from him.

'Um,' he said. 'How are you?'

'Fine. What's going on?' Because Stuart never said 'um'. And he looked terrible. 'What I mean is,' she went on, a bit more calmly, 'is everything all right? Are you all right? Oh! Have you come from work? Was it really busy?' She stopped herself.

'I'm fine.' He touched his car key with his forefinger. 'Amelia and I finished up last night.'

'Oh.' Her breath went out of her throat in an ugly-sounding half-laugh. 'I hope you're OK,' she amended. She relaxed her shoulders and prepared to have a mature discussion about how this news might affect the children. Would they get the impression that all adult relationships were disposable? Although, all things considered, that was bound to be the least of their issues. 'Would you like a cup of tea?' she asked.

He laughed. 'Yep,' was all he said.

She stood up and flicked the switch on the kettle. Out of her peripheral vision, she saw Essie run across the deck, shooting an enormous water pistol at Lachlan, who was hiding in tree ferns.

'Did you just give them those?' Bec asked. He nodded. They both smiled. Turning her gaze away from his was like throwing away a

369

pile of the kids' old baby clothes. She took two white cups out of the cupboard, and watched them as she placed them very carefully on the bench. She heard the chink of the china on the marble.

'Bec.' She looked up at him. 'This.'

He didn't have to say what he meant.

'Bec,' he repeated. Sometimes, when he said her name, he said it in a really lovely way. Almost like a chant, as if he really enjoyed the sound of it, as if he felt happy that he was the one who was allowed to say it like that.

She left the cups and sat down again. He swallowed.

'When I was seventeen,' he said, 'I went into Mum's study one night. Must have been during my year twelve exams or something. It was really late, but she was up working.'

Bec nodded, sombrely, although she was wondering where on earth he was going.

'Mum was sort of frowning at her screen, and she looked up.' He paused. He was deep in the memory. 'She goes, "I'll tell you this, Stuart. Any paralegal or trained monkey can report the data. The job is to make the call."'

Despite everything, they exchanged a that-is-*so*-typical-of-her look. They even laughed a tiny bit.

'Yeah,' he said. 'Obviously at the time I just hoped she didn't say things like that in front of her paralegals.' Then his face changed. 'But. Lately I've been thinking about that a lot. You know?'

Bec must have looked a bit confused, because he said, 'I've been thinking that things can look a certain way on paper, but really sometimes how things look isn't the whole story. And that's what Mum was getting at. That sometimes it can be difficult to look beyond the obvious, but what you have to try to do – as a judge – or as a doctor, or a . . . a husband, or just as a person – is to see things as they really are, and then have the guts to make the right call.'

'I see.' But her voice sounded tentative, because she very much didn't want to get her hopes up, and maybe he was talking about schools or Amelia or houses or something.

'You know. Bec. Bec? All those times?' He looked away for a moment, then back at her. 'We'd be here' – he rotated a hand to indicate their kitchen – 'and you'd be stirring a cake or something, and telling Essie to pick up her shoes and checking a text and pouring us a wine and saying people who were too tired to move their shoes were too tired to stay up for ice cream. And you'd be telling me about Lachlan's reading or a homelessness report off the radio or how my dad had hurt his knee again or – I don't know – did I think Mathilda was getting enough iron. And I'd be, just, leaning against the cooker, half-thinking about someone's pancreatitis or the laparotomy I had on the next morning. You know?'

There was a silence.

'Yes,' she said, because she did know. And astoundingly, there was a trace of anger in her voice. 'Yes. That's how it was.' Tears would start in a minute. 'That's exactly how it was, Stuart.'

They looked at each other. It was just him. The hostility had gone. The *amicability* had gone, too. And somehow, their hands had made their way towards each other across the bench, and two of his fingertips were touching the side of her wrist.

'I've cut back, lots, already, and I was thinking that if you wanted I could—'

But she was already nodding, nodding, nodding, in a way they knew meant *yes, please, come home, come here, come back to us* and she didn't want to move her hands, so there were tears on her face.

'I'm sure we can work it out,' he said, in a thick voice. 'We can – whatever you think will work.' He cleared his throat and went on more steadily. 'Because, I want to be with you, Bec. And I think we should get back together.'

Their fingers had interlaced themselves without her having to make any effort. She moved her wrists forward, and so did he, so that their palms touched.

There was a long precious quiet.

Stuart said, 'Bec?' He kept his hands where they were. 'After we . . . after you told me. I had sex with a lot of different women.'

Bec nodded. What could she say? It was to be expected.

'Sometimes it was really amazing.' He definitely wasn't gloating. 'It was mainly about loneliness and feeling, um . . . unwanted. And I can imagine that maybe that's how you were feeling too. Last year. In our relationship. I wasn't around enough. Or, when I was here, I wasn't properly present.'

'Have you been seeing a *counsellor*?' she said.

'Can you tell?' Semi-ironic.

'Your *feelings*! Not being "present".' She actually laughed. 'And I . . . oh look, Stu. Whoever you slept with. Whatever. As long as you don't, anymore, if we . . . are going to be together, again.'

He shook his head, in a way that meant *course not, not if we were together*.

'OK. Well. Thanks for telling me. I guess.'

He laughed, when she said 'I guess'. But it helped, oddly, him telling her.

She found herself thinking: the kids will be here any minute, it's a miracle they've left us alone this long, those water pistols were genius, but let's not push our luck, we can't be sitting in here crying and talking about sex when someone comes in for a Band-Aid.

So she said, 'Stuart?' It came out very clear. 'I'd love for us to be together again.'

He made a little noise. So inarticulate, so unlike himself. He nodded. He squeezed her hands, very hard.

Kate

The car park was a concrete mess, but above us the still evening sky was fading from palest blue to palest pink. 'I'm a bit numb,' I said, as we approached my car. 'Maybe you could drive home?'

''Course I can,' he said.

Once we were strapped in, Adam rattled the car key in his loose fist, and kept his eyes on the windscreen. An older woman in a crafty, emerging-local-designer-type outfit clipped efficiently past. When she'd gone, he turned to me.

'You OK?' he said.

'Scans.' I made a wild sort of gesture with my hand.

'I really think it's going to be all right. I really do.'

'I'm *forty*,' I snapped, and I nearly started crying. 'Sorry,' I added. He touched my leg.

It was like if you went to an Irish pub and everyone started singing folk songs while a kindly old man played the fiddle and a handsome farmhand whirled you about in a rollicking jig. You'd think: Can this actually happen in real life? Is it actually happening? To me?

Like that, except about a million times more.

'Show me that again,' said Adam. He put one of his hands on my belly, and I held out the shiny slip of paper that curled at the edges. On it was an ultrasound image.

'Good size for thirty-four weeks,' the obstetrician had just said, and I'd relaxed my sweaty grip on Adam's hand a little bit. 'All looks excellent. Nearly there.'

The woman in the arty clothes was way over the other side of the car park now. I stared down again at the black and grey splodges on the shiny little slip of paper. A photo.

Our baby. Our daughter. Our beautiful little girl.

Acknowledgements

A huge amount of credit is due to Tegan Morrison for her expert editing and her brilliant ideas. Enormous thanks also to the rest of the Bonnier team, both in Australia and the UK. Particular thanks to Katie Lumsden for her insights and Jon Appleton for copyediting.

Thanks to Ros Calita for meticulous attention to names and for helping with early drafts of the final scene.

Thanks to Claire Bryan for telling me about medieval textiles, Helen Cushing for gardening advice, Claire Donoghue for mountain-climbing lingo, Mardi George for helping me understand Kate's occupational therapy, and Steve Karpeles for patiently explaining aspects of criminal law. To Sophie Ricketts, awe-inspiring surgeon and generous friend, thank you for your expert explanation of sarcoma management, and for telling me about how surgeons look after their hands. Thanks to the staff at the State Library of Tasmania for retrieving many, many old editions of *Vogue*. Thanks to others, too, including the unknown resident of Melbourne with the INCWINC number plate. Any mistakes are mine, of course. I took artistic license when necessary.

The Medical Practitioner Regulation Authority that investigates Stuart is a fictional entity. The real-life Australian Health Practitioner Regulation Agency (AHPRA) is the body charged with regulating doctors in Australia. Their website, and the report on the 2017 Senate enquiry into AHPRA's methods of dealing with complaints against doctors, were useful in writing about what happened to

Stuart. The books *Sarcoma*, edited by Robert M. Henshaw, and *One Step Beyond*, by Warren Macdonald, were very useful in my research, as was a medical journal article called *Unexpected Resection of Soft Tissue Sarcoma* (2000), by K. Siebenrock et al.

To the beautiful school community I am lucky to belong to: thank you so much for all the great times, and I'm very glad this is a work of fiction. Thanks to Katie Daniels, Fiona McIntosh, Ian McMahon and Frank Meumann for rock-solid career guidance. To Gillian Tsaousidis-nee-Ahluwalia – I don't think I could write about sisters if not for you. (Thanks also for the voicemail about the pronunciation of 'obviously'.)

To all my family: I started listing the ways you helped with this book, but it was going on for *far* too long, and then I started crying (in the happy way). Thank you. Special thanks to my mum, Trish, and my dad, Ian.

To Cuthbert and the B-factor, you help make my world. Thanks for everything.

And very deepest gratitude to my beloved husband, Phill.

If you or someone you know is suffering from mental illness, you can call Anxiety UK on 03444 775 774, the Samaritans on 116 123, or Mind on 0300 123 3393. You can also visit the Mental Health Foundation at www.mentalhealth.org.uk.